T0304830

SECRETS AND LIES

Quintin
Jardine
SECRETS
AND LIES

HEADLINE

First published in Great Britain in 2024 by
HEADLINE PUBLISHING GROUP

1

Cataloguing in Publication Data is available from the British Library

Hardback ISBN 978 1 0354 0292 2
Trade Paperback ISBN 978 1 0354 0293 9

Typeset in 12.5/16pt Electra LT Std by Jouve (UK), Milton Keynes

Printed and bound in Great Britain by Clays Ltd, Elcograf S.p.A.

MIX
Paper | Supporting
responsible forestry
FSC® C104740

HEADLINE PUBLISHING GROUP
An Hachette UK Company
Carmelite House
50 Victoria Embankment
London EC4Y 0DZ

www.headline.co.uk
www.hachette.co.uk

This work is dedicated to my son and daughter, AJ and Susie. They know how I feel about them, and always will, now and in the other place, wherever that is.

One

'Bertie's been twitchy for a few weeks now, every time we've walked past this thing . . . and we do, every day, sometimes twice, hail, rain or shine.'

Maisie Berry looked down at her dog. 'We believe that the bad days are the price we pay for the good ones,' she declared, philosophically. 'Isn't that right, Bertie?' The spaniel grunted, as if it knew that confirmation was needed. 'He's been stopping, sniffing at it for a few days now,' she continued, nodding towards the huge square white tent that covered the pavement and more than half the width of the blocked off cul-de-sac. 'Yes, for at least a week, maybe more. My sense of smell isn't anything like it used to be, but yesterday I detected something too. I put it down to a blocked drain at first, but it was pretty clear by this morning that was coming from this camper van thing. So I called the police, and . . .' she shuddered. 'Horrible,' she said, shuddering. 'Imagine, such a thing happening here.'

'How long has the vehicle been here, Mrs Berry?' Detective Sergeant John Stirling asked.

'Miss Berry,' she countered, a little sharply. 'At least two months, I'd say, maybe more. We all woke up one morning in early July and it was there, parked most inconveniently, and with a wheel clamp on it too. At first, I think each of the residents assumed that it belonged to one of the others. Obviously, this being a new estate we don't know each other very well, not yet, but gradually it became clear that nobody knew anything about it. After a couple of weeks one of the neighbours did call the police to complain, but basically he was brushed off. He was told that as it wasn't in a restricted road, it was far enough away from the nearest house not to be blocking anyone's access, and it hadn't been reported as stolen, there was nothing they could do. But finally,' she harrumphed, 'when I called, again, this morning, and reported the alarming smell, a uniformed officer deigned to come along. He decided that he couldn't force entry without permission so he called in someone else, a man in plain clothes. He arrived and took a sniff, went back to his car and produced a crowbar, prised the door open, went in and . . . Well, you know the rest.'

Stirling's right eyebrow rose, momentarily. 'Yes, I am the rest,' he said.

'How do you fit in alongside the other plain clothes officer?' Miss Berry asked.

'I'm from serious crimes, in Glasgow,' the DS explained. 'My team covers the west of Scotland. The other guy was a detective constable from area CID.'

She winced. 'Serious Crimes. So there really is a dead person in there? Not that I had much doubt after the officer who went in came straight back out and was sick all over the grass.'

Stirling nodded. 'I'm afraid so.'

'Dead for how long?'

'I've got no idea,' he said. 'I only stayed in there for a second or two, because the forensic team were working and the space was limited. Once they've completed their initial sweep, the body'll be taken to the mortuary for examination.'

'You must have some idea, surely.'

'He's new to this kind of work,' a third voice advised, as its owner bore down on them. 'Me on the other hand,' she continued, 'I've been to more of these events than are good for me, enough to know that at this stage there are too many variables for us to be guessing. My name's Detective Chief Inspector Charlotte Mann,' she volunteered. 'I'm his boss.'

'So this really is a crime?' Maisie Berry asked. 'A murder? Here in sunny Irvine?'

'This is where I say "No further comment", madam,' Mann replied, 'thank you for your help, and ask you to return home or to carry on walking your pal here.'

Miss Berry frowned at the large woman, noting the positivity of her stance, the resolve that showed in her eyes and last of all her bronzed complexion, unaided by make-up. *Where did she get a tan like that given the weather in Scotland this month?* she wondered, before deciding that it was best to accede with dignity to the DCI's request. 'Of course,' she said. 'If there's anything else you need . . .' she added, with a gentle tug on Bertie's lead as they went on their way.

'She's a piece of . . .' Stirling murmured, as he watched her leave.

'She's a retired teacher,' Mann declared. 'Probably a headmistress, I'd say.'

'You know her?' the DS exclaimed, puzzled by her certainty.

'No, but trust me. I'd bet your life on it.'

'How do you work that out?'

She sighed, then raised an eyebrow. 'I'm a bloody detective, John. I have these instincts. Plus, in her attitude and mannerisms she's a dead ringer for my Auntie Annie. She was a primary head, and a right battle-axe, God rest her. She left a trail of terrified weans behind her in a forty year career. Back in the days when you could, she used to belt one every morning; boy or girl it didn't matter. She said it made all the rest behave themselves.'

Stirling shuddered, then handed her a set of crime scene overalls, identical to his own, and held her rucksack as she struggled into them. 'What's in the thing?' she asked as she tucked her hair into the tight fitting hood. 'Is it Male? Female? Canine?'

'Female,' he replied. 'That's all the lead soco said . . . other than that she's been dead for a while . . . which was painfully obvious in the few seconds that I was in there. I didn't stay any longer than I had to, or get any closer than I needed.' He winced forcefully. 'The body's absolutely mingin', boss: you should wear a mask when you go in there.'

'She, then,' Mann continued. 'Is there any obvious cause of death?'

'None that the soco or I could see, but like I said, it's a mess.'

She frowned. 'Were you here when the vehicle was opened?'

'No. A local CID guy opened it,' her DS told her. 'With a crowbar, so Miss Berry said. The bloke's a veteran; he's in his forties but still a detective constable. Not a deep thinker, without being too judgmental. Just like the old dear said, he went in, came back out, threw up, and called us. I stood him down when I got here . . . I had to, he had boak all over his jacket . . . but I told him we'll likely need him and others later, for most likely this is going to turn into a major investigation.'

She threw Stirling an atypical grin. 'A crowbar?' she muttered. 'Forensics must have loved that when they got here. Messing up their crime scene.'

'It wasn't a crime scene until DC Brown opened it,' he pointed out. 'Don't be too hard on him.'

'Can we say for sure that it is now?' Mann wondered. 'Until

there's been an autopsy, can we rule out sudden death by natural causes, or a suicide?'

'Suicides aren't usually found lashed to a chair with yards of gaffer tape . . . Gaffer. I was in there long enough to register that.'

'I'll grant you that one.' She paused. 'Even so, how come we were called in so quickly? From what you're saying this was flagged as one for serious crimes as soon as the vehicle was opened. From what you're saying DC Brown didn't even refer back to his own office before pressing the panic button.'

Stirling beamed. 'It wasn't quite like that, but almost. Let's just say that if the Scotland rugby team had passed the ball as quickly and efficiently as the buck was passed here, they'd have won the World Cup. This is a public holiday, right?' Mann nodded. 'So, when the uniform who turned out first phoned his sergeant's mobile, he was told to, and I quote, fuck off and call someone else, because the sergeant was one, off duty and two, in the second hole of a golf tie. In the absence of that someone else, the PC, who's now helping man the press exclusion zone that you'll have passed through getting in here, called the CID office in Kilmarnock. They were short-handed too, so only Detective Constable Brown was sent to the scene. The rest you know, more or less. After the van had been opened and Brown had seen what he saw, he called his office, where his DS, the only other person there, was wise enough or cynical enough, depending on how you look at it, to tell him call us.'

Mann gazed at him. 'And when you got the message, was there nobody else that you could have called, other than me?' she murmured. 'My man and I were halfway through putting the lunch together when you belled me. Plus,' she intoned, 'I was supposed to be off today. Like you said, it's a public holiday.'

'Boss,' Stirling pleaded, 'you know the answer to that. We're short of a DI. I had to call you. But if you remember I didn't ask you to turn out.'

She nodded, grudgingly. 'I know, I'll grant you that,' she conceded. 'I'm sounding like that sergeant, but at least I'm here. No, you did the right thing, John. ACC Stallings promised me someone six months ago then did eff all about it. Now that she's out of the picture and Detective Superintendent Haddock's effectively in charge of all the Serious Crimes teams, I'm hopeful we'll have progress on that front. There was some talk of DI Singh being transferred to Glasgow when DI McClair comes back from maternity leave, but . . .'

'I heard. There's a problem with that?'

'Two problems,' Mann said. 'The first, it'll be six months before Noele's back in action, and the second . . . big Tarvil's none too keen on leaving Edinburgh. Normally you might say "tough on him, it's a national force", but he's a bit of a folk hero these days, after he took down that bomber before he could atomise Sauce Haddock.'

'Could DI McClair be transferred through instead when she comes back?' the DS asked.

'No chance. She's a single parent, and as well as having the new baby, her boy's halfway through primary school. She relies on her mother for support. It's not just her they'd be moving, it would be her whole bloody family.' She drew a long breath. 'Bob Skinner was right all along, you know. He said loud and long that a national police service would never work in practice, and that cost savings were over-riding common sense, but the politicians . . . Skinner's then wife among them, by the way . . . ignored him. He was a great cop, Big Bob, a, the, role model for the people who're at the top now, McIlhenney, McGuire and

Mackie. He taught them all. He'd have been great as the first chief but he stuck to his principles and walked away.'

'He's done all right out of doing that from what I've read,' the DS observed. 'Isn't he the chair of an international media company now?'

'Global, John,' she said, 'it's global. He'll likely be in the job for a while too; I heard from Sauce that he's moving his family to Spain.' She flexed her shoulders suddenly, rippling the tight-fitting tunic. 'Come on then, back to business. Let's take a look.'

The two detectives stepped into the huge tent, which was floodlit by four lamps on stands, one on each corner, all of them powered by a generator that was positioned outside. The area in which they stood was dominated by the vehicle but the putrescent odour emanating from it filled the space entirely. She had been warned to expect it, but she reacted nonetheless, slipping on a filtered mask. 'Jesus,' she whispered, her voice muffled. 'You weren't kidding about the smell.' She looked at its source. 'I wasn't expecting the thing to be that big. It qualifies as a motor home, not just a bloody Dormobile. What is it? American? A Winnebago?'

'No, it's German,' Stirling replied. 'It's called a Schlossneues, if that's how you pronounce it. I didn't do German at school. I checked it on my tablet; I couldn't see the manufacturer's name anywhere but I identified it using the logo on the back. Whatever you want to call it, it's well over a hundred grand's worth.'

'RJ08WRJ.' She read the registration plate, then glanced at Stirling, a question in her eyes.

'I've checked, boss,' he answered. 'Inevitably, they're stolen: according to the DVLA it's a Renault Clio, belonging to a woman in Dumbarton. We'll try to trace it through the chassis number, but it's a left-hand drive vehicle. There's a better than even chance it was first registered in Europe, rather than the UK.'

'Get somebody on it anyway, John,' the DCI instructed. 'I'd better take a look inside. Is Professor Scott here yet?'

The DS frowned. 'Who's Professor Scott, boss?'

'Ah sorry, you haven't met him yet. He's the lead pathologist: he took over from Graeme Bell a couple of years ago. He works out of the Queen Elizabeth Hospital in Glasgow.' She paused, reading hesitancy in his eyes. 'You have called for a pathologist, haven't you?' she asked.

His brow furrowed. 'Ah, er, no,' he admitted. 'I called out the Forensic team. Isn't the pathologist part of that?'

Mann shook her head, briefly. 'No, Graham's a separate entity.' She nodded. 'His predecessor had the same name, but a different spelling, and he's a very different personality. Is Doctor Bramley with the scientists? She's head of the unit,' she added, in further explanation.

'Yes,' Stirling said. 'That is, I think so. The one who briefed me was female and the other two in the team are men. When they built the tent she seemed to be giving the orders.'

'Where are they now?'

'Back in their vehicle. They stopped work when they heard you were on the way; their boss thought you should see the scene as it was.'

'Not all of them stopped, only the lads,' a woman called out as she emerged from the motor home. 'It got overwhelming with three of us in there so I stood them down for a while. That was the excuse I used; these macho types, they need to be handled carefully or their pride will get in the way.' She stepped briskly down the two steps and on to the pavement. She was of medium height, fresh-faced, possibly a youthful forty; a dark curl had escaped her sterile hood. 'Hi Lottie.'

'Jenny,' Mann responded, glancing once again at her DS. 'John, this is Dr Bramley. Jenny, Detective Sergeant Stirling'.

The scientist smiled, apologetically. 'My bad, John. I should have introduced myself properly when we got here, but I was in a hurry to get the enclosure built.' She returned her gaze to Mann. 'What about the pathologist? We can't begin a proper sweep until he's seen the body in situ.'

'We're about to call hm,' the DCI advised. 'John, I'll flash you his number. Get in touch with him and brief him. You'll probably make his day. The messier they are, the greater the challenge; that's how Graham sees his job.' She sighed. 'Me, I'm the opposite, but I suppose we'd better take a look. Are you up for going back in, Sergeant?'

Stirling winced, as did Bramley. 'Brace yourself, Lottie,' she advised. 'Most of the flies vacated the premises when the door was first opened, but there are still a fair few in there.'

Two

'This is a lifetime first for me,' Sir Robert Skinner confessed. 'I've never had physiotherapy before. Lots of other stuff, but never physio.'

'That's no great surprise to me,' Camilla Knorr said. 'You've obviously lived an active life, and you still do from what you've told me. For a man of your age your muscle tone is excellent. What sort of training do you do?'

'I work out regularly, on my home equipment and in our office gym in Spain. I run whenever I can find the time and the place. Running's what I like best: or I did, before my right knee packed up on me.'

'Don't be daft, Sir Robert,' the physiotherapist protested. 'It hasn't packed up. It's a long way from doing that.'

'Bob, please.'

'Bob, then, and I'm Cammy. Your knee is basically okay; your kneecap is out of place, but I think that's because your hips are a bit tight. I'm going to tape it back in the proper position, and give you some exercises that will help. Also, there's a procedure that I can show you; it's one that a partner can do for you. Do you have one?'

He nodded, grinning. 'Yes I do, Sarah, but she prefers to be called a wife. She'll love that, especially if it hurts.'

'Does she have medical knowledge?'

'Sure, she's a doctor: actually she's a pathologist. Having a living subject will be a pleasant change for her.'

'Couldn't be better; with her help we can sort this in no time.'

'Does it mean I'm on the road to a hip replacement?' Skinner asked.

'Hell no!' Knorr exclaimed, laughing. 'I can't see twenty years into the future, but at the moment there's no reason to expect that. Mind you it would be handy to know why this has suddenly occurred. Remind me, when did you become aware of it?'

'Last week, at home when I was going upstairs. Until then it was fine.'

'Mmm, I see. Tell me: we know your exercise programme is good; have you had any lifestyle changes? For example a new office chair? A new chair at home?'

'Nope,' he replied, firmly.

'Car?'

'No. I haven't changed lately, in Scotland or in Spain. The fact is I don't drive a lot these days. I take a taxi to Edinburgh Airport, and I'm picked up at Girona.'

'You fly a lot?'

'Every week; there and back again.'

'Do you travel Economy or Business class?'

Skinner's smile hinted at embarrassment. 'We have a company jet,' he confessed.

'Wow!' Cammy Knorr exclaimed. 'Big time indeed.'

'It's not that glamorous,' he assured her. 'It's a Cessna Citation. Bigger than a Lear Jet but still I can't stand fully upright in it.'

'And the flight is how long?' she asked.

He frowned. 'That depends on wind direction, whether it's a tail wind or against us, but on average two and a half hours is probably a fair guess.'

'Is the seat comfortable?'

'Very.'

'Still, I think that might be the root cause of your problem.'

'What can I do about it?'

'Get a bigger jet?' She paused, smiling. 'Or failing that,' she continued, 'double down on the exercise programme and the hip manipulation. Or failing that . . . go back to your old job. I'm sure they would have you in some capacity.'

It was Skinner's turn to laugh out loud. 'I miss it,' he admitted, 'but nowhere near that much.'

Three

Lottie Mann ensured that her mask was firmly in place, before stepping up and into the motor home. Although she had prepared herself mentally for what she would encounter she flinched nonetheless as she entered the space. The stench that greeted her in the tent was even more intense. Behind her she heard Stirling retch, then swear, softly.

All of the vehicle's windows had been blacked out. Its blinds had been reinforced with plastic sheeting taped over each one, but the lighting that Bramley's team had set up inside flooded the scene, leaving nothing in shadow.

The body was seated in a faux-leather armchair, on a swivel base, beside a rectangular table that took up half of the width of the van. As the detective sergeant had said, it was held in place by broad brown tape wound round the arms and legs and securing it firmly in the seat. It appeared to be female, but from its attire alone, a long-sleeved blouse that might have once been pink, and black leggings. The head was covered by a plastic Tesco supermarket bag, lashed around the neck with the same brown tape, making it airtight beyond doubt.

'Fuck!' Stirling whispered.

'Couldn't have put it better myself,' his senior colleague affirmed.

The chair and the carpet beneath it were stained, as was the clothing of the corpse. 'What . . ?' the DS began.

'Body fluids,' Mann murmured, 'waste and God knows what else. The body gets bloated, gases build up, organs liquify. The old dear was right; I'd say she's been here for at least a couple of months.'

'She looks quite chunky: it must have been quite a task, lashing her into that chair.'

'Like I said, John, a body gets bloated as it decays. Let's make no assumptions. We'll wait for the post-mortem examination to give us facts.' The DCI shuddered. 'Come on, let's get tae fuck out of here. There's nothing useful we can do other than acquire memories that'll stay with us until we're in the same state as that one there. Go on, move it. Let's get some fresh air before we boak like that DC Brown did earlier.'

Stirling led the retreat from the awful place, down the steps, through the tented enclosure and into the street outside. Bramley and her colleagues were waiting there; one of the two men was vaping. 'Not a regular habit,' he told the detectives, 'but I find that it helps at a locus like this one.'

'Can I stand close to you and breathe some in?' the DS asked.

'No time for that,' Mann told him. 'We've got work to do. We need to get door to door enquiries in place. I want every household interviewed, every resident, in this cul-de-sac and beyond. Someone might have seen the vehicle being dumped here; with a bit of luck they might have seen who did the dumping. I'll get that under way. I'll want DC Brown, the one you stood down, and his DS, back here, and as many uniforms as we can round up.' Her eyes narrowed. 'Where's that PC? Ask him the name of that sergeant who's in the middle of his golf tie. He's getting pulled off the course right now.' She grinned, momentarily.

'While I'm doing that, John, you contact the manufacturer of this thing . . . what did you say it's called?'

'*Schlossneues.*'

'Indeed? Newcastle in English.'

Stirling looked at her, surprise in his eyes. 'You speak German, boss?'

'Why shouldn't I?' she retorted, fiercely . . . then grinned. 'I don't, not really. When I was at high school, we'd a young German supply teacher. He and I had a brief but passionate affair, and I picked up a few words, "*Schlossneues Braunbier*" being two of them, that being Newcastle Brown Ale in German, or so he said.'

'Maybe it's you should call the company, gaffer,' the DS suggested.

'Hell no. For all I know Dietmar might answer the phone, such being fate. The headmaster saw us in the pub; Dietmar got the sack and I got . . .' Her eyes went somewhere else for a few seconds. 'Come to think of it, I didn't get anything. I was quizzed by the guidance teacher about our relationship, but I was sixteen going on seventeen at the time, so I told her to fuck right off. She did.' She paused, coming back to the present. 'No, you go ahead and contact them yourself, John. I don't need you here; we're only half an hour from the office so get back there, where you've got a desk and a proper internet connection. When you speak to the manufacturers, ask where we'll find the chassis number on the vehicle; with that we can track down the registered owner through the DVLA.'

'Will do, Boss, but whoever that is, they're hardly likely to have dumped a body in their own van, are they?'

Mann laughed, softly. 'Assumptions, John. What do I keep telling you about making assumptions?'

Four

'Could you?' Sarah asked. 'If you wanted to, that is? Go back to policing?'

Bob grinned back at her across the table. 'Technically, I never left. Maggie Steele gave me a special constable warrant card, remember. I still have it. However, I was never a fan of pounding the beat; not even in my most sentimental moments would I ever want to go back to that. My first day as a detective constable was one of the happiest of my career. And another was the day I made chief constable. Since Neil McIlhenney's in the chief constable's chair, and will be until he retires, going back at the top doesn't appear to be a possibility.'

'The very fact that you've told me about your physio's remark has to mean that you've thought about it,' she asserted.

'No,' he countered. 'It means that occasionally I miss my old job, that's all. Keeping the streets safe, keeping the traffic flowing, catching the bad people, yes, it gave me a buzz. But the higher up the command chain that I climbed the more that buzz was diluted. The job I'm in now, executive chair of the Inter-Media group, I'm right at the top of the command chain there too, not of a geographical region in Scotland, but of an international media company. I'm making operational decisions every day and

I have input on policy at the highest level. The only things that I take to Xavi Aislado, as owner of the group, are matters that affect its future development, like the expansion into the US that we're planning with our Spanish cable news operation. I love it, and they pay me a fucking fortune to do it all. No way am I going to give that up, not until Xavi's ready to come back. So,' he continued, smiling, 'that leaves Cammy's other two suggestions for sorting my knee problem. A bigger jet is not undoable, given the US thing, but I'm not going to be the one to propose it. So I'll go for the cheapest option, manipulation of my hips, that's if you're prepared to help.'

She looked at him over her glass. 'I've manipulated most of the rest of you over the years, so why not? When's she going to show us what to do?'

'She's sending me a video link.'

'Okay.' She set the glass down in the table. 'By the way, what did you think of James Andrew's reaction when we told him and Seonaid that we're proposing to move to Spain? Do you think he only said "Yes" because he knew that's what we wanted to hear?'

'He didn't say "Yes", my love. He said "Magic". And he meant it. Jazz doesn't do diplomacy: he's started to think about his future, and he knows it isn't in Gullane. You have to be aware of that.'

'I'm only too well aware,' she admitted. 'And of his career plans. Hopefully he'll grow out of all that. It was bad enough being a cop's wife. Being a soldier's mum, that would be a whole different level of anxiety.'

Bob frowned, pausing as their waiter removed the dessert plates. 'I won't be any different,' he confessed. 'I'll worry as much as you. But you know as well as I do that he isn't going to grow out of it. The opposite's happening: he's growing into it, if anything.'

17

'Couldn't you talk him out of it?'

'Maybe I could; I don't know. But, would I talk him out of it? No, I couldn't be that selfish. My dad wanted me to be something nice and safe, a provincial family lawyer like him. He always felt that he lost my brother Michael to the military . . . although in reality he lost him to alcohol.'

'And to PTSD possibly?' Sarah whispered.

'That's what my dad thought, but I never believed it. In all his time in the army Michael never saw combat. He served in Northern Ireland for six months, but never in a high risk area, always in a background role. Anyway, he was on the piss well before that.' He shrugged. 'Whatever . . . my father wanted me to go into his legal practice. When I said "No" after I left university, and told him that I was joining the police, I knew he was disappointed, but I admired him for never trying to talk me out of it. There are many doors to other careers that I could open for Jazz, but I won't, not unless he asks me.' He sighed, leaning back to allow the waiter to serve coffee. 'Who knows?' he pondered. 'Maybe a few years in Spain will make him see the future differently . . . but don't hold your breath.'

'How about his big sister?' she mused. 'She's always adored him. How does she feel about his joining the army, do you think?'

'Alex? We haven't talked about it, but she probably feels the same as me: apprehensive but stoic. Anyway, Alex is very focused on her own life at the moment.'

'How do you feel about that?'

He gazed back at her. 'First and foremost, I have always wanted my oldest daughter to be happy. She is; she's happier and more content than I've ever seen her. And as for my friend Dominic, he seems to be the same. I tell you, love, my fingers have never been so tightly crossed for the pair of them.'

'Will they marry, do you think?' Sarah asked.

Bob blinked. 'Honestly, I've never thought about that,' he confessed. 'She's got a lot of her mother in her . . . not all of her, thank God . . . so she's a traditionalist at heart but . . .' He stopped in mid-sentence, reflecting. 'She isn't wearing a ring, third finger left hand. Remember, when she was with Andy Martin, the first time, they were engaged. But if you think back, you'll recall that she never once talked about them actually getting married. So in answer to your question, Sarah my love, I just don't know.'

'Babies?' she suggested. 'What if Dominic wants them?'

He shook his head. 'No,' he replied firmly.

'Why so sure?'

'Have you ever heard him talk about his past life, when he was Lennie Plenderleith, before he went to prison, earned his psychology degree and his doctorate, and adopted a new identity?'

'No,' Sarah admitted. 'No, I haven't.'

'Exactly. Can you imagine him trying to explain all that to his children? Or alternatively the pressure on him and Alex of trying to keep the secret in the years to come?'

'Maybe not,' she conceded. 'Changing the subject: how about your oldest son? How do you feel about him and his evolving relationship?'

'Ignacio and Pilar? Likewise, I couldn't be happier for them. I would say their relationship's evolved. They've both finished their chemistry degrees. Neither has any idea what they want to do with them, but they have all the time in the world to make their minds up. Meantime, Nacho's having a ball working on his mother's radio station.' Skinner looked up, as the waiter passed by. 'Angelo, could I have a nightcap?' he asked. 'Port, if you have it. We have twenty minutes until the taxi arrives.' He glanced at his wife. 'Sarah?'

'No, I'm good. Might they decide to live in Spain, do you think?' she continued. 'Pilar might like to be closer to her parents in Madrid.'

'She might,' he agreed. 'Her prospective mother-in-law might not be too keen on that though. Mia got up to some very dodgy stuff while she was raising my secret son over there, and she's never been back since they left. It's maybe as well that Pilar's dad, Señor Sanchez is a banker, and not a cop.'

'How about her mother? She might be one, for all you know.'

'Señora Hoverstad? She isn't. She works in advertising.'

She grinned, twisting a lock of her silver hair between two fingers. 'You checked them out? Seriously?'

He returned her smile. 'Actually she checked me out. She contacted me in Girona a few weeks ago, by email. When I saw the address at first I thought she was pitching for business. I almost binned it without reading it, until the name, Inge Hoverstad, threw a switch so I read it. All she was doing was introducing herself as Pilar's mum. There was a mobile number. Rather than replying by email I called it, feeling full of guilt that I hadn't reached out to them before, giving that our kids are now officially living together, with no pretence of being campus roommates. She's met Nacho, of course, as we've met Pilar. We spoke for about fifteen minutes, we got on, and we agreed that the two of us will meet her and her husband at the first opportunity, either in Barcelona if her husband's business . . . his name's Raul, by the way . . . brings him there, or we'll go to Madrid once we've officially moved to Spain. I'm sorry, love, I should have told you about this at the time, but the US expansion blew up at the same time, and then there was that other stuff with Merle Gower.'

'No worries,' Sarah said. 'Let's make it Madrid. It'll give me an excuse to go and look at Picasso's *Guernica* for another half hour.

Do you know if she's reached out to the Widow McCullough as well?'

'Mia? I don't, but if she has I'll bet the only thing on offer will be a visit to Scotland. I don't know if Spanish law enforcement was ever looking for her, but I doubt that she'll want to find out.'

Five

'Do you ever have days when you hate your job, Graham?' Lottie Mann asked.

The pathologist beamed back at her as he stepped out of his protective shoes and stripped off his stained gloves. 'Yes,' he replied, 'but this isn't one of them. I love a challenge and that person in there is certainly one of those. I know, I know,' he continued quickly, catching the detectives' expressions of disbelief. 'It stinks to high heaven, but that's nature folks, it's part of the process of decomposition. Every subject that comes to me has started down that road. You ask my esteemed colleague in Edinburgh, Sarah Grace, and she'll tell you the same thing.'

'Fair enough, Professor,' John Stirling countered. 'I get that, but where's the challenge here? Somebody tied her to a chair then suffocated her with a plastic bag. That's it, clear as day.'

'Is it?' he chuckled. 'It's one possible scenario I'll grant you, but the Tesco bag proves nothing.'

'Assumptions, John,' Mann said. 'What did I tell you?'

'That's right,' Scott concurred. 'It may be that the perpetrator, having despatched his . . . or her . . . or their . . . victim by another means couldn't bear the sight of the dead face, maybe even the reproach in the vacant eyes,' he added colourfully, 'and

22

chose to cover it up. To be frank, I can't even guarantee that the cadaver is female, let alone the means of its execution. We're going by the clothes, that's all. It, he, they could be a cross-dresser, for all we know.'

'Did you take it off, Graham?' the DCI asked. 'The bag.'

'No, I've left it in place. My people will remove the body very carefully. I'm not going to disturb the remains until they're on my table. There, I'll peel everything off piece by piece and we'll see what's inside. It'll be pretty messy, mind.'

'We?' the detective sergeant murmured.

'Oh yes,' the pathologist declared. 'This is a criminal investigation. That being so, the Crown Office requires that my work be witnessed.' He looked at Mann. 'Tomorrow morning, I think, if you're okay with that, Lottie. Ten a.m.?'

She nodded. 'That'll do; I'll include that information in the statement that I'll have to give the press office.'

'Yes, you will,' Scott agreed. 'There was a media presence when I came in here. I'm known to these people, so my very presence will have tipped them off that something serious is up.'

'Neighbourhood chat and social media would have done that anyway,' Mann grumbled. 'We'll be doing door to door enquiries on WhatsApp before I'm too much older. Graham,' she continued, 'if you're going to reserve your position on the cause of death, is there anything that you can tell us now? For example, the period when we're told that the vehicle was dumped indicates that the subject's been dead for a couple of months.'

'No, it's longer than that,' he declared. 'Even from the little I could see of the flesh, we're looking at a minimum of four months, probably longer. The body itself isn't going to give us an exact date of death. It might not even give us a cause, unless it's something that's still clear and obvious. If it was asphyxia that killed

23

the victim, the lungs aren't going to be a reliable indicator, not after all this time. You're right, Lottie, no assumptions. I'll see you both tomorrow.' He picked up his case and headed out of the covered enclosure.

Six

'Our officers have knocked on every door in the development, ma'am,' Sergeant Brian Knox reported, stiffly formal. Mann surmised from his manner that he was still carrying a grudge over his interrupted golf tie. *'Three up wi' four to play and she calls me in,'* she had heard him grumble to his colleague, DC Brown. 'About a quarter of them, we got no reply, but we'll re-canvass those tonight. So far nobody's had any knowledge of the vehicle and nobody saw it being parked.' He paused, then continued. 'But, we do know for sure when it was left, within a seven day window. Davie Brown had a bright idea, for once. His brother Alec works on the bin lorries. They still empty them once a week here, so Davie asked him if he could remember when the thing first appeared. The eighth of July, he said; that was the first day they saw it, so it must have been dumped between then and July the first, the previous Monday. Alec said the driver's been bitchin' about it ever since. It's been tight for the lorry getting by.'

The DCI nodded. 'Give him a gold star from me,' she said.

'Wi' that window you could check CCTV, couldn't you?' Knox suggested.

'That's possible,' Mann agreed. 'The only problem is, this being a new scheme there won't be any in the immediate area.

25

But,' she continued, 'all of this is one big cul-de-sac, fed off the main road. To be thorough, I want you to have people check on its coverage.'

He nodded. His resentment seemed to have been set aside. 'There's a couple of traffic cameras on that stretch, I know that. I'll look into it.'

'Thanks Sergeant. The footage will be stored somewhere, either locally or in the Cloud. The problem may be, how long do they keep it. The public get very sensitive about the nanny state, so I'm pretty sure there's a limit. Thirty days runs in my mind, unless there are very specific reasons for keeping it longer.'

'I'll check it anyway, ma'am.'

'Do that, thanks. By the way,' Mann added, 'I'm sorry about the golf tie.'

For the first time, Knox smiled. 'Ach, that's all right. It worked out okay. We've got a local rule that calls for a replay if a tie's interrupted by an emergency. My opponent knew he couldn't beat me in a month of Sundays, so he conceded. I'll report back when I've got something concrete.' He made to leave, took a few steps, then froze. 'Ma'am,' he called out, turning partly back towards her, but pointing away. 'That house there, the one directly opposite the vehicle: It's got a Ring doorbell, and that'll have a camera built in. I know because I've got one, and it works bloody well. I've had to warn my neighbour when it caught him pretty much falling out of his car when he came home after a late night. Depending on how it's set, the motion sensor might be triggered by someone as far away as the driver of the vehicle would have been when he got out. If they've got the right package, it'll store video for up to six months. The occupants are on the list to be re-canvassed. I'll come back this evening and do them myself if you want.'

Mann looked back at him, with what might have been a hint of a smile in her eyes. 'Thanks, Sergeant . . . Brian is it? . . . but we've done enough damage to your day off as it is. John and I will take care of that. But what you could do before you go, since you know the tech, is take a look at every house in this street to see who else has one of those Ring things. Even if the one across the street doesn't have the right settings or the right package, there might be someone else who does.'

She watched him as he set off on his task, but her mind was on Stirling and his search for the owner of the motor home. She was about to call him when her ringtone sounded. 'Det Sup Haddock,' the screen told her.

'Sauce,' she answered, switching the call to video.

'Where are you, Lottie?' the young detective superintendent asked.

'On the outskirts of Irvine,' she replied.

'The body in the camper?'

'That's right. You know about it already?'

'Yeah. I'm given a list of active investigations across the country at the end of every day. Helps me keep a handle on our clear-up rate, region by region. What's it about, and why's it for us rather than the locals?'

'That's what I asked when John called me, but yes, it is ours. The victim's so far unidentified, but it's homicide beyond a shadow, and a nasty one. At the moment we know a little less than fuck all, in that the pathologist won't even tell us what gender the victim is, so all we can do is gather as much information as we can about the location, the circumstances and the vehicle.'

'Can I help you with resources?' Haddock asked.

'To be honest I don't know. Once the autopsy's done and once I know whose vehicle it is, everything might fall into place very quickly.'

'What's your gut saying?'

'Other than "Feed me", you mean? My instinct and experience say that it won't. This doesn't look or feel like a spur of the moment crime. It was planned to delay discovery for as long as possible.'

'By dumping it in a residential area? How was that supposed to work?'

'It has,' Mann pointed out. 'It's been here for two months, with the victim decomposing inside, but, Graham's sure that death occurred well before that. Think about it, Sauce. If it had been left in a caravan park, it might have been one among many but the owner, would one, have wanted paying, two would have taken a closer look at it before now and three more than likely could identify the perpetrator. And if it had been left in the countryside, it would have stood out.'

'Granted,' the superintendent conceded. He paused as if he was considering something. 'Okay,' he said, finally. 'Listen Lottie, I'm aware that you're flying a bit light in Glasgow. I've been thinking about this for a few days but now I'm going to do it. I've got Jackie Wright here; she's DS level and ready for a step up, but she needs broader experience to take her on to the next stage. I'm going to assign her to you for the rest of this year. She's got seniority over Stirling, and I'd make her acting DI, but HR won't wear that: budget constraints, as usual. I could involve the deputy chief and ask him to override them, but I've only got so many favours in the bank with Mario McGuire and this isn't a sufficiently rainy day. You can manage her any way you like, but I want her ready for a promotion board by the end of the year. You good?'

'More than,' Mann exclaimed. 'I know Jackie and I rate her.' She smiled at the camera. 'If I can have her in Glasgow by ten tomorrow morning she can come to the post-mortem with me. Jackie won't throw up, but I reckon John Stirling might.'

Seven

'You're off the hook, John.'

'What do you mean, boss?' Stirling asked, phone to his ear. 'Why was I on it?'

'What I mean is that you don't have to go to the post-mortem tomorrow,' Mann replied. 'Sauce is giving us Jackie Wright for the rest of this year, so you're stood down.'

He smiled. 'That's good news,' he confessed. 'My imagination's been painting some colourful pictures. For example I've been seeing the professor cutting off the clothes and what's inside just running all over the floor and forming a big smelly puddle.'

'It might not be that bad,' the DCI chuckled. 'But it won't be pretty, that's for sure.'

'Jackie Wright,' Stirling said. 'I don't think I know him. The name means nothing to me. Is he a DI?'

'He's a she,' Mann told him. 'And she's a DS, for now, but as far as the command chain's concerned, she'll sit between you and me.'

'Does that mean I report to her from now on?'

'Not really: I see the three of us as a team. But, if Jackie asks you to do something, it won't be a request.'

'Understood, boss. I don't have a problem with that.'

'It wouldn't matter a damn if you did,' she said, 'but it's good to know. Now, the crime scene. Any progress in tracking the owner?'

'Limited, truth be told,' the DS admitted. 'The manufacturer has dealerships in the UK but no subsidiary, so I had to get on to the factory in Germany. There I was connected to the PR department, where they speak most languages. They were helpful: my contact there said that they're used to dealing with police enquiries; their vehicles are high value, so a few of them have been nicked. One was found in Poland, on its way to Russia through Belarus they believed. Her name was Deborah by the way, the PR person, not Dietmar,' he added. 'I meant to ask you, did you ever see him again?'

'Not that it's any of your business, but yes. He got in touch couple of years later, from Munich. I was with someone else by then, but we sneaked in a week in Gran Canaria. That was it, though. Enough,' she said firmly, ending the digression. 'Carry on.'

'Yes boss. Deborah told me where to find the chassis number: under the carpet in front of the driver's seat. Rather than go back down to Irvine and look for it myself, I got Dr Bramley's number from the soco office in the Crime Campus and rang her. She found it for me. I fed it into the DVLA . . . and got a nil return.'

'Which means it isn't UK registered,' Mann sighed.

'Exactly.'

'So we have to check on a country by country basis until we find it?'

'That's what I thought, boss . . . until the lovely Deborah came up trumps. I called her back, and asked if she could think of any shortcuts. She said there's one and it's very obvious. The motor homes . . . she got humpty with me when I called it a camper van . . . are covered by manufacturer's warranty, and have benefits attached. So, when each vehicle's sold and put on the road . . .'

The DCI finished the sentence. 'Ownership details go back to the manufacturer.'

'Exactly. I gave her the number that Doctor Bramley gave me and she came back to me inside ten minutes. It's a *Grose Kabine* model and it's owned by a company, registered in Jersey under the name Artisan de Boite Limited, in English, roughly that means Boxcraft.'

'You speak French too, John?'

'It's about as good as your German.'

'Mmm,' she mused. 'Maybe I should have shagged the French teacher as well. But then again maybe not; she was fat, fifty and had a moustache. Who owns Boxcraft?'

'That, Deborah could not tell me,' Stirling replied. 'For that I'll need to speak to the Jersey Financial Services Commission . . . but I won't be able to do that until tomorrow; it's closed for the day. That said, if you think it's necessary, I could ask the State of Jersey police to dig up a contact in the Commission.'

'It wouldn't gain us anything other than an enemy, John,' Mann observed. 'Tomorrow morning will do.' She paused. 'Will they be able to tell us who owns the thing, though? Don't these offshore companies often work through nominees?'

'Yes they do, but my limited research suggests that in Jersey you can't hide behind them. There's a register of beneficial ownership and an agreement at government level between Jersey and the UK that allows for information sharing with police forces.'

'You have googled Artisan de whatever, I take it?'

'I did boss,' the DS said, 'but all I've come up with is a seventy-seven year old French cabinet maker in a place called Pérouges, near Lyon, and I very much doubt that it's him we're looking for.'

Eight

'Are you all right with that, DS Wright?' Sauce Haddock asked.

And if I wasn't? she thought, but kept it to herself, knowing that few senior officers would even have asked the question.

'I believe it's a good move for you,' the detective superintendent continued. 'If it had been down to me you'd have made DS before you did. I see this as a shortcut in your future career path.'

'But no promises?'

'I can't make any. There's *x* number of DI positions around the country. I expect one to open up in the next six months, but with budgets under constant review by Holyrood, nothing in this service is nailed on.' He frowned. 'Bob Skinner's pathological hatred of politicians used to amuse me, but now I'm with him one hundred per cent. Mind you, I'm not about to let it show in the way he did. I'm not that secure.'

Jackie Wright stared at him. 'Sauce,' she laughed, 'you must be the most secure polis I know, even more than the DCC. Your wife's even richer than his, by a factor of ten, probably more. You could walk away tomorrow; we all know that.'

'You do?' he murmured, his expression suddenly so serious

that she was afraid she had pushed friendship too far. 'Well you're all wrong. The very fact that Cheeky inherited most of Grandpa McCullough's wealth, that ties me even tighter to my career. If I walked away from it what would I do? Pretend to manage a couple of the businesses she owns? Call myself a security consultant and do eff all but cruise around the pro-am golf circuit? No, I've always set out to be the best officer I can possibly be, and now I'm driven even harder.' His smile returned. 'Plus, we're going to have another mouth to feed next year. Cheeky's pregnant again . . . and you have the privilege of being the third person to know.'

'Wow,' Wright exclaimed. 'Congratulations. And yet . . . Sauce, I appreciate the career planning you're doing for me, but . . .' she hesitated '. . . you're assuming that's all the ambition I have. Just because I'm gay, that doesn't mean I can't get broody.'

Haddock winced. 'You're right, of course.' He held up his right hand. 'Obviously I flunked the people management section on the command course. Note to self: even police officers have private lives. And are you, Jackie, broody?'

'Personally, no. I'm not so sure about my partner, but she's just started a new job and that'll rein her in for a bit. You can bank on one thing though. Unlike our colleague Noele, I'm not going to have a one-night stand with some bloke and get myself knocked up.'

'Does all that add up to a "yes" to the Glasgow secondment?' Haddock asked.

Wright nodded. 'Yes it does. I heard someone calling DCI Mann "Godzilla" in the canteen. It'll be interesting to find out whether she lives up to the label.'

He laughed. 'She doesn't, I promise. That being the case,

meet her in the pathology suite in the Queen Elizabeth Hospital in Glasgow, ten o'clock tomorrow.' She nodded and turned to leave his office, but he called out, 'Hey Jackie, what do they call me in the canteen?'

She turned back to face him. 'Are you serious? When you get to be chief constable, they'll still be calling you Sauce.'

Nine

Despite the apology that had been proffered and accepted, Sergeant Brian Knox was still seething over the peremptory manner in which he had been summoned from the golf course, but quietly, for he had the common sense and experience to keep his feelings to himself. He reasoned that the best way for him to recover from the slight was by making a significant contribution to the investigation, one that the formidable Detective Chief Inspector Mann would acknowledge in her eventual report to the procurator fiscal.

His visit to the house opposite the abandoned motor home and crime scene had told him very quickly that its owners would not be helping him to do that. They made only the most basic use of their Ring device, and had neither of the storage packages that Amazon offered.

Sighing inwardly he had thanked them and left, resigned to an hour of door knocking that would in all likelihood prove fruitless. Less than ten minutes later his spirits, and his faith in old-fashioned thorough door-knocking were restored. Number Twelve Dredgerton Way, neighbour but one to the home that had given him false hope, had exactly that, a big old-fashioned brass knocker, with no buzzer in sight. He had almost passed it by, but seeing that it was on the list of homes to be re-canvassed, he had done his duty.

A lady had opened the door; early thirties, blonde, hair askew, a curious jam-smeared three year old half-hidden behind her. 'Is that a policeman, Mummy? What have you done?'

'Quiet, Camila,' the mother hissed. 'What have I done, Sergeant? Nothing, I hope. Is this about that van up the street?'

'Yes, it is, Mrs . . .'

'McColl, Janie McColl.'

'Thank you. I'm sorry to bother you; officers did call earlier, but you must have been out.'

'I was. I'm a private nursery assistant; Camila goes there, so it's handy. What do you want to know?'

'Whether you've seen anyone around the van recently, or at any time since it was dumped there.'

She shook her head, then ran her fingers through her hair in an attempt to restore it to some sort of order. 'No, I can't say that I have. We tend to keep to ourselves . . . unlike the woman in number sixteen, Mrs Galloway. She probably knows everything about everyone in this street by now, the nosey cow. If you speak to her and she tells you who shot Kennedy you'd better believe her.'

Knox smiled. 'I'll leave that one to the CIA,' he said. 'Although maybe they did it. Again, I'm sorry to have bothered you.' He turned to leave.

'Hold on,' she called out. 'I haven't seen anything, but our security system might. There's a camera covering the front garden and the street beyond with one hundred and eighty degree coverage. There's another out back too.'

'What?' the sergeant said. 'I didn't see . . .'

'You wouldn't, it's that discreet. Jordan, my husband had it installed as the house was being built. He's sales director of a company that makes industrial environmental control systems for an international market. He travels all the time . . . he's in Dubai right now . . . and he's obsessed with security, as am I. My parents live in Bearsden and one of their neighbours has been burgled three times in the last ten years.'

'The street camera,' Knox ventured, 'it's not just for effect, is it?' He realised the stupidity of the question as soon as the last words had left his mouth. 'But it wouldn't be, would it, since I never saw it. Do you know if the coverage is stored anywhere?'

'I'm sure that it is,' Janie McColl replied. 'Sergeant, come in. There's a file on the computer with all the details. If I can leave Camila with you for a minute, I'll find it.' Curiosity must have showed in his expression, for she added, 'No, she's not called after the queen. There's a Spanish singer called Camila Cabello and I'm a huge fan.'

She showed him into a living room with modern minimalist furniture, chosen possibly for practicality with a jammy toddler in the house. 'I'll be as quick as I can,' she promised. 'Camila, behave yourself.'

Knox took a seat in a firm white chair, appraising his temporary charge. He had a daughter of his own, a thirteen year old who had been named after a grandmother who had been named in turn after Princess Margaret Rose. 'You going to give me a song, Camila?'

She beamed, eyes widening then astonished him by doing just that. 'Said you hated the ocean but you're suffing now,' she chirped, 'said you'd love me for life but you just sold our house.' The lines seemed to be all that her three year old memory could store, for she repeated them over and over, tunefully, until her mother returned.

'I must teach her the rest,' Janie said, handing him a printed page. 'That's the company's contact number,' she said, 'and that's Jordan's client ID. If you need consent to access the camera coverage, get back to me and I'll get in touch with him.'

He accepted it and stood. 'Thanks, Mrs McColl,' he exclaimed, then looked down at the child. 'And thank you, Camila. You've got a big future ahead of you. You're lucky, Janie,' he told her mother. 'My kid sings Lizzo songs all the time. Some of them should have an "Explicit" warning, but she mumbles her way through the rude bits.'

Ten

DCI Lottie Mann's formidable reputation extended well beyond her home city of Glasgow. It had been born out of her insistence in taking part in a police boxing tournament, for men. The crowd, the great majority of them serving officers, had laughed when the rookie constable was introduced, only to be silenced less than a minute later as the referee counted to ten over her prostrate opponent.

She had felt so sorry for the poor guy, she suggested to friends a few years later, that she had married him. The union had not been ideal; there had been a few return bouts, of which she had lost more than she had won, but its one positive was a son, Jakey, who was growing up straight and true under the tutelage of her second partner, Dan Provan.

DS Jackie Wright had heard the whole story, and knew that a slot on Mann's team was a privilege rather than a punishment. Nevertheless on her first day on the job she was determined to make a good impression. For that very reason, she allowed so much time for the commute from her home in West Lothian, that she arrived at the pathology suite only a minute after the technician who was opening it up, and spent the next twenty making small talk and waiting for her new boss and the pathologist to join her.

Mann appeared first, at three minutes to ten. 'Jackie,' she said, hand extended. 'Welcome to No Mean City. Events like this are all in a day's work through here. The body count's much higher than it is in Edinburgh.' She glanced at her wristwatch. 'If Graham Scott's on time it'll be a first. He likes everything to be ready for him when he turns up.' She looked at the technician. 'Isn't that right, Goran?'

The man, in his thirties, powerfully built and with a solid jaw, accentuated by a light beard, grunted an affirmative as he positioned a gurney alongside the examination table. It bore a shapeless mass under a white cover, with a rubber liner beneath.

'Need help transferring it?' Mann asked, but he shook his head. He was a powerful man, and made light of the transfer of body to table and of easing the rubber sheet out from under it.

He had finished aligning the body, and was arranging instruments on a tray when the doors swung open and Professor Scott appeared, gowned and gloved. 'Good morning officers,' he boomed, eyeing them up and down. 'You might wish to dress appropriately,' he suggested. 'There's no clinical need for you to wear protective clothing but as you know, Lottie, this one is ripe.' He glanced towards Wright once again. 'Did DS Stirling call in sick?' he asked. 'He'd be by no means the first to do that if he did.'

'No, he's on other duties this morning,' she replied. 'DS Wright here is joining the team for the next few months.' She looked at her colleague. 'I think we'll take his advice, Jackie, if only to keep the smell from clinging to our clothes and our hair. If you think it's bad just now, wait until he peels off the wrapping.'

The two detectives accepted the gowns, hats and masks that Goran offered to them. When they were clad, Professor Scott picked up a pair of long narrow scissors from the tray. 'Let's see what it looks like under the Tesco wrapping,' he murmured as he went to work, cutting through the tape that held the bag in place. As he slipped it off, blonde hair, lacking any lustre, came with it in clumps.

'Almost certainly dyed, I would say,' Scott murmured. 'We'll know for sure soon enough. And yes, Lottie your victim is female.' He felt the exposed neck with a gloved hand. 'It's not definitive but the size of the Adam's Apple is a reliable indicator.'

'Are you saying women have got one, Professor?' Wright asked. 'I thought . . .'

'As do most people. Yes, Eve had one as well. It's the cartilage that covers the front of the larynx, but it grows bigger in males during puberty, and that explains why men have deeper voices than women . . . and louder too,' he added, 'until the ladies have a few drinks, that is.'

'Less of the gender stereotyping, Graham,' Mann said. 'I get quieter when I get pished. Don't you, Jackie?'

'I don't get pished, boss,' the DS replied. 'I learned not to when I was a teenager, the hard way.'

The flesh of the murder victim was blackened by decomposition. 'Can you tell the ethnic origin?' Mann asked the pathologist as he measured the corpse with a tape.

'She's either Identity Code one or two, light skinned or Hispanic European. Could be either. The DNA profile will tell us, when it's extracted. She was approximately five feet eight inches tall, solidly built but not overweight, as far as I can tell at this stage. Any body fat will have liquified by now.' He turned to his assistant. 'Goran, would you please cut off the clothing and remove it carefully. As always be careful to leave any labels intact, in case the officers have no physical means of identifying the victim and have to use the barcodes.'

The body was dressed in blue jeans and a long-sleeved red and white check shirt: both garments were heavily stained. 'Wranglers,' the technician said, quietly as he cut his way through the trousers. 'The shirt too, I think from the logo. There's something in its pocket, by the way.'

Mann felt her stomach heave as the clothes and underwear were removed. She thought that her reaction had gone unnoticed, until Scott turned from his assistant to look knowingly in her direction. 'We can take a break now,' he said. 'Goran will spray-wash the subject before I open her up. I tell you now, the organs will have deteriorated badly, but I can give you a possible cause of death; or one of them at least, there could have been a combination of factors. She was hit before or after the bag was put in place, hard enough for there to be blood and hair sticking to the inside. Goran will take her to be scanned and X-rayed. When I see the results I'm expecting to find a significant skull fracture. While he's doing that, let's go for a coffee.'

'I don't think they'll let us into Costa smelling like we must,' Wright observed.

'No,' the pathologist agreed. 'That's why I keep a percolator in the ante-room.'

Eleven

From the name of the registered owner of the motor home, John Stirling had feared that his French might be put to the test, when he began his search for information about Artisan de Boite, but he was soon put at ease. 'I'm trying to trace the owner of a company registered in Jersey,' he told the switchboard operator. 'My name is Detective Sergeant . . .'

'You should speak to Mr Vassell, Head of Registry,' the man said. 'I know he's busy just now, but if you give me a landline number I'll have him call you back when he's free.' Clearly the rank had been a trigger. The call back, he interpreted as a standard security procedure. Mobiles were just that, but landline numbers were verifiable. That assumption was more or less confirmed as his phone rang within two minutes.

'Elwyn Vassell,' the caller announced, 'Jersey Information Commission. I wasn't given your name, Sergeant. Our switchboard can be a bit trigger-happy I'm afraid.'

'Understood. John Stirling; I'm a member of the west of Scotland Serious Crimes Unit.'

'Do you suspect this company to be engaged in criminality?' the executive exclaimed.

'Not at this stage,' the DS replied. 'This is just one strand of an investigation.'

'Can you give me the name? Again, I wasn't given that significant detail.'

'Artisan de Boite.'

'Do you have a registration number?'

'I'm afraid not.'

'Doesn't matter. Our company names are unique. Let me consult the alphabetical list. It shouldn't take me long to find an A,' Vassell chuckled. 'No indeed,' he said, almost immediately. 'Here it is. Artisan de Boite, a general investment company. It could be a trust of sorts; a device for someone to keep their wealth in a single place. The company has one officer listed, that's all. His name is Marco Gialini. I know him; for all the name, he's as British as you and me. Marco's a front for several registered companies, where the beneficial owner prefers to stay in the background. I'll give you his number, but he can be hard to pin down sometimes. He's a Jersey resident, but he has another home somewhere and he's there often. He has a very relaxed lifestyle.'

Stirling was curious as the call ended. 'Very relaxed lifestyle' was open to interpretation in many different ways. *Only one way to find out*, he thought as he punched in the Jersey number he had been given.

The call went straight to voicemail. 'This is Marco Gialini. I'm skiing right now, but if you leave your name and number I'll call you back. If you need to find me sooner than that, I've sure you'll work out how.'

'Skiing?' Stirling muttered. 'In fucking September?'

'Leave your message at the beep.'

The detective obeyed, leaving his name and number, then

waited. His hope that the man would respond as quickly as Vassell. 'Fuck that,' he growled, then logged on to Facebook and entered a search for Marco Gialini. It returned twenty-four hits: he began to scroll through them. The posts on the first ten pages that he visited were all in Italian. Those on the twelfth were predominately English with a little French mixed in. He checked Marco's 'about info', smiling as he found a UK mobile number. Five minutes later, having eliminated every other of the listed pages as a possible, he called it. The ringtone repeated seven times before the call was answered.

'Marco,' Stirling heard a drowsy voice mumble.

'Mr Gialini,' he began, 'this is DS John Stirling, from the police in Glasgow. I need to talk to you?'

'Right now?' the man complained. 'I'm in fucking Wanaka, mate. If you don't know where that is, it's in fucking New Zealand, South Island, it's past my bedtime and I've got company.'

'I'm sorry about that, Mr Gialini, but this is an urgent enquiry and you seem to be the only person who can help me.'

'Can't it wait?'

'If it could I'd have hung up by now. I need to find the beneficial owner of a Jersey company, in which you're a nominee director.'

'Which one out of the fifty plus,' Gialini sighed.

'It's called Artisan de Boite Limited.'

'Yes, that's one of mine. What's the problem?'

'I've been tasked with tracing the owner of a *Schlossneues* motor home that's been found abandoned in Scotland, possibly stolen, and I find that it's registered to Artisan de Boite.'

'That's right; I bought it on the instructions of the client, but I've never seen it. We sent the registration plates to the factory in Germany and it was collected from there. No theft's been reported to me, Sergeant, but if it was stolen, thanks for recovering it. I'll make some calls and arrange for it to be picked up.'

'It's not quite as simple as that, Mr Gialini,' Stirling said. 'I need to speak to the actual owner of the vehicle, not to the company. That means, the person behind Artisan de Boite, the person you represent. I'm hoping we can do this informally, but be under no illusions, this is not a request, it's a requirement. I can make it formal if you like, even if that means you being on the first flight back from New Zealand.'

He heard a great exhalation. 'Okay,' Gialini conceded. 'Let me make a couple of calls and someone will be in touch with you.'

'Today?'

'If that's at all possible.'

'It had better be,' the DS warned. 'If I haven't heard by three o'clock this afternoon, I'll be calling you back. And please, don't think about switching your phone off, Mr Gialini. Now I know where you are, I can trace you. I doubt that your companion would appreciate the police battering on the door in the middle of the night.'

Twelve

The autopsy of Van Woman, as Graham Scott had named her, was not the first post-mortem examination that Jackie Wright had attended, but as it progressed she knew that there was not a single detail that she would ever forget.

Much of it was routine; the detailed examination of the body, the Y incision, the spreading of the chest cavity, the removal, examination and sampling for laboratory of the main organs, the noise of the saw cutting through the skull to reveal the brain. She had seen all of that before in other homicide investigations, but, with the single exception of long buried skeletal remains, those had all been carried out within two days of the victim's demise. The remains had been fresh, not swollen with the skin rendered mottled green and black by advancing decomposition. Van Woman, Scott determined had been dead for at least four months, possibly as many as six, and her decay had been accelerated by the conditions in which she had been kept.

'It will have been warm in that vehicle, ladies,' he said, when his work was complete, 'and that will have speeded up the process. Recently Sarah Grace did one in Spain, where, from what she's told me, she will now be spending some of her professional life, and most of the personal. The stiff she had to work on there

48

was literally so. He had been stored in a chest freezer and had to be thawed out for two days before she could open him up. Van Woman's insides were the opposite; they were like a slurry pit, and her brain looked like something a window cleaner had thrown away. At some point in her life she'd had her appendix removed, but other than that I can tell you little or nothing about her medical history because her organs were just too degraded. Skeletally she was almost intact; the X-rays showed no healed fractures. The shape of the pelvis suggests that she never had a child, or at least never carried one full term. The uterus and ovaries were still there, but degraded like everything else.'

'How old was she?' Mann asked. 'Can you tell us that, Graham?'

'Between thirty-five and forty-five, I'd say. That's going by the state of the skeleton; she had a solid frame and was possibly fairly fit. What I found was flesh, with little sign of fat. She weighed in at seventy-one kilos, in the state that you saw her. Take five off for the soiled clothing; alive I'd put her around ten and a half stone.'

'Did you remove any jewellery from the body, Graham? A wedding ring, for example?'

'No, Lottie, I didn't. The only thing on her was that piece of paper in the shirt pocket, but it's illegible. Maybe it can be recovered but don't hold your breath while you wait for it.'

The DCI wrinkled her nose. 'That doesn't surprise me. Jenny Bramley's team found absolutely no personal effects in the motor home; nothing else either. The thing was stripped clean.'

Wright raised a hand, as if she was in a lecture theatre. 'Cause of death, Professor? Can you give us one now?'

'I can't be definitive,' he confessed. 'Nor could any other pathologist, although I can think of a couple who might claim to be. There is indeed, the X-ray revealed, a depressed skull fracture to match the blood, hair and tissue adhering to the inside of the Tesco bag. The size suggests that she was hit with your classic blunt instrument. That, and the site of the blow, could have, yes I'd say would have, proved fatal, but would she have expired before she suffocated? The lungs are too far gone to give or even suggest an answer to that question, I'm afraid.' He shrugged. 'But actually, Jackie, who cares? Ultimately her body died because her brain did, and no jury on this planet is going to find that happened as the result of anything other than a deliberate act . . . other than possibly one in Russia.'

Thirteen

'He said no, Hector,' Bob Skinner told the chief executive of the InterMedia Group. 'I told him it was the most significant expansion we've ever made and that as the President of the company, as he still is, he should be seen to be there in America when our Hispanic cable news channel goes live. He wouldn't wear it. He said that it would undermine me as chairman. I said I didn't give a fuck about that, but he said he did; he argues that I'm the one with the high level contacts in Washington, so I should be the face of the business. He also said that he's only keeping the President's chair warm for his daughter Paloma, when she's gathered enough experience to take over.'

Hector Sureda sighed, spreading his hands wide in a gesture of defeat. 'There's no persuading him?'

'None.'

'I shouldn't be surprised,' the CEO admitted. 'He will not even talk to me these days unless you are there: "undermining" being the word he repeats over and over. Looks like you and me on the first of October, then.'

'Yes. I'll have our secretary book the flights. You good to go on the Sunday,' Skinner asked, 'two days before the launch?'

'Sure, but aren't we taking the Cesna?'

'No fucking way! That's fine within Europe, but we're not crossing the Atlantic in it. It doesn't have the range.'

Sureda smiled. 'I'm glad you said that.' He paused. 'Bob, if it pays us to have a company jet, now that America is coming on stream, shouldn't we have an aircraft that's capable of flying there direct?'

'There is a case for it,' Skinner agreed. 'My physiotherapist would agree with you one hundred per cent, by the way. But it's not one that I can bring to the board myself; you neither. Take it to the chief financial officer and ask her to look at it, long term, against the cost of business and first class flights to and within the US for up to a dozen people. It's not a luxury, it has to be justifiable financially. If she says it's a go-er, she can present the case to the board. It won't happen in three weeks, though, so I'll have the flights booked regardless.'

'Will we fly first class or business?'

'That'll depend on how good our travel agent is at screwing upgrades out of airlines.' He grinned. 'Whatever, it'll be an unusual experience for me, flying with other people. I haven't done that since Xavi asked me to take on this job.'

Sureda was laughing as he returned to his own office, leaving his chairman to turn his attention to his lunch, a chorizo-filled mini-baguette that he had baked and prepared that morning, before leaving his apartment in Girona. Skinner's life was going to change very soon, when Sarah and the three youngest children moved to Spain from Scotland. He was looking forward to the change, and yet apprehensive also, hoping that Jazz and Seonaid would settle into the English language schools that had been chosen for them. Dawn, the toddler, was no problem; Trish, the children's carer was moving with them.

The move had been triggered when Sarah had been offered

part time university tenure in Barcelona. Originally they had imagined her commuting in the way that Bob did, but the idea had evolved, driven forward by the enthusiasm of both Jazz and Seonaid, once they were assured they could spend at least six summer weeks with their friends in Gullane.

As he ate he imagined the family fitting into the duplex. It was spacious for him, and had five bedrooms, but would it work? If not, the fallback was to live in the seaside holiday home he had owned in L'Escala since Alex was a child. 'You grew up in a bungalow in Motherwell, now you're a property millionaire,' he mused.

His ringtone broke into his thoughts. The screen showed a Spanish mobile number, one that was not in his directory. He answered it, curious.

'Sir Robert,' a male voice began. 'This is Raul Sanchez, the father of Pilar. I hope I am not disturbing you. I know you are an important man.'

He swallowed a mouthful. 'No, not at all,' he said. 'It's good to hear from you. As for importance, we all breathe the same air whatever it says on the office door. And the name's Bob. What can I do for you? The kids are all right, yes?' By which he meant, he realised instinctively, 'You're not going to tell me your daughter's pregnant, are you?'

'As far as I know they are fine,' Sanchez replied. 'I have not heard from Pilar for ten days at least. Her mother may have but I haven't.'

'Ten days is okay,' Skinner assured him. 'I haven't heard from Nacho since I saw the pair of them in L'Escala two weeks ago. When my daughter Alex was their age, a month could go by without her touching base. Mind you, she was setting out on her career by then,' he observed.

'I hear what you are saying. This concept of a gap year did not exist thirty years ago, not in Spain.'

'If it did in Scotland back then, Raul, nobody told me about it. Even now it's normally taken between leaving school and starting university, rather than after graduation. Nacho's lucky, in that he's leaving with no debt hung around his neck.'

'And Pilar the same,' Sanchez added, quickly.

'Good. I don't influence the editorial stance of InterMedia titles, but neither do I hide my personal belief that the nations should invest in their future, and that means equating higher education with health provision. It's a tough political sell though. People are afraid of death, but not of ignorance.'

'I like that,' the banker laughed. 'Bob, the reason I call, I'm going to be in Barcelona on business on Thursday. I wonder if we could meet for dinner? I would be happy to come to Girona, if that made it easier for you.'

'It probably would,' Skinner admitted. 'I'm flying back to Edinburgh on Friday morning for an afternoon meeting. Why don't you stay over Thursday night? There's plenty of room at my place . . . for now.'

Fourteen

'How did it go?' Sauce Haddock asked the face on the screen.

'How did it go?' Lottie Mann repeated. He saw her pause for a moment to consider the question. 'Among the experiences I would not want to live through again,' she concluded, 'it runs childbirth a close second.'

'That good, eh? Does it leave us any closer to identifying the victim?'

'It rules out the chunk of the population that isn't female and IC one or two, but apart from that, no. We can only hope that her DNA is on the database, or failing that, a label on her clothing gives us a pointer. If we have to go to dental records we're stuffed; the X-rays show that she had perfect teeth. How do you search for somebody like that, Sauce?'

'What about the vehicle?'

'I've got John Stirling looking into that. He's identified the owner, and yet he hasn't. It's a Jersey company, but doesn't tell us much. He reported to me ten minutes ago that he's tracked down a contact who's currently in Wanaka, New Zealand. Skiing, would you believe?'

'I'd believe most things. Does he need to go there to interview him?' Haddock chuckled.

'That option didn't occur to him, thank Christ. No, his man said he would arrange for someone else to contact him. If that doesn't happen, there are legal steps we can take to identify the beneficial owner.'

'Fine, Lottie, but how long will that take?'

'I've no idea,' she admitted. 'John threatened the guy, Gialini, his name is, with a visit from the Wanaka police. We know that's bullshit, but hopefully Mr Gialini doesn't.'

'What's the level of media interest?' the superintendent asked.

'Modest so far. All we've told them so far is that a body's been found in a motor home. The press office called the death "unexplained" rather than "suspicious", but I'm going to have to front up and upgrade that before the day's out. Unless you want to do it as head of serious crimes?' she added, hopefully.

'And undermine you? No way. I will report it to the DCC, but I'm pretty sure big Mario will be content to leave it to you. Trust me, you want that: if he got involved you'd be under much more scrutiny.'

'I know. I'll wait until five. By that time John might have got a result. That or Jackie might have made progress on identifying the buyer of the clothing, but the outer garments are all big brand stuff, which will probably make it more difficult.'

'What about the underwear?' Haddock suggested.

He saw Mann's frown. 'Why do women have to cut the labels off their bras and knickers? Don't they know it makes them impossible to track down?'

'When will you have the DNA profile?'

'Mid-afternoon, I hope. It's all we'll have: Jenny Bramley says the inside of the vehicle was absolutely clear.'

'Still, if the victim's on the database . . .'

'Yes, but how many people actually are, Sauce?' She shook

herself, quickly. 'Fuck it,' she snapped. 'Come on Charlotte, think positive. This one will be, and as soon as we know who she is, and know who and what were in her life we'll have ourselves a list of suspects.'

'That's the spirit. Check in with me please, before you do the media briefing. There's bound to be some bugger'll come back to me looking for a little extra.'

'Will do, Sauce.'

She clicked the red X on her screen and her boss disappeared, leaving her free to accept the incoming audio call that had been signalled. 'DCI Mann?' the newcomer began. 'It's Brian Knox here, in Irvine, about the canvass of the area around the van.' The man sounded excited, a world away from the dour individual she had encountered the day before. 'I've made some progress,' he said. 'Not with the house nearest the van. That was a dead loss, but. There's one just down the road with a much better security system, with long-term video storage, and I've been given access to it.'

Mann felt a surge of renewed energy running through her. 'Excellent,' she exclaimed. 'How do we view it?'

'The owner's given me a link. All I need is a computer with a decent screen.'

'Come to my base in Glasgow,' she said. 'We've got that here, and some extra manpower too. The more we have looking the sooner we'll see who's on there.'

Fifteen

As morning skipped seamlessly into a warm autumn after-noon, John Stirling's impatience grew. He was the new guy in the team, and felt that status keenly. Jackie Wright's arrival from Edinburgh had done nothing to boost his confidence. While he had not been looking forward to witnessing the post-mortem he had seen it as an endorsement in a way. Yes, he had been given an important task instead, but he had a sense that the assignment had less to do with Lottie Mann's faith in his problem-solving skills, as she had put it, than it had with her fear of him emptying his breakfast on to the floor.

In an attempt to keep his frustration at bay, he called the Jersey Financial Services Commission once more, to see whether there was any way that the procedure could be short-circuited, but found Elwyn Vassell to be intractable.

'There are formal procedures,' the official declared. 'They were put in place for a reason; to protect the civil rights of people who choose to incorporate here. We are not part of the United King-dom, Sergeant Stirling, but we are its closest international partner and have been for hundreds of years. Constitutionally we're a Crown dependency; the relationship is through the UK sover-eign, not its Parliament and we have the rights of self-government and of judicial independence. Whatever information I might hold by virtue of my position, that belongs to my government, and can only be shared within the framework of a formal agreement with yours. In other words, you can badger me all you like about the ultimate ownership of the company Artisan de Boite, but you will get nothing out of me.'

'What if Marco Gialini called you and said "Go ahead"?' Stirling countered.

'He's not going to do that, son,' Vassell sighed wearily. 'If he did that his other clients would find out and dump him overnight. Look, how about sharing yourself? You've told me as much as I've told you, zilch, other than saying that you don't suspect Artisan de Boite of being crooked. Is that really true?'

Stirling reflected on the question. 'Maybe not,' he admitted. 'The company owns a motor home.'

Unexpectedly, Vassell laughed. 'You're not going to tell me it's parked on a politician's driveway are you?'

'It would be a bloody sight easier for us if it was. In fact, it was parked, legally, in a street in Scotland a couple of months ago. It was only when it was opened yesterday, on public health grounds, that a body was discovered inside.'

He heard a gasp. 'My God,' the man said. 'And you're a detective so . . . Okay, I get it, I get it. I still can't help you, but what I can do is message Marco Gialini and tell him that if I find him being obstructive in any way, I won't forget about it. People like him need to be on my good side.'

'Thanks for that at least. Hopefully you won't hear from me again,' the DS said as he ended the call.

He would never know whether Vassell's hand was behind it, but twenty minutes later his landline rang. 'DS Stirling, serious crimes,' he said as he snatched the phone from its cradle.

'Sergeant,' a male Scottish voice drawled; Glaswegian, he judged. 'My name is James Bonar. I'm a solicitor, senior partner in James Bonar and Associates and I've been asked to call you by Mr Marco Gialini. I believe you and he had a conversation earlier on today.'

'That's correct. Am I speaking to the beneficial owner of Artisan de Boite?'

'No, you're not.'

'Then with the utmost respect, Mr Bonar,' Stirling sighed, his patience hanging by a single strand, 'why the hell am I speaking to you?'

'Because my firm acts for the beneficial ownership of the company. We're instructed to speak on their behalf, but under no obligation to reveal their identity, any more than Mr Gialini is, without an order from the Jersey Parliament. Even less in fact, because he'd only tell you that it's me. Now, what's this about?'

'It's about a badly decomposed corpse that was found yesterday in Irvine, tied to a chair in a motor home purchased in Germany by Mr Gialini for your client's company and registered in Jersey.'

'You fuckin' serious?' Suddenly James Bonar's accent had become even more Glasgwegian. An image of Detective Inspector Jim Taggart appeared in Stirling's mind's eye.

'Never more so.'

'Whose is the body?' the solicitor croaked.

'That's what I was hoping you could tell me.'

'I don't know, for Christ's sake. Look I'll need to get back to you on this.'

A switch was thrown in Stirling as the last thread of his patience was severed 'No,' he barked, his thick shoulders hunching. 'Mr Bonar, we're now in territory where I believe you may be obstructing a homicide investigation. You give me an answer now, or I'll have uniformed officers at your office within five minutes and we can continue this conversation in mine. You might not have met my boss, DCI Mann, but I'm pretty sure you'll have heard of her.'

'Okay, okay, okay!' Bonar cried out. 'The owner of Artisan de Boite isn't a person, not as such. It's the beneficiary of the estate of the late Mr Leo Speight.'

Sixteen

'How are you doing through there?' Detective Inspector Tarvil Singh asked.

'I don't really know,' Jackie Wright confessed to her surprise caller. 'My feet haven't really touched the ground yet. My new boss and I spent all morning contemplating the ultimate fate of humanity, and now I'm looking across an open plan office watching my new DS colleague . . . who may or may not be happy to see me here: I haven't figured that out yet . . . tear lumps off someone on the phone.'

'How do you know that, if he's across the room?'

'Body language, Tarvil. He's a big lump of a boy . . . not as big as you but big enough . . . with a US marine haircut. He was having what appeared to be a polite conversation, then all of a sudden he turned into Brock Lesnar.'

'Not Lottie Mann?'

'No, Lottie has an even temperament. She's intimidating all the time, without meaning to be.'

'What are you doing through there, anyway?' Wright's former colleague asked. 'All Sauce told me was that it's a messy homicide.'

'That's an understatement,' she said. 'The crime scene's a big mobile caravan . . . false plates, naturally . . . and the victim's been dead for up to six months, so the pathologist said. I'll leave you to imagine what the autopsy was like. A further mess is that we don't know who she is, and whoever killed her's gone out of their way to make it hard for us to find out. The crime scene's absolutely clean. Even the steering wheel and information display were wiped.'

'Age?'

'Forty, give or take a few. Dark hair, dyed blonde. Fit, GSOH as they say on the dating sites.'

'Did you recover DNA?'

'Yes, there was no problem with that. I've been given a profile; now I'm waiting to see if the database throws up a match. Meanwhile I'm trying to trace her through her clothing. She was wearing Wrangler shirt and jeans. I'd hoped the distributor might have been able to narrow down the area where they were bought. Far from it; when I sent an image of the labels, they told me that it could have been in France. Hold on,' she said. 'That's a text in from Gartcosh. Ah shit,' she sighed as she read it. 'Her DNA isn't on our database, or any other.'

'And yet . . .' Singh murmured.

Wright waited. And waited. 'Come on,' she said. 'And yet what?'

'Nothing really,' he admitted. 'It was just . . . You said the vehicle had been wiped clean of prints.'

'Yes. It's back on the Crime Campus now; the socos are still working on it but so far they've found nothing.'

'Okay. Thing is, you're obviously dealing with a very careful perpetrator. I'd be assuming that they wore gloves in the crime scene, so, why did they bother to wipe everything down?'

'Just in case they had left some.'

'Possibly Jackie. But . . . could you recover fingerprints from the remains?'

'No chance,' Wright said. 'They were too far gone.'

'So, might the perpetrator have wiped the scene because they knew, or had reason to believe that the victim's prints were on the system?'

'That's a thought,' she conceded. 'You're no' just a big dumb Sikh, are you?'

'I never was, Jackie,' Singh laughed. 'I'll take that as a compliment by the way.'

'You know me well enough to realise I couldn't have meant it any other way.'

'Yeah, you're the least Woke person I know.'

'And I'll take that as a compliment. Any other flashes of insight?' she asked.

'Just one. Having had some experience of caravan holidays, I will bet you there's one place that wasn't wiped down. Beneath the toilet there will be a removable cassette that holds . . . let's say waste. If your victim used that vehicle herself, and travelled in it, she'll have emptied it regularly. Unless she was super-hygienic and used gloves when she did, there could be prints on it.'

'That's a great thought, Tarvil, but how would we know they were hers, with no comparison?'

'Because she'll have left her DNA as well, Sunshine, along with the prints. You might want to pass that on to Jenny Bramley. I know she's very good, but as Joe E Brown said to Jack Lemmon, nobody's perfect.'

Seventeen

As Lottie Mann and John Stirling stepped into James Bonar's twelfth storey glass-walled office, each had a momentary feeling that they were hovering over the centre of the Clyde. The block was positioned at a slight bend in the river, on its southern bank, offering a view of its bridges and beyond, of the city's Victorian heart.

As they entered, the solicitor gazed at them, two bulky figures whom he realised he would much rather be receiving on his turf than visiting on theirs.

Mann caught his appraising look and returned it. The man was of medium height with a slim build and a haircut the cost of which, she guessed, might have fed her family for a fortnight. He wore a dark jacket and waistcoat over pinstripe trousers, complemented by a royal blue shirt with a white collar and tie. He had the appearance of a court practitioner, but the chief inspector had never seen him there, and surmised that he was dressed purely to impress.

'Officers,' he said, as they approached. 'Let's sit over here.' He led them towards a quartet of chairs set around a low table. 'Nobody has a worry about heights, do they?'

In fact, Mann had a full blown phobia. It had been

65

accentuated by a helicopter flight to the top of a nine thousand foot mountain a few weeks before, but there was no way she would admit it to the lawyer. She took the seat closest to the glass wall, but with her back to it. Stirling took the place facing her, so that they were flanking Bonar.

'Coffee?' he asked. 'Tea? Something stronger? Ahh,' he chuckled with a forced smile, 'but you're on duty, aren't you?'

'That wouldn't bother us,' the DCI replied, 'but John's driving, so we'd better not. Enough of the pleasantries, Mr Bonar. We're here to discuss Artisan de Boite, and the estate of Mr Leo Speight.'

'You know who he was?' Bonar asked.

She glared at him. 'Of course I do. A Scottish boxing champion, maybe the greatest, from Paisley. He died in a bizarre accident a few years ago. At first his death was flagged as suspicious; I was the SIO in the investigation so of course I bloody know about him. I remember everything about the case, all the circumstances, but what I don't remember,' she added, 'was Leo ever having a company registered in Jersey. In fact I was told that he didn't, by somebody involved.'

'Whoever told you that didn't know the whole picture. About a month before he died, Leo approached me personally. I'm from Paisley too; I knew him at school although we weren't close. He told me that he had just rewritten his will, but he was afraid that in the unlikely event of his death, hell would be raised by the mother of two of his children. Against that possibility he wanted to hide some of his assets. He asked me to set up an off-shore company that would hold the bulk of his liquid assets invested in various long term and fixed interest bonds, accessible by him or in the event of his death by the beneficiaries of his estate.'

'Speight died a while back,' Mann said. 'Was this holding declared to HMRC for inheritance tax purposes?'

'There's no inheritance tax in Jersey.'

'Who administers the company now?' Stirling asked. 'You, or Gialini, your nominee in Jersey?'

'I don't think I have to tell you that,' the lawyer replied. 'I'm not even sure we should be having this discussion without the permission of my client. I did try to locate her before you arrived, by WhatsApp and by a direct call, but I've had no response.'

'Her,' Mann repeated. She felt a cold fist grip her stomach. 'When did you last hear from her?'

'April, when we had a six monthly management review with the Jersey company's financial adviser. There's been no contact since, I'm afraid.' He frowned, sitting upright. 'Look, that's as much as I can tell you. When I do contact her, and I have her permission, we can continue this discussion.'

'Mmm,' the DCI murmured. 'That may be sooner than you imagine, Mr Bonar. It's possible that we may have found her for you.'

Eighteen

'What do you think he wants?' Sarah Grace Skinner asked her husband.

On her screen, Bob smiled. 'Dinner?' he suggested.

'Yes, but more than that, surely. They know we're moving the family here at the weekend. That'll make you much more available. Did he sound anxious in any way?'

'He sounded like a busy bloke trying to fill his diary, love,' he said.

'Do you think Ignacio might have upset him in some way?'

'How? Nacho's in Dundee, filling in for one of the presenters on Mia's radio station, and Pilar's understudying the manager at Black Shield Lodge, the resort. My son is more likely to upset me, but he hasn't. Anyway, Nacho and Pilar are grown-ups. If Raul had a problem, I'm sure he'd sort it out directly rather than come running to me.'

'Come on, you've got daughters. What would you do?'

'What did I do? you should ask. It wasn't plain sailing when Alex was growing up. There was one time when she was fifteen, the mother of a lad at North Berwick High came to me complaining that she'd burst her son's lip open. I apologised and said

68

to her that next time her kid put his hand up my daughter's skirt, I'd deal with it personally.'

Sarah gasped. 'You did? Alex told me about the incident, but she didn't mention that.'

'Alex never knew about it. She told me about the thing when it happened, as did the mother of one of her Gullane pals. I weighed it up and decided that justice had been done.'

'What would you have done if you'd met the boy?'

His eyebrows rose. 'I don't actually know. But I hope I'd have talked to him and pointed out that a fat lip was getting off lightly, compared to a listing on the sex offenders' register.'

'You'll miss not being close to Alex when we're gone, you know,' Sarah said, 'much more than you're letting on.'

'I've missed her since she left home for Glasgow University aged eighteen. The year before we met,' he added. 'But that's life. I have this theory; so far it's mostly based on observation, but with Mark off to Cambridge it'll be proved soon. When daughters go, they go for good. Sons, they never go completely, not until they have a family of their own.'

'What about Ignacio? He doesn't come back here.'

'Where is he now?' Bob countered. 'He's at his mother's. Where's Pilar? Not in Madrid, where she grew up; she's with him.'

'When they're ready, they'll set up home. Maybe that's why her dad wants to meet you. He's going to demand that your son make an honest woman of his daughter.'

'Maybe. We'll see. Meanwhile . . . are the kids ready to fly here on Saturday?'

'Jazz is,' Sarah said. 'He can't wait to get on the jet. Seonaid, she's a little less so. She's very close to Noele McClair's Harry, and she's just fallen in love with Matilda, the baby. But as I've told her, she used to be the same with Dawn, her little sister. Now, she says she's a pain in the ass.'

'She's learning life. Nothing is forever.' Suddenly he frowned. 'Hey love, I've got to go. I have an incoming voice call from Mario McGuire. I wonder what the hell he wants?'

Nineteen

'There's no doubt,' Jenny Bramley declared, looking at the two detectives across her desk. 'The name you suggested to me yesterday afternoon, Lottie, it's her.' She shook her head. 'I have no idea how you came up with it. That's why you're the cops and I'm the scientist.' She smiled at Jackie Wright. 'Yours was a good shout too, Sergeant. I can't put my hand on my heart and say for sure that my team would have looked there without you prompting them. When they did, they found clear fingerprints and DNA that matches the profile of the body. The fingerprints match those of an Alexandra Bulloch, as you said they would Lottie.'

'Yeah,' Mann sighed. Her eyes were set and fixed on a point behind the scientist. As Wright glanced at her, she was disturbed to see that they were glazed.

'What I don't quite understand is why her fingerprints are on record but her DNA isn't. It's standard practice these days with people when they're arrested.'

'Sandra was never arrested, Jenny,' the DCI murmured. 'Her fingerprints were recorded for elimination purposes at crime scenes. She wasn't a criminal, she was a police officer. As a matter of fact she was my boss, until she left the force a few years ago.' As she stood, she turned to Wright. 'We need to see DCC

71

McGuire, Jackie. I told him, and Sauce, about my suspicion as soon as I left the guy Bonar's office. The big man said if I was right I should take it straight to him. He told me that he's on the Campus today, so hold on while I message him.'

Wright and Bramley looked on as she took out her phone, keyed in a text then waited. Less than a minute later a click signalled a reply. She glanced at the DS. 'Now,' she said. 'Jenny, where do I find the conference rooms in this zoo? I don't know my way around.'

They followed the scientist's directions through the complex building, taking several minutes to reach the corridor where the great dark figure that was Mario McGuire stood waiting, his expression as serious as that of Mann. 'In here,' he said quietly, opening a door behind him and ushering them into a small room with a view across open countryside from its single window.

'Well,' he growled. 'This is a can of worms, no mistake.'

'Too right,' Mann agreed. 'The media haven't shown too much interest in the story up to now, but this will get everybody's attention.'

He nodded. 'You bet.' He glanced at his watch. 'Briefing in Glasgow at two?'

'I'd rather it was later, sir. Say five?'

'Why?' the deputy chief constable asked.

'Don't we have to tell Faye Bulloch before we announce it? As far as I know she's the next of kin.'

'I've done that already,' he told her. 'I sourced her phone number and called her myself. We've got no valid reason to delay, Lottie. We don't gain anything else by holding it back. I pulled Sandra's file from HR: yes, Faye's her next of kin. Apart from Faye's children by Leo Speight . . . her niece and nephew . . . her only other living blood relative's an elderly aunt of hers on her father's side. The file hasn't been updated since Sandra left the service, not that you'd expect that. When I had the aunt's address checked out, I discovered that she's now in a care home in Biggar, in South Lanarkshire. I've told the division to send a ranking female officer down there to break the news before we announce it. It'll be done within the hour, so you brief the media this afternoon. Or if you feel it's necessary I'll front it myself. Do you?'

'It's your call, sir, but I'm okay to handle it.'

'Then you do it, that's fine. Let's treat this like any other suspicious death. I'll keep a low profile, but . . . when Faye Bulloch is interviewed, as she will have to be, I'd like to be there. I'm not saying for a moment I don't think you're up to it, but I remember the woman from last time. She'll insist on having a lawyer present. I imagine that'll be Moss Lee, same as before. If it is, frankly, I want to intimidate that little bastard.'

'Sir?' Jackie Wright ventured, her tone questioning.

He looked at her. 'Jackie,' he murmured, 'you don't have a clue what we're on about, or who, do you? You were on the other side of the country, maybe even in uniform, when the thing kicked off. This is what happened. A few years ago . . . don't press me on the date . . . Detective Chief Inspector Sandra Bulloch was the head of the serious crimes team you've just joined; DCI Mann, then a DI, and DS Dan Provan reported to her. One day they had a call-out to a suspicious death in a big house in Ayr. The victim was Leo Speight, the recently retired undefeated world champion boxer.'

The DS nodded. 'I remember his death, sir, but I didn't realise he was murdered.'

'That's the thing,' McGuire said. 'He wasn't, but the medical examiner suggested that he might have been poisoned. Sandra was early on the scene, followed by me, followed by Lottie and

Dan. Almost immediately, Sandra recused herself as SIO, by advising us that Leo Speight was her brother-in-law. But that was actually deceitful. There was a lot that she didn't tell us. In fact she and Leo weren't formally related at all; he had two children by Faye Bulloch, her sister, but Faye and Leo didn't cohabit nor had they ever. Speight also had an older child, a son, from a teenage relationship, and a kid in Las Vegas with a woman that he regarded as a friend rather than a partner. When he was in the US he usually stayed with her and the wee one. When Sandra stood aside as an investigator, DI Mann took over and that's the situation her team uncovered.' He glanced at Mann. 'Do you want to carry on, Lottie?'

'Yes, sir, can do.' She looked at Wright, then continued. 'It wasn't until well into the investigation that we were led in another direction. Certain forensic evidence was found in the house that led to Sandra Bulloch being interviewed herself. Under questioning she admitted that she and Leo Speight were actually together; they had become a couple, and were even planning to marry. That would have been a first for Leo, and for her for that matter. She didn't know it at the time but this had to come out. Shortly before his death, Speight had changed his will making her the principal beneficiary. In the process, Faye was disinherited. When she found out she went apeshit . . . so much so that she might have gone to jail for attempted murder. She was actually charged but the Crown Office decided the evidence didn't give a high enough chance of a conviction.'

'So how did Speight die,' the sergeant asked, 'if he wasn't poisoned?'

'Accidentally; let's just call it misfortune. Look it up, Jackie,' she said. 'There was a book published about his life, and his death. To carry on, Sandra's reticence would have been a disciplinary matter if she'd chosen to stay in the police service, but she didn't, she resigned, forthwith, and left the country. I can't speak for everybody she ever worked with, but I've never heard from her or of her from that day on, and I know for sure that Dan hasn't either. Basically she's been gone from our world since all that stuff happened. I'm now gob-smacked that on Tuesday I watched her being unwrapped and filleted without having the faintest idea that it was her.'

'When did it first dawn on you that it might be?' Wright asked.

'As soon as John Stirling mentioned Leo Speight's name after speaking with Bonar. When he did, I knew for sure.' She sighed, looking at McGuire. 'Where do we go from here, sir?'

'You tell me,' he countered. 'You're the SIO.'

'Well, I'd say we begin by reviewing the record of the investigation into Leo Speight's death,' she said. 'Also we should talk to everybody she ever worked with, just in case there was someone she kept in touch with.'

'Everyone?' the DCC drawled. 'That's a big ask. But there is someone I can help you with. You two get back to Glasgow and I'll call him, right now.'

Twenty

'Bob,' Mario McGuire began, as his friend and mentor picked up his call, 'I have something to tell you. Three days ago, officers were called to a motor home in Irvine. It had been parked there for weeks, the neighbours were complaining and it was starting to smell.'

'I know,' Skinner said. 'They found a body inside. Remember, mate, the *Saltire*'s one of our newspapers, so I scan it every day, whether I'm in Scotland or here. I saw the reports, both of them, the discovery, then the second one labelling it as suspicious. What is it? Drug related? A gang thing?'

'No, it doesn't appear to be either of those. We haven't a fucking clue what it is, other than a very brutal and callous murder. The thing is, and the reason I'm calling . . . Bob, we've identified the body. It's Sandra Bulloch.'

McGuire heard a quick intake of breath, then silence. He was about to ask if Skinner was still there when he spoke. 'Sandra?'

'Yes.'

'Beyond doubt?'

'Beyond a shadow.'

'How?'

SECRETS AND LIES

'She was tied to a chair, a bag was put over her head, and she was hit.'

'Who did the autopsy?'

'Graham Scott.'

'Mmm. He's the second best in the business, after my lovely wife. What actually killed her, then? The blow to the head?'

'We don't know for sure,' McGuire admitted. 'It could have but equally it could have been asphyxia that finished her off. She'd been dead for months, Bob; four, five, six. She was killed well before the vehicle was dumped where it was found. She was only identified after the crime scene team found fingerprints in the only spot that hadn't been wiped clean of any traces to her. We've only just had confirmation of the ID.'

'Jesus,' he hissed. 'The poor lass. Lottie's the SIO, I take it. Or is Sauce leading?'

'No, he's not. It's DCI Mann's area so she leads, with Jackie Wright as number two. Obviously she'll get all the backup she needs.

'Suspects?'

'Not yet. I'm not sure where Lottie can begin. The sister will be interviewed for sure, but other than her there're no obvious leads. As of now we know absolutely nothing about Sandra's life after she left the police. Lottie'll have to piece that together. But first she and her team will have to talk to former colleagues, on the off chance she's kept in touch with somebody.'

'That should include me,' Skinner said. 'In my brief tenure as chief of the old Strathclyde force, Sandra was my exec.'

'I'd forgotten that,' McGuire told him. 'How soon can she speak to you? Where are you just now? Here or there? What's your availability in Scotland?'

77

'It's very limited,' he admitted. 'I'm going home tomorrow morning. Twenty four hours later, the whole family are flying to Spain. It's moving day, Mario. I suggest that Lottie calls me tomorrow afternoon if she can. If she prefers a face to face, I suggest we meet at Edinburgh Airport.'

Twenty-One

'Sergeant Knox?' John Stirling rose as the uniformed figure approached his desk in the squad room.

'That's me,' the newcomer confirmed, extending a hand. 'Brian. And you'll be DS Stirling I guess.'

'John, yes.'

They shook hands; Knox looked around. 'So this is the nerve centre,' he said.

'I prefer to think of it as the hive,' his shirt-sleeved colleague replied, ''cos it's where the queen bee lives.'

The newcomer laughed. 'Nice one. Is she about?'

'No, she and DS Wright are at the place in Gartcosh, hoping to confirm the identity of the victim. I've had no feedback so far, so I don't know if we have it yet. Anyway it's not relevant for what we've got to do. The boss said you've got a video link for us.'

'Yes, that's right.' Knox paused. 'Have you ever been to Gartcosh, John?'

'Inside it? No. But I've driven past it often enough.'

'What is it, exactly? It's just a name to us country plods.'

'As I understand it, it's where all the specialist services are located. For example, it's where the forensic scientists do their science. That's who the boss and Jackie have gone to see. It's not

79

just them though; there's all sorts there. Somebody told me once that HMRC are there; that they have their own investigators. I don't know that for sure, though,' Stirling added.

'Mmm, those bastards are everywhere. They sent me a text yesterday saying I'd be fined unless I gave them the information they needed. Bastards!' Knox repeated, vehemently.

'You didn't respond, did you?' his colleague asked.

'I had to, didn't I? I don't want to be fined. It can affect your credit score and everything.'

'Fuck me,' the DS whispered. 'It's a scam, Brian. HMRC never send text messages, and they never ask you for personal information.'

'Seriously?'

'If you don't believe me, fucking google it.'

'Jesus, what'll I do? Where do I report it? Gartcosh?'

'There's little point in reporting it anywhere. What you do need to do is change all your passwords, on your banking apps, credit cards, subscription services, the lot.'

The visitor stared back at him. 'What sort of a world is this, John?'

'A very complicated and dangerous one, mate. I had a text myself on Monday from the Royal Mail. It said that a delivery had been delayed because of incorrect information, and asked me to log on to a link and then resend it to an online address. I almost fell for it, until I looked at the link and saw that it led to somewhere in Italy. Last night I had an almost identical text from another courier company. In both cases I deleted and reported as junk. For a while I thought that might be part of the scam, but no, that option's genuine. You'd better change those passwords now. Use the boss's office. Give me that video link before you go, and I'll get started.'

The sergeant nodded. 'I'll just write it down rather than text it. Nothing seems to be safe online.' He pulled a notepad across Stirling's desk, scribbled on it, then handed it over. 'That's the link to the security company's monitoring site, and the client password. I'll join you as soon as I've made myself safe again.'

As he left, the DS settled into his swivel chair, and pulled his computer terminal closer. Opening his browser he keyed in the link that the uniformed sergeant had left. It took him to the home page of an entity calling itself Busara Security Solutions. It described and depicted the services offered by the company, with heavy emphasis on discretion. 'Overt security relies on deterrence,' the opening paragraph read. 'Discreet solutions are just as effective and better at identifying property predators.'

Stirling smiled. 'Property predators,' he murmured. 'I'll bet someone in a marketing consultancy got a bonus for coming up with that line.'

He looked at the menu, found a section labelled 'Client Portal', and entered the password when prompted. A page opened, revealing the personal profile of Jordan McColl, of Twelve Dredgerton Way, Irvine. He scanned its contents until he found a further link leading to footage from the system's six cameras. Two were external, front and rear, four indoors, named as 'Living', 'Kitchen', 'Hall' and 'Camila bedroom'.

'They don't have one on their own room,' he observed. 'A wise move considering what Knox is doing right now. Any bugger could hack in there, find all sorts and post it anywhere.'

His fingers were crossed mentally as he clicked on 'Front'. He sighed with relief as he saw, beside an image that appeared to be live, given the light and weather conditions, a calendar. He selected a time window covering July and clicked again, on the first day of the month. The image grew to fill most of his screen.

'Now,' he whispered, as he hovered his cursor on an arrow beneath and pressed it. In the bottom right corner of the screen a date and time indicator, that had been still, began to move more rapidly than he could follow. Above it the image remained still.

'It's got a motion sensor, ya beauty,' he said, just as the picture came to life, showing a female figure, Miss Berry, no less, walking her dog on the pavement, past the parking bay where the motor home had been left. As she passed out of shot, the image and the clock froze once again, until it was triggered once more but only for a few seconds, by a car passing through the camera's field of vision.

He searched the indicators for a fast forward option and found it, doubling the speed of his review and then trebling it as he played his way through the first twenty four hours of footage. As he had expected, having no through traffic the area was quiet, with very few cars and not many more pedestrians. Miss Berry walked her dog twice a day; as did three other owners, everyone in the senior age bracket.

At nineteen minutes past eleven on the fifth of July, just under an hour after an elderly man and his Labrador had triggered the camera, with darkness fallen on an apparently moonless night, the screen sprang to life as a large white vehicle appeared from the left of the frame. Instantly, Stirling hit the 'Stop' icon. As he had been able to accelerate playback, so he was able to slow it down before restarting. As he watched the reactivated recording, he saw the vehicle settle carefully into the parking bay. It had been designed to accommodate at least two cars, but the motor home's positioning left no room for any other. He paused playback again, studying the image. The camera's night vision was excellent, but the view of the windscreen was affected by the reflection from a streetlight on the periphery of its range of vision. Focusing on it he advanced the video frame by frame, and was able to see a blind being drawn within the van.

'What's happening now?' he whispered, as the recording crept on for a few more seconds, then stopped. He could only guess the answer. Both the driver's and the cabin doors were on the left, hidden from his view. Possibly, the driver was still inside, sanitising the space, removing any identifying traces. Or possibly that had been done elsewhere, in which case the perpetrator had emerged and was fixing the clamp to the rear nearside wheel. And a further possibility, that he or she had made their exit from the scene without ever being captured by the camera. There were no homes on the other side of the motor home, only an open field.

Stirling was resigned to that outcome and to the video trawl having been a waste of police time, when the still image changed, subtly. There was a slight alteration in the reflection of the windscreen. A windvane in the McColl garden, which had been still throughout began to veer from side to side. A cyclist appeared in shot heading right from behind the motor home, on the pavement, but for less than two seconds before disappearing from sight down Dredgerton Way.

'Yes!' the DS hissed. He froze the play once more then rewound, frame by frame until he had a still image of the mounted cyclist. He saved it to his computer, zoomed in as far as he could, then saved it for a second time.

As he leaned towards the screen, he felt a hand on his shoulder. 'You got something?' Brian Knox asked. 'The driver?'

'Has to be,' he replied. 'Eleven thirty at night there can't be much cycle traffic on that estate.'

'Male?'

'Christ Brian, who knows? Whoever it is, they're wearing train-ers, tracksuit bottoms and a hoodie. It's not loose either, like hoodies nearly always are. It's tied at the neck, to hide the face as much as possible. Whatever the gender is, male, female, non-fucking-binary, that's our killer and they're leaving nothing to chance.'

'Maybe we can get an ID from the clothing,' Knox suggested. 'Or the bike. I've always thought they should have number plates.'

'Yes, and maybe if I let the video run for a couple of minutes more it'll start to snow. I'll send the image to the specialists at Gartcosh and see what magic they can work, but I reckon this is even beyond Harry Potter.'

Twenty-Two

'What does your gut say, John?' Mann asked as she studied the magnified image of the cyclist that Stirling had extracted from the video still. 'Male or female?'

'My gut?' Stirling repeated. 'Well . . . my gut says he's a man, but,' he added, glancing at her with a half-smile, 'that's perilously close to making an assumption, boss. The clothing's too loose; it could be either. It's a Trespass logo on the hoodie, but there's bloody millions of them. That won't take us anywhere.'

'No, it won't,' she conceded. 'Did you and Knox stop your playback when the vehicle appeared in shot or did you carry on further?'

'First off we reviewed it right through until the eighth, when the bin truck turned up. Quite a few people stopped to look at it but most of them were dog walkers, apart from a few curious neighbours, among them the male householder of the camera owner. But we didn't stop there, boss. We scanned right up until Monday when Miss Berry got her phone out and called the police again. I say again, because on July the thirteenth there's footage of one of our cars arriving at the locus. The driver and his partner spoke to a guy from the house next door to the camera, and drove off again all within five minutes. They didn't even look at the vehicle. Brian knows them. I think he was embarrassed by the way they brushed off the complainant. No I don't think so, I know, he was steaming after he saw it. He said he'd be taking it to the station commander.'

'He won't be the only one,' Mann growled. 'I'll be rattling their cage too. If they'd had the nous to check the registration number, Sandra's body could have been discovered then.' She turned to Jackie Wright. 'Has anyone followed up the owner of the stolen plates?'

'No, but we know they were taken in a supermarket car park in Drumchapel, in Glasgow, on June the twenty-eighth. The theft was reported on the same day.'

'A week or so before the motor home was abandoned. Jackie, I want to know if it was acted upon, if patrol vehicles were warned to look out for the number.'

'I'll find out, boss,' the DS promised, 'but even if it was, the likelihood was that the thing was off the road until the perpetrator was ready to dump it.'

'I agree,' the DCI conceded, 'but the fiscal's likely to ask when we submit a report so I want everyone's arse covered. On the positive side,' she continued, 'if we can look at it that way, we can take it from the video review that there was only one person involved in the dumping of the vehicle. Right John?'

Stirling nodded. 'I would say so, ma'am. We looked at the disposal footage several times, with that in mind, just in case we'd missed somebody else heading off in another direction.'

'Okay.' She leaned forward, forearms on the meeting table in her office and looked at her two colleagues. 'That's what we know so far: only a little more than bugger all. In a little over half an hour, at two o'clock, I'm going to have to tell the media that a former senior police officer, someone that quite a few of them will have known, has been murdered. I'm not going to share any more than I have to but I'm going to be asked all sorts of questions, and very few of those I'll be able to answer. I worked with Sandra Bulloch, but we were never close, nowhere near friends. She was above me on the ladder, DCI to my DI, and I was never happy reporting to her. I hope I'm nowhere near her as a line manager. If I am, I apologise. The truth is, I didn't like the woman, pure and simple. She was rude, peremptory and rarely cracked a smile. Because of that I knew very little about her, just that she'd dumped a long term partner, and had no friends anyone knew about, male or female. When it all came out about her and Leo Speight, I was as surprised as everyone else. You know the story, Jackie, about her and Leo, from our meeting with the DCC. For John's benefit, when he was found dead in suspicious circumstances, and a major investigation began, she was one of the first on the scene, but said nothing about them being together. In fact she actually lied to us. There was a very hush-hush internal inquiry, run by Bob Skinner . . . probably a mistake because she'd worked for him and he did rate her . . . and she never came back to work, just went away.'

'Where to?' Stirling asked.

'I don't know, John. Speight had property all over the place. There was a place in Las Vegas where his youngest child lived with her mother . . . Rae Something her name was, and the kid was called Raeleen. It went to her, then there was the mansion in Ayr where he died, and I believe there was a house in the Caribbean, possibly in the Bahamas. They went to Sandra in the will along with his wealth, apart from some hotels that he owned, a few specific bequests and the trusts he left for his kids.'

'What about the sister?'

'Zilch,' Mann said. 'She was a cow. She was a serious suspect at the time. Sandra obviously couldn't be part of the investigation, but looking back, I reckon she did her best to point us in Faye's direction.'

'So there was no love lost there?' Wright suggested.

'None at all.'

'Which makes the sister a person of interest, doesn't it?'

The DCI nodded. 'When we have a list she'll probably be at the top, but before we get that far we need to know all we can about Sandra herself. While I'm away telling the press who the victim is and trying to downplay the inevitable hysteria that'll follow, that's what I need you to be doing. Find out where she lived? How did she live? Who did she live with, if anyone? But start with the motor home. Find out everything there is to know about it and see where it takes us.'

Stirling raised a hand. 'Boss, does the thing have navigation? Could we track its movements before it was dumped?'

'The socos have looked there already, John,' Wright told him. 'They found that system was disabled, and any information on it had been deleted. Nobody's making this easy for us.'

Twenty-Three

'Bob?' the man ventured, although he seemed in no doubt as he approached Skinner in the Girona station forecourt.

'Raul,' he replied, extending his right hand. 'Good to meet you and thank you for coming all this way. It makes life easier for me. I have a lot going on over the next couple of days.'

'It's my pleasure,' Raul Sanchez assured him. 'I like this city, and it's very easy to get here. Fifty minutes on the high speed train from Barcelona.'

'Let's go,' Skinner said leading the way to the parking area outside. 'I've booked us a table in a Japanese restaurant close to my place. I can dump the car, we can walk there and I can still get you back for the return AVE. You're okay with sushi?' he asked.

'Of course. It's obligatory in today's Spain, and especially in Madrid. I've heard of a place that gives the sushi chef an armed guard, in case its rivals try to kidnap him.'

Skinner drove the short distance from the station to his home. Spotting a vacant slot outside their dinner venue, he parked there and programmed a payment through an app on his phone before stepping inside.

'To drink, gentlemen?' their waiter asked, after seating them.

'Corona zero,' Skinner replied.

'Sounds good to me,' his guest agreed. 'I have heard that there is now a zero alcohol Guinness, Bob,' he said. 'Is that true?'

'It is. Someone told me they both taste the same, but I don't like the standard version so I haven't tried it. The Corona zero does the job for me.'

The waiter returned with menus and the drinks, each with the obligatory wedge of lime in the neck of the bottle. 'Standard platter's my usual,' Bob told his guest, as the young man hovered.

'That will be fine by me. Cool, I believe you say in English now.'

'Hah,' he laughed, 'not in the version I've always spoken. So, my friend, are you happy with the way our offspring are progressing?'

'Very happy,' Sanchez replied. 'And I speak for Inge also when I say that.'

'Ignacio has . . . how do I put it? . . . an interesting history. You know that?'

He nodded. 'Yes, I do. The first time we met, the first time that Pilar brought him to Madrid, he told me his life story; how he was brought up in Spain by his mother, never knowing who his father was, the things they got up to, how he met you, what happened when his mother took him to Scotland, the spell in prison. He told me everything, I think.'

'Yes. My boy had quite an upbringing.'

'It's quite a tale. I admired his courage in being open about it from the start.'

'Have you met his mother yet?'

'No, we have not. But she has invited us to visit her in Scotland. What's she like, Bob? Can you talk about her?'

'Sure,' Skinner said. 'Hers is quite a tale as well. Mia Watson McCullough, she's a piece of work. She came from a notorious extended criminal family in Edinburgh; the Watsons and the Spreckleys. They were low rent hoodlums, not masterminds, any one of them. Her mother,' he paused, searching for an adequate description, 'she was an absolute brute, pure evil. Mia was the only one of her brood with an IQ above a hundred, way above as it happens. She broke free of them as soon as she could: not because she was inherently honest, but because she didn't want a life on the wrong side of society. And yet,' he said, 'that's where she wound up for a while.' He frowned at the memory.

'I met her when I investigated the murder of her brother. He had upset the wrong people. He had information they wanted so they took him to an indoor swimming pool and kept throwing him off the high diving board until they got it out of him.'

'That sounds like fairly gentle persuasion,' Sanchez observed.

'The pool was empty at the time, Raul, hence the murder investigation. The dead boy, he'd have been Nacho's uncle. When he was killed, Mia was a radio presenter on an Edinburgh station . . . Mia Sparkles, she called herself . . . with a big teenage audience. My daughter Alex was one of them. I was single at the time, she was frankly gorgeous, and she wasn't directly involved in the investigation so . . . that's how Nacho came into being.'

Sanchez nodded. 'That's what Ignacio told me.' He smiled. 'Not in so much detail but I couldn't expect that.'

'He probably doesn't know all the details. I doubt that Mia told him, and I never have. For example, I doubt he's aware that Mia had . . . unwittingly . . . set her brother up to be killed. When her mother found out, and she would have eventually, Mia would have been a target herself; that's how dangerous her mother was. I couldn't have guaranteed her safety, so I told her to disappear, fast. She followed that advice so literally, that I didn't hear from her or learn of my son's existence for almost twenty years.' He paused. 'I'm telling you all this, Raul, about all of Igna-cio's genetic inheritance, because it's important to me that you and your wife are fully aware of it. Pilar knows the story. Nacho promised me that he told her as soon as it became serious between them.'

'Yes,' Raul Sanchez said. 'He did. Bob, my friend, Inge and I, we have discussed all this, and we accept your son for what he is, not what his ancestors were. This too, he may have his mother's DNA, but he has yours as well. You are the person I see in him and that makes me feel very secure and happy for my daughter.'

'Thanks for that,' Skinner replied. 'I've a good feeling about the pair of them too.'

'What do you make of Mia now?' he asked. 'Or would you rather not say?'

'I've got no trouble with that. First and foremost Mia's a sur-vivor. When she met and married Cameron McCullough she knew exactly what she was doing . . . and so did he. He saw her as a problem solver. She saw him as a safe bet, and it paid off. If Mia ever gives you a tip about a horse in a big race, you back it, because she'll be right. One other thing I can tell you about her: she likes your daughter. She doesn't give anything away but I can tell.'

'I sense that you admire this woman, Bob.'

He drew a breath. 'I rate her abilities, but that's as far as it goes. The young Mia that I briefly fell in love with, she's long gone. The older version, she's someone you'd want on your side, rather than the opposite. She's moved on from her origins, no doubt, but I reckon there's one thing she did inherit from her awful mother; her ruthlessness. Anyone whoever threatened her son and his partner, they'd discover that very quickly.' Skinner smiled.

'Actually, when I think about it, the same's true of me. Is that what you wanted to know?' he asked.

'Is that why I wanted to meet with you, do you mean? No it isn't. I simply felt that it was time I got to know you. With us both being busy men, my business trip to Barcelona today seemed like a good opportunity.'

'I'm glad we've taken it. Speaking of business, I took a look at your bank and I talked to our CFO about it. You don't have any relationship with InterMedia at the moment but should a need or an opportunity arise in the future . . . she'd be open to a discussion.'

'That is very good to know,' Sanchez exclaimed, just as the sushi arrived, on two large plates.

The two men settled down to eat and to get to know each other better. The conversation began with business. Skinner radiated enthusiasm for the second career that he had never imagined on the day he walked away from the police service. He described the way in which InterMedia had grown since his involvement . . . coincidentally, he insisted . . . and explained its plans for a Hispanic cable news service in the United States. 'As a foreign company we thought we'd have problems with the regulators,' he said, 'but I know a couple of people with influence in the right places.'

'Do you think this new venture is bankable?'

He laughed. 'Our US bankers do, and that's what matters. Raul, there isn't a high capital cost in the set-up, and the potential revenue from advertisers looking to address the Hispanic market directly, well that's scary.'

'Still, it's a risk. Have you always been a risk-taker, Bob?'

He shrugged. 'I dunno. I've never walked away from a challenge, whatever the odds. You might say that makes me a risk-taker, but I've always had faith in my ability to get a job done. You're a vice-president of your bank. Surely you have too?'

Sanchez sighed. 'In business situations, I suppose so, yes. But life is more than business, and away from there, I . . .'

Skinner sensed a sea change in the man. 'Raul,' he murmured. 'what's up?'

The banker looked at him, across the table, across the platters of sushi. 'In Barcelona,' he said, 'someone has threatened to kill my wife.'

Twenty-Four

'Sandra Bulloch never lived in Speight's house,' John Stirling told the team, gathered for a morning meeting in the Glasgow office. 'The executors had sold it, for three and a half million, by the time the will was filed with HMRC. It was bought by a stockbroker.'

'Where did she live?' Mann asked. 'After she left the service?' she added.

'I don't know yet,' the DS admitted. 'Her passport and driving licence still have her at the address in Glasgow, in North Kelvinside, that she shared with her former partner, Craig Goram, until they broke up, but I've established that she sold that after they split and moved into a small flat on the south side of the river.'

'Could she actually have lived in the motor home?' Wright suggested.

'Not ever since she left the police, because it's too new. Recently, I suppose that's possible, Jackie. I've tasked a pair of DCs with tracking down every Alexandra Bulloch on the electoral register, and everybody of that name who's currently paying council tax. If she doesn't show up on either of those, well, it might even be probable.'

'Who handled the sale?'

As Stirling turned to the DCI, he wondered if her question was a test. If so, he had passed. 'An estate agent. She remembered it well. The property was in Bulloch's name alone and had been since she bought it, but Goram turned up at the completion, wanting a share of the proceeds and threatening legal action if he didn't get it. He wanted fifty per cent, but settled for ten after they had a brief private chat.'

'That was quite a climb-down,' Mann observed. 'Do we know where Goram is now?'

'He wasn't hard to find. He's a teacher; English, in a school in Dumbarton.'

'We should talk to him. Put him at the top of the list in fact, John. If Sandra talked him down from demanding fifty per cent to taking ten in a couple of minutes, it suggests to me that she had something on him. Who else will be on the list?' she asked.

'I've been looking at the Speight investigation file like you asked, boss,' Wright volunteered. 'Based on that, and what you've told me about it, we have to put Faye Bulloch, the sister, right at the top, above Goram. Leo disinherited her completely when he and Sandra got together.'

'One hundred per cent,' the DCI confirmed. 'Faye was our chief suspect back then, until we found out how Leo really died. Yes, we will interview her as soon as I can arrange it. When I say we, I mean me and the DCC. He wants to be involved in that one, for his own reasons. When we do,' she added, 'my plan is to go straight for her, to make it clear that she's our number one person of interest. Maybe we'll get lucky; maybe she'll fold and confess. Maybe,' she muttered, 'but I won't be betting the house on it.'

'When are you seeing her, ma'am?' Stirling asked.

'Soonest. The DCC's arranging it. I'm assuming she's still

living in the house in Troon that Leo bought for her and their kids. Is that right, Jackie?'

'I don't know,' Wright admitted. 'My priority's been to find out as much as I can about the victim's life, who were her current associates, and what could have led her to be killed as she was. I'm pretty clear that Bonar and the Jersey guy, Gialini, can't give us any more than they have already, so I plan to speak to the executors of Leo Speight's estate. There are two of them, a man called Charles Baxter, and Gino Butler, who was Leo's manager.'

'Gino was also his boyhood friend,' Mann added. 'He was closer to Speight than anyone, apart from Sandra latterly, and maybe Rae Letts, the woman in Las Vegas. Yes they should be priorities but we'll likely need to speak to every adult beneficiary in the will, as well as them. Baxter, he was Leo's property adviser. I might speak to him myself.' She stood. 'Okay, that's clear. Jackie, you progress that line of enquiry. Prioritise Goram, then the executors. John, you build a profile of Sandra from leaving the police until her death. The Faye interview, big Mario and I will do that whenever he tells me. As for me right now, I have another interview lined up, one I'll do by myself.' She checked her watch. 'Which means I need to get to Edinburgh Airport to be there when his plane touches down.'

Twenty-Five

'Why doesn't he go to the police?' Sarah asked.

'That's the second question I asked him,' Bob replied. 'They have done, but they're not impressed by progress.'

'The first question being?'

'Why?'

'What did he say?'

'He said it has to do with her work. She's a director of an advertising agency, Diaz Hoverstad, an equal partner, not majority owner. It has an office in Barcelona that took on a commission for a client in the soft drinks industry, to handle the launch of a new product, one that was a bit of a departure from the company's norm. The brief they were given was to reach all sections of the market; all ethnic groups, all faiths, all genders. They came up with a campaign that was supposed to be light-hearted but completely inclusive, using all media; press, radio, tv, social. It launched in June, when the Spanish school holidays began. It's gone down reasonably well,' Raul said, 'without starting any fires. The early sales figures have been okay, that's all, but it's early days. The campaign itself though, it's been well received. Public awareness has been great, so good that it's been shortlisted for an industry award. Everything was hunky-dory until the creative director's car was firebombed . . . she's the Diaz half of the business. She wasn't in it, thank Christ, but she was meant to be. She got in there, triggered the car's information package, plugged in Apple CarPlay and was about to start the engine, when she realised that she'd forgotten some artwork that she needed for a meeting that morning. She jumped out but was only halfway to her front door when the car went up in flames. It was an electric vehicle, with a lot of plastic bodywork that just melted, making it a total write-off. A fire crew attended and a couple of traffic cops, but at the time no crime was suspected. The insurance company's assessor couldn't be certain of the cause of the fire, but he put it down as a wiring issue and settled the claim without question. But, a couple of days later, the woman received a letter at the office. Paraphrased it said, "You were lucky last time, but we'll be back for you and all your blasphemer owners." The signature was "Las Hermanas de la Trinidad", the Sisters of the Trinity. Yes, she reported it to the Mossos d'Esquadra, but Raul said they were sceptical to say the least.'

'I can see why they might have been. That sounds like the work of random nutters,' Sarah observed. 'Was the car fire reported in the media?'

'There were a couple of newspaper stories, but not much. One of our titles carried a piece. It named her and mentioned the company.'

'So what? A mischief maker's still the likely source. Why,' she asked, 'is Raul so worried?'

'For two reasons. One, the letter was delivered inside an empty bottle of the advertiser's new product. Second, three days ago, Inge had a parcel arrive at her office in Madrid. It was dumped in the mailbox overnight and addressed to her, personally. Inside there was a dead rat with the product label pasted to it and a note that said, basically, "You're next," signed again by the Trinity Sisters. She took that to the Policia Nacional, but they were apathetic too, and wrote it off as the work of cranks, like the Barcelona cops.'

'And they're probably right. Why do you sound so concerned?'

'Because Raul and Inge are concerned, love,' Bob said. 'They're family, near enough.'

'Fine, but what can you do about it?'

'For openers, I'm going to have a word with Comissari Roza, the Mossos officer who helped Lottie Mann when she was here a few weeks ago. I'll tell her the story and ask her if she can have someone take another look, maybe an investigator rather than the patrol officers they assigned before.'

'What if she says sod off?' Sarah persisted.

'She won't.'

'God, you are good at getting your own way!' Her eyes seemed to sparkle as she laughed, on screen.

'You should know, baby,' he shot back. 'How are things at your end? Did Jazz and Seonaid get off to school?'

'Yes. It's the last day for both of them. I told Jazz he could stay at home if he wanted rather than catch the bus to North Berwick, especially as they finish at lunchtime, but he insisted. We've been speaking Spanish about the house since you've been away. I plan to keep it up.'

'You probably need the practice more than they do,' Bob said. 'I know the University is effectively bi-lingual, but not all of your students are going to speak English.'

'You forget, my love,' Sarah corrected him, 'that although I'm from New England originally, I practised medicine in a neighbourhood in New York City. My medical Spanish is plenty good enough.'

'It's got to be better than your shopping Spanish,' he laughed. 'Remember that time in Carrefour when you couldn't remember the word for carrot?'

'Just one word,' she protested. 'And zanahoria doesn't exactly trip off the tongue does it. Speaking of shopping, is the fridge stocked in the apartment? We'll be feeding a family of five plus Trish there, as from Sunday.'

'McDonald's will feed us on Sunday.'

'Us if you like, but not Dawn. She's far too young for a Big Mac.'

'It's okay,' he assured her. 'I did a late shop last night in Cort Ingles, after I dropped Raul at the station. Dawn can have a pizza; double pepperoni if she fancies it.'

'Bob!'

'Or failing that fish fingers.'

'Now you're talking her language.'

Twenty-Six

'How are your searches going, John?' Jackie Wright asked.

'They're still incomplete,' Stirling replied, 'but so far we're drawing a blank. There's an Alexandra Bulloch in Orkney, another in Castle Douglas and one in Cumbernauld, but none of them are possibilities. The team are still working on it.' He frowned. 'Meantime,' he continued, 'I've been looking for her on social media, on all the main channels, Instagram, Facebook, Twitter, Snapchat etc. You know what? I've come across a few Sandras, but all of them are spoof pages, people pretending to be the actress who spells her name with a K not an H. Our Sandra doesn't appear to have a social profile at all. I ran an internet search for her as well as the sites. There I had a couple of hits, but they were from press coverage of court cases, criminal trials in which she was a police witness, nothing current or anything like it. She's virtually invisible. How usual is that these days, Jackie?'

'It's not impossible,' she suggested, 'but I'll grant you, for somebody her age and stage it's not what you'd expect.'

'I even broadened the search, looking for her and Leo Speight together. He's all over the place, naturally, even though he's been dead for a few years, but there's nothing in his coverage to link him to Sandra.' He paused, smiling. 'Her sister, on the other hand, she comes up alongside him all over the place. She actually calls herself Faye Speight on her Instagram profile. There are three users with that name, but she's by far the most active. She's Faye Bulloch on the others, but she still posts often about Leo; memorials on his birthday and the day he died, that sort of stuff.'

'How touching,' his colleague drawled.

'Yes, but you wouldn't say that about the posts that mention her sister. There aren't many, but a couple of them . . . I don't know how they survived the Facebook taste police.'

'Indeed?' Wright exclaimed. 'Maybe print out some of those pages, John. They could be useful when we interview her.'

Twenty-Seven

'If you ask me to, Señor Bob, I will,' Comissari Lita Roza promised. 'I understand why my officers did not get excited when your friend complained. The incident with the fire was reported, so it was public knowledge. That being the case, we both know there are people who live for nothing more than to make mischief for others.'

'Of course, and I agree that if everything was investigated, no matter how trivial, you'd be doing nothing else. But the second incident,' Skinner said, 'it makes this one a little different. Madrid's about five hundred kilometres away from Barcelona, so the car incident wasn't reported there. Yet both packages were hand delivered, indicating we are looking at a network of sorts. Even without the link to the client product, it's worth investigating.'

'There I agree with you, and so I will. I'll assign two investigators to revisit the case. Does Señora Hoverstad or her company still have the packages that were delivered?' Roza asked.

'I'm assuming she disposed of the rat,' Skinner chuckled, 'but otherwise yes, hers and the one in Barcelona. I told her husband to make sure they were wrapped to prevent further contamination. As things stand they've only been handled by the recipients and an assistant in each office. Will you talk to the Policia in Madrid?'

'Yes I will. You're right when you say that the second incident is a significant escalation. I will take the threats seriously, I promise. Do you know if the company has any sort of security at its offices?'

'Yes, I asked that. Each one's within an office block. The owners employ security staff. In Madrid they're ex cops: in Barcelona, I'm not so sure.'

'They should be briefed. I'll speak to someone senior in Madrid and ask that your friend's home be put under discreet observation and the same with the Barcelona partner. I'll have my people look at the first package. If we get anything from that, I'll pass it on to the Policia, or get their agreement to send my team there. I'll let you know how things develop. For now you can give your friends a little reassurance.'

'Thanks, Comissari,' Skinner said, ending the call just as his aircraft came to a halt, close to the border control area to the south of Edinburgh Airport. Normally, after customs clearance he would have been picked up by a taxi, from the area beneath the multi-storey car park; instead, he walked the short distance through the tram station to the Doubletree Hotel. Lottie Mann was waiting for him in the foyer, as she had told him in a text.

'I'd have come to the terminal building if you'd wanted, sir,' she said as he approached.

'Hell no!' he exclaimed. 'I hate that fucking place and everything it's become; a big engine for screwing as much cash as possible out of the travelling public. If there was another private airport in reasonable distance I would use it. Come on, let's get a coffee. I had one on the flight but it's worn off.'

He found a table in the hotel foyer, and gave a quiet order to the waiter who approached them. As he withdrew, he turned to the detective. 'So, Sandra Bulloch: that's the biggest shocker I've had since . . .' He stopped for a few seconds. 'You know what? It's the biggest shocker I've had since I was told that Sandra had left traces of herself all over Leo Speight's bed. Do you remember that the chief constable and deputy asked me to interview her after that came to light?'

Mann nodded. 'Yes, I do sir, and that's partly why we're having this discussion. My team are operating in an information vacuum. We know nothing at all about Sandra's life after she left the force. We don't even know where she lived. It took us two days to identify her and that was pure luck. When she resigned from the service, her DNA was taken off the database, since it had only been there for elimination purposes. The same should probably have been done with her fingerprints but it wasn't. There was one print left at the scene and we found it. Otherwise . . . we might never have known who she was.'

'Maybe that would have been better all round,' Skinner said quietly.

She stared at him. 'Why do you say that?'

'For her sake, I suppose. Sandra was a private person with a very sad back story. She left the police under a cloud, after she held back facts from you and Dan Provan. Now she's dead, you're investigating and it's all going to come out. I'm sorry for her, that's all. I always have been, truth be told.'

'She shagged her sister's partner,' Mann pointed out.

'Ex-partner,' he corrected her. 'And they were due a free pass on that one. You know what Faye was.'

'Yes, I do. But it's not relevant. There's been a murder, and it has to be investigated. Where would you look if you were me?'

'You just brought her up. Faye Bulloch must be your first port of call. When are you seeing her?'

'Later on today. DCC McGuire and I are going to interview her at her place. She's still in Troon; hasn't moved.'

'Will you do it under caution?' Skinner asked.

'I'm not quite at that stage. We'll see how it goes, how she reacts, what information she volunteers. If it becomes necessary I'll be prepared to stop the proceedings and advise her that she has the right to a lawyer.'

'She didn't do it,' he said, abruptly, taking Mann by surprise.

'Why are you so sure of that?' she asked.

'Lottie, sororicide went out of fashion with the fall of the Roman Empire. It's very rare, and when it does happen the majority of victims and offenders are young. If Faye was going to kill Sandra she'd probably have suffocated her in her sleep when she was a kid. Granted they didn't like each other: I knew that before the Speight investigation. But still . . .'

'How did you know?'

'When Sandra worked for me in Strathclyde,' he explained, 'she mentioned Faye a couple of times, and each time she almost spat on the floor, as if the very name left a bad taste.'

'Why would that be?'

'I never asked; I understood the feeling. I always hated my older brother. I almost killed him once, but my dad hauled me off him.'

'Hazard a guess,' Mann challenged.

'A lifetime's experience? Or possibly . . . possibly Sandra carried a torch for Leo for far longer than she admitted to me at interview. She told me that Faye got pregnant on purpose with her first child, and that story holds up. However . . . and this is just me thinking you understand . . . Sandra and Speight got together when Faye was giving him serious grief, taking him to court. If he felt vulnerable that would have been a new experience for him. Did Sandra use that to set him up in her own way?'

The DCI seized on his hypothesis. 'If so, might that not have provoked Faye? Aren't you arguing against yourself, sir?'

He shrugged. 'Who knows? You're right, Lottie. Ignore me and keep an open mind when you see her.' He paused as the coffee arrived and as the waiter poured. 'How else can I help you?' he asked, as the man withdrew.

'You were pretty much the last person in the circle to see Sandra,' she replied, 'when you interviewed her, when Chief Constable Steele asked you to. My big problem is finding out what she's been doing since then. My people can't trace any recent activity or any movements; nothing at all. They can't even find bank records. Did she say anything on that day that might point me in the right direction?'

He shook his head, vigorously. 'Back then? No, she didn't. She was still in shock; I mean finding him dead, Lottie. The girl was in bits, just too tough to show it to you and Dan at the scene. She said nothing, but . . . I did. I gave her a piece of very specific advice.'

'What was it?'

'By that time,' he continued, 'when I interviewed her, we knew about the will, and that she was the main beneficiary of a multi-million pound estate. By that time I also knew its components, or most of them. Leo had property in the Bahamas that she was going to inherit. I suggested to her that she get the keys from the executors, at their discretion in advance of the estate being confirmed, and that she piss off there, to let her get her head back together. Charles Baxter was the property specialist in the executry team, as I recall. You might ask him if she listened to me and did that.'

'He's on the interview list, sir. I'll raise it with him. I do know already that the house in Ayr was sold very soon after Speight's death.'

'She was always going to do that, wasn't she?' Skinner observed. 'Could you live in a house where your partner died an unnatural death?'

'Some people have to,' Mann murmured. 'I've known a couple of neighbourhoods where there was a suicide and afterwards the bereaved wife couldn't sell the house for love nor money.'

'It would have been different with the Leo Speight mansion though,' he countered. 'I will bet you it went for a large chunk above the asking price. You ask the man Baxter about that too when you see him. Not that the answer will help you trace the movements of Sandra Bulloch.'

He paused to drain his coffee cup. Refilling it from the cafetiere, he looked at her across the table. 'Lottie,' he said, 'it looks like this will be a proper investigation, one without shortcuts, where you have to rely on old-fashioned pre-computer detective work. When I lecture on that subject, my favourite analogy involves seagulls in winter, when the ground is hard and you see them standing there, like they do on my lawn in Gullane, pounding the grass with their feet to see what sticks its head out, and then harvesting it as it does. That's what you and your people need to do, Chief Inspector. You have to keep drumming up worms.'

Twenty-Eight

'Thanks Maya,' John Stirling said, as the tall detective constable returned to her desk after delivering her report.

'For what?' Jackie Wright asked as she approached him.

'For nothing, really. DC Smith co-ordinated the trawl through the electoral register. Sandra Bulloch's sense of social responsibility was lacking, I'm afraid. She hasn't been a registered voter anywhere since she left the address in North Kelvinside. Nor,' he added, 'can I find her paying council tax anywhere in Scotland. It's beginning to look like she really was a travelling person.'

'When was the motor home bought?'

'The manufacturers say that it was ordered in February last year, but it wasn't collected until October.'

'When did she actually inherit? Do we know that?'

'As soon as Speight's estate was cleared,' Stirling said, 'and inheritance tax was paid. Such as it was: he must have had a fucking brilliant tax adviser. The sale of the house in Ayr pretty much took care of it.'

'And what did she inherit? How much?'

'Property, a specific bequest of five million pounds, and thirty per cent of the residue of the estate, the other seventy going into trusts for each of his three minor children, Leonard, Jolene and

110

Raeleen. Gordon, his older son, was eighteen when his father died. When he turned twenty-one he inherited property in London and a number of hotels.'

Wright persisted. 'Fine but what did her share add up to? In money?'

'I'd need time and a slide rule to get it right,' her colleague replied, 'but it has to be at least twenty million. Possibly more, because the property element is hard to nail down.'

'Could it be that we're looking for her recent past in the wrong place. Have you thought about checking Monaco?'

'I've thought about it,' Stirling replied, 'but get me the resources. Anyway,' he added, 'wherever she was, she turned up dead in Irvine, and my experience such as it is, tells me that the motive for her murder and her killer can't be too far distant from there.'

'I might argue with that,' Wright countered. 'But there's some-thing else that I've thought about. I was going to take it to Lottie but I'll try it on you first. Are we sure that we're looking for the right person?'

'What the hell do you mean by that, Jackie?'

'Not too long ago,' she replied, 'a pal of mine was bereaved, in her late thirties. Her husband contracted cancer and didn't make it. She grieved, deeply, for a year at least, until she decided that she had half of her life in front of her. She considered her options, and she talked them over with me. She's a nurse, and retraining to become an oncology specialist was at the top of her list. I pointed out that if she did, it would remind her of Billy every single working day. "Fuck it," I said to her. "Do something out of character: go on a singles cruise and take it from there." She did, for a month, and came back with a new partner. She was Mrs Betty McGurk. Now she's Mrs Elizabeth Lindsay, and she's happy again. Sandra Bulloch could have afforded to sail round the world for a year; maybe she did and reinvented herself like my pal. Could she have become Mrs Alexandra Something Else?'

'Fuck,' Stirling muttered. 'You're right. Would you like to tell DS Smith to do a search of the General Register Offices in Scotland and England or will I?'

Twenty-Nine

Being a large lady, Lottie Mann rarely felt dwarfed by another human, but the sheer bulk of Deputy Chief Constable Mario McGuire always had that effect on her; even more so when he wore uniform, as he did, standing at Faye Bulloch's impressive doorway.

When it was opened, they were greeted by a man, instead of the woman they had come to interview. 'Moss Lee,' McGuire said, with a humourless smile on his face. 'I take it that you're not here as a family friend.'

'I might be,' the solicitor advocate replied, 'but as it happens my client has requested my presence at your meeting.' He tilted his head as he looked up at the DCC's colleague. 'Detective Chief Inspector now, I hear. I suppose congratulations are in order.'

'If they're offered, thank you,' she said. 'Yes, I was a DI last time we met. I'm sure you remember that occasion. You've put on a bit of weight since then,' she observed, 'but you're better without the gangster moustache.'

Lee's expression froze for an instant. He had represented her ex-husband and his parents in an attempt to seize custody of her son in a hearing before a sheriff, only for his case to be eviscerated by Alex Skinner, appearing on Lottie's behalf. 'Vaguely,' he murmured as he ushered them into a large reception hall. 'My client's in the drawing room. I'm sure you remember the way from your last visit.'

'I do, but lead on. Earn your fee.' McGuire's right eyebrow twitched as he threw her a half smile.

Faye Bulloch was waiting for them in a large reception room. She stayed seated as they entered, her back to its bay window, a cigarette between two fingers. 'How often do you see that these days?' the DCC whispered to his colleague.

The police officers took seats facing her on the white semi-circular couch. *It could do with a clean*, Mann thought, remembering how immaculate everything had been when she and Dan Provan had visited, in the aftermath of Leo Speight's death.

'I hope this won't take long,' she snapped. 'I've got a client coming in forty-five minutes.'

'A client?'

She looked up at the DCC. 'I'm a podiatrist,' she replied. 'And you are?'

'Deputy Chief Constable Mario McGuire. Podiatrist,' he repeated. 'That's the same as a chiropodist, isn't it.'

She nodded, and for an instant Mann imagined Provan beside her, whispering in her ear, *It sounds better, that's all.*

'I've had to go back to work,' Bulloch said, indignantly. 'My late husband left our children well provided for, but he left me nothing of my own.'

'Apart from a multi-million pound house and the funds to run it,' the DCI observed.

As she spoke, Moss Lee leaned forward and laid his phone on the coffee table. It was set to record. McGuire shrugged his broad shoulders, took his own from a pocket in his tunic and did the same. 'I want to begin,' he said, 'by offering you and your children the sincere condolences of the police services for your loss. Regardless of its end, Sandra had a distinguished career as an officer, and that hasn't been forgotten.'

'I'm sure Moss will note that,' Bulloch replied, icily. 'He's here because . . .'

'We know why he's here,' the DCC interrupted. 'You don't need to spell it out: he's watching your back. Now, bearing in mind your time frame, can we begin?' He nodded in Mann's direction, as if giving her a cue.

'How do you feel about your sister's death?' she asked, abruptly.

Bulloch stubbed out her cigarette in an ashtray on the table: the detective made no attempt to keep her distaste from showing. 'No comment,' the woman hissed.

Lee's back straightened as he sat stiffly upright. 'We were told this was an informal interview, Mrs Mann,' he exclaimed. 'I don't appreciate that question.'

Mario McGuire leaned forward in his chair, his gaze fixed on the solicitor advocate. 'That's Detective Chief Inspector Mann to you, chum. And let's be clear about your role. You're here to advise your client if that's necessary, at her request, not as a legal entitlement. You do not address DCI Mann directly, or me, and you don't interrupt us.'

Lee looked back at him, not quite in the eye: his mouth opened as if to argue, but he thought better of it and settled back down.

'When were you last in contact with Sandra?' Mann continued.

'I haven't seen her since Leo died, the poor love,' Bulloch replied. 'Neither have my kids; her own nephew and her niece and she's cut them out of her life. Imagine that! Why are you talking to me anyway?' she exclaimed. 'You've told me she's dead, so what's all this about?'

'We're trying to establish your sister's movements in the period leading up to her death, Ms Bulloch,' McGuire said.

'I prefer Mrs Speight.'

'But you never were that, Faye,' Mann sighed. 'Face the facts for once, please. Leo fathered your children, and he gave you this very nice house here in Troon, practically on the beach, but he never lived here for more than a few days at a time, and he never married you. He didn't marry the mothers of his other children either, but he was going to marry your sister. Hence my question, how do you feel about her death?'

Moss Lee laid a hand on his client's sleeve, but she shook it off. 'No, I'm going to answer her. Put it this way,' she snapped. 'I won't be front row at the funeral. I won't even be in the fucking back row. If they're having cheerleaders, then I might show up. The fact is, Sandra's been dead to me for as long as Leo has, because that's when I found out about the cow moving in on my man.'

'This image of Leo that you keep trying to sell to us,' the DCI said, 'it's at odds with the way you behaved when you found out that Leo had changed his will in your sister's favour. As we both know, I had enough evidence against you then to charge you with trying to kill him.'

'That scandalous accusation never made it to court,' Moss Lee blustered, with a sidelong glance in McGuire's direction.

'Technically it did,' the DCC countered. 'Your client was charged, and she did make a brief appearance in the Sheriff Court. You should know; you were there representing her. It was the decision of the Crown Office not to take it to trial. The Advocate

Depute felt that there was too great a risk of an acquittal to justify the cost. To be frank, I disagreed with that at the time, and nothing's happened since to make me change that view.'

'Regardless of the fact that the cause of Leo Speight's death was established, and had nothing to do with my client?'

McGuire laughed. 'Seriously? Imagine that I dragged you into the sea out there and held you under for five minutes, but when they did the post-mortem it was discovered that you'd suffered a brain aneurysm that had absolutely nothing to do with your immersion, and that you were in fact dead before you went into the water. Is it your legal opinion that that would absolve me of prosecution for trying to kill you? For sure, if I ever need a lawyer it won't be you, mate.' He glanced at Mann. 'I'm sorry Lottie. Carry on, please.'

'Yes sir. Faye,' she continued, 'you and I both know what happened. It's history now, but even you'll understand why, with your sister dying the way she did, and her body being found five or six miles from your house, it makes us take a look in your direction. So think hard, have you never heard from Sandra since then, or heard of her?'

'I haven't, and I'm not in touch with anyone who might have either. Leo's mate Gino, he doesn't speak to me anymore, and he's the only possibility.'

'Gino,' she repeated, 'with whom you were having a fling behind Leo's back. You're about as trustworthy as a paper condom, Faye. Did you mean it when you said she'd cut herself off from the children?'

Bulloch frowned. 'Yes, I did,' she confirmed. 'Although she has sent them Christmas cards.'

'Do you still have them? I know I always keep mine,' the DCI added.

She winced. 'I binned them. But,' she added, 'Leonard saw the envelopes that a couple of them came in and kept the stamps. He's into that. He's upstairs. Give me a minute, and I'll find out if he's still got them.'

As she left the room, Moss Lee reached out and picked up his phone. McGuire watched him as he stopped the voice recording, then appeared to delete it. He made as if to retrieve his own, then smiled and left it where it was, preserving the solicitor advocate's legal gaffe for possible future use.

Faye Bulloch returned in under two minutes. As she resumed her seat she laid down two colourful stamps and a postcard. 'He had those,' she said. 'One of them's from the Bahamas, and the other's American. There's franking marks on each of them that'll tell you when they were sent.'

'And maybe more,' Mann murmured. 'What about the card?'

'Take a look; it's addressed to the kids. I'd never seen it before or I'd probably have trashed it. Leonard said it came on a Saturday, when he wasn't at school and got the mail in.'

The DCI picked it up. The photo side displayed a composite of London scenes; Big Ben, the Tower, Trafalgar Square and Wembley Stadium. On the reverse, the names of the recipients, Leonard and Jolene Speight and their address, alongside a message that she read aloud. 'Hope you're good and doing well at school. Love, Auntie Sandra.'

She handed it to McGuire. 'Bought in London, I guess,' he said as he peered at the faint lines of the postmark. 'But posted in Guildford, in February. Congratulations Lottie: your first lead.'

'And well done, Leonard,' she added.

As they looked across the table, they were astonished to see the change that had come over Faye Bulloch, as she listened to her sister's words. 'That stuff I said earlier, about Sandra and her funeral. Life's too fucking short,' she murmured, tears welling up in her eyes. 'At the end of the day she was my wee sister and somebody's killed her. Let me know when you're ready to release the body. I'll arrange the funeral and the kids and me will be in the front row.'

'What did you think of that?' McGuire asked Mann, a few minutes later, as they walked back to the DCC's car. 'Faye finally showing that she does have a human side.'

'Aye,' the DCI said. 'Or it's Faye finally figuring out that unless Sandra's left a will or a surprise husband somewhere, she'll be her next of kin.'

Thirty

'I thought I'd let you know, given your connection with Sandra in the past,' Mario McGuire told his friend, 'but I'm sorry to drop in out of the blue when you're so busy. It's a nice day and there won't be many more chances to take wee Eamon to the beach this year. Paula's there with him now.'

'The beach, such as it is,' Bob Skinner commented. 'It was battered to hell by all the storms and high tides we had last winter. There are exposed rocks down there that nobody here has ever seen before, not even octogenarians who were born in Gullane. Don't worry about the surprise visit,' he said. 'You weren't to know this is moving day. As it is, we're all packed and ready, and the airport taxi's booked. We don't fly until two-thirty and with the company plane there's no need to clear security.' He laughed. 'You and Paula should get one.'

'That'll be right,' McGuire snorted. 'The Viareggio family business isn't that profitable.'

'Anyway,' he continued, 'they're beginning to make progress on the Sandra investigation, are they?'

'A wee bit. We now know that she did go to the Bahamas after Leo Speight died, that she was in Philadelphia four years after that, and that she was in England at the beginning of this year.

The motor home she was found in was bought through her Jersey company just over eighteen months ago and was serviced by a specialist firm in Worcester, a month after she sent a postcard to her sister's children.'

'What did it have on the clock when she was found?'

'Thirteen thousand miles.'

'Seven hundred miles a month, give or take, on average,' Skinner calculated. 'Who paid for the service?'

'The Jersey company, through a credit card. It goes back to a lawyer in Glasgow, but he's not being co-operative. His line is that his ultimate client is the Speight estate, and that he can do nothing without its approval. But effectively the Speight estate means Sandra, and she's dead.'

'I get it; Jersey won't volunteer company information, so you have to go through the UK government to get it.'

'That's right,' McGuire said. 'Young John Stirling, Lottie's new DS, is looking at that, but he's being told it'll take time and it's not a given that Jersey will agree to a formal request. It's very sensitive about its sovereignty, it seems.' He grinned, and shook his head. 'Be glad you're out of all this. I've never known an investigation where we had so little background information. We don't even know where Sandra Bulloch banked. It should be far simpler than it is. People can't hide, no matter how rich they are. Okay, maybe if you're at the head of a drug cartel, but not a Scottish ex-cop surely.'

'People can hide if they have the right corporate structure,' Skinner countered. 'What do you know about Leo Speight's businesses when he was alive?'

'We know he invested a lot of his money in hotels; they went to his son Gordon in the will. We know that he set his women up with houses in their names, and that the rest was in cash and investments, the balance of which went to Sandra after the kids were taken care of long term.'

'And how much do you know about those investments?' Skinner asked.

'Personally not a lot,' McGuire admitted. 'I'm assuming they were recorded in the will.'

'Maybe yes, maybe not. There are three people you need to talk to. One is Joy Herbert, Speight's solicitor. Lottie'll remember her from the investigation. The others are the executors.'

'Butler and Baxter.'

'That's right. I don't expect Butler to help you too much. Yes, he was styled as Leo's manager but mostly he was his mate, and did what he was told . . . apart from restarting an old relationship with Faye Bulloch. But Baxter, he's on a different level: has an office in Charlotte Square, across from the First Minister's official residence. He was Leo's property adviser, and he is what my youngest son would call a serious dude. I spoke to him after Leo's death and he opened up to me, in a way he probably wouldn't have to a serious crimes detective. You should ask Mrs Herbert what happened to the property holdings under the will and ask Baxter to tell you all about them. They were big, Mario, maybe nine figures big, and if someone wanted to hide behind them, they could. Now,' he exclaimed as he rose from his chair, 'I do have to kick you out. I've promised my wife one last lunch in the Members' Clubhouse.'

'What about the kids?' McGuire asked, as they walked to the door.

'They want to eat on the aircraft. They've been looking forward to it, although God knows why. It'll probably be sandwiches from Greggs.'

Thirty-One

'Will this take long?' Craig Goram asked, casting a meaning-ful glance at the wall clock in his kitchen; it showed two minutes after midday. 'I'm a Rangers season-ticket holder and we've got a home game.'

'That'll be up to you,' Lottie Mann replied. 'But as I recall you're playing Hibs, so you know the result anyway. DS Wright's a Hibs supporter, aren't you, Jackie?'

'Worse,' the sergeant sighed. 'Livingston.'

'Somebody has to support them, I suppose. Me, I'm Celtic through and through.' In fact the only football matches she had ever attended had been as a uniformed officer; the lie was intended to unsettle Goram, no more.

He glowered at her. 'Somebody has to be, I suppose. You might as well sit down. My partner and our daughter are out, so we can use the sitting room.'

His home was a two bedroom flat in a relatively new develop-ment in Port Glasgow. It looked across the beginnings of the Firth of Clyde towards Dumbarton, where the detectives knew that he worked. He offered them uncomfortable faux leather chairs but remained standing himself, in an attempt, Mann surmised, to retain some level of control. *This isn't the classroom, chum*, she thought.

'Right,' he said. 'What's this about? All the sergeant said when she called me at the school yesterday was that it related to a current investigation.'

Mann gazed up at him. 'Are you telling us you can't guess?'

'Yeah,' he snapped.

'Do you have a big family, Mr Goram?' she asked. 'Parents, siblings, grandparents?'

He nodded. 'My folks are still alive, and I've got a brother and a sister.'

'So, you're asking us to believe that even if you don't read newspapers yourself, that none of those has picked up the phone to tell you that Sandra Bulloch, a woman you lived with for several years, was found dead earlier this week?'

'Sandra?' he sighed. 'Is that what this is about? Okay, Sandra and me, we used to live together, but that was seven years ago.'

'But you did live together,' Jackie Wright said. 'Look,' she sighed, exasperated, 'sit down please, Mr Goram. Enough with the games.' He scowled at her, but he complied.

'We're contacting everyone who knew Ms Bulloch,' the DS continued. 'Our problem is that she's been out of our orbit since she left the police service, so we know nothing of what she's been doing over the past few years.'

'Well she hasn't been doing it with me,' he snapped.

'You've had no contact with her?'

'None at all. I wouldn't want any?'

'Are you saying that you didn't part on good terms?' Wright asked.

'You must know that,' Goram retorted. 'I know she didn't have too many close friends . . . as in none; I was being kind . . . but I'm sure she'd bitch about it to somebody at work.'

'You're correct,' Mann said. 'She did indeed. She told

someone that you'd been having a relationship with a sixteen-year-old pupil, and that as soon as the girl left school, you dumped Sandra for her. She also implied that it wasn't the only time you were unfaithful, but that's not relevant to this investigation, not yet at any rate. The pupil, she's your current partner, yes?'

'Yes.'

'And the mother of your daughter?'

'Well, obviously,' he sighed, rolling his eyes.

'Thanks for confirming that. It kind of ties in with something we've discovered in the course of our enquiries. We've been told that when Ms Bulloch completed the sale of your former home, which was in her name, you turned up at the signing, demanding fifty per cent of the proceeds, because you said the place had been a matrimonial home. Is that correct?'

The DCI had built a career on reading facial expressions. She recognised the apprehension that she saw in Goram's eyes as he looked back at her. 'Yes,' he murmured.

'After you'd done that you and she had a private discussion and just like that, you settled for ten per cent. Is that true as well?'

The apprehension deepened. 'Yes, but . . .'

' "But", indeed,' Mann repeated. 'That was quite a generous concession given that you might actually have had a case.'

Goram relaxed, and shrugged. 'I'm a generous man, Chief Inspector. And I suppose I felt sorry for Sandra, at the time.'

'I'm sure you're the soul of generosity, but also, I suspect, you're a realist. You see, Mr Goram, before we came here we did some homework. As a teacher you'll appreciate that. We checked the records that are open to us as investigating officers, and we found out a few things. When she left school seven years ago, and your relationship went public, your partner . . . Hazel, isn't it? . . . was sixteen years and five weeks old. Your daughter, Beech, was born

125

on the seventh of February the following year, three days before Ms Bulloch completed the sale of your former home.' The DCI shifted in her uncomfortable chair. 'You can see where I'm going with this, can't you?'

Goram's face had gone ashen. His mouth opened then closed again, like a sprung trap.

'I'm no mathematician,' Mann said, 'and neither are you, you're an English teacher, but I do know about gestation, having had a kid myself, and I can work out that since Hazel's medical history shows that she went full term before giving birth, and even had to be induced, she must have fallen pregnant sometime in May, when not only were you still her teacher, *in loco parentis* as they say, but she was still only fifteen. If I can work that out . . . well, Sandra Bulloch would have too, seasoned police officer that she was. Ten per cent?' she exclaimed. 'You could have got ten years, man. Did Sandra still have a soft spot for you, to let you off with a crime? Maybe, but more likely, having known her, she didn't want any of the muck of a court case splashing on her.'

He looked back at her. 'Are you going to . . .?' he began.

'Charge you?' the DCI exclaimed. 'Now? No, we're not. Not out of any sympathy for you, but for Beech's sake. Your child doesn't deserve to suffer for your criminal behaviour.' She paused. 'But, Mr Goram, you shouldn't be teaching. I will give you until the end of the year to find a new career, otherwise . . . Hazel's school record will still be accessible somewhere. One phone call to your employer and that'll be that.'

He stared at her for several seconds. 'Okay, I'll do that,' he murmured. 'I hate the fucking job anyway. Is that us?' he asked. 'Are we done?'

'Hell no! Are you so naïve you don't realise that makes you a reasonable suspect in Sandra's murder investigation? So I'm going to ask you again. Have you ever seen her or heard from her since that day at the estate agent's?'

'No,' Goram replied, vehemently. 'I heard back then from someone we both knew that she'd left the police, but that's all. Honest.' He frowned, eyebrows knitted. 'But,' he murmured, 'there was one time, maybe a year or so ago, a guy called me out of the blue, someone I'd never heard of, asking if I knew where Sandra was. I told him no, I didn't. It was a one-off and I've never heard from him since.'

'Would his number still be on your phone? Or was it a land-line call?'

'No, it was to my mobile, and I remember, the caller number was withheld.'

'Write down your number anyway,' Mann ordered. Goram fetched a Post-it label from a block on his sideboard and did as she asked.

'Thanks,' she said as she took it. 'Can you remember the man's name?'

'Yes. He was called Stoddart, Bryce Stoddart.'

'Okay,' the DCI said abruptly, as she pushed herself upright, 'thanks for that if nothing else. You might still make the kick-off. I hope your team loses, by the way.'

Wright stayed silent until they were outside, in the street, admiring the river view. 'Well?' she ventured. 'Did that name ring a bell?'

The DCI nodded, eyebrows knitted. 'Oh yes,' she replied. 'A fucking big one. Seconds out, Round One. But there's only one problem . . .'

Thirty-Two

'Bryce Stoddart?' the deputy chief constable repeated. 'Leo Speight's boxing promoter?' There was heavy background interference on the call; wind noise, Mann guessed.

'That's what he said,' she assured him.

'But Bryce Stoddart's still in jail. Isn't he? He hasn't found a soft-hearted parole board, has he?'

'No, I've checked. He's still serving his sentence. Currently he's in an open prison in Suffolk, but up until nine months ago he was in a Category B jail in Oxfordshire.'

'He could have used a phone from there,' McGuire said.

'Yes he could,' the DCI agreed. 'If he did, the call might have been recorded, and the number might have been withheld as a security measure. But, think back, sir, to the Speight investigation. I don't recall that Bryce Stoddart ever met Sandra Bulloch. Indeed, Leo was so coy about their relationship, that he may never even have heard of her. So why should he, banged up in jail, be trying to track her down?'

'I can't give you an answer to that beyond the obvious suggestion: that someone used his name rather than give his own.'

'But why give that name to Craig Goram?' She heard what she thought was a laugh.

128

'Go on, Lottie,' McGuire chuckled, 'you're cooking by gas. Tell me.'

'Because he thought it was a name Goram might recognise from the time he was with Sandra, one that she might have mentioned, or that Goram might even have heard from Leo Speight himself. He and Sandra were a couple, and Leo was her sister's part time lover. Goram and Leo may well have met.'

'Ask him if they did. Call him as soon as we're done.'

'I'll wait for a bit,' she replied. 'I doubt that he'd hear me just now over the noise from crowds at Ibrox.'

'No chance,' McGuire agreed. 'They're playing my team, too. Good luck in identifying the mystery caller, but you have one thing going for you. Whoever used Stoddart's name didn't pull it out of the ether. He must have known who he was, quite possibly even knew him. Since Stoddart didn't feature in the Speight investigation, the caller's unlikely to be someone looking in from the outside. He's most likely to have been part of the inner circle himself, and that gives you a fairly short list of suspects. I've got to go now. Paula needs rescuing from the waves; she likes the sea but she can't bloody swim.'

She was about to end the call, until: 'Ah, Lottie, I almost forgot! One more thing, and it's important . . .'

Thirty-Three

'Well?' Bob murmured as he gazed westward from the terrace across the outskirts of Girona to the mountains beyond. 'I know it's only our first morning here, but what do you think of our new family home?'

'Honestly?' Sarah said.

'No punches pulled.'

'Okay, I agreed to the move, and I still see all the benefits for the kids and for us. I don't doubt any of it.'

'But?'

'But . . . this is probably the best duplex in the city, it's a great investment, it's beautiful, it's big enough for all of us, and it's well situated for your work and for mine, yet my gut is telling me it's not the total answer. It's Sunday, it's sunny but where are the kids just now?'

'They're out with Trish, exploring L'Espai de Girona shopping mall.'

'We've been there,' she reminded him, 'and on a Sunday too. The place is a zoo. It's mobbed, people come from everywhere. I heard as much French being spoken there as I did Spanish or Catalan. Trish will only be able to find a parking space because Dawn still needs a stroller, otherwise . . . Jazz and Seonaid don't start school until Wednesday. What are they going to do Monday and Tuesday? What are they going to do next weekend?'

He nodded, lips pursed, but remained silent.

'Bob, we are the most privileged family I know. We can move here without needing to sell Gullane, and leave it to Alex to look after it and for Ignacio to use it when he wants to go there. We've got this, which you bought to use up the silly money InterMedia pays you as its executive chairman. But we also have the house in L'Escala, by the sea, which you bought with your inheritance from your dad and which we've been expanding. Now we've made the move, we need to experience it and decide which will really be our home, there or here?'

He smiled as he took his mug from the table. 'We could go to Cort Ingles next weekend, instead of L'Espai,' he murmured.

'Bob!' she exclaimed. 'I'm fucking serious.'

The smile widened. 'I know you are . . . speaking of which, the kids will be out for at least another hour and it is Sunday morning . . .'

His suggestion went unspoken as his ringtone sounded. 'Fuck,' he hissed. She nodded. He picked up the phone without checking the caller number.

'Señor Robert,' a woman said, 'this is Comissari Roza. I have had a report, five minutes ago, from my investigators about the matter you reported to me. I thought you would want to know straight away. Through the insurance company my people found what was left of the car that went on fire: it was in a yard close to the Ronda Litoral, waiting to be crushed. When they examined it, they found definite traces of a device. It had been placed above the rear wheel. They are not able to prove it, but they believe that it was meant to be triggered by the driver closing the car door after getting in.'

'But she didn't do that, did she?' Skinner exclaimed. 'Raul Sanchez told me that she realised she'd forgotten something and went back indoors.'

'That is correct. And so when she closed the door she was not inside the vehicle.'

'If she had been . . .' he began.

'. . . it would probably not have been fatal,' Roza told him. 'It was an incendiary device, not explosive. She would have had time to escape before the fire took hold. I will call my colleague in Madrid and tell him his people should take another look at the package sent to Señora Hoverstad.'

'Did your team find any traces on the other one?'

'They found no fingerprints, but there was a hair inside the bottle that we will assume came from the person who put the letter inside. That should be as good as a print, maybe even better. As for the bottle, the label is intact. It may be we can match it with the one in Madrid.'

'That's good to hear. You'll continue to keep me in touch?'

'As far as I can,' she replied, 'but as a former police officer I am sure you will understand that with a criminal investigation under-way, there will be a limit to what I can share.'

'Of course,' Skinner said, with as much sincerity as he could muster. 'One thing I forgot to ask Raul Sanchez,' he continued. 'What's the product in question? I didn't ask him and he didn't mention it by name. You might as well share that Comissari, for I'm sure he will.'

She laughed. 'Yes I think I can do that. It is a drink, one that is . . . I believe the English word is fortified. It has a little alcohol, maybe more than a little. It's called *Ciervorapido*. The manufac-turers, Compostella SA, say it is based on a recipe from a convent in the eighteenth century in the south of Italy, but nobody believes that. They invented it themselves and created a legend around it.'

'The Sisters of the Trinity might believe it,' he countered.

'Yes,' Roza reflected. 'Perhaps they do, if they are real.'

Skinner ended the call, returned his phone to the table and looked up at his wife, who was standing by the glazed terrace enclosure. He grinned. 'As we were saying . . .'

She shook her head. 'No, as you were saying. Anyway, the moment's past.'

'Are you sure?'

She nodded her head, and made a gesture, downwards, towards the street. 'Very. Trish and the kids are just about to drive into the garage.'

Thirty-Four

'Did you have a good weekend, John?' Jackie Wright asked as she draped her jacket across the back of her office chair.

'I can't really say that I did. My girlfriend took me away on Saturday morning for a surprise trip, but she could see that my head was still in Glasgow, working on the investigation.'

His colleague smiled. 'Oh dear, girlfriends don't like that. I was in the same boat as you. Mine gave me a hard time for going to interview the guy Goram with the boss. She made me pay for it, literally; when I got back, she told me we were going for dinner to the Peat Inn, or rather . . . she told me I was taking her for dinner in the Peat Inn, and staying there afterwards.'

He whistled. 'I've heard of that place. It's my mum's lifelong ambition to go there, but my dad still hasn't got the message. Good?'

'Brilliant, but jeez, I hope a promotion comes up soon. It put a big lump on my credit card balance. You? Where were you taken?'

'The Atholl Palace in Pitlochry. A big Victorian place up on a hill.'

'Was it good?'

'It was okay. I liked it: it's old but it's kind of beautiful. Funny place, Pitlochry,' he mused. 'Half the shops sell hiking gear; you'd think that there's nothing to do there but walk.'

'Has it got a caravan park?' Both detectives turned to see Lottie Mann, framed in the doorway.

'I suppose so,' Stirling guessed. 'Why?'

'Sandra Bulloch was the outdoors type. She must have toured that van around, given the mileage.' She shook her head. 'But that's well down our list of places to be ticked off. You two carry on. I have an appointment in the city centre. I did some digging yesterday.' She paused as she realised that both detective sergeants were staring at her. 'What?' she asked.

'You were working on a Sunday?' Wright exclaimed. 'We've been comparing notes on getting pelters for bringing our work home with us.'

Mann laughed as she came towards them. 'As normal people might expect. But normal people don't share their lives with Dan Provan. Plus, when the deputy chief makes a suggestion, from the beach, on a Saturday, it's best not to add it to the Monday morning to do list. I'm going to see a woman called Moira Mansfield. She's the managing partner of a law firm called Herbert Chesters. They were Leo Speight's lawyers, and they handled the processing of his estate. Herbert Chesters wasn't a bloke, by the way, they were two people. The Chesters half is dead now. Joy Herbert, the other partner, retired a couple of years ago, although she's still on the letterhead as a consultant, and no doubt still collects a profit share. Ms Mansfield was her senior associate and took over the running of the firm.'

'I've never heard of them,' Stirling confessed.

His boss shrugged. 'I'd be impressed if you had. They're a very discreet operation. The *Glasgow Herald* even called them "reclusive". They manage the affairs of high net worth individuals, in Scotland and beyond.'

'Something like James Bonar's firm?'

'Way, way, way above his level, John. Leo Speight was by no means their richest client.'

'If they're that discreet,' Wright asked, 'how come you were able to dig all this up at the weekend and get an appointment?'

'Like I said, I live with Dan Provan. Law firms here are regulated by the Law Society of Scotland, right? Dan pointed out that it's got a PR department. I got in touch with them and their guy did all the research, even arranged my date with Ms Mansfield.' She looked at Stirling. 'While I'm there, John, I have another task for you . . . some proper detecting, Sergeant.'

Thirty-Five

S tirling sat at his desk, his computer terminal pushed to one side to accommodate a stack of old-fashioned files. He knew that he was too young to be a traditionalist, but in his short CID career he had learned that it could be quicker and easier to work with paper than sort through a list on screen. The investigation of Leo Speight's death had been comprehensive and wide ranging, although Mann had made him aware that one name he would not find there was that of Sandra Bulloch. Every mention of her and of the circumstances of her departure from the police service had been excised from the report to the Crown prosecutors.

'Maggie Steele,' she had said, ' the chief constable of the day, ordered that she shouldn't be named. She decided that Sandra's deception at the beginning of the thing was a matter for her and not for the fiscal, so she took it out of the record. Everything else is there, John; that includes a list, with descriptions of everyone interviewed in the course of an all-embracing search for a murderer who at the end of the day didn't exist.'

'Can I ask you one question, boss? Why are we focusing on the Speight investigation for a lead to Bulloch's killing?'

'Because it's all we have. Her CID career was relatively brief, and it was certainly uneventful. When Skinner arrived in

Glasgow, I was a DI and she was a uniformed inspector. Somehow, she became his exec. When Andy Martin took over from
big Bob as the head of the national force, she carried on in that
role, but only for a very short time, until she got bumped up to
DCI and became my boss in serious crimes. She was SIO in a
couple of linked armed robberies, but Dan and I did all the hard
work on those. Sandra just signed off the reports. If her death
relates to her police career, that can only mean the Speight investigation, and that links in with her inheritance of his wealth. Yes,
there's her personal life and I had wondered about Goram, but he
couldn't have done it. I knew that before I went to see him.'

'How come?'

'I had a full background check done on him,' Mann had told
him. 'DC Smith handled it, very efficiently. When the motor
home was dumped in Irvine, Goram was in Ibiza, with his partner and their kid. However, he is one of the few living links to
Sandra's life outside the police, so he's a person of interest from
that aspect. When he told Jackie and me that somebody had
called him claiming to be Bryce Stoddart, Leo's fight promoter,
that interest multiplied. Stoddart's in the nick, plus he never
knew Sandra, so it's really very unlikely to have been him. Assuming that, whoever did phone Goram knew who Stoddart was, and
plucked him out as cover. Go through the files, John, tell me who
the caller might have been, and we'll pay the candidates a visit. I
have my own idea, but I'd like you to confirm it or knock it down,
as the case may be. We have to go now; I'm being taken to my
meeting. It's in the middle of our new low emission zone, and my
car isn't compliant. That Thunberg kid? She doesn't know the
half of what she's done.'

Stirling was still smiling at Mann's exasperation as he laid the
box on the floor beside his chair and removed the top file, a

summary of the detailed report to the prosecution. The opening
section described the structure of the police investigation, from
the discovery of Leo Speight's lifeless body in his house in Ayr . . .
one of several homes . . . after he failed to appear for a meeting
with a publisher in the Turnberry Hotel . . . '*I might not have
turned up there either,*' Stirling murmured as he read . . . through
the compilation of a list of people of interest, to their interviews
and elimination, one by one, the emergence of a strong line of
enquiry that implicated Faye Bulloch only to conclude abruptly
after forensic evidence that pinpointed the cause of the ex-boxer's
death rendered the entire process irrelevant.

Delving deeper into the box, he found the files that he was after,
individual reports on the people interviewed, their background,
relationship to the dead man and their recent involvement with
him. He opened the first, and read.

Gene Alderney: not a man, as he had assumed, a woman in a
male-driven business, matchmaker for Stoddart Promotions, the
company Speight had chosen to guide his career after leaving the
amateurs as an Olympic silver medallist. She was the partner of
Benny Stoddart, long retired and living in Arizona. Her identity
was false. In fact she was Russian, real name Lyudmila Brezinskova, mother of one Yevgeny Brezinski, an opponent of Speight
as both amateur and professional.

Charles Baxter: Leo Speight's property adviser and co-executor
with Butler. Chartered surveyor and partner in an Edinburgh
firm. Outside Leo's professional boxing circle but still close, and
the only man who knew the full extent of his property holdings.

Gino Butler: Leo Speight's accountant, manager and friend
from youth. Knew everything about Speight's business. With
Faye Bulloch before Leo, and it was he who introduced them.
That relationship may have been renewed for latterly they were

close. Gino knew everything about Speight's business and was involved in obtaining a UK passport for Swords/Mechikov, and a false identity for Gene Alderney. Profound dislike of Bryce Stoddart. Suspected of encouraging Faye to take Leo to court. One of Speight's two executors, with Charles Baxter.

Augusta Cambridge: Live event artist and friend of Leo, painted all his fights and gave him a 5% commission on her subsequent print sales. Present at Leo's retirement party and gave the investigating officers several leads.

Rae Letts: Leo's Las Vegas girlfriend and the mother of his child. She knew most of the people in his circle and was present at the retirement event that preceded Speight's death, but was a peripheral figure in the investigation.

Aldorino Moscardinetto: an Italian film director who had been making a documentary on boxing in collaboration with Leo Speight, and who had interviewed several people in his circle. Murdered by Swords/Mechikov when he had interrupted him trying to steal his laptop from his hotel room.

Gordon Pollock: Leo Speight's son with Trudi Pollock, his teenage girlfriend. Not yet twenty when his father died and kept away by him from the boxing business, so had no involvement in the matters uncovered following Leo's death. Inherited his hotel businesses, which were considerable.

Trudi Pollock: Leo Speight's teenage girlfriend. Fell pregnant by him and gave birth to his son, Gordon. Never a suspect, but influenced events when she discovered that Leo was planning to marry Sandra Bulloch and was provoked into revealing it to Faye. Worked as Gino Butler's secretary. Left £1m in Speight's will.

Bryce Stoddart: son of Benny, running the promotion company after his retirement. Lightly regarded by Speight, but aware of the illicit relationship with Zirka, a Russian promotional company and of secret payments being made by his own company to the Russians. Ordered the break-in that led to the murder of Moscardinetto and imprisoned in consequence.

Billy Swords: another transplanted Russian, real name Uilyam Mechikov. Ring announcer for Stoddart production and for Zirka, which Alderney ran, from a distance. Currently in prison in Scotland having been convicted of the murder of Aldorino Moscardinetto, in which Alderney and Bryce Stoddart were implicated.

Stirling replaced the folders and leaned back in his chair, considering the options. He began with Bryce Stoddart, the man Craig Goram had named as the mystery caller. Mann had thought it unlikely that it had been him, but thoroughness demanded that he be eliminated. He searched for and found the phone number of Longstone Prison in Oxfordshire, where Mann's check had led her.

His landline call was answered quickly; he asked for and was connected to the Governor's office where a female staff member picked it up. 'This is Detective Sergeant John Stirling, serious crimes team, Glasgow,' he began, quoting his service number. 'I'm working on a homicide investigation and the name of one of your inmates has come up. He's not a suspect, but he's alleged to have made a telephone call to one of our witnesses. I need to confirm whether or not that that's the case.'

'I don't know if we'll be able to help you,' the woman said, 'but I'll try. What was the prisoner's name?'

'Stoddart.' He spelled it out, letter by letter. 'Bryce Stoddart. I'd like to know if he made any calls using the prison landline, and if they were recorded. This is the number that he'd have called.' Once again he spelled out Craig Goram's mobile number, digit by digit.

'I'll ask an assistant governor to look into that and call you back, Sergeant. I have your number on my screen.'

He had barely replaced the clumsy handset in its cradle when his mobile sounded. 'John,' Lottie Mann said. 'I'm just about to go into the meeting. How are you getting on?'

'I'm waiting for a call back from Stoddart's last prison,' he told her, 'but to eliminate him more than anything else. From what I've read he seems to have been a lightweight really, taking his orders latterly from Speight and Alderney. Also I'm finding it hard to see any connection between him and Leo's private life. But,' he cautioned, 'that doesn't necessarily mean there wasn't one. On the face of it you wouldn't think that Rae Letts had ever heard of Charles Baxter, given the geography between them, but she actually met him.'

'True,' the DCI murmured. 'I'd forgotten that.'

'However, boss, the person I would put at the head of the list for a visit would be Gino Butler. He was by Speight's side from the very beginning, knew everything about him. He was Faye Bulloch's boyfriend before she went after Leo, and they were close again before his death. Everything I've read about the guy, it's telling me he's not to be trusted. He's top of my list as Goram's mystery caller . . . that's if we're right and it wasn't Stoddart.'

'He's top of mine too,' Mann admitted. 'I didn't commit myself before because I wanted you to stay objective. Let me get through this interview and we'll pay him a visit . . . that's assuming we can find him.'

'I'll take a look at his social media,' Stirling said. 'See what's been posted lately. That may tell us where he is.'

'Are you sure he had a profile?'

'I know he has, boss. Last week I looked at everyone who was a contact of Sandra Bulloch, direct and indirect. She didn't herself, but I was looking for recent references to her. Gino Butler's on Instagram and X.'

'Okay, do that now. I've just been called in to see Ms Mansfield.'

Stirling pulled his monitor towards him and touched a button on his keyboard to bring it back to life. He was waiting for the system to fire up when his landline rang. He snatched it up.

'Detective Sergeant Stirling,' the caller began. The DS detected a faint Irish accent 'Ronnie Bush, assistant governor, Longstone. I have the information you were after. If you'd called next week, we'd probably have binned these records, but you're in luck. Prisoner Bryce Stoddart made very few calls during his time with us, and all of them were to the same number in the United States. They were international so he had to tell us who he was calling. The recipient was one Lyudmila Brezinskova. I don't know anything about her, I'm afraid.'

'I do,' the DS said. 'She's Stoddart's father's partner.'

'Late father,' Bush corrected him. 'I found a note on his file advising of his death, while he was with us. But his next of kin was listed as Genevieve Alderney.'

'One and the same. She took the Alderney name when she applied for a British passport. It was dodgy, so probably wouldn't have passed the scrutiny of US immigration. That's the extent of his phone records then? Calls to her?'

'Outgoing, yes, and they stopped after his father's death. But,' the assistant governor continued, 'he did have one incoming call during his time here. It lasted for twenty-one minutes. That would include the time it took to bring Stoddart to the phone.'

'Did the caller identify themselves?'

'Of course, that's a requirement. His name's listed here as Gordon Pollock.'

143

Thirty-Six

'That is very good of you, Bob. I'm pleased that the police are finally getting off their backsides. But,' Raul Sanchez paused, 'it makes me afraid for Inge and her colleagues.'

'Don't be,' Skinner assured him. 'They're safer than they were without police involvement. It means that everything coming into their offices will be scanned, and they'll have discreet personal security too. Your household mail will be scrutinised too, by the *Correos* and private delivery companies.'

'Will they catch these people, do you think?'

'It depends on how good they are, and how careless the senders have been. From what I've been told they've made one mistake already. What about the client, *Ciervorapido*? Has Inge said anything about their reaction?'

'They are anxious, she says, very sympathetic. They said they're afraid that the agency will give up their account, given all the effort and investment that's been committed to the project, but Inge and her colleagues have told them that is not going to happen. Also, Inge says they are most relieved that the incidents have not become known to the public. I think that's their big worry. It's a new product and they're afraid that being targeted by fanatics like these will affect its sales. If that happens,

I can tell you as a banker, they will be in big trouble, because their lenders will be likely to minimise any losses and walk away.'

'To be frank, Raul,' Skinner said, 'my surprise is that the incident hasn't hit the press yet. I didn't have a lot of experience of this sort of thing in my police career, but from the little I did, I'd be expecting these holy bloody Sisters or whatever they are to be splashing themselves all over the news cycles. I've done an internet search for them, but can't find a trace. It could be they're scared that if they do reveal themselves they'll lead the police straight to their door. If that's the case they really are amateurs.' He chuckled. 'I hope you realise that you've landed me on a very horny dilemma. I'm the head of an international media group. I am the fucking press, you've given me a cracking news story and here I am sitting on it.'

'My God!' Sanchez exclaimed. 'That had not occurred to me! In that case my friend, do not let me compromise you. Of course you must do your duty to your company. Whatever the consequences are, they must be borne.'

'Let's not rush into anything. Yes, it's a news story. I'm no journalist, but I'm learning, and it seems to me that it's one that needs to be developed, before it's broken, ideally with the arrest of these Sisters of the Trinity. I don't want to downplay the Mossos, but my people are pretty good investigators too. Let me talk to my senior colleague and see if we can make progress without stepping on their toes. Do you know,' he asked, 'whether the agency retained images of the letter and the packages that were delivered, specifically of the two labels.'

'I think they still have them,' Sanchez replied, 'but I can find out with one phone call to my wife.'

'Then make it,' Skinner instructed him. 'If they did, have

them emailed to my personal address, which I will text you. Top quality please, soon as you can.'

'I will do that, Bob,' his friend promised, 'right now.'

The call ended. Skinner leaned back in his chair, gazing at the ceiling for a few seconds before returning to his phone and placing a call to his closest colleague. 'Hector?' he said as it was answered. 'Got a minute? I might have a scoop for us.'

Thirty-Seven

'I don't know if I should be taking this call,' Bryce Stoddart said. 'I've said everything to you lot that I ever want to say. Frankly, mate, if I didn't have a parole board coming up, I'd tell you to fuck off.'

'I'll treat it as my lucky day,' John Stirling replied. 'I want to ask you about another phone call, one you received when you were detained at Longstone Prison. I'm told that the caller identified himself as Gordon Pollock, and that you spoke for around fifteen minutes. Is that correct?'

'It's a year ago, so I'll take your word about the duration, but yes, it was young Gordon that called me . . . Leo Speight's boy.'

'Can I ask why?'

'I dunno, really. He said he was just ringing to see how I was getting along. Said he thought I was unlucky to have wound up inside, seein' as how the guy who did the actual crime did it off his own bat, like. I told him I agreed with that one hundred per cent and if he'd like to tell my brief as much it might do me a bit of good come the parole hearing. Dunno if he did though.'

'How well do you know Mr Pollock?'

'Gordon?' Stoddart exclaimed. 'Like I said, he's Leo's kid, in' he. Leo Speight, my boy, my champ. He 'ad him the lad with that

Trudi girl, the one that worked for Gino Butler, when they were just kids themselves. Tell you the truth, when I was told it was him calling me, I wondered if he was going to ask me to manage him when I get out. Leo would never let him near a boxing ring, although I know the boy was keen. Mind you he'd have been wasting his time if he had asked me. Stoddart Promotions is pretty well fucked. The Board of Control cancelled our licence when I got sent down, and I won't be getting it back any time soon. Not that I'll need it, mind. Leo made me a ton of money and the lawyers haven't taken all of it.'

'And did he? Ask you to promote him?'

'Nah. Never mentioned it once. Just asked how I was getting on, said we might meet up when I got out. Said 'e lives in London now. He didn't find it comfortable livin' in Scotland after Leo went. If people found out he was 'is kid, it put a bit of a target on 'is back. I can understand that.' Stoddart paused; somehow Stirling sensed him smiling. 'I was in Glasgow with Leo one night,' he resumed, 'at a black tie do, and this big bloke, a proper gorilla with a couple of drinks in 'im, started mouthing off at 'im.'

'What happened?' Stirling asked.

'Nuffin'. Nuffin' at all. Leo just looked up at him, straight in the eye, and said '"Really?" very quiet like. Straight away the big guy knew what sort of trouble he was askin' for, he thought about it and he just disappeared. Lot of fighters, big name fighters, have security, muscle, around them to take care of stuff like that. Leo never needed those. He was a lovely guy, but he could be fuckin' terrifying. Young Gordon, though, 'e couldn't have handled that, so he's better off out of it.'

'Have you kept in touch since he called you?'

'No,' Stoddart said. 'I wouldn't know how. He didn't leave a number and 'e's never called since. Mind you,' he added, 'he might not know I've been moved 'ere.'

Stirling felt that he was approaching a dead end. 'Was that the extent of your conversation?'

'More or less. He did ask me one thing, though. Asked if I knew what the Bulloch woman was doing? "What? Faye?" I asked him but he said no, the other one, 'er sister. Told 'im, "How the fuck would I know mate?" And how would I? I never met the woman.'

Thirty-Eight

'On the face of it,' Hector Sureda said, 'we have enough information to run the story now.'

'We do,' Skinner agreed, 'but if we do we risk compromising police investigations in both Barcelona and Madrid, and in the process I will burn a very good contact in the Mossos. Not just her,' he added, 'but more than likely her boss too, Major Teijero. He's a guy we need to be alongside as an organisation.'

'I know that,' the CEO admitted. 'And yet, we have a public duty as journalists to report the facts as we know them.'

'I accept that, Hector, but . . . maybe this story would be the better for a little more in depth investigation. You and I, we're not journos but you have the trade in your blood, and so do I in a way, after thirty years as an investigator.'

'The problem with that,' Sureda observed, 'is that if we set a journalist to work on this story, they will report to Mario Fuentes, the editor of *GironaDia*. Mario is an absolute zealot, who would compromise the Pope as a source out of sheer principle. How do we get round that?'

'I can think of a way.' A light smile showed on his face as he looked at his colleague. 'Could you find me a promising young reporter, out to make a name, and too pragmatic to get hung up on those principles?'

'Sure I could.' Sureda nodded, vigorously. 'I can think of the very one: Dolça Nuñez, she joined InterMedia as a graduate trainee a year ago and has been picking up experience on several titles, print and broadcast.'

'Where is she just now?'

'Copy-editing in the Girona broadcast newsroom, five floors below us.'

'Then send her up here,' Skinner said. 'I'll brief her on the evidence that we have at the moment, and send her out to get more. She'll report back to me, not to Fuentes or any other editor. When you and I decide that we have a story that will make the police love us rather than hate us, then we'll publish, right across the group.'

Thirty-Nine

Moira Mansfield did not fit the popular image of a Scottish private lawyer. Having done a little research in advance of the meeting, Mann knew that she was thirty seven years old, but if she was a suspect in an ID parade the line-up would have been filled by women ten years younger. Her long hair was honey blonde with darker streaks, natural, she guessed, and her clothing, a colourful dress with short sleeves, also defied convention. Her only jewellery was a simple gold neck chain. Appraising her, Lottie had a momentary vision of a reporter on a sports programme that was becoming Dan's default TV choice.

'Detective Chief Inspector, Detective Sergeant,' she greeted them as Wright closed the door behind her. 'Welcome to Herbert Chesters. Your visit's a bit of a departure for us, I confess . . . especially as it's on a Sunday.' There was nothing surprising about her voice. Fast-talking Glaswegian, probably from south of the river, the DCI surmised.

'Not the first, though,' she said. 'I've been in this room before. We were involved with you a few years ago, when Mrs Herbert was still here.'

'That's right,' Mansfield agreed. 'I remember you coming to see Joy.' She smiled. 'You probably won't remember me, though.

The dress code was a bit different then. Joy was conservative in that respect. Being a private law practice for Hinwies,' she paused catching Wright's puzzlement. 'High net worth individuals,' she explained. 'Given that, our client profile's inevitably going to be older than average and still predominately male, so Joy felt they should have the sombre approach. I take the opposite view. I believe in reminding them that they're still alive.'

'Are you in complete control of the firm now?' Mann asked.

'Not quite. Joy has a seven-year profit participation exit deal. It's a buy-out by another name. Once that's done I will be. I'll even be able to put my name over the door if I want.'

'Will you?'

'No chance, whatever my husband says. The name holds the reputation of the practice. If I changed that, even slightly, I'd be throwing most of that away.'

'Is your husband a lawyer?' Wright asked.

'No, he's an accountant. His name's Butler, Gino Butler.' Reading the detectives' surprise, she continued, 'I might as well get it over with. Yes, that Gino Butler, the late Leo Speight's manager, long-time friend and joint executor. He and I met when he and Charles came into the office to consult on the executry. Our paths hadn't crossed until then. I was only involved with the estate in the background, sorting out the details and reporting to Joy. Leo was a beneficiary of course. His bequest bought us a stunning art deco flat out near Anniesland, and a paddock for Gino in the hills behind Bowling where he keeps his horse. He's got two of them; he spends most of his spare time there: not me, though, horses scare me. It's not that far,' she said, smiling. 'He can actually cycle there. He's a bit of a gent, is my Gino, although he does his best to keep it hidden. Now to business,' she continued briskly. 'You want to ask me about Sandra Bulloch, yes?'

'That's correct,' the DCI said.

'Poor woman,' Mansfield sighed. 'Her life was a bit of a tragedy really. Gino told me that her previous partner, before Leo, was a bit of a shit. He was really pleased for the two of them when they finally hooked up. And then Leo died, and now her. It's just awful, don't you think.' She paused. 'That said, in your job you're dealing with tragedy all the time.'

'But not with the murder of a former colleague,' Mann pointed out. 'We're all trying to be objective, but there is that personal element.'

'I can imagine,' the lawyer agreed. 'I suppose you'll have met her awful sister, the Faye creature.'

The detective frowned. 'It's my turn to say "no comment",' she replied.

'Understood. It still rankles with me that she and Gino have history. He says that she was okay until he introduced her to Leo. Then, he says, it was as if he could see the £ signs spinning in her eyes. Of course Leo fell for it; Gino said that women were his weakness. In fact he said that if Scotland had an Olympic shagging team, he'd have been captain . . . until he and Sandra got together. He was a changed man after that, as his revised will demonstrated, I suppose. God,' she exclaimed, 'when Faye heard about that! She and Gino had been getting close again, but that put an end to it. Finally he realised what an evil cow she was.' Mansfield paused. 'She must be at the top of your suspect list, surely?'

'I refer you to my previous answer,' Mann said, grimly.

'Of course. She threatened to challenge the will in court, but she had absolutely no grounds. Even her solicitor, that slimy turd Moss Lee, had to recognise that. We handled the processing of the estate in spite of her noise, just as we would with any other client. That meant formally, establishing the assets and liabilities, calculating and agreeing Inheritance Tax payable with HMRC and getting its authorisation code so that the estate could be submitted to the Sheriff Court for confirmation. That's how the process works. I suggested that we meet here in case you needed access to the documentation.'

'No, we don't,' the DCI told her. 'Later possibly, depending on how the investigation progresses but not at this stage. How much tax was payable?' she asked.

'About three million.'

'What!' she exclaimed. 'I was expecting six figures.'

'No, three million, give or take,' the solicitor retorted. 'If you don't believe me, check with the Sheriff Court. We're good at what we do, Chief Inspector. Plus, our late client Leo was a very clever man; not your stereotypical fighter. You know that he was an LSE graduate?'

'Yes, I'm aware.'

'Then you can be assured that prepared him very well for his boxing career. He made a hell of a lot of money from his fights, a spectacular amount. Most of them, the really big ones, took place outside the UK and only a small percentage of the profits ever touched down here. The rest was banked or invested offshore, much of it by Charles Baxter, the property guy. He actually knows a lot more about the overall picture than we do . . . and when I say "we" I include Gino in that too.'

'How's that going to help us get an idea of Sandra Bulloch's movements over the last five years? That's what we need to do.'

'The fact is, it's not,' Mansfield replied. 'The truth is I've never actually met Sandra Bulloch. I had no need to, given the nature of the work I did for the executry. And although he had a fling or two with her sister, the truth is that Gino was never very close to her either. Yes, he knew about her thing with Leo, but not that they were planning to marry. That only came out after he was dead when Joy Herbert opened the final handwritten will that he left. The way things were concluded, Leo's wealth was sheltered in his Jersey company. After the kids were taken care of, most of his cash and investments, and the property, apart from the hotels, went to Sandra, but I have no idea what she did with it. The way it was set up, the only person in Glasgow who can really help you is James Bonar . . . if he chooses.'

Forty

'I've done that, Sarge,' Maya Smith replied. 'There's no Gordon Pollock on any social platform that comes close to matching our guy. Plus, I've looked at the files from the Speight investigation. There are contact details in there, but they're out of date. Even his mobile's discontinued.'

'What about Trudi, his mum?' Stirling asked.

'She's his mum?' the DC exclaimed. 'I saw another Pollock on the list, but I wasn't quite sure whether she was his mother or his sister. I'll try to contact her then.'

'No, Maya, leave it to me. I need to touch base with as many people as I can that knew Sandra Bulloch.' He crossed to the table where the case files sat and rummaged among them until he found what he was after, a list of addresses and numbers for every interviewee in the investigation. There were three numbers for Trudi Pollock, home, office, and mobile. He chose the third, and keyed it in.

'Hello?' a hesitant female voice answered.

'Is that Trudi?'

'Yes.'

'This is DS John Stirling, Ms Pollock. Is it convenient for us to speak?'

'I'm with a customer just now,' she said quietly. 'Can I call you back? Or you could come here if you'd rather do that.'

The DS was seized by a sudden urge to get out of the office. 'Yes, I will. Where are you?'

'The shop's called "Flowers by Trudi". It's on Dumbarton Road, in Whiteinch, near the doctor's. You can't miss it.'

'Got it,' he told her.

'I should be done by then,' she murmured, 'but it's quite a complicated order.'

After messaging Mann to tell her of his mission, Stirling jogged downstairs to the car park exit. Whiteinch was on the other side of the river, but easily accessed by using the Clyde Tunnel. Trudi Pollock's shop stood out, its sign being a rectangle of bright colours that blended sympathetically with three storeys of red sandstone tenement above. He found a parking space around thirty yards distant, where the clock on his dashboard told him that his journey had taken only seven minutes. Thinking of Trudi Pollock's complicated order, he waited, passing some time by consuming a Twix bar, washed down with a can of zero calorie Tango. He had just finished when a man emerged from 'Flowers by Trudi', bearing a large floral arrangement in a basket. Taking that as a cue, Stirling exited his car and headed for the shop.

One of the statements in the box of files had referred to Trudi Pollock as 'chubby'. Either that had been an exaggeration or she had done something about it. The woman was almost slender, in a full length green apron that was tied at the waist, but her face was a little gaunt, with a hint of a yellow pallor that made him wonder whether all was well with her. Or maybe it was her make-up choice, he conceded. She wore no jewellery other than a silver chain around her neck, half hidden by the apron.

Her smile was full of life, dispelling his thoughts about her health. 'Detective Sergeant Stirling?' she began. 'I don't remember you from five years ago.'

'I wasn't around five years ago,' he responded. 'Not in CID. Back then I was a uniform PC driving a patrol car.'

'And I was a slightly depressed wee woman working in Gino Butler's office.'

'Why the change?'

'I inherited some money, enough to let me realise an ambition I'd had since I was a girl. This is it. Floral arrangement was a hobby, but I'd always wanted to own a shop. The legacy let me do that. I wish Leo was still here so I could thank him.' She frowned. 'That doesn't quite make sense, does it? What I should say is I'd give this up if it would bring him back.' She looked him in the eye. 'What are you doing now?' she asked. 'Now you're not a traffic cop any longer. Silly question though. Detective Sergeant. There's a clue in there somewhere.'

He smiled. 'Fine deductive powers, Ms Pollock. Maybe you should join us.'

'I can deduce why you're here as well,' she said. 'Sandra Bulloch. I read about her in the *Record*. It was a hell of a shock, I'll tell you. It made my stomach turn, something like that happening to a woman like her. Who was it did it? Somebody she'd arrested when she was with you?'

'If we knew that,' Stirling replied, I wouldn't need to be here. But,' he added, 'that's not high on our list of possibilities. The truth is we have no idea who killed her or why. In fact we have no idea what she's been doing since she left the police service after Leo Speight's death.'

'Neither have I, I'm afraid. Not that 'I expected to. I met her once, I think, when she and Leo came into the office. She was

Faye's sister so I didn't think anything of it at the time, but I was pleased for them both when they got together. She was the one for him, no question about it, unlike that cow of a sister of hers. It was just terrible the way that ended up. She should have gone to jail, that Faye woman.'

'The Crown decided it didn't have a strong enough case against her,' the DS said.

'She should have gone to fucking jail anyway,' Pollock replied, cheerfully. 'You'll have gathered I hate the woman,' she added. 'I called her a cow. Not fair: she'd give cows a bad name. From the little I saw of Sandra, she was the complete opposite. She was reserved, polite. She didn't say much, but what she did say was spot on.'

'And you're sure you've heard nothing about her since she left?' the DS asked her.

'Absolutely,' she declared. 'Why would she keep in touch with me? She barely knew me, plus Leo and I were a teenage thing . . . even if we did leave evidence behind us.'

'How about Gordon?'

She frowned, taken slightly aback. 'I would say that would be more likely,' she said, 'but if she has, he's never mentioned it to me. You should ask him.'

'I would if I could find him,' Stirling told her. 'I don't have an address for him, and he doesn't seem to have a social profile.'

'I can give you his address no problem, and his phone . . .' She stopped abruptly, as the shop door opened and a woman entered. 'Excuse me, please,' she whispered. 'Yes madam.'

The detective waited patiently while she dealt with the customer. He was impressed by her knowledge, her assessment of the lady's needs and the way she guided her towards making the correct choice.

'Next time I need to impress, I'll come here myself,' he promised, as the door closed and they were alone once more.

'The bigger the sin, the greater the cost,' Trudi Pollock advised him, 'but I'll give you the special polis discount.'

'Thank you in advance. Happily I'm not a sinner. Now . . .'

'Yes. Gordon's details.' She recited a London address, complete with postcode, a mobile number, and an email address. 'That's not the house that Leo left him, by the way. He sold that and bought an apartment with a river view. And you're way off about the social profile. He's very active; he's one of these lifestyle influencers, and he's good at it. Folk pay him to advertise on his page because of the number of followers he's got. He's on Instagram, but not under his own name. He's called @completepollocks: that's all one word, no capitals with one of those squiggly things in front of it. He reviews stuff, hotels, shops, bars, restaurants, could be anything, anywhere. He was going to review me, but I told him, "Gordon no. I don't want daft kids knocking my door down. I'm happy with the business I've got." He could be anywhere right now, on a cruise, at a Taylor Swift concert in Australia, anywhere. And he's still only twenty-three.'

'Quite a lifestyle from the sound of it,' the DS observed.

'You can say that again. But he can afford it, given what his dad left him, those hotels and the money.'

'What did he do with the hotels?'

'Gino looks after them for him. Gino Butler. I mentioned him, the man I used to work for.'

Stirling nodded. 'He was Leo's manager, yes?'

'That's right; now he's Gordon's in a way, with the hotels. Not that Gino's a hotel expert, but he does know business. He's taken the hotels into an international group, with a brand name, like Best Western, only higher class. They take a cut of the profits and so does Gino, a small percentage, but Gordon's still getting income.'

'Has he ever reviewed one of his own hotels?'

Trudi Pollock frowned once again. 'I don't know. Would that not be illegal?'

'I have no idea,' the DS confessed. 'To be honest I don't care. My interest is Sandra Bulloch, and her life in the last few years. I have information that suggests Gordon may have been asking about her too; that's why I need to speak to him.'

'He has? Again that's news to me. Who would he have asked?'

'A man called Bryce Stoddart, and possibly someone else.'

'Bryce Stoddart?' she repeated. 'He'd have known eff all. Anyway, isn't he still in jail?'

'Yes, he is, but he's still contactable.' As the door's warning bell tinkled again, Stirling realised that the conversation had reached a natural conclusion. 'Thanks Trudi,' he said. 'You've been very helpful. I'll see you again, and I won't forget that discount.'

Forty-One

Above Skinner's office door, on both sides, there were two lights, one red, one green, their purpose being to indicate to those outside whether the chairman was available or engaged, and to remind the chairman himself of his own status. As Dolça Nuñez knocked and entered, he pressed the button that changed the display from green to red.

'Welcome,' he greeted her. 'Thanks for coming up at short notice.' Normally his conversations with colleagues were in Spanish, or occasionally Catalan, but he spoke English.

If the young journalist realised that it was a test, she gave no indication. 'Not at all,' she replied. 'When the bosses say "Come" I assume that they mean "Come right away." Anyway,' she added, 'I had just finished the story I was working on.' Skinner detected a hint of American in her accent, but he read nothing into that. His son Ignacio had been raised as a Spanish speaker and the same was true of him. He attributed it to the influence of Netflix.

He grinned at the thought of it. 'You've been with us for a year now, Ms Nuñez. How are you finding InterMedia?' For a moment she seemed puzzled. 'Are you enjoying us?' he added. 'Is the company as you expected?'

'It is, sir, and more. I am enjoying it very much. I'm grateful to have been chosen.'

'That was mutual. You chose us too, and from what I've been told by Señor Sureda, we're as grateful as you are. We've given you a range of experiences so far,' he continued, 'a little broadcast, a little newspaper work, reporting. You're currently sub-editing, I believe. Do you have any preferences yet? Don't hold back, tell me. This isn't a test.'

'I don't want to be a sub-editor,' she replied, instantly, almost fervently. 'Subs don't originate, and the reporters dislike them when they alter their words. I want to be an originator, sir. I want to find things out.'

'How much do you know about me?' Skinner asked her suddenly. 'I'm willing to bet that when you were asked to come up here you did a quick net search. Right?'

There was a touch of guilt in the smile that lit up her otherwise serious features. Her dark hair was tied back, her eyes were as brown as her skin tone. He knew from her HR file that her mother was Thai, her father a seaman from Valencia. She nodded. 'Yes, I did. But I did not have time to read much. I know you were a cop, at the head of a force. It must have been a big one for them to have made you a knight.'

'It was,' he replied, 'but I didn't get the gong for that: it was for something else. Whatever, knowing that, you'll understand that I made a career of finding things out. I'm sure that's why I've been able to fit into this business, for I cannot break the habit. My problem is that I can no longer get out there and knock on doors, ask the questions, find the answers. That's where you come in. I have an assignment for you, one that's off the books of any Inter-Media outlet, for now. I'd like you to be my eyes, ears and legs, and to report to me and me only until I tell you differently. You must be discreet, and share with nobody, but I know already I can trust you in that respect. Are you up for it, Dolça?'

'Am I ever,' she exclaimed. 'When do I start and where do I begin?'

'You start in Barcelona and you begin right now. I'll move someone into your sub-editing slot right now. If anyone down-stairs asks you, tell them you're being given some experience in the chairman's office, no more than that. Now, this is what we're investigating . . .'

Forty-Two

The James Bonar who greeted Jackie Wright was a far cry from the version that Mann and Stirling had described after their earlier visit. Whether this was because he knew that his client was dead, or whether his cage had been rattled by Moira Mansfield, she did not know, and if she had she would not have cared.

'DS Wright,' he said, quietly as she came into the room with the view. 'I'm pleased to meet you. I'm sorry I couldn't help your colleagues last time, but obviously the circumstances have changed now. I'll do everything I can.'

'That's gratifying,' she replied as she took a seat that offered her a view of the famous Squinty Bridge and the museum piece crane that stood as a tribute to the halcyon days of Clyde shipbuilding. 'Did you ever meet Ms Bulloch?' she asked.

'In the flesh, no. We spoke a few times via WhatsApp, but that's all. In fact I never met Leo Speight either. His instructions were brought to me by his manager, a man called Gino Butler, and I followed them. When documents needed signed, Butler picked them up and brought them back.'

'Was that okay?' Wright asked. 'How did you know that Speight actually, signed them?'

'That's what witnesses are for, Sergeant. On those documents

166

the witnesses were always the same, Butler and a woman called Trudi Pollock. There's no problem with that.'

'Sandra Bulloch was never mentioned in this process.'

'Never. The first I heard of her was after Speight died. That was almost two years after the offshore company was set up. Butler came here with his co-executor, an Edinburgh guy called Baxter. They told me what was in the will, and who was the beneficiary. I say they, but actually it was Baxter that did all the talking.'

'Charles Baxter?'

'That's correct. He's a surveyor. I don't know a lot about that crowd, but from what I've heard he's one of the top players in property. His firm's called LJMcF, and he's the main man. It's what they call a multi-disciplinary practice: that means it's got its own legal division so it can do all of its deals in-house.' Bonar drew a breath. 'Baxter's a cut above Butler, that's for sure.'

The DS frowned. 'What do you mean?'

'How can I put it? He was much more authoritative, had much more of a presence. The guy's a decision-maker. Gino, I got the impression he liked to style himself as the brains behind his boss, but he wasn't. There were a few occasions where significant decisions had to be made, and it was clear to me that he didn't have the authority, and probably not the brains either.' Bonar held up a hand. 'Don't get me wrong,' he exclaimed, 'Gino has the qualifications. He's a fully fledged CA, but if he was in one of the big firms, I doubt he'd make partner level.'

'Okay,' Wright said. 'They came, briefed you and left. What happened after that?'

'They went away, the estate was confirmed and as the principal beneficiary Sandra Bulloch became our client. She was in the Bahamas at the beginning, but latterly I haven't really known where she was. Through the Jersey company he's a client of an international bank, and papers are referred to us. She might have a bank account somewhere as an individual, but most of her spending, maybe even all of it seems, seemed, to be done through the Artisan de Boite account. She has, had, a debit card in the company name, and the statements come here as the registered address.'

'Would they give us any useful information about her?'

Bonar smiled. 'I thought you'd ask me that,' he said, 'so I looked through all of the bank records. I can tell you that she moved into Leo Speight's Bahamas house by arrangement with the executors even before the will was confirmed. Mr Speight had been involved in a project there at the time, with a few other sporting investors, but that was completed within six months of Ms Bulloch moving out there. I'd assume that Baxter was involved in that at some level, so he'll be able to fill in any blanks. Also, very soon after her arrival she joined a country club on the island. That seems to have been the centre of her life for at least three years; until she started to go travelling, that is.'

'Where did she go?'

'According to the bank statements, it was mostly in the US, until she's shown as flying from Miami to Frankfurt last October.'

'That's when we know she picked up the motor home,' Wright said.

'That would square with the bank debits after that. Most of them were in euros, then at the beginning of this year, sterling buys start to appear. The last debits I can find were in late April. A fuel stop in Chipping Norton, a supermarket shop in South Tyneside, and more petrol bought in a Morrisons in Berwick. That's the last card buy she made.'

'Can we have all these records?' the DS asked. 'We're trying to get an understanding of Sandra's life. They might let us do it in detail.'

'Technically,' Bonar replied, 'they still belong to an estate as they did before. The difference is, it's now Ms Bulloch's estate and I have no idea who'll be handling that. But what the hell, you can have them. I don't think she's going to sue me.'

Forty-Three

John Stirling was a twenty-nine-year-old man who saw himself as a member of the new generation, but occasionally something would test his self-belief. The phenomenon of influencing was one of those things. He had chosen to ignore it until his meeting with Trudi Pollock had removed that option.

'Do you know what an influencer is, Maya?' he asked DC Smith.

She looked at him with a frown that bordered on severe. 'Of course. Usually it's someone with a big social media following. But it could be a broadcaster, a sports pundit, someone like that.'

'What do they do?'

The frown became questioning. 'They . . .' She paused. 'They . . .' She paused again. 'I suppose, when you think about it, what they do is, they make people believe in them, then follow their advice when it comes to lifestyle choices.'

'How?'

'Because of who they are I suppose: or who they appear to be,' she corrected herself. 'Because of the personalities they project through the media they're using. It could be something like Facebook, or they could have a YouTube channel, or it could be a podcast. It's how they appear, how they communicate and how they use it.' Her eyes fixed on him again. 'You know that TV pro-gramme, "The Traitors"?' she asked.

'Know it?' the DS laughed. 'I'm an addict. Claudia,' he murmured.

'My grandpa knew her aunt,' Smith said. 'She was a photog-rapher, and he says she had the same black hair. Anyway,' she continued, 'what they're doing there ... Thousands and thou-sands of people will apply to be contestants, but what the producers do, out of them all they choose twenty-two that they reckon have the ability to influence others, and they put them in closed surroundings. I suppose the winner is meant to be the one who's best at it. I mean, look at the people who get to the end, look at what they do afterwards. They've all got big followings on Instagram.'

'That I knew,' Stirling conceded, 'but none of them come any-where near Gordon Pollock. He has well over a million on the Gram ... and he's on YouTube.'

'Then he's probably making a fortune out of it. Why don't we access his bank accounts and his tax returns?' she suggested.

'We've got no cause, Maya. He isn't a suspect ... not yet, at any rate. The first step's to contact him, and that might not be easy. He posted on Instagram yesterday from something called a young singles' safari, in Kenya, and put up a piece of video on YouTube, him and the tour guide.'

'I wonder how much he's been paid for that,' the DC mur-mured, a trace of envy in her tone. 'Six months' salary for me, I'll bet you.'

'I'll be sure to ask him ... not ... if we ever make contact. I called him on the number his mum gave me, but it went straight to voicemail. He's not on WhatsApp and I can hardly leave him a post on Instagram, so all I've been able to do is leave a voice message and follow that up with a text asking him to call me. If he's out in the bush, heaven knows when that'll happen. Young singles safari,' he chuckled, shaking his head. 'God help the wildlife.'

He rose from his desk and crossed the room, to the refreshment table. He made himself a coffee in the Nespresso machine that Lottie Mann had donated to the squad . . . 'I can't stand instant, people' . . . and had barely returned to his desk when his landline rang. He guessed who the caller would be before he picked up the phone. Most of the calls he made and received were by mobile, but when messaging first time contacts, he always left the police landline number.

'Is that Detective Sergeant Stirling?' Gordon Pollock said. Lottie Mann had described a slightly awkward Paisley-reared teenager, but five years had wrought changes. The accent was still Scottish, but smooth. It had no hint of a rough regional bias, but there was anxiety.

'It is. Mr Pollock?'

'Yes.'

'Good, so you got my voicemail.'

'Is it my mum?' he asked. 'Has something happened to her?'

'No, it's okay,' the DS assured him. The connection was clear but there was background noise, city traffic, he thought. 'Your mother's fine. It was her that gave me your contact details in fact. I believe you're in Kenya. Is that correct?'

'As of this moment yes, but actually I'm at Jomo Kenyatta Airport, in Nairobi, waiting for my flight back. I'm due in Glasgow tomorrow, paying my mum a surprise visit. Do you need to see me?'

'Not at this stage,' Stirling said. 'Can you speak freely now? Before you do, I need to tell you that this call's being recorded.'

'I have no problem with that and yes, I can speak. I'm in the departure lounge, but it's no more than a quarter full. What's up?'

'I'm guessing you've been out of the reach of UK media for a few days,' Stirling replied. 'If so what I'm going to tell you will come as a bit of a shock. Sandra Bulloch was found dead last week. It's being treated as a homicide and I'm part of the investigating team.' He stopped, allowing Pollock to assimilate the news he had been given.

The line was silent for a few seconds, until he heard a long, loud exhalation of breath. 'How?' the young man continued, eventually.

'The cause of death isn't quite certain, but there's no doubt that she was murdered. She was found in her motor home, and she'd been dead for quite some time.'

'Jesus,' he whispered, almost reverentially. 'Where was she found?'

'Irvine, in Ayrshire.'

'Irvine?' Pollock repeated. 'That's near where Faye lives. She didn't do it, did she? I wouldn't put it past her. The bitch did her best to kill my dad. But if it was Faye, who's looking out for Leonard and Jolene, my brother and sister?'

'Slow down, Mr Pollock,' the DS said.

'Gordon, please.'

'Fine, but still, slow down. There are no suspects yet, Gordon, but there's no reason to assume that Faye Bulloch would be one. Frankly, our investigation's hampered by our lack of knowledge of Sandra's life since she left Glasgow. She's been, reclusive, you might almost say.'

'I wouldn't say that,' Pollock countered. 'Not with me, she hasn't.'

'I'll ask you to expand on that in a second, but first, there's something I need to ask you. A few weeks ago, did you call a man named Craig Goram, pretending to be Bryce Stoddart?'

'Yes I did.' The reply was instant, without prevarication.

'Why hide your identity?'

'Because I met the guy once. It was at a birthday party my dad threw in the house in Ayr for my wee brother Leonard, when he was five. Sandra was there, Leonard being her nephew, and he was with her. It was the first time I met her, way before she and my dad got together. I'd have been about fifteen at the time. I didn't like Goram then, and I liked him even less when Sandra told me why they'd split up, that he'd been banging a sixteen year-old in his class, and maybe a couple of girls before her, she thought.'

'Why did you call him?'

'Same reason I called Stoddart. Because I was worried about Sandra, and thought there was an outside chance she might have been in touch with him. I called anyone in my circle I thought she might have been in touch with. I even called Leonard.'

'Are you in regular contact with him?' Stirling asked.

'Of course. He's my kid brother, for Christ's sake. I've kept in touch with him ever since our dad died; Jolene too. Gino Butler and Faye aren't connected any longer, so he needs an adult male figure in his life. He hadn't heard from her either.' He paused. 'Look, this idea Gino has that Sandra was a recluse, it's wrong. She got in touch with me about six months after my dad died. She didn't say as much but I think it was because she saw me as a connection to him, and to Leonard and Jolene . . . even though she was their auntie,' he added. 'The rift between her and Faye, that was unbreachable, on both sides.'

'Understood, but back to Goram. Why did you use Stoddart's name?'

'I didn't want him to know it was me, simple as that. I thought that if I told him who I really was, he'd just hang up. He didn't, but he couldn't tell me anything useful.'

'Okay. You say you were worried about Sandra, but why?'

'Because she seemed to have dropped off the planet. The game plan was that she was going to visit her old auntie in the care home, then park the motor home somewhere and maybe come back south to stay with me for a while in London before she went back to the Bahamas. But she never showed up. I tried to call her but her number was dead. I tried the Bahamas number but no result. I had no other options, and she didn't do social so . . . eventually I stopped trying. I thought . . . well I don't really know what I thought; probably that she'd just got bored hanging with me and gone off somewhere else, on her own.'

'Hanging with you?' the DS repeated.

'Yes. Look I've told you that Sandra and I were quite close. We spoke on the phone a lot from the very start, after Dad. It was Sandra that encouraged me to move to London as soon as I turned twenty-one and make a life that wasn't connected to my birth or my upbringing. My mum was onside with that too, by the way. She was worried there were hooligans out there that might try to take advantage of me. It was Sandra that told me I should sell the London house and buy something that was better suited for me. She found me an estate agent through a guy in Glasgow, and she even came over and helped me choose my flat, and furnish it. I've been to the Bahamas too, to her place, that my dad left her. It's cool,' he added, 'like he was. It was Sandra who realised that I was quite good at social media and encouraged me to work on it. And before that, when I was still in Glasgow, she told me I should get off my arse, and plan my life. She told me to forget my dreams of being a boxer, because that would only work if I was as good as my dad, and that I never would be. Instead, she suggested that I enrol in a drama school. "Your life's been a fucking movie anyway, Gordon," she said. So I did. For a year. I even got a bit of TV work, bit parts in series set in Scotland. There are more than you imagine.' He fell silent for a few seconds. 'You know, Sergeant,' he whispered, 'telling you all this, it makes me realise, Sandra was like another mother to me, and that's what she'd have been if my dad had lived long enough to marry her.'

Forty-Four

'The woman that Gordon Pollock described to Stirling: that is not the Sandra Bulloch that I knew as a police officer.'

'Me neither,' Mario McGuire agreed. 'But,' he added, smiling on screen, 'suppose your Jakey, in a few years, was to describe you, do you think that any of us would recognise that Lottie Mann?'

'Probably not,' she conceded. 'Certainly not since I've been together with Dan.'

'Did Pollock help?' Sauce Haddock asked, joining in from Edinburgh.

'To an extent,' Mann said. 'He told John that in the second half of last year he had a call from Sandra. He told him that she had bought a motor home from a company in Germany and that she was flying to Frankfurt to pick it up. She asked him if he was free, and if so whether he fancied going native for a while and touring Europe. He said that he was, and that a road trip could be quite good for him business-wise, if he could plan ahead.'

The DCC shook his head. 'Influencing's a business now?'

'You'd better believe it,' Haddock said. 'Isn't that right, Lottie?'

'So it seems, and Sandra was fine with it, Gordon said. She gave him a list of places she wanted to visit, and he planned around that. Mostly they were cities: Lyon, Barcelona, Milan, Amsterdam and Paris. Luxembourg too, if that counts as a city, not a country. He was able to fix up a promotional link in each place. There are records of every stop in his YouTube channel. They went as far as the south of Italy, and brought in the new year there, until Sandra said late January that she wanted to head back to Britain. She was having a crisis of conscience, she said, about not having visited her Aunt Sally . . . yes, that was really her name . . . in her care home in Biggar. So they did; they took the mobile home on the ferry, then rather than take it into London, Sandra dropped Gordon off in Guildford, where she posted a card to her nephew and niece, then headed north. We know she got as far as Berwick, but that's all. After that, effectively she disappeared.'

'Did she visit the aunt?' McGuire asked. 'Do we know that?'

'John checked that straight away. The home manager said there's no record of her being there. The bank records that the man Bonar gave Jackie, they back all this up. Through fuel stops and parking fees we can build up a pattern of her movements that's almost as good as the disabled navigation system in the van would have given us, until it stops, abruptly.'

'That should pinpoint where she was when she was taken out, shouldn't it?' the DCC suggested.

'Not at all, unfortunately. Her last buy was fuel, in Berwick. Given the range of the thing she could have been anywhere within a three hundred mile radius.'

'Sod it,' Haddock whispered.

'Exactly, Sauce,' Mann agreed, 'but . . . all this might tell us where she was, but it doesn't take us anywhere near a motive for her murder. Gordon Pollock didn't tell us anything that would help in that respect. I need a complete picture of Sandra

Bulloch's life from the time she moved to the Bahamas to the day she died, and I'm not going to get that through phone interviews or video calls like this one. We have to talk to people on the ground. I need to send Jackie Wright or John Stirling over there, probably Jackie, since she has seniority.'

'She does but is she senior enough for an assignment like that?' Haddock wondered. 'I agree with you, we need to go there, but I think it needs a higher rank . . . for example Detective Chief Inspector.'

'I can't go. I'm the SIO. Can't we make Jackie acting DI?'

'I suppose . . .'

'Yes but,' McGuire exclaimed. 'I'm sorry to hose you both down, but I need to. I sat in on a meeting yesterday with the Chief and a couple of suits from the Scottish government. It was all about budgets, or to be more specific, budget cuts. From now on, all of our spending will have to stand up to public scrutiny, and our financial decision making will have to be spotless. For example, if the victim in a homicide was, let's say, an ordinary punter who'd been in a foreign country and might have upset somebody there badly enough to get bumped off once he was back home, would we send officers there to investigate the background? Most probably not; most likely we'd share information with the locals and ask for their assistance.'

'Hold on sir,' Mann argued. 'I was sent over to Spain earlier this year.'

'Yes, you were, but that was to assist the Spanish. Plus, there were American interests, and there were secret squirrel factors, with Bob Skinner getting kidnapped and such. In this case the victim was killed in this country, months after she left the Bahamas, and, she was a former police officer. That leaves any decision I take about overseas deployment open to comparative scrutiny.

179

Would we be applying different standards because she was one of our own? I hear what both of you are saying, and personally, I agree with it, but: the sad fact is that we have a chief financial officer. She's not a cop, so she isn't part of the command structure, but she does have oversight of everything we do. She might not have the power of veto, but she does have the ability to make a fuss. Look,' he sighed, 'I've thought about this, and if this was put to her, she'd point out that the Royal Bahamas Police Force predates our service by about a hundred and seventy years, it has a commissioner and fourteen assistant commissioners. That's more than we do. Sorry, I can't justify sending anyone, regardless of rank. Lottie, you have to ask the RBPF for assistance.'

'And where will we stand in its priority list?' Haddock protested. 'Not very high up, that's for sure. Fuck it!' he exclaimed. 'I've got about a month's accrued leave, and I want to take Cheeky somewhere warm before she gets too pregnant to fly. I'll go, on my own time and at my own expense, and fuck the bean counters.'

Forty-Five

Dolça Nuñez was excited, but it was not in her nature to let it show. She had been surprised by the invitation to the chairman's office, a little apprehensive initially until she had reasoned that if she was going to be fired she would have been told to report to someone in HR.

The outcome was not something she could have imagined, ever. She had a flair for investigative reporting, one that she had demonstrated on a student newspaper by outing a plot by a right wing nationalist group to infiltrate the campus. She had the courage that had to go with it also. She had not ignored the potential threats made to her personal safety. Instead she had included them in her story, which had caused the perpetrators to be expelled from the university and to be placed under judicial investigation. And yet the episode had featured nowhere on the CV that she had presented when applying for a trainee position with InterMedia. She had been concerned that if she had included it she might be flagged as an agitator herself, but on the left of the political spectrum, and turned down on that ground.

She thought of herself as a strong personality, capable of holding her own in any company, and yet in hindsight, she realised that initially she had been a little intimidated by Sir Robert

Skinner. The man had an intensity about him, a personality that was almost visible. Like most of Spain's journalistic community she had been surprised when he had been unveiled as the successor to Xavi Aislado as executive head of the InterMedia group. Xavi himself had succeeded Josep Maria Aislado, who had purchased what was then little more than a regional daily newspaper with a bad reputation. Old Joe had begun by clearing out the Francoist influence, and had been expansionist from that point on. He had been a pure businessman, but Xavi was a journalist from his bootlaces up. He had taken a view that was even more global than his predecessor. Among those who knew him the expectation was that he would groom his daughter as his successor, and stay in post until she was ready, until the death of Sheila Craig, his wife, Paloma's mother, had derailed everything.

InterMedia's rivals had stopped short of celebrating Xavi's emotional collapse and withdrawal from business and public life, but they had anticipated that they would benefit from it as their rival declined without its leader. When Skinner had been unveiled as his successor, and they had looked at his background, those expectations had increased. And yet a year later they were in full retreat; the InterMedia group's operations across Europe had been strengthened and it had posted record profits. Most striking of all, Skinner and his chief lieutenant, Hector Sureda, had surprised the industry by announcing an expansion into the US, and obtaining approval to launch their upcoming Hispanic cable news outlet. From being a curiosity, Sir Robert Skinner had become a story himself.

And he had chosen her, Dolça Nuñez Otero, as his undercover agent. When she had left his office, clutching the folder he had given her, to settle into the small room he had assigned her on the executive floor, Mount Olympus, as they called it downstairs, she knew that she had been handed a career-making opportunity . . . or career breaking, if she screwed it up. 'But I won't do that,' she murmured.

Opening the folder she found herself looking at several photocopies. Two were photos of the packages delivered to the Diaz Hoverstad offices. They were as Skinner had described them: a message in a bottle, and a deceased rodent with enclosures. She shuddered at the latter; she had grown up in an underprivileged neighbourhood in Valencia where rats were an everyday presence. The notes were there too, photocopied. Explicit, to the point, and threatening. No wonder the poor woman had been scared, she thought. The other enclosures were also photos, close-ups of the barcodes on the bottle received in Barcelona and the label that had been affixed to the rat. There for a reason, she thought, but . . .

'Do I take these to *Ciervorapido*?' she asked herself. Inge Hoverstad had kept this thing between the company and the police, the boss had told her. Sure, the Mossos and the Policia would go to the company, but if she did, the assumption would be that the media were on to the story. For sure *Ciervorapido* would issue a press statement, aimed that hosing down a fire that did not actually exist.

'No,' she decided. Discreet, Sir Robert had said, so discreet she would be. But, share with no one, that was a different matter. In her university career, Dolça had built a wide circle of friends, people of many talents and skills, most with an alternative outlook on life. She took out her phone, found a number and dialled.

She and Jorge Poch had met in her first post-graduate year, which she had spent in Sevilla, looking for the right employment opportunity while making ends meet by working as a waitress by day and a call-girl by night, seven hundred euros a trick. Not for the first time: Dolça had put herself through university by any means necessary. She had grown up poor but had no wish to stay that way.

Jordi Poch Hierro was like-minded, a boy from a background similar to hers who had earned a degree with distinction in computer science. If he had chosen to pursue a Masters it would have been in online stealth. He was an investigator of sorts, one whose specialty was, as he put it, accessing information without its owner ever being aware that his pocket had been picked. He was a hacker, a data protection officer's worst nightmare. He moonlighted also, as a security adviser, plugging holes for his clients that he had created, undetectably, himself.

'Baybee,' he greeted her as he took her call. 'How are the provinces?'

'More interesting than I had expected.'

'Are you still doing two jobs?'

'No.' She paused. 'I don't waitress anymore.'

Jordi gasped. 'You're . . .'

She laughed. 'No, I'm kidding. This is a small city; I couldn't keep such a secret here.'

As she spoke, she gasped involuntarily, as a throwaway remark by the chairman returned to her. '*I know already I can trust you in that respect.*'

'*And he did,*' she realised. '*They had another Jordi look at me, and still they hired me. God, maybe it was him! But no, he wouldn't have told.*'

'So why the call?' he asked, breaking into her moment of realisation. 'Have you finally realised that you love me?'

'I knew that a long time ago, my dear, as you love me. Now I want to take advantage of it. There's a pocket that I want you to pick.'

Forty-Six

'So, we meet again,' Gino Butler said, as Lottie Mann lowered herself into a tight-fitting leather chair in the golf club members' lounge, while John Stirling chose the easier option of a sofa. 'Too bad that it's in the same circumstances as the last time.'

'Not quite,' she countered. 'This one is very definitely a murder investigation.'

'As you thought Leo's was too, until things got more complicated. You and your wee sidekick were dead certain of it. I remember you on the day I found his body. Where is he now, by the way?'

She checked her watch. 'Right now? Lecturing at the police college.'

'I'd like to be in that class,' Butler chuckled. 'He was a peppery little bugger. He had me down as suspect straight away . . . even though it was me that found the victim . . . assumed victim,' he corrected himself.

She made herself return his smile. 'Being first on the scene doesn't automatically rule someone out as a person of interest. I can think of a couple of precedents, incidents where the perpetrator came back, called it in and made a great show of having found the victim.'

'Well I didn't,' he said, suddenly grim. 'I will never forget it. I walked in and there he was, my best mate, dead in his chair.'

'And your employer,' Stirling observed. 'A double hit.'

Butler stared at him and whistled, then looked back at Mann. 'Has this one been in your ex-partner's class? He's got the same direct approach.'

'He's had a few tips,' she conceded, then continued. 'Sandra was there that morning as well.'

He nodded, frowning as he gazed at the table between them. 'How could I forget . . . but I never knew that she would be until she turned up. If I'd known she was coming I'd have been waiting for her outside, to warn her.'

'But you didn't know then that she and Leo were a couple.'

'No, I didn't, but I knew they knew each other. She was Faye's sister, for Christ's sake!'

'Yes,' the DCI murmured. 'Faye.' She glanced at him. 'And you and she were . . .' She allowed the remark to hang in the air.

'Yes we were, but as you know, I've moved on from there; moved a long way as it happens.'

'Yes I know,' Mann agreed. 'I've met with your wife. Your life's taken quite a different turn . . . unlike Faye's. She's still sitting in her nice house by the beach raging at the world.'

'Whatever she says, DCI Mann, remember this. Faye's a congenital liar, and vicious with it. You talked about people of interest. She's got to be one, hasn't she? You must rememeber what she did when she found out about Leo and Sandra.'

'I do but I can't comment on it, or on any other aspect of our investigation. Nobody with a potential grievance against the victim has been ruled out yet, that's all I can say.'

'Not even me?' Butler ventured.

'Nobody,' she repeated. 'It struck me at the time that given how close you and Leo were, you had a relatively minor bequest. What was it again? The cars in the garage at Ayr and a paltry half a mil?'

He grinned, shaking his head gently. 'Yes,' he chuckled. 'That's what quite a few people thought, but none of them ever looked in the garage. The place was more like a motor museum. There were six cars in there, every one a classic, high value vehicle. The prize exhibit was a nineteen fifties Ferrari, that had actually belonged to Enzo himself. I sold that at auction for three and a half million, net. No, Chief Inspector,' he said. 'I'm not disgruntled. Far from it: I'm probably the most gruntled person . . . if that's a word . . . in this room.'

Mann was taken aback, but she maintained her legendary impassivity. 'When did you last see Sandra, Mr Butler?' she continued.

'Gino, please.'

'We'll keep it formal if you don't mind. Are you going to answer me?'

'Yes. I haven't seen Sandra Bulloch, not face to face, since that morning in Ayr. Obviously as one of Leo's executors, I had contact with her during the processing of the estate, but it was all done long distance. We spoke a few times, and I emailed her stuff to be Docusigned, but she didn't come back to Scotland and I didn't go out there. Once all the legal stuff was done, I distributed all of the bequests, my own, Trudi's, Gordon's, the kids', then handed all the rest over to Sandra through the state lawyers and went away. I've never contacted her since then, nor did she ever get in touch with me.'

'How about Mr Baxter?' Stirling asked. 'Has he seen her?'

'I can't speak for him. I know they didn't meet while we were preparing the estate for confirmation, but it's possible they've met since then. He's the property guy and that all went to Sandra . . . apart from the hotels, that is: they went to Gordon, as you'll know.'

'Which you manage for him,' Mann said. 'We've spoken to him.'

'Yes, that's right,' Butler confirmed. 'I was his trustee until he turned twenty-one and he didn't have a clue, so I had to take decisions. The ownership was a shambles: Leo had bought the properties individually and run them as such, with managers. I wasn't much involved then, but as Gordon's trustee I was able to bring them all together into a holding company, hire an experienced general manager and give her oversight.'

'Do you take a percentage?'

'I didn't as a trustee, but when he took ownership as an adult, Gordon, and Trudi too, asked me if I'd continue, in a different way with . . . what do I call it? . . . appropriate remuneration. By that time, Gordon had moved to London and was completely obsessed by growing his online persona . . . at which he's bloody brilliant by the way. The hotel GM's still in place, and reports to me. At a fairly early stage she proposed that we buy a brand . . . you'll have heard of Best Western? Same idea, only a different name . . . but that didn't work out too well so now they just trade as Pollock Hotels.'

Mann nodded. 'Who's the trustee for the three minor children?' she asked.

'For Raeleen, the kid in Las Vegas, the youngest one, her mother is; Rae Letts. Leonard and Jolene, theirs is Herbert Chesters, solicitors: in other words my wife.'

'Not their mother, that I understand, but not Sandra either?'

'No.' Butler hesitated. 'If you remember, the final version of Leo's will was written very quickly, by him alone. Trudi was a witness, but only to his signature. Its purpose was to make Sandra his principal beneficiary. It would have made sense for him to make her the kids' trustee, but Leo never thought of that. Why do you ask?'

'I'm trying to establish reasons for Sandra to have come back to Britain,' she replied, 'other than to visit her aunt in her care home.'

'Then I can't help you. The first I knew of it was when her death was reported in the press. Like I said, I never saw her after Leo died, and I haven't spoken to her since the estate was confirmed.'

Mann frowned. 'I'm wondering, did Sandra come back for Leo's funeral?' she asked. 'It wasn't an issue for us, since the case was virtually closed by then, so we wouldn't have asked. Now I think about it, I don't remember there being much media coverage of it.'

'That's because there wasn't one,' Butler retorted. 'Leo donated his body to medical research; it went to a teaching hospital in Birmingham that was running a study on the long term effects of combat sports. He thought it was the right thing to do, given his profession,' he added. 'Baxter and I did discuss having a memorial service, but Joy Herbert said that wasn't part of our remit as executors, as it wasn't mentioned in the will. I did ask Gordon what he thought, given that technically he was the next of kin as Leo's oldest child. He asked his mother but Trudi said "no way", in case Faye turned up and turned it into a circus with her drama queen act.' He shrugged. 'Anyway, Leo was an atheist.'

'Moving on,' the DCI said, 'were you aware that Sandra and Gordon have been in touch?'

'That I did know. He mentioned it a year or so back.'

'Did you know that the pair of them had been touring Europe in Sandra's motor home?'

Butler's eyebrows rose; he shook his head. 'No, I did not know. I spoke to him three weeks ago, but he never mentioned it.' He looked her in the eye. 'You need to understand, DCI Mann, that although I oversee the hotels his dad left him, Gordon and I aren't all that close. Okay, he was Leo's son and his mother worked for me, but I never saw much of him as a kid, and we didn't discuss each other's everyday lives. That said,' he added, 'he did ask me how he could get in touch with Charles Baxter. Now that struck me as odd.'

Forty-Seven

'This is a bit whirlwind, isn't it, Sauce?'

Harold Haddock smiled at his wife. 'You're always accusing me of not being spontaneous enough,' he countered. 'I act on impulse and now you're questioning it? You can't have it both ways, Cheeky.'

'I'm a woman, love,' Cheeky McCullough said. 'That means I can. You call me from work, you tell me to pack for a fortnight for a warm destination, but what you don't say until you get home is that we're leaving for the airport at three-thirty tomorrow morning. And you still haven't told me where we're going other than it'll be warm. It's just as well we got a passport for Samantha. Where are we going anyway?'

'Lynden Pindling.'

'Who the f u . . . is Lynden Pindling?'

'He was a controversial figure when he was alive but now he's dead, he's an international airport, in the Bahamas. We're booked into a resort hotel there. You need it, you deserve it, there's a creche and . . .'

'You can take your golf clubs?' she suggested.

'Correct.'

'Put that on the table, please.' She handed him a bowl of salad. 'And what's the catch?'

'Why should there be a catch?' he protested.

'Sauce,' she laughed. 'This is you. When we got married you thought Aberystwyth would be a nice place to go for our honeymoon.'

'It would have been,' he protested. 'It's remote and yet it's by the sea.'

'So are the Seychelles. Come on,' she persisted. 'What's the catch? You didn't just up and think "Hey, let's go to the Bahamas tomorrow? Cheeky would like that." There's more to it than that.'

'Well,' Haddock admitted, 'while we're there, I might have to talk to a couple of people about what Sandra Bulloch did when she lived there . . . that's all, I reckon, just a couple . . . and report back to Lottie.'

'What?' Cheeky exclaimed. 'I thought she reported to you.'

'She does, but . . .'

'Why can't she go?' She paused. 'Not that I'm complaining about you doing stuff, mind. You couldn't sit still for a fortnight anyway.'

'Mario said he'd never get it past the CFO.' He frowned. 'Yes, you heard me, she's investigating the murder of a former police officer, and she was being handicapped by finance.'

'I can understand that,' she commented. 'If she went and it became known the Holyrood opposition and the press would be likely to yell that there was special treatment because the victim had been a cop. Yet if it was a civvy victim, the same people would be outraged if she didn't go.'

'That's a PR argument, Cheeks. The CFO has an accountant's brain. Either way I was outraged that she had any say. That's why I did my nut at the meeting, and said I would do it on our tab. I confess it was only after that, I realised it was something I should have been doing anyway, getting you away for a last holiday as a mother of one.'

'Hah!' Cheeky retorted. 'I've been a mother of two ever since Samantha was born. Come on, let's eat then crash out. We'll get four hours sleep if we're lucky.'

Forty-Eight

'You're becoming a regular here,' Trudi Pollock told Stirling as he stepped into her shop. 'It's about time you bought something.'

'Find me a nice cactus,' he said. 'I'll take it back to the office. It'll be a metaphor of sorts. Gordon said to meet him here. Is that okay?'

'Yes, I know he did. He's in the back shop.' She nodded towards a door behind the counter, taking a step to one side to make way. 'Just go in.'

Gordon Pollock's tan was newer than that of Lottie Mann, but probably deeper than hers had ever been. 'DS Stirling?' he exclaimed as the detective joined him in a store room cum office that was almost as large as the public area. 'Is this okay to meet? I've got no hang-ups about coming to a police office, but this is closer to Mum's.'

'No worries,' Stirling said. 'This is much better. How's the jet lag?'

'Minimal,' Pollock said. 'At this time of year there's only a two hour time difference between here and Kenya. Three in our winter,' he added. 'It's equatorial so they don't need daylight saving. The big challenge is getting used to our climate again.

Fucking freezing. They say it's sixteen degrees today. It was twice that in Nairobi, even though that's more than four thousand feet above sea level. And the humidity? Forget it.'

'You were on a safari, according to Instagram. What was that like?'

'A terrific experience. The Kenyans are very proud of the big five, lion, leopard, elephant, rhino and hippo, and we got to see all of them. It was purely photographic, of course, although there were a couple of tossers from Belgium that were disappointed we didn't get to shoot anything. The same boys wanted to swim with the hippos. The safari guides should have let them; those things kill more people in Africa than any other animal. If you want to see it, take a look at my YouTube channel in a day or two, once I've had time to process it all. There's a couple of clips on Instagram already, but the full works will be much better.'

'Including the Belgians?'

'Definitely not. They'll be edited out, for the sake of the client.'

'Client?' Stirling repeated.

'The safari company. That's how I think of the people who use me, as clients; they pay me, and I promote them. It works for us both; I give them low cost access to a well-defined target group, and they give me money . . . and perks like free safaris. It's a form of advertising for them and I'm becoming a leading provider.' He smiled. 'My dad was the leader in his business. I'm out to emulate him in mine. I'll never make as much money though,' he chuckled. 'So Sergeant,' he continued. 'What else do you want to ask me? I'm sorry again about the false name when I called the guy Goram. I just didn't fancy telling him who I was.'

'Fair enough. We're over that. Thing is, Gordon, as a serving police officer Sandra was way before my time, and she was noted for keeping her private and professional lives apart. And now she's a murder victim, with no obvious suspects. That means that I, we, the team, need to build as complete a picture of her as we can. You're better placed than anyone else to help us, as you've seen her most recently. Our knowledge of DCI Bulloch ended when she left the service after your father died.'

'It seems to me you should be asking your questions in the Bahamas,' Pollock observed. 'That's where she's been for most of that time.'

'We are,' the DS said. 'A senior officer's on his way there now.'

The younger man laughed. 'The bosses get the big trips while the other ranks are stuck in Glasgow?'

'You could look at it that way,' Stirling agreed, 'but it's not as bad as it sounds. Did you ever visit Sandra there?' he continued.

'No, I never did. I was planning to, later on this year. But now . . .' His voice tailed off.

'Did she talk to you about her life there?'

'A wee bit; not much, probably because there wasn't much to talk about. She liked it there though, the isolation, the peace and quiet. She'd played a bit of golf since she was a girl, and she took it up again out there. Otherwise, I'd say she lived a quiet life. She wasn't a recluse, though. She mentioned a few friends, ex-pats mostly, but she did say that she was very pally with a pro golfer who was attached to her club. Also she did yoga. I know that because she mentioned her teacher. She was from Tyneside originally, Sandra said, but she moved on and Sandra became more interested in golf.'

'When you were touring in the mobile, how did she seem?' the detective asked.

Pollock gazed at him. 'What do you mean?'

'How was her mood?'

'Good, no question about it. She wasn't grieving any more,

put it that way. My mum is, although she never lets it show. She's a sweetheart but the fact is she's been grieving quietly for my dad ever since he left Paisley and moved to London, only she never told him or gave him or anyone else a hint of it . . . apart from me, I could tell. Sandra, though,' he continued, 'she'd moved on finally.'

'Did she have any new relationships?'

'There might have been in the Bahamas, but while we were touring she definitely wasn't interested. A couple of guys tried it on in places where we stopped, but she fended them off by dropping hints that I was her toy-boy.'

Stirling drew a breath. 'I suppose I have to ask you this, Gordon,' he said. 'Were you?'

The young man grinned again. 'I suppose you have to,' he agreed. 'Answer, no, I wasn't. The thought never crossed my mind. Not because of the age difference between us: Sandra was fit, no question. We went to a sauna once in Switzerland, so I can tell you she was in good shape. But I've sort of said it before; she was like a stepmother. That's how she acted and that was cool as far as I was concerned.'

'Fair enough. When you toured, was it planned?'

'No, it was pretty much instinctive. We had her list, but it wasn't exhaustive. Sandra would pick a place and we would go there. We shared the driving fifty-fifty; and the cooking when we ate in . . . which we didn't do much.'

'You were touring in the winter. Was that not a bit . . .'

Pollock finished the sentence. 'Cold? On occasion, but we had the gear for it. Sandra loved it. She'd been living in the Caribbean for four years, remember. She said it was great to wear a heavy jacket and to be in cities again.'

'Those cities, what did you do there?' the DS asked.

He shrugged. 'Nothing special; we parked the van on a site and did the tourist thing. Stayed for a couple of days, sometimes in a hotel for a break from sleeping on wheels, then we moved on. Apart from Luxembourg: we took a quick look at the city centre and left as soon as we could. That place didn't feel right. I've nothing against immigration . . . as far as I can see it benefits most countries . . . but I read somewhere that forty per cent of the population of Luxembourg are immigrants, and that quite a few of them are illegals. Sorry,' he said. 'I really am a liberal, honest.'

'Ultimately, though,' Stirling persisted, 'who chose where you went?'

'Sandra did; it was her van. I was happy with that; I posted everywhere we went, and I made some money, so it felt like a business trip.' Pollock paused. 'That's as much as I can tell you, really. Sandra was happy all the time we were away, and she was happy the last time I saw her, when I made her drop me off in Guildford, on the eighth of February, rather than try to get into London.'

'What did she say she was going to do from there?'

'Like I told you before, she was going to Scotland to visit her Aunt Sally. Then, she said she was going to take care of some business, and after that come back to see me on her way home.'

'Take care of business,' Stirling repeated. 'What did she mean by that?'

'I don't know. She didn't say.'

'And that was the last time you spoke to her? In Guildford?'

'Not quite,' Pollock replied. 'I called her a couple of days later, to see how she was getting on, and how her aunt had been. She said that physically she was fine but mentally she was in her own wee universe.'

The DS nodded. 'Okay, that's good, Gordon. But just one more thing. Gino Butler told my boss that you asked him how you could contact Charles Baxter, his co-executor. Is that true?'

'Yes, I did,' he confirmed.

'Why him?'

'Because he was the only person from back then that Sandra mentioned by name all the time we were away. It was in Luxembourg, in the city centre. We were looking at the architecture, buildings and stuff and out of nowhere she said, to herself, rather than me, "Mmm, I must ask Charlie about that." Baxter's the only Charlie I could think of. I've never met him, only had an idea of who he was, and that's why I asked Gino for his number.'

'And did you call him?'

'Yes, I did. It wasn't easy but eventually I got past his secretary. I asked him if he had heard from Sandra but he hadn't. I told him what she'd said in Luxembourg and asked him if he'd any idea what she'd meant. He said "No, but even if I had, Gordon, I couldn't discuss it with you." Then he hung up on me, just like that.' Pollock's eyes narrowed. 'I haven't forgotten that,' he murmured. 'I'm going to find a very public way of sorting him out.'

Forty-Nine

'*Ciervorapido*'. Dolça Nuñez whispered as she looked at the brand's website on her laptop in her small office. 'Where the hell did they come up with a name like that?'

Her research had told her that the product had been launched quietly at the beginning of the year, cheap and cheerful, ostensibly targeting the younger market but with just a nod to another group, stay at home women who were not averse to keeping a little buzzed without it being too apparent to those around them. The home page told a story of its invention three hundred years ago by Italian nuns who had kept the secret until the current generation had decided that the time had come to share it with the outside world. 'They should have called it Mierda de Toro,' she said aloud, 'because that's what the story is.' And yet, the convent did exist, as did the sisters. Dolça was fairly sure that if Jordi could access their bank account he would find that a substantial deposit had been made within the last two years by Compostella, the manufacturer. The secret formula tale was a fine romance, but the obligatory list of ingredients shown in one of the images revealed that it was actually red wine, laced with tequila and a little sugar. Of course she had sampled it; she and one of her boyfriends had shared a bottle the night before.

He had drunk most of it, and had been of no use to her thereafter.

The sound of her mobile interrupted her. 'Jordi,' she said as she took the call. 'What have you got for me?'

'As much as there was to find from the codes,' he replied, in the lisping accent of his Andalusian Spanish. 'Both of the labels that you sent me came from the same batch. They were bottled in the Compostella plant in San Cugat, near Barcelona on the seventh of July. The company does a whole range of non-alcoholic drinks.'

'Yes, I know. I can see that from the website. It's very informative.'

'What it won't tell you,' he countered, 'is that the company has taken a big gamble with this product. A much bigger group has expressed interest in taking Compostella over but the owners, two brothers, Emil and Sancho Blazquez Gallardo, want to fatten it up, to boost its turnover as quickly as possible and increase the sale price. That's what *Ciervorapido* is all about. The brothers have thrown everything behind it, including a big advertising and PR spend. It seems to be paying off, as the sales figures for the first month are very good and getting better. It's all good news for them so far.'

'But if there was some bad news?'

'Their borrowing is high, and their liquidity is about to be eaten into by a big tax bill. Any more negativity and there's a better than even chance they'd be fucked. Basically, they need the sale. Otherwise, even if *Ciervorapido* becomes an international success, effectively they'll be working for the banks for the next ten years at least.'

Dolça whistled. 'Boy, this is good stuff. But what about the labels? Did you get anything else from them?'

'Of course,' Jordi said, dismissively. 'They were delivered to a wholesaler, Grau, in the town of Lleida. It supplies all the super-markets as well as selling directly to the public itself . . . at standard prices so that it never undercuts its main customers.'

'How many of those supermarkets are there?'

'All of the big ones, basically, and many smaller places, Spar stores and the like.'

'Mmm,' Dolça murmured, slightly disappointed. 'Still, it's a start.'

'It's much more than that. Grau's systems are very good; you can track everything. Both of the labels were from bottles deliv-ered to a Mercadona store in Calle Manuel de Palacio, Lleida. Mercadona's systems are not so good.'

'Still, that's great,' she exclaimed.

'Not so good,' he continued, 'so even more accessible. Both bottles were sold to the same person on the seventeenth of August. I had hoped to tell you who it was, but the buyer was one of a rare breed today; they paid cash. Also the store's camera sur-veillance is shit.'

'You are a genius, Jordi.'

'Yes,' he agreed, 'but that won't stop either of us going to jail if another genius hacks into a record of this call and works out what we're doing.'

'Is that possible?'

'No, because I will remove it.'

'Is there anywhere you can't go?' Dolça asked.

'I'd have trouble telling you the size of Kim Jong Un's under-pants,' Jordi replied, 'but if they're imported, I could probably find out where he buys them. Closer to home,' he continued, 'I discovered that Emil Blazquez has a personal reason for wanting the sale to go through. He has a mistress, a woman named Silvi

Urquel, who wants to be more than a mistress, and is threatening to out their relationship. If she does . . . Emil's wife owns twenty-five per cent of Compostella already, and as he told Silvi in a very indiscreet email, a decent lawyer would have a field day with his share. That bad news we were talking about, it would be fucking terrible for him."

'What about Sancho, the other Blazquez?'

'Spotless.'

'Interesting,' she murmured, 'but probably not relevant to my enquiries. Thank you, my love. When am I going to see you again?'

'As soon as you like. I could catch an AVE to Girona and be there in time for dinner.'

'Just you do that,' Dolça said. 'I'll meet you at the station. But,' she added, 'you've said nothing about the other name I gave you.'

'That is very true,' Jordi agreed, 'and I'm not going to. I'm not even going to mention him. I cover my tracks, as you can appreciate, and now I am hoping that I cover them well enough. I found the biographical stuff easily enough, but when I tried to dig a little deeper I came up against a very thick wall, too thick even for me. It's called the British security service, and they are not to be fucking messed with. You said you were curious, that's all. Don't be any longer; let it lie. See you later; you're buying dinner and I want Italian.'

Fifty

Lottie Mann took pride in being open-minded. She was not one of those Glaswegians who hated Edinburgh in principle, believing that such people were displaying their feelings of inadequacy for all to see. Nevertheless, when she stepped from the train on to the Waverley Station platform she could not help feeling that she was in another country and that the ticket inspection point was, in reality, passport control.

She rode the escalator to Princes Street, and headed west, striding purposefully past the Scott Monument, wondering as she did why she had never read any of the writer's nineteenth century works, and indeed how many of her contemporaries actually had. As she neared the National Galleries she glanced up towards the Castle and its esplanade, where the grandstands that had enclosed the Edinburgh Military Tattoo were being dismantled for another nine months. 'Why do they no' just hold it in Murrayfield?' her ancient grandfather had said, every time the annual show had appeared on television, and she had to admit that given the cost, there had been sense in his grumpy argument.

Passing the galleries and the Mound, she made to cross the street, but was delayed by a passing tram, moving so slowly that if asked, she could have given eye witness descriptions of all four passengers. Even her parents had only vague memories of Glasgow's legendary equivalents, standout exhibitions in the modern era in the Transport Museum that was a favourite haunt for Dan and Jakey.

Having reached the northern pavement, she walked up the pedestrianised Castle Street, then turned towards Charlotte Square, where the office of Charles Baxter's firm, LJMcF, a global practice of property advisers, was located. Rather than search number by number, she used Maps to pinpoint the address, a classic terraced building on the south side of the Georgian square, facing another that she recognised from television coverage as the official residence of Scotland's First Minister.

Stepping into the reception area, Mann had the distinct feeling that she was entering a hotel rather than an office. A young man, tall, blue-suited, with a rugby forward's build, stepped out of a side room to greet her. 'Detective Chief Inspector Mann?' he began.

'Is it that bloody obvious?' she retorted.

He smiled. 'You're our only female visitor today, so from that point of view it is. You're here to see Mr Baxter? Give me a moment and I'll let him know you've arrived.' He returned to his bolt-hole, but only for half a minute. 'The boss is ready for you,' he said. 'First floor, his room is facing you when you get to the top of the stairs.'

The direction was unnecessary for he was waiting for her in his doorway. She had no doubt that it was Baxter; there was a presence about him that only a boss could have assumed, and survived. He was as tall as the man in reception, and as solidly built. Mann wondered if they had both played for the same club.

As she approached he peered at her, over the same narrow gold-framed spectacles that she had seen in the photos she had found in preparing for the meeting. Professionally, LJMcF was a firm of chartered surveyors, but in practice it was much more. 'Strategic global property advice and management,' its online presence declared.

'Welcome to Edinburgh, Chief Inspector,' Baxter said, offering a handshake. 'You are only the second police officer to visit this office, and the first wasn't serving when he came here. Sir Robert Skinner. Did you ever meet him?'

'Oh yes,' Mann replied. 'He was my last chief in Strathclyde, and I've encountered him since, quite recently in fact.'

He ushered her into what she acknowledged silently as a magnificent room, furnished and presented in the way its architect had envisaged more than two hundred years before, its windows looking across at the more celebrated building opposite with something that might have been taken for disdain.

'Ironic,' Baxter sighed, 'that his visit here was in the aftermath of Leo Speight's demise. Now you're here investigating poor Sandra's.'

'When was the last time you saw her?' Mann asked as she settled into the leather armchair that he offered her.

'Probably just over four years ago,' he replied. 'After she inherited I went out to the Bahamas to brief her on her property holdings and to take her instruction on how they should be managed.'

'And how was that?'

'How were they managed? Remotely, as far as Sandra was concerned. That's what she wanted. She was honest enough to admit that she knew nothing about the property business and told me that as Leo had trusted me, then she would too. It was just what I wanted to hear, to be honest with you. Nothing's worse than a hands-on client.'

'You haven't seen her since? Never?'

He shook his large head. 'Never. The plan originally was that I would visit to brief her every six months, but when the pandemic happened that was shelved, and we did our business by video link.'

'That business was routine, was it? Forgive me,' the DCI said, 'I know as much about the property market as Sandra did . . . she used to be my boss, by the way, so I did know her.'

Baxter removed his spectacles and gazed at her. 'Can I ask you what you thought of her? Or is that not allowed?'

Mann met him eye to eye. 'I'm used to asking the questions,' she replied. 'But since this is informal . . . I didn't like her. I thought she was remote, peremptory, rude at times, and frankly not the team player she should have been at her rank and in her job. But now, through this investigation I can see that she had some issues in her personal life, specifically a former partner, that might have affected her.'

'I don't know about those,' Baxter admitted, 'but I can see where you're coming from. She was pretty crusty initially in the Bahamas, but I put that down to grief. I don't suppose you ever met Leo . . .'

She shook her head. 'I investigated his death but no, I never met him.'

'No, well: Leo Speight was a brilliant individual, and I don't simply mean in the boxing ring. He's had very few peers, historically, in his sport. I've studied some of them since then and reached the conclusion that to make it to his level one needs to be intellectually superior also. That's not only the case in boxing; I see it in other sports as well, golf being a good example. Leo had a very quick mind, one of the sharpest I've ever encountered. He was capable of reading and analysing any situation. I learned just

how capable very early in our relationship. When he first contacted me and asked me to help him invest his wealth in property,
we had a meeting in this very room. I'll be honest, I was expecting a roughneck in a leather jacket and trainers with scar tissue
and a bent nose. The man who arrived couldn't have been further from that stereotype. He had an aura about him . . . I can't
put it any better than that . . . his suit was tailor made and his
shoes had probably come from his own last. I gave him a run-
through of the property business, rather pompously in hindsight,
but realised very quickly that he'd done his own research and
knew it all already. He told me how much he wanted to invest,
and where. Most of it was in dollars, lesser amounts in sterling,
euros and yen: he explained that this was money earned through
what they call pay-per-view, post-tax, and retained in the original
currency. He asked me for a list of prospective investments in the
relevant markets.'

'Very interesting,' Mann said, 'but I'm investigating Sandra
Bulloch's murder, not Leo Speight's business dealings.'

'Yes, yes,' Baxter acknowledged, testily. 'I'm trying to set a con-
text. Over the next few years I helped Leo build a significant
property portfolio, all legal and incorporated in tax-advantageous
locations. Through that period he was the most hands-on client
I ever had, but a complete contradiction to the norm. He was
quick, he would originate ideas, he was mercurial, but there was
an air about him, a sense almost of danger.'

'Menace?'

'No, not really. It was as if he was living on the edge, in pursuit
of something without quite knowing what it was. Until,' Baxter
paused, 'about a year before he died, he changed completely,
almost overnight. He was almost unnaturally calm and content,
as if he had finally reached his destination. I didn't realise it at

the time, because he dropped no hints, but in hindsight, it coincided with he and Sandra becoming a couple.'

'And then he died.'

'Yes. And the relationship that she had been as keen as Leo to hide from her sister came to light, along with the will changes that removed Faye and made Sandra and his children the beneficiaries. As you investigated the death you will know that the stuff hit the fan for Sandra, professionally on top of her bereavement. That's why, acting on Skinner's advice, I believe, she went to Butler, my co-executor, asked for access to the Bahamas property and moved out there . . . where she and I finally met.'

'Good,' Mann sighed. 'And when you did . . .?'

'I found, to an extent, the woman you described earlier. Remote, a little suspicious, not rude, but on the edge of it. But she'd just lost her man, she had the family complications, she found herself in totally unexpected circumstances. I actually asked her if she felt she was living a dream. "No, but you could call it a nightmare." That was how she replied. It was only towards the end of that meeting, maybe after getting to know me a little, that she revealed that her biggest worry was that the four children had been treated fairly. I was able to tell her, as co-executor, that they had. I even had her added as a trustee for her nephew and niece. There was no need to do that with the boy Pollock: he was nearing majority by then. As for the youngest, in America . . . what's she called? Raeleen . . . I had actually met her and the mother, when I went to Vegas to have Leo sign off a property purchase, so I was able to assure Sandra that she would be fine. With all that in place, Sandra began to change. Not as quickly as Leo had but gradually for a year or so, until she was a different woman, relaxed, content, I would almost say happy. As she appeared to be at every one of our online meetings, until she disappeared.'

'Your business dealings: how were they?'

'Uneventful. I managed the estate, if you want to call it that, secured the income, recommended and made a few strategic disposals. Sandra had no wish to grow her holdings. She wasn't like Leo. She had no real interest in the sector.'

'Not even in Luxembourg?' the DCI suggested.

Baxter frowned. 'Luxembourg,' he repeated. 'Again. Sandra doesn't . . . didn't have property in Luxembourg. Yes,' he admitted, 'young Pollock did mention something about that when he called me a few days ago. I brushed him off, I'm afraid. Why should you be asking about that now?'

'She was there with him not long before she disappeared,' Mann told him. 'He heard her make a remark; said she'd have to talk to you about something. Since it was you, the assumption is that it was a property matter. She never did ask you?'

'No, absolutely not. How could she have if this was just before she went out of sight?'

'She didn't contact you, or try to?'

'I repeat, no, Chief Inspector, absolutely not.'

'Did you know she was coming back to Europe, Mr Baxter?' Mann asked.

'No, I did not.'

'She didn't mention buying a motor home and touring Europe?'

Baxter gasped. 'Of course not, whyever would she? That would have nothing to do with me. I was her property manager, that's all. Her other wealth was sheltered in a Jersey company that Leo set up years ago, run by a shifty Italian called Gialini, through a Glasgow solicitor whose name I can't recall. If she wanted to buy a toy she'd have done it through one of them.'

'She did. I just wondered if she'd mentioned it to you, that's all.'

'Well she didn't. Look, Chief Inspector,' he exclaimed, 'you're making me feel like a suspect. This is becoming an interrogation.'

'It's not,' she assured him. 'In a homicide investigation, every box has to be ticked, and every question has to be asked, whether it turns out to be relevant or not. With this one, there are no suspects, because there is no apparent motive.'

'No suspects?' Baxter challenged. 'I would have thought there's one prime suspect, front and centre. The sister, Faye Bulloch, the mother of Leo's middle two kids. I remember her behaviour after the truth came out about Sandra and Leo. Threatening, vindictive, you name it. She tried to make as much trouble as she could when Butler and I were winding up the estate. She used a weaselly like lawyer from Glasgow, but Mrs Herbert, whose firm did the donkey work, was more than a match for him, and her. She was beyond vitriolic. I don't want to teach you your job, Ms Mann, but I wouldn't look past her, sister or not.'

Fifty-One

'Is that Detective Sergeant Wright?'

'Yes it is,' she replied. The light mellifluous tone of the caller's voice made her think of puff candy. Lottie Mann had described her as radiant; at once she understood why.

'This is Rae Letts. I'm sorry it's taken me so long to return your call. I was out of town visiting my mother in Fresno, and I only just got back.'

'Thank you, that's understood. I . . .'

'Before you say anything else,' Letts continued. 'I know why you reached out. Gordon . . . Gordon Pollock, my little girl's half-brother . . . messaged me to tell me about Sandra having died. I called him back, so I know how. It's terrible. Why would anyone do such a thing to a lovely lady like Sandra? It makes my skin crawl. I don't know what I'm going to say to Raeleen; not the truth that's for sure. You caught the son of a . . ?'

'No,' Wright admitted. 'We haven't got that far, I'm afraid. We're still interviewing people who knew Ms Bulloch and who might have spoken with her recently. From what you've just said I assume that you've been in touch with her.'

'Yeah. We speak often. She's visited me here by the lake.'

'The lake?'

'Lake Las Vegas, it's where I live, me and Raeleen. Not in the city but close enough for me to get to my job.'

'What do you do?' Wright asked.

'I work in reception in a golf course; there are over fifty of those in Vegas. I used to be a dancer, but I don't do that no more. Leo left it so I'd never have to, but Raeleen's going on eight years old now, and I can't sit around the house alone all day.'

'You don't have a partner?'

'No, not since Leo. It's a funny thing, none of Leo's ladies ever have, since him. I dunno what that says.'

'A lot about him, I suppose. You said that Sandra's visited you in the past.'

'Yeah, we've been in contact since not long after she settled in the Bahamas. I took Raeleen there once, when she was five, and Sandra visited with us a couple of years ago. There was a PGA golf championship at one of the fifty, and a friend of hers was playing, so she came to follow him on the course.'

'A friend?' the DS said.

'Yeah, just a friend, not a partner. That's what she said, and I'm pretty sure she meant it. She went other places with him, she said. I never met the guy, though. I think his name was Ryan something.'

'Were you surprised when Gordon told you that she'd gone back to Europe?'

'I guess I was, a little bit, but not a whole lot. She talked about her auntie a couple of times. She said apart from Faye, who she hated as much as everyone else does, the old lady was her only blood relative left . . . her father's sister, she said . . . and sometimes she went on a guilt trip for leaving her in that old people's residence and only ever sending her a birthday card, 'xcept the trip never lasted too long, 'cos it wasn't Sandra that actually put

213

her in that place. The old lady, she was a widow; she had a step-daughter from that marriage, a woman that Sandra had never met so she didn't count her as family. It was her that put the old lady away.'

'It's been suggested to us,' Wright said, 'that she was planning to visit her aunt when she and Gordon finished their travels around Europe.'

'Then I guess she would have,' Letts said. 'She talked about her often enough. She said places like that, they gave her the horrors. When she was young she saw one of her grandmas pass her last days in one of them, and she was half convinced that she was helped on her way. Sandra, lately she had no anger left in her she said, apart from that. She said she'd never forgot it and never would.'

Fifty-Two

Lottie Mann hung her coat on a hook, smiling as she glanced through her office window at the impressive stonework of the main grandstand of Ibrox Stadium. It was one of the images that defined the city of Glasgow in her mind and the sight of it made her feel happy to be home.

She stepped out into the squad room, where Wright and Stirling sat, their desks not far apart. Maya Smith and three other detective constables were in a group beyond them. As she approached her eye was caught by a new addition to the refreshment table.

'Where did that come from?' she asked, pointing towards the cactus.

'Me, via Trudi Pollock's shop,' Stirling replied. 'A wee present for the team.'

'If you knew my other half,' she chuckled, 'you'd never have done that. "We've got enough pricks in here already," he'd say. I can hear him now, the only thing being that women are in the majority now. But thanks John, it's the thought that counts. I'd have brought us back some Edinburgh Rock, but I can't stand the stuff. So,' she continued, 'I had my audience with Mr Baxter. A man who likes to make an impression.'

Wright smiled. 'Kate, my partner would agree with that. She's a surveyor, like him, but with a firm on a much lower level. She says that LJMcF is so far up itself that it hasn't seen daylight for years, and that it's Charles Baxter that sets the tone. He got one cap for Scotland rugby, as a replacement off the bench, and he's dined out on it ever since. But, he is international class in the property business, no doubt about that.'

'Maybe so,' Mann said, 'but he didn't exactly fill any gaps in my knowledge of Sandra Bulloch's property holdings. I'd like to know more about them; John, that's your task. Find out what she had, how it was owned and where. From what Baxter said, it'll all be held within a company, or a series of companies, in tax havens. Do that, but without referring back to Baxter or LJMcF, if you can.'

She turned to Wright. 'Jackie, the one thing Baxter did say that I reflected on during the train journey back: Faye Bulloch. My fault, but I think she's been given too easy a ride up to now. Re-interview her, without that bastard Lee in the room, if you can manage it. Ask her to account for her movements from the last time Gordon Pollock saw her until the day that Sandra's motor home was dumped in Irvine. Let's take nothing and nobody for granted . . . especially not her.'

As her sergeants set about their tasks, Mann returned to her personal space, a glass walled office with internal venetian blinds that could be closed but never were. Alone, she took out her phone and made a call.

'DCI Mann,' Bob Skinner exclaimed. 'This is a surprise.'

'Can you speak, sir?'

'I have a couple of minutes. Do you have news for me? Have you made an arrest?'

'Not even close. We're following various lines of enquiry but none of them are leading us anywhere significant. I've found out more about Sandra's movements in the weeks leading up to her disappearance. She toured Europe with Gordon Pollock in the motor home. He seems to have been her protégé. As it stands, he's the only significant witness we have.'

'Could he be a suspect?'

'No chance. I did have someone check his movements after they went their separate ways. When Sandra made her last petrol purchase, he was in New York, where he stayed for two weeks. From there he went back to London and stayed there until he went to Kenya a few months later. He's ruled out. We are having another look at Faye Bulloch, though,' she said.

'Look all you like,' Skinner replied. 'She didn't do it.'

'What makes you so sure?' the DCI asked.

'Experience.' He paused. 'Plus,' he added, 'Faye isn't a complete idiot. If she did kill her sister, in her very own camper van, she wouldn't have dumped the bloody thing within a few miles of her own bloody house. You'd have found it a hundred miles away, and you'd be tracing her through a rail ticket from wherever that was back to Ayrshire. So,' he exclaimed, 'why are you calling me, Lottie? I really do have to be somewhere else in a minute.'

'I wanted to ask your opinion, sir, about the man I've just interviewed. You met him, just after Leo Speight died. Charles Baxter, the property adviser, and co-executor. He's been managing Sandra's portfolio since she inherited, and I have evidence that she was planning to call on him or speak to him when she got back to Britain. I interviewed him this morning and he's adamant that she never did. Maybe your meeting is too far in the past for you to answer this, but I wondered . . . what was your opinion of him, in terms of reliability?'

Skinner was silent, for so long that Mann thought the call had been discontinued, until . . .

'Let me put it this way,' he murmured. 'If I was you and I had two conflicting descriptions of the same event, one from Charles Baxter, and one from my late granny's budgie, if I wanted to judge the truth I would lean towards Joey all day long. Good luck and keep me in the loop, if you'd be so good.'

Fifty-Three

Preferring to interview her subjects face to face, Dolça Nuñez had thought of driving to Lleida, but two factors had dissuaded her. The first was that the journey would have taken up to three hours, depending on the traffic. The second, she did not own a car. Yes, she could have requisitioned one of the InterMedia pool vehicles but that would have required her to state her purpose, and compromised the privacy of her mission for Sir Robert.

Instead she stuck with basics and sourced the phone number of the Mercadona store in Carrer (online directories often used the Catalan word rather than the Spanish Calle) Manuel de Palacio, and called it, hoping that it was not one of those that closed during the afternoon hours.

'Is the manager available?' she asked the gruff woman who answered.

'A moment.'

She waited, for several moments. Eventually a man responded. 'I am the manager, madam, Carles Adamo. How can I help you?'

'Good afternoon,' she said, adding an edge of excitement to her voice. 'My name is Dolça Otero, I'm a market researcher employed by the makers of a new product called *Ciervorapido*.

I'm looking to assess the brand's impact, both with stores and with customers. Can you help me?'

'Not a lot, I'm afraid,' Señor Adamo confessed. 'I know the brand you're talking about, but only because it was forced on to my shelves by my regional management. I told them it was one of those gimmicky products that might be okay for the big cities, but not for this city or for my branch, not without a special promo, but there wasn't the budget for that apparently. I told them so but as always they know best and sent the stuff anyway. I'm sure you know how that is.'

'Yes,' Dolça ad-libbed, 'I've heard the same from other supermarket managers.'

'And they probably told you the same as me, that we were right. You know what? So far I have sold only two bottles of the stuff, and they were to the same customer. The rest, I'm going to send back to Grau, the wholesaler.'

She made a conscious effort to curb her excitement. 'I don't suppose you know who that customer was,' she ventured. 'It would be good for my survey if I could interview them too.'

'I know who she was, but I can't put you in touch I'm afraid. She's a regular; a street musician, I think. Not a big spender; always pays cash. I was there when she bought the stuff. Her name's Maria, Maria Gallardo, but I don't know where she lives. That's too bad for her, if you were going to pay her for her thoughts.'

'Yes, too bad,' Dolça sighed, 'but thank you anyway. That will blend very nicely into my research. Good afternoon.'

She ended the call, and leaned back in her chair. 'Gallardo, Gallardo, Gallardo,' she thought. 'Why is that name . . ?' She sat bolt upright. 'Of course.' She grabbed her phone from the desk and made another call. 'Jordi,' she exclaimed as the connection was made, 'where are you?'

'Can't you hear?' he replied. 'I'm where I told you I would be. On the AVE, heading for Madrid then on to Girona, and linguine with a nice sea food sauce.'

'Good, I can't wait. But right now, do you have your laptop?'

'Of course I do. It's chained to me, you know that.'

'Is there Wi-Fi on the train?'

'Yes, of course.'

'Even better. There's something else I need you to do for me, someone I want you to find. Her name is Maria Gallardo, she lives in Lleida, and I think she might be a busker. I need to know everything there is to know about her, ideally by the time you get to Madrid.'

'Then hang up and let me get on with it,' Jordi said. 'This train goes very fast.'

Fifty-Four

Cheeky smiled up at her husband from the poolside lounger in the Bright Islands Resort Hotel. 'I love it when you act on impulse,' she said. 'Samantha's in the resort creche making new friends, you're off to work and I'm here with nothing to do but relax and fight off the urge to be completely decadent and have a morning strawberry daiquiri. I love you, Sauce Haddock; don't take too long.'

He returned her grin. 'I won't,' he promised. 'Every hour I spend away from here is an hour off the golf course. It looks like a beauty.' He dropped to one knee and kissed her, then headed for the exit.

Their rental car, part of the package deal they had bought, was a Lexus hybrid with voice activated controls. 'Plot me the fastest route to the Foxlake gated community,' he said.

'Exit left onto the highway and proceed for three miles, then exit onto Reynolds Road,' a female American voice instructed.

'Yes ma'am,' he murmured and obeyed.

The Foxlake community where Sandra Bulloch had lived was seven miles from the hotel. 'You have reached your destination,' his guide told him, but she failed to mention the barrier that blocked the entrance. The Lexus purred quietly as he waited for the security guard to make his way from his booth, at a leisurely pace.

'Your business, sir,' the young man drawled. His shoulder badges bore the insignia of a private security company. He was unarmed, but a large wooden baton swung from his belt.

Haddock took his Scottish police warrant card, in its enamelled case, from his pocket and held it up for inspection. The guard made to take it from him, but he shook his head. 'No,' he said quietly. 'Look, but don't touch. I'm looking for Ms Bulloch's residence, number eleven. Your manager's meeting me there. Please let him know I've arrived.'

'I didn't catch the name, sir.'

'Haddock, Superintendent Haddock.'

The guard grinned. 'Really? Like the guy in Tintin?'

Harold Haddock was known to friends and colleagues, junior and senior, as the most amiable of men, but there was one button they all knew better than to push and that was his surname. He was happy to be called after a condiment by those who knew him, but nobody made fun of his family. He stared silently back at the man, stone-faced, until the grin vanished, he nodded, 'Yes sir,' shuffled back to the booth and raised the barrier.

The road within Foxlake was one-way and kidney shaped. The community contained seventeen residences; when he arrived at number eleven, Haddock could see the entry barrier in the distance, and watched it rise to admit, without stopping, a car dressed in what the blue light on its roof made him assume was police insignia.

Each of the homes had a flagpole beside its entrance doorway. Some were bare others were dressed. Sandra Bulloch's stood out from the rest because it flew the Scottish saltire. 'Rock on,' he murmured, as he stepped out of the Lexus. The house was smaller than the mental picture he had carried with him, but still substantial, on a package of land that a satellite scan had told him was generous.

'Mr Haddock!'

Sauce turned to see a dark-skinned woman walking towards him. On the land enclosed by the roadway an eighteenth house stood, from which he guessed she had emerged. 'Jane Way,' she announced as she approached. 'I'm the community superintendent. I have Ms Bulloch's key. The cops got in touch with me to tell me you were coming, but nobody's told me what the issue is.'

As she spoke, the police car reached them, drawing up behind Haddock's. A uniformed officer emerged from the passenger seat. The Scot glanced at his epaulettes, his reading of them confirmed when their bearer spoke. 'Superintendent Haddock?' he began, hand extended. 'Superintendent Alan Dossor, Royal Bahamas Police. Welcome to our islands.'

'I'm not tuned into the Bahamian accent yet,' Haddock said, 'but that doesn't sound like one.'

'It's not,' the newcomer confirmed. 'I started my career with Greater Manchester Police. I made inspector and was happy with that, until my wife and I were watching "Death in Paradise" on telly one night, about five years ago, and she said, "That looks like a good idea." We laughed but she'd planted the seed. I started to look out for opportunities and to my surprise, I found one here. Level transfer, but I've worked my way up.' He held up a document. 'I have the document from the court that lets you enter the premises.'

'Can I see that?' Ms Way asked. 'Maybe it'll explain what this is about.'

'It may not,' Haddock suggested, 'but I will. Ms Bulloch is deceased, and her death's being treated as suspicious. I'm head of the national serious crimes squad in Scotland and we're investigating.'

'Oh my!' Jane Way exclaimed. 'How horrible, she was such a pleasant lady. Who'd do that to her?'

'That's what we're working to find out,' he replied. 'And it's why I'm here in person,' he glanced at Dossor, 'rather than asking our colleagues in the RBPF for assistance. I'm sure they'd have done the same job as me and probably better but this is going to wind up in court in Scotland.'

'Trust me,' the Bahamian officer said. 'We're very glad that you are. Sure, we're good, but we have three thousand officers, tops. You have five or six times that. Do you want me to hang around, Superintendent, or are you okay on your own?'

'Please stay. We have this thing in Scotland called corroboration.'

'I take that to mean I could still be called as a witness?' Dossor asked.

'In theory, it does, but . . . I don't expect to find anything that's going to help our investigation. I might, but chances are I won't. Suppose I do, all you'd have to do was confirm my discovery. In those circumstances, the defence would probably accept a witness statement and waive cross-examination.'

'Pity. I'd like to visit Scotland again.'

Haddock grinned. 'You still hanker for the wind and rain, do you? Let's go, if we may. Ms Way, you have the keys?'

She nodded. 'And the alarm code,' she added. 'Without that, there will be a hell of a noise. This is a very secure community. Ten of these homes lie unoccupied for most of the year, but we've never had a home invasion, not ever.'

She led the way up a slight incline to the entrance door of Sandra Bulloch's home. The two superintendents watched as she unlocked and opened it, wide enough for her to punch a six-digit code into a keypad. After three seconds, a sound rang out. 'Clear,' she said. 'It's all yours.' As she stepped aside, she handed Haddock a slip of paper. 'The code, should you need it again.'

'Thanks. Has anyone been in here since Ms Bulloch left?'

'Only the cleaners,' Way replied. 'They go in once a week regardless, but they're super reliable.'

'They have keys?'

'They sign for them, in and out. They know the codes, but that's all. I'll leave you now. I'll be in my office if you need me again.' She walked away, leaving Haddock and Dossor to step into the dead woman's home.

An inner door gave them entry to a spacious hall, but it was more than that.

'Jesus,' the Bahamian superintendent whispered, 'what's this? It's like . . .'

'It's a trophy room,' Haddock said, quietly, 'dedicated to the memory of Leo Speight, undisputed, undefeated world middle-weight champion, the man Sandra Bulloch was going to marry, until he went and died on her. If it was all back in Glasgow, there would be a long line of people ready to pay good money to see this stuff.'

Facing them was a pedestal, on which stood a huge trophy, overlooked by display cases which covered all the available wall space. They were filled with more trophies, smaller but no less impressive, and with signed, framed, photographs of Speight, embracing beaten opponents and shaking hands with household name celebrities.

Dossor pointed to one of them. 'Is that . . .'

'Barack Obama? Looks like him. And I can see three British Prime Ministers and two Scottish First Ministers. And is that

Sharleen? I think so.' The cabinets had as their backdrop an array of championship belts. Most were big, garish and colourful, but two stood out less ornate, a mix of gold and ribbon. 'That's a Lonsdale belt,' Haddock murmured. 'British champions get them, but they only get to keep them after three or four defences. Next to it, that's the Ring Magazine belt. Only the very best get one of those, and he was.'

'What's all this worth, Superintendent Haddock?'

'Call me Sauce, please. In the right auction house, properly promoted, it's got to be millions. But I guess to Sandra it was all priceless.' He frowned. 'But it's not what I'm looking for. Let's move on.'

The two men moved on, beginning their search at the top of the house, a glazed turret that an estate agent would have called a belvedere. There was enough room for a table, a small bar, and two chairs, from which the occupants could enjoy a spectacular ocean view.

'Our constables start at under twenty-five thousand dollars a year,' Dossor said. 'And for that they protect people with this level of wealth.'

'I know,' Haddock sighed. 'The clown in the gatehouse probably gets paid more than that.'

They moved downstairs, inspecting each of the five bedrooms in turn. Four gave no sign of recent use, but the largest, with a balcony that also looked beyond the garden and swimming pool towards the sea, had been left with make-up and a hairbrush, on the dressing table. There were three drawers on either side. The Scot checked them, finding underwear, socks, and a small jewel box that contained earrings and a few costume rings. Similarly the wardrobe unit held nothing exceptional, only clothing and shoes.

'How old was Ms Bulloch?' Dossor asked as he emerged from the en suite bathroom.

'Forty.'

'Forty and single. There's no sign of a man ever having been in there, and in my experience they always leave a trace. She had a vibrator, but so what? I saw no condoms and no contraceptive pills. The cleaners could have been more thorough,' he observed. 'There's a toe-nail clipping on the floor, but it's painted, so I'd guess it's hers. Did you see any sign of jewellery?'

'Only a few things in a box,' Haddock said. 'Nothing significant. That fits with the description of her style that I have from people who worked with her.'

The staircase was wide enough for them to descend side by side. As they did, they were surprised to see a woman standing in the hallway. She was silvery blonde, buxom and, Haddock knew instinctively, British.

'What's going on here?' she demanded, in clipped tones that might have been modified Essex. 'Who are you guys?'

'Does my uniform give you a clue, madam?' Dossor said, icily.

'Should it?' she challenged. 'All you guys wear uniforms of one sort or another. Okay, so you might be police, but that doesn't give you the right to go looking through people's houses in a closed community.'

'This does.' Haddock held up the court warrant. 'Superintendents Haddock and Dossor.'

She peered at him. 'You're not from around here, love. Scotland, innit, from that accent.'

'Wow,' he exclaimed. 'We could make a detective out of you. Any vacancies, Alan? The lady's about to introduce herself, aren't you madam?'

She sniffed. 'Liz Brown,' she replied. 'Live next door at number ten, me and my old man. I came in to see what you're up to.'

'I commend your public spirit,' the Scot said, 'but we're not going to discuss our business. If you'll oblige us by going back home, when my colleague and I are done, I'll come and see you, and we can have a chat then. Meanwhile do you know your neighbour well?'

'Well? Not well, but yeah, I know her.'

'Right, we can discuss that but for now . . .'

Liz Brown sighed. 'I know, fuck off.'

Involuntarily, Haddock smiled. 'I wasn't going to put it quite like that, but yes please, off you fuck, and I will see you shortly.'

She left, holding her dignity round her like an invisible robe.

'Twenty-five thousand a year,' Dossor repeated. 'She probably spends that much at the hairdresser. Come on Sauce, let's do the rest.'

The ground floor, behind the entrance gallery was open plan, kitchen and dining area to the right, a large television with one armchair to the left. The central area was seated, but it was not large. The house had been designed for mainly outdoor living.

Haddock was admiring the layout when his colleague called out. 'What's this?' He turned to see him standing by a door beyond the television area.

'Toilet?' he suggested.

'If it is,' the Manchester Bahamian countered, 'it's the only room in the house with a Yale lock. That could be a problem if you were in a rush.'

Haddock crossed the space to join him. As he did so he took the key-ring from his pocket; studying it he saw no Yale key. 'Bugger,' he muttered. 'Do you have a locksmith on call?'

Dossor smiled. 'Yes,' he replied, 'but first . . .' From his trouser pocket he took what seemed to be a collection of long narrow tools. 'You might not want to witness this,' he chuckled, as he turned to block the door, shielding his actions. 'The warrant doesn't cover it.' He went to work. A few seconds later, there was a click and the door opened. 'I'm old school,' he explained. 'Whenever I have a job like this I always come equipped, just in case.' He stood aside as Haddock joined him.

'Not a toilet,' the Scot murmured.

The room was, in fact a small office. It was furnished only with a desk, a swivel chair and a set of Harman/Kardon candle-stick speakers, that were connected to an Apple iMac computer. Haddock felt a surge of excitement. 'This,' he murmured, 'could be gold dust.'

'What do you mean?'

'The location, the place where Sandra's body was found, it had been stripped clean of every trace of her. There was no phone, no tablet, no laptop, although we know for sure that she had all three of those. This,' he said, pointing at the desktop, 'if we can get into this, we could find her whole life on here . . . that's assuming she actually used it. But even if she didn't, it might connect to the Cloud, where almost everything's backed up these days.'

'Do you have Ms Bulloch's email address?'

'Yes, and the Glasgow team have looked at it, but she doesn't appear to have used it since she left for Europe, other than to make final arrangements to pick up her motor home in Germany. If we can get into this thing . . .' He switched it on and waited for a few seconds, as it booted up. An image of Leo Speight and Sandra Bulloch appeared, a selfie, taken in what might have been a Highland location. At the foot a cursor flickered, awaiting a password. On impulse Haddock pulled the keyboard across, typed in 'Champion' and clicked, only to see the asterisks in the space bounce as it was rejected.

'Do you have an IT department?' he asked.

'Of course,' Dossor said. 'We can help you with that. The warrant authorises the removal of personal items at our discretion. I have some clever men and women who should be able to get in there. I'll take it to them.'

'What level of internet infrastructure will this place have?'

'Ms Way will be able tell you, but if it isn't full fibre I would be surprised.' He leaned over the desk. 'Yes, there, behind the computer, that's the router. It's the same as the one I have at home, so I'd bet that BTC'S the provider. I'll have someone contact them and check. However it's just possible that the service is provided centrally, through the community. Whatever, leave it with me.'

'Thanks, although the main thing will be to get us into this computer. Minimum, it'll show us her search history up until her departure. Progress at last, Alan.'

'Yes. Let's unplug the thing. I can take it back to my office now, so my people can get to work. That'll let you go and finish your conversation with the delightful lady next door. D'you want me to do a background check on her, by the way?'

'To cover all the bases, yes I would. I don't expect any surprises, mind but I preach thoroughness to my team until they're sick of hearing it, so I need to practise it myself. Let me help you take this down to your car, Alan, before I go into number ten.'

'Yes, thank you. Everything must be in there, Sauce, if you think about it. The lady doesn't appear to have kept any paper records at all.'

'She must have; nobody's completely paper free. We just

haven't found them yet. I'm probably going to need a more detailed search, Alan,' he warned.

Haddock carried the computer down to the police vehicle, while Dossor took the keyboard, mouse and cables. As he closed the rear door, his colleague took a card from his pocket and handed it over. 'Contact details,' he said. 'Can I have yours, please?'

'I'll text you,' the Scot promised. 'That'll put my mobile in your contacts. We're staying at the Bright Islands Resort.'

'We?'

'Wife and daughter. It's a dirty job . . .'

'But someone's got to do it,' Dossor laughed, as he slid behind the wheel of his car.

Haddock returned to Sandra Bulloch's mansion, where he conducted another, quicker, search with no more success than the first. Frustrated, he reset the alarm and locked up, before cutting across the grass to the neighbouring property.

Liz Brown's front door opened as he reached it. She had changed from day pyjamas into a swim suit covered with a diaphanous robe. The carpet slippers she had worn earlier had been replaced by yellow plastic clogs. 'Come through to the garden,' she said, as he stepped inside.

He glanced around. The entrance was different from number eleven, more conventional, square, with a staircase to the right and beside it a glass-fronted lift. The white walls were hung with prints and framed photographs, showing Brown and a white-haired man in a variety of locations and situations.

The woman read his mind. 'Yeah, I know. We don't have any trophies to show off, Bry and I, just our memories. Mind we've got loads of those.'

'Where is your husband, Mrs Brown?' Haddock asked. 'It is Mrs, yes?'

'Oh yes,' she replied, with emphasis. 'Call me Liz. My maiden name was Dors, would you believe. I 'ated it, got fed up early doors, with people calling me Diana, so I was more than happy to change it when Bry and I got hitched. He's out just now, as he is every morning, at the country club; golfing. He's getting on a bit now, but he can use a buggy so it's okay.'

'I don't think you have a choice out here,' Haddock observed. 'Carts are compulsory. Good news for the caddies.'

'You a golfer, Superintendent?'

He nodded. 'I am.'

'What's your handicap?'

'At the moment it's two, but I can't practise as much as I used to.'

'Bloody hell. Bry's twenty-two. He won't let me play with him anymore, 'cos I always beat him.'

She led him through the house. The furniture was dark, leather seating, wooden tables. 'We brought all this stuff with us when we moved, eight years ago,' she explained, as if reading his thoughts. 'We sold our big house near Chelmsford when Bry retired. We still have a little flat there for when we visit our boys and the grandkids, but otherwise we're here for good.'

'What did your husband do?' Haddock asked. He had no real interest in his career, but experience had taught him that when interviewing a compulsive talker, it always helped to feed the addiction.

'He was a consultant. That's what I usually tell people and usually that's enough. Actually he was a proctologist. Know what that is?'

The detective nodded.

'Yeah. Arseholes, that's what people normally think when I tell them, but it's much more complicated than that. A colorectal surgeon, that's what he was. He did some NHS work, but latterly it was all private. He had quite a client list. Film stars, MPs, a couple of oligarchs, even some Royals; half the crowned arses in Europe, he'll tell you when he's had a few. Have a seat,' she said, as they reached a suite of brown rattan garden furniture. 'Would you like a drink? I don't mean booze. I've got that but I don't myself. Got to take care of Bry. These days he shifts enough for both of us.'

'Anything with ice in it would be good,' Haddock told her.

She left him in the garden, feeling slightly enclosed by the flanking trees, high enough to block the view from Sandra Bulloch's balcony and from the home on the other side.

'Here you are love,' Liz Brown exclaimed, handing him a tall glass of a bubbling yellow liquid decorated with mint and slices of lime. 'Barley water and soda. Can't beat it. Makes me think of Wimbledon. Went there once. One of Bry's clients got him seats in the Royal Box. We sat behind Tom Cruise, and String.'

'String?'

'Ah sorry, Sting. I always get his name wrong.' She settled into a chair, rubbing her back against its cushion as if she was relieving an itch. 'Well,' she exclaimed. 'What's the news about our Sandra? She's a deep one, but I didn't expect to find cops raiding her house. What's she done?'

'She's dead, I'm afraid,' Haddock said.

'Fuckin' 'ell!' She sat bolt upright the itch forgotten. 'What? How? What happened?'

'She was murdered. I'm head of the team that's investigating her death.'

'Fuckin' 'ell!'

Haddock said nothing, allowing the woman to absorb and process the shock, and to react in her own time.

'How?' she asked, when she was ready. Her strident tone had become little more than a whisper.

'I won't go into detail,' he replied. 'All I'll say is that she was killed a few months ago, but was only recently that her body was discovered.'

'Who done it?'

'That's what we're trying to establish. Sandra Bulloch was a private person; she was also a former police officer. I didn't work with her but several of my colleagues did. None of them really knew her, though. We need to find people who did. Did you, and your husband?'

Brown stared at her shimmering swimming pool, as if she had lost the power of speech. For a few moments Haddock feared that she had, until, 'I suppose,' she said, almost a concession. 'I suppose we did. Certainly we knew her better than we know anyone else in this place. This is a fucking ghost town, truth be told. A very hot ghost town, but that's what it is. It took us a while, mind,' she added, her voice regaining its former timbre. 'We knew Leo, before Sandra arrived here. He was some machine. A quiet man but an absolute fucking killer.'

'In the ring,' Haddock agreed. 'Yes, that was his reputation.'

'Not only there,' she countered. 'Anywhere, I'd say. One time, he was having dinner with us, and he got talking about a Russian guy he said had stolen his gold medal in the Olympics, because the judges were bent. He'd have killed him, given half a chance, I could see it in his eyes. I met a couple of blokes in England that were hoodlums that had never been caught. You could tell with them, and Leo was the same, only far more dangerous.'

'Did they ever come here together, Sandra and him?'

'No, love. Sandra only moved out after he died. We thought it was just to get over it, but she stayed on here, full-time. She kept herself to herself, for, oh, must have been the first year she was here, but finally she came in to ours for a drink, then for dinner. After a while we invited guys along, to make up a four. Attempted match-making I suppose you'd call it, but she wasn't interested. She did a return dinner once with one of them included, but that was it. He told me later that walking into her house, he'd been fucking terrified. It was like Leo Speight's ghost was intimidating him, that's what he told me afterwards. The only man I ever saw her with more than him that was Ryan, but he was definitely only a friend.'

'Ryan?' Haddock repeated.

'Ryan Pilgrim,' Brown explained. 'He's a pro golfer, a touring player attached to the country club. Sandra was a member too. He gave her a few lessons when she joined. She liked him and they became a sort of a couple, like I said, friends. After that, if Sandra had us in for dinner, he'd be there unless he was away playing somewhere.'

'Friends with benefits?'

'Definitely not. Sandra was done with men, she told me one night when she'd had a couple of drinks. She said she'd had a bad experience before Leo. After that, and what happened to him, her bedroom door was definitely closed. "With a combination lock, Liz," she said. There was one, apart from Ryan, that she was close to, she told me, back in Britain, but he was like a son. He was Leo's boy from when he was young; Gordon, she said he was called, her project. In fact, the last time I saw her . . . Christ, nearly a year ago, when I think about it . . . she said she was going back to tour Europe with him, and to sort a few things out.'

'To what?' Haddock asked.

'Sort a few things out; that's what she said. "Things or people?" I remember I asked her. She shook her head and said "Just business." That was all. I knew she'd inherited millions from Leo, but she never really talked about that side of her life. She dropped the odd name . . . an Italian called Giuli-something that she said was nutty, a guy called Charlie she said was her property guru, and another called Gino . . . but that was all.'

'What about her sister? Did she ever mention her?'

'Sister? I never knew she had one. That sums her up, my neighbour Sandra, really.' To Haddock's surprise, Liz Brown's eyes glazed. 'A woman of mystery,' she murmured, her voice faltering, 'right up to the end.'

Fifty-Five

'This is a little off piste, Dolça,' Bob Skinner observed. 'I tend to hold all my meetings in the office, not in a city centre coffee shop.'

'I know, sir,' she replied, 'and I wouldn't have dreamed of suggesting it, but I didn't want to have to sign Jordi into the office. They might have wanted to know who he is, and why he's here.'

'I could have fixed that, but never mind.' He looked at their companion, a lean man in his mid-twenties with sandy hair and a pointed chin that gave him a fox-like appearance. 'Now I'll ask. Who are you, Jordi, and why are you here?'

'He's my research . . .' Dolça began but he held up a hand to stop her.

'Let him tell me.'

'I'm her researcher,' Jordi Poch said. 'I've been helping Dolça with the investigation that you asked her to undertake.'

'Do you live in Girona?'

'No, I'm from Sevilla.'

'That's a long way from here. How have you been helping her?'

'I do my research online.'

'Anyone can do that these days. What's your added value?'

'I can go where other people can't.'

Skinner's smile did not reach his eyes. 'That's a diplomatic way of saying you're a hacker.'

'Personally, I hate that word,' Poch retorted. 'I'm an online researcher. That's what I do.'

'By breaking through layers of data protection if you have to. I was a cop, son, before fate threw me into the job I do now. I have contacts in various places. If I were to ask them if they'd ever heard of you and if your name was on a list of people they wanted to locate, what might they tell me?'

'Nothing sir. I'm not so stupid that I'd put myself in that position. My business is to uncover information for my clients, but within the law. Okay, the law can be grey and the lines can be wavy, but I manage to stay on the right side. If my subjects have systems that can keep me out, good luck to them. If not . . . they should have.'

'Which of those categories do I fall into, Jordi?' he asked, quietly.

The question drew an intake of breath from Dolça Nuñez. 'Jordi?' she whispered, staring at him, but he waved a hand as if warding her off.

'The second,' Poch replied. 'How did you know?'

Skinner chuckled. 'Are you fucking serious?'

The young man winced. 'I'm sorry sir, but when you involve my girlfriend in an off the books investigation, I want to know whether she can trust you or whether you're setting her up as a . . . fall girl.'

He nodded. 'That, I respect. Okay, that's dealt with, and I've already told the people you woke up in London that they can go back to sleep.' His gaze switched to Nuñez. 'Dolça, tell me your story.'

'It's a scam,' she said, instantly and vehemently. 'The whole Sisters of the Trinity scare. A complete scam, a set-up.'

'Set up by whom?'

'I'll get there . . . but I wouldn't have got anywhere without Jordi. The two labels, the images that you gave me, he traced from the bottling hall in San Cugat to a small Mercadona store in Lleida. They were bought by the same person, the manager told me, a woman called Maria Gallardo. That surname, I recognised. The company that makes *Ciervorapido*, it's owned by two brothers, Emil and Sancho, and they are planning to sell it, for big money, maybe more than it is really worth. Blazquez is their first surname, their father's name. The second, their mother's in Spanish custom, is Gallardo. Maria is their cousin, the daughter of their uncle, their mother's brother. It took Jordi no time at all to trace her, and to find where she lives in Lleida. His train to Girona from Madrid stopped there, so I told him to get off and I met him there.' She paused, looking at Skinner. 'I had to hire a car, sir. Can I put in on expenses?'

He gazed back at her, took five one-hundred euro notes from his wallet and handed them to her. 'Enough?'

She smiled and nodded. 'We found Maria after a short search. One of her neighbours sent us to a shopping centre where she said we'd find her singing. That's how she makes her money, it seems. We did. When I told her what I had found, she collapsed, she went hysterical. We calmed her down . . . at least Jordi did, he's very good that way. When she was able, she told us that her cousin Emil had paid her to buy the bottles and to deliver them in packages to the offices of an advertising agency in Barcelona and then a few days later to an address in Madrid. She told us Emil has personal problems that means he needs to get as much money as possible from the sale of the company. I asked her if she knew that one of the agency people's car had been fire-bombed. She was genuinely shocked, sir.' She turned to her companion. 'Isn't that right, Jordi?'

'Yes,' he confirmed. 'She gave a little scream that she couldn't have faked. She's a singer, not an actress. She said that Emil, when he was a student had spent some time as a labourer in a quarry, and knew how to handle explosives.'

Skinner nodded. 'Let me get this right,' he said. 'What you're telling me is that the Blazquez brothers have bet their future on this new drink. Only it's a bit of a turkey, as far as sales and customer satisfaction are concerned despite the creative success of the advertising campaign. That's a leap on my part, but am I right?'

'Yes sir, that's my belief.'

'Okay so the brothers, believing that no news is bad news, come up with a scheme to get the product on to the front page.'

'Only Emil,' Dolça interrupted. 'I have no evidence that Sancho is involved.'

'Right, Emil on his own. Maria plays her part, by delivering the threatening mail, and he boobytraps the car. The flaw in the theme is the advertising agency. It knows only too well that most news is bad news, so it protects the brand by covering up the incidents and carries on with the account. That's it.'

'That's it,' she agreed.

'What have you done with this,' he asked, 'other than talk to me?'

'This morning we phoned Emil Blazquez,' Jordi replied. 'Maria gave us his mobile number. We placed the call through my laptop, so that we could record it.' He took the computer from the backpack that lay at his feet, laid it on the table and opened it, then looked around to check that there was nobody within hearing distance. 'This is where it gets serious. Dolça's told him what she's found and asked him to comment, and he says,' he clicked his trackpad.

'What do I have to say, lady?' a rough voice snarled. 'Let me give you some advice. As you found my cousin, so she can lead me to you. If I have to do that, the bomb on your doorstep won't be a fake, the milk you feed your cat will be poisoned. If you have children, one day one of them won't make it home from school. These things I promise you. Now fuck off or die.'

As the pair looked at Skinner, waiting for his reaction, they saw his expression change. What had been simple interest became something else, something that made Dolça and Jordi feel a little afraid.

'What do we do, sir?' she asked.

'InterMedia will run the story,' he replied. 'It will go online at sixteen hundred hours, and into print after that on all our titles. You and I, Dolça, will meet with Hector Sureda and Mario Fuentes, the *GironaDia* editor, and we'll brief them both. It'll be your by-line all the way, and you'll do the story to camera for the video, and sound for the audio outlets. By that time you'll have met with Comissari Lita Roza of the Mossos, and made a full statement to her.'

'But what about Emil Blazquez?' Poch exclaimed. 'What about his threats.'

For less than a second, Skinner's eyes narrowed. 'Don't you worry about him, son. He's all mine. Dolça,' he said, 'go outside and get us a taxi. I'll join you when I've squared up for the coffee and croissants. On your way out, tell the waiter to bring me a bill.'

As she left, he turned back to her associate. 'You're quite impressive, mate,' he told him. 'I appreciate that you might prefer to be self-employed . . . and that might suit us best too, all things considered . . . but how would you feel about the InterMedia group putting you on an exclusive retainer?'

Surprise showed on the fox-like features. 'That would depend on the size of the retainer,' he murmured.

'You and our HR people can agree that, and sort out legal terms too. It'll have to come through me, meaning there will be no problem.'

'Would I have to live here?'

'Not if you don't want to. You and Dolça . . .?'

'Very good friends,' Jordi said, 'but I know she would rather keep me at a distance.'

'Understood. Be accessible, all the time, wherever you are, that's all I'll ask.'

'In that case, thank you very much sir, I accept.'

'That's good,' Skinner declared. The younger man made to rise, but he waved him back to his seat. 'Before we part,' he continued, 'I have another project that I'd like to give you. Nothing to do with InterMedia, nor for reporting anywhere else. This will be entirely between you and me, not a whisper to Dolça or anyone else. There's someone I'm interested in. I want to know everything there is to know about him . . . as soon as you can tell me, starting right now. Stay here, drink as much coffee as you like on expenses, but get it done. This is the brief.'

Fifty-Six

'I'd hoped to tell you by now,' Alan Dossor said, 'that my people had accessed Sandra Bulloch's computer, but no such luck. When she was serving did she have any experience of investigating cyber-crime? They reckon she had a very high-level password.'

'I have no idea,' Sauce Haddock replied, 'but I can find out. Would it help if I did?'

'Probably not, but there's one thing you could do. Beyond the password, the keyboard requires fingerprint access. Are Ms Bulloch's on file?'

'Yes, they are. I know that for sure. I'll get them to you, highest quality possible. That should do it.'

'Thanks. One more thing,' he added. 'I ran that check on the neighbours, the Browns. He was a car dealer in Colchester before he moved out here, and, he was on the police radar in Essex. He was suspected of providing the wheels for a couple of armed robberies, but it could never be proved. He must have felt the wind in his sails though. Not long after the last incident they sold up and moved here, with the assistance of a lottery win; two and a half million.'

244

Haddock laughed. 'That's priceless. Liz told me he was a consultant proctologist.'

'Did she indeed? That fits with what I was told about her. She had a sideline: she was quite well known in the Essex clubs as a stand-up comic. She must have seen you as a chance to keep her hand in.'

'It's as well for her I've got a sense of humour,' he said, 'otherwise I might be asking you to charge her with wasting police time.'

'Apart from taking the piss, did she tell you much?' Dossor asked.

'Nothing we didn't know before, but she did confirm our understanding of why she left the Bahamas and went back to Europe. She also gave me a lead to a friend of Sandra's, a golfer who plays out of a club here. My hotel has access to it, so I'm going to hit a few balls there and look for him.'

'Your wife's okay with that?'

'Two days ago she thought she'd be in Edinburgh for at least a year. Right now, she'd be okay with most things.' Haddock paused. 'Alan, there's something else that's been niggling away at me. I've had a couple of mentors in my career. One's still around. He's not in the police any longer but we still speak quite often. Both of them used to hammer on at me about covering all the basics, turning every stone, etc. Both of them are in my head right now, saying the same thing. You and I did a quick search of Sandra Bulloch's place this morning, and found nothing apart from the computer, but that's all it was, quick and perfunctory. As I said earlier, I need more than that. I know you've got manpower issues like everyone else, but if you could spare a team to look the place over, I'd be grateful. I'm not talking about a full forensic examination, understand, just a detailed search by people who know what they're doing.'

'Sure,' his colleague replied. 'No problem. It'll be tomorrow morning, but I can do that. You'll need to let my people in, as you've got the keys and the code. I'll have them there at nine. While I arrange that, you get me those fingerprints.'

Fifty-Seven

'What's the worst job you've ever had?' John Stirling muttered, mimicking his grandfather mimicking a comedian from an era before his grandson was born.

'What?' Maya Smith asked, overhearing him.

'Nothing,' he replied. 'I was having a conversation with my grandpa, that's all.'

'What was it?' she persisted.

'What?'

'The worst job he ever had?'

'Trust me,' he assured her, 'you don't want to know. In my case this is running it close, trying to determine what it was that Charles Baxter did for Sandra Bulloch. His online profile, and his firm's, is big and brash, but it doesn't actually tell you anything. They publish a client list, but all of them seem to be big international property outfits; there are no individuals included in the list.'

'Could Bulloch's property holdings be incorporated, held by companies?'

'Probably but if they are, they must fall beneath whatever the benchmark is for inclusion in the LJMcF website. They boast

247

about individual transactions, but only for the listed clients. I'm wasting my time here, Maya.'

'Maybe look at his personal socials?' she suggested.

'I did, but they told me two things: sod and all. Charles Baxter does have a Facebook profile, but he hasn't posted on it for eight years. Coincidentally,' Stirling added, 'that's when his original firm, Delgado Baxter, became part of LJMcF. LJMcF isn't just Charles Baxter,' he explained, 'although looking at the business press I think he likes to give that impression. It's Canadian in origin. It was founded thirty-seven years ago by the merger of two practices, McFarlane's, of Toronto, and Lionel Jinks and Partners, of Vancouver. McFarlane's was founded in the fifties by a Scottish immigrant, but getting information about the other one, that's like drawing teeth. Together, though, they grew and grew; they expanded strategically in North America, the site says, absorbing partner firms in New York, Houston, Philadelphia, and Los Angeles. In ninety-nine, they began to expand out of North America, going into Paris, then Malaysia, then Milan, then Madrid.'

'Not London?' Smith asked.

'Strangely no. I found a *Financial Times* article about the firm that suggested the London market was too big for them to find a strategic partner of the right size. If that's true then Charles Baxter may have had his eye on them before theirs ever fell on him. He had family money, his rugby connections and three years' experience with another Edinburgh surveying firm when he started Delgado Baxter and he used that to build up the practice pretty quickly.'

'Who's Delgado?'

'There never was one. Delgado, in Spanish, means slim; Baxter eventually confessed to a journalist that he called the firm after his old football idol, from an era way before Messi and Cristiano, back in Bobby Charlton's time.'

'Why didn't he pick a rugby idol, since that was his game?'

'He was asked that. He said his idol was Gareth Edwards, who is, unfortunately Welsh. Anyway, if you look at the growth of Delgado Baxter you can see that it was an ideal fit for the LJMcF profile, with a lot of its client list good sized English businesses, not just Scottish. Eventually the invitation to join was made, and Baxter seems to have made the most of it. He'd been in the group for only two years when he moved into his present office, the one the DCI says is a listed building. I say "seems to have", because his financial performance is hidden. Legally LJMcF is what you call a general partnership, as was Delgado Baxter before it. That means that none of the individual members or the Toronto parent have to file annual accounts.'

'What about the companies it advises?' Smith asked. 'Don't they have to publish accounts?'

'That depends on where they're incorporated. Half of those on the list are offshore.'

The DC pursed her lips. 'Baxter might be a big fish in Scotland, but how big is he in the group?'

'Pretty big, I'd say. He's on the management board, and that's only five people. The listed head of the partnership is, believe it or not, one of the founders, Mr Jinks. He's life president, in his mid 90s. Looking at Baxter's public persona, my guess is that he sees himself as his eventual successor. But none of that helps me find out what he did for Sandra Bulloch, or why, according to Gordon Pollock, she was intendng to see him.'

Fifty-Eight

Emil Blazquez Gallardo had digestive problems, a sensitivity that made him liable to bouts of debilitating acid reflux. It could be triggered by several factors, but stress was at the top of the list. The call from the journalist woman had unsettled him, even though his terrified cousin Maria had given him advance warning.

He had been ready for her, and would be if he could find her, or if she approached him again. Emil was a man of his word, as a would-be union activist had discovered when he had attempted to organise strike action by the company's work force. He had been dissuaded by a couple of hired guys with baseball bats, and by two broken kneecaps. That would be nothing on the vengeance he would visit on the journalist woman when he caught up with her, as he would. The business editor of *GironaDia* was a schoolfriend of his uncle. When he heard of Maria's surprise visitor, he would be sure to help trace her, he reckoned, as another wave of stomach acid bit hard.

He was standing by his drinking fountain, in the act of washing down a third omeprazole tablet, when his office door swung open and a large man strode into the room. He looked to be in his fifties, with grey hair and weathered features, but he moved like someone younger, and with authority.

250

'Who the fuck are . . .' Emil began as the newcomer moved towards him, only to be cut off in midsentence as a large, hard hand clamped round his throat and lifted him clear off his feet, before slamming him against the wall.

'I'm your worst fucking nightmare,' the invader said. He spoke English, which Emil understood, but with an accent that he could not place.

The hand squeezed harder. Emil could feel his face redden as he fought in vain for his next breath. His eyes swam and his feet kicked; the panic that had engulfed his anger turned to fear. He felt his bladder loosen.

And then the man threw him away, literally. He flung him across his desk like a discarded garment, leaving him scrabbling on the floor on the other side.

'Get up!' his attacker snapped, in Catalan but with an accent that was close to impenetrable, as the first had been. 'Get up, you little bastard,' he said. 'You want to play at being a hoodlum? Okay, this is what the game involves, if you overreach yourself. I've heard your threat to my reporter, Blazquez. I know you're full of wind and piss, but you scared her. You do that, and you deal with me, personally: such things I don't delegate. Son, you're lucky there are people in this building. You're even luckier that the police are on their way here and will expect to find you in one piece, otherwise I'd spend the next ten minutes kicking you around this room.'

Emil pulled himself to his feet then into his chair, as if it was a safe haven. His lips moved but no sound came out. He wanted to scream, but his throat was too sore.

The man checked his watch. 'This is what's going to happen next,' he said. 'I was kidding about the police being on their way. Actually they're outside, but they gave me five minutes with you, to explain your situation. When I leave, they'll come in. They'll arrest you and they'll take you into custody, past the film and still photographers that I have waiting outside. As they're booking you in, you'll become front page news as my company breaks the story of your dirty little plot. Tonight or tomorrow, you'll be charged with whatever the prosecutor in Barcelona decides he can make stick. Given the firebomb that you planted in the advertising lady's car, I expect that to include terrorism. That's got a very broad entry threshold and could put you away for fifteen years.'

He checked his watch again. 'My five minutes are nearly up,' he said. 'Before I go, though, one more thing. Half an hour ago, my colleague Hector and I, and Comissari Roza of the Mossos d'Esquadra, met with your brother and your wife and told them what you've been up to. Their thinking, as they expressed it to us, is to cancel the sale of your company, discontinue the *Ciervorapido* project, which they say was your idea in the first place, and take legal steps to forfeit your shares. Oh yes, and your wife said she's going to leave it to you to tell your girlfriend. So long Emil,' he called out as he reached for the door handle, 'it's been rotten knowing you.'

Fifty-Nine

In his teenage years Sauce Haddock had wondered when a golf club became a country club. As he drove into the Bright Islands complex, the question resurfaced. 'When they add a clubhouse like a sultan's palace, tennis courts, a swimming pool and a spa complex,' he murmured. 'And a pro shop the size of Harrods,' he added, as he was greeted in the driveway by a youth in a uniform, on a mission to park his car.

'How can we help you today, sir?' another clean-cut student with a vacation job asked as he stepped into the shop, carrying the driver, mid-irons and wedge that he had brought with him.

'I'd like to hit some balls,' he replied. 'I'm a guest in the resort hotel. I hope to play a couple of rounds, if I can find a partner, but for now I'd just like to loosen up.'

'You'd be Mr Haddock, yes?' she asked.

He nodded, cautiously.

She grinned. 'The hotel briefs us on new arrivals. They told us that you were coming from Scotland. Love the accent,' she added.

'Yours is okay too. New England?'

'Yes, I'm impressed. How did you know?'

'My old boss's wife's from that part of the world. She lives in

253

Scotland now . . . or she did until a few days ago when she and her family moved to Spain.'

'Oh, Espana,' the young woman purred. 'I'd love to go there. When I graduate my plan is to visit Barcelona, Madrid, all those cities.' She switched to business mode. 'The driving range, sir,' she said. 'It's over there, to your left beyond the clubhouse. I know that there are plenty of bays available. The balls are stacked for you.'

He thanked her. 'Are there any pros around?' he asked.

'Yes, would you like a lesson?'

'Not today,' he replied. 'But I am trying to find one. His name's Ryan Pilgrim. He may not be a teaching pro, but . . .'

'He isn't,' she confirmed, 'but Ryan is around today. I saw him earlier. If you go to the range, I'll locate him and ask him whether he would like to join you.'

Haddock followed her directions, walking around the palatial clubhouse until he saw the practice area. First there was a short-game zone, a large area surrounded by a mix of rough and bunkers with four flags marking the target holes for the six members who were honing their skills. Beyond that lay an immaculately cut undulating nine-hole putting green where two elderly ladies appeared to be having a contest. Finally, there was the driving range itself, twelve numbered bays with a pyramid of golf balls stacked beside each one. As the pro-shop girl had promised, it was lightly used, with only three golfers at work on their games. He chose bay number eleven.

'Good day sir. Do you have everything you need?'

Haddock turned to see an attendant approaching him, of the same vintage as the other two and wearing the same uniform. *'Fuck me,'* Haddock thought. *'These kids all go to politeness school.'*

'I didn't bring any tees,' he replied, finding himself anxious to offer the boy some way, any way, to help him.

'That's okay, sir. There's a box next to the balls. That will last almost for ever, but if you need another stack I'll roll one across.'

'Thanks,' he said. 'I'll let you know.' He laid down his clubs, loosened his belt by one notch and began the yoga-based stretching routine that he performed before every round. When he was finished, and feeling supple, he picked up his seven iron and went to work. The bay had an artificial surface, but the contact was clean; 'Hit the little ball first, the big ball second,' he told himself; the serious golfer's mantra before every iron shot. He hit twenty-five balls with the seven, twenty more with his four iron. When he was satisfied with the consistency of both distance and trajectory, he switched to his driver. He was teeing up his sixth shot when he became aware that someone was watching him. As he looked around, the man approached; he was tall, with a brown complexion, clean-shaven, age range early to mid-thirties.

'Are you Mr Haddock?' He nodded. 'Ryan Pilgrim,' the newcomer said. 'I thought it had to be you from the way you hit the ball, low. It's as if you grew up allowing for the wind. I've competed against a few Scottish players: I see it as their trade mark.'

'I can't argue with that,' Haddock admitted. 'But it can also give us an advantage. The higher you hit the ball, the greater the margin for error.'

Pilgrim looked him in the eye. 'You wanted to see me, Joanne said. I can guess why. It's about Sandra, isn't it.'

He nodded. 'Yes, it is? You know?'

'I do. An English guy, Bryan Brown, who's a member here: he was spreading the word in the bar earlier. He had a call from his wife. He said that Sandra's dead and the cops are calling it a homicide.'

'Yes, and I'm one of them. Detective Superintendent.'

'Pretty unusual way to be investigating a murder,' Pilgrim observed.

'Pretty unusual circumstances,' the Scot countered. 'Do you know that Sandra used to be a cop herself?'

'Yes, she told me. She wasn't close to many people here, but she told me stuff.'

'Just how close were you?' Haddock asked.

'Did we sleep together, you asking? No. She and I were friends, good friends. I think we both knew without saying, that anything more would just have made things complicated. We got to know each other here, in this place, oh, about three years ago. I'm what they call a touring pro in the US; Bright Islands is my listed home club. They pay me a modest retainer for the limited exposure that brings, plus I have a cabin on the property. Mostly I play the secondary PGA tour, but occasionally my ranking will get me a start on the smaller events on the main tour.'

'How did you and she meet?'

'I saw her first on this practice ground,' Pilgrim said, 'just like I saw you. I don't give lessons; that would be taking bread from the resort's assistant pros, but I could see a flaw in her set-up and I mentioned it. She was an okay player, mid-handicap. You're lower than that, I can see. What are you?'

'The lowest I've been's plus one, when I was just a sergeant. I'm two point one right now. Every promotion I've had's put a shot on my handicap. How was Sandra?' he continued. 'Even as a police officer she was a bit of an enigma.'

'How was she?' the American mused. 'When we met, she was just beginning to get over her thing. She was damaged, Mr Haddock.'

'Sauce.'

'What?'

'Sauce,' he repeated. 'It's what everyone calls me. Truth is I prefer it to Harold or Harry.'

Pilgrim smiled. 'I get it. As I said, Sandra was damaged. She acquired a reputation as a loner when she moved out here. Spoke to nobody she didn't have to, just sat in her house watching the sea, like Tennyson's Lady of Shalott.' He smiled at the flicker of surprise that showed on Haddock's face. 'I'm a college boy, Sauce. Even on a golf scholarship we had to study stuff. I majored in English lit.'

'Me too,' the Scot murmured. 'That's why I became a cop. I reckoned that if you weren't going to be a writer, you could only teach it. I didn't fancy being part of an academic time loop, so . . .' He paused. 'Sandra was damaged, you said. How much of her story did she tell you? Or did you know of Leo Speight before she arrived?'

'I knew of him,' the golfer said. 'Who didn't? Have you been in the house yet?' he asked.

'Yes, I have.'

'Then you've seen the trophies. Everything that Speight ever won is in those cases . . . apart from one item.'

'What's that?'

'His silver medal from the Olympics. The only fight he ever lost, although the world knows that he was robbed. After that he wore it everywhere he went, Sandra said, to remind him not to take anything for granted ever again. After he died, so did she; never took it off. I never met Speight,' he continued. 'He died two weeks after I moved here. Sandra and I arrived around the same time, for similar reasons, as it happens. I was damaged too. I'd been trying to make my way through to the main tour, totally focused on my game, travelling every week from my home in Arizona, so it came as a complete surprise when my wife went off with a real estate salesman from Phoenix. She also took our car and our furniture, but she was kind enough to leave me with the mortgage.'

'Ouch.'

'Say that again. I was bust. I'd have had to take a club pro job . . . or maybe even teach English lit . . . if my agent hadn't found the Bright Islands opportunity. It let me recover emotionally, and keep playing. My finances still aren't right, but I'm getting there.' He smiled, sadly. 'Sandra offered to sponsor me, but I couldn't allow that.'

'Why not?' Haddock asked.

'Pride, pure and simple,' Pilgrim replied. 'She understood that, but she did insist on paying for a couple of lessons with a swing coach in Las Vegas. That was last year and they paid off. I've had eight top ten finishes and two wins since then, which makes me a certainty to graduate to the full tour next year. I'd been looking forward to her coming back, so I could thank her properly.'

'Have you heard from her since she left?'

'I did, WhatsApp messages from time to time. She told me she was touring with Leo Speight's oldest kid, her virtual stepson, she used to call him. Sent me pics from all the places she went. In one of her last messages, she said she knew someone who was a big wheel in the European media, and maybe could get me a sponsor invitation to a DP Tour event in Spain.'

'One of her last?' the detective repeated.

'Yeah. It was late February. She said that on her trip she'd been researching, and had found out some pretty interesting stuff. Said she'd be off the radar for a while, but she was looking forward to getting back and catching up. She'd been following me when she was away, she said. I'd had three top tens by then, including a third place finish in Mexico. She said congratulations and . . .'

258

He paused, as if for thought. Eventually, he took his phone from a trouser pocket and scrolled through its contents. 'Sandra's very last message,' he murmured as he handed it to Haddock. 'She sent it six months ago.'

It was a WhatsApp. 'I saw what you did in Mexico,' he read. 'Fantastic. Congrats. This is only the start. My business is almost done, I'll be back in a week or two and ready to go on 🏌 tour, full time. I want to be the woman you 🌝 at the eighteenth green when you have your first win. ❤'

'How did you feel about that?' he asked.

'Surprised. Good. Warm,' Pilgrim replied. 'I realised that I wanted that too. But it'll never happen now.' His mouth tightened and his eyes glistened. 'I've spent the last six months waiting for that week or two to end. Wondering, but too proud or more likely too scared to go looking for her.'

'I'm sorry,' Haddock murmured, awkwardly. 'Ryan,' he ventured, 'can I ask you to do something? Would you be prepared to forward Sandra's messages to my WhatsApp account? They might be relevant to our investigation. Will you do that? They'll be kept private, I promise . . . unless they're ever used in evidence in a trial.'

'Key in your number to my phone and it's done,' he promised. 'I want whoever killed her as badly as you do, maybe worse.'

The Scot entered his mobile number and handed the phone back to its owner, who summoned a few images then clicked. 'It's done. How else can I help you, Sauce?'

'You can tell me about the times she did go with you?'

'You mean did we share a room? No, we didn't. Our thing, like I said, it was platonic and we were good with that. Well, I was and I'm sure Sandra was too, for that time. We were comfortable together, peaceful, you get what I mean?'

'I do, but it's not what I meant. Where did you go?'

Pilgrim scratched his head. 'Where?' he murmured, 'let's see. There was Jacksonville, Florida, the first time. Then there was Seattle, then Chicago. And Vegas. And Baltimore,' he added, almost an afterthought. 'I got a start in a PGA tour event in Baltimore. That's not a cool place, but Sandra said she'd always wanted to run up the Rocky steps in Philadelphia and it's close by.'

'Was that unusual? Her going sight-seeing?' the Scot asked.

'Nope, she did it every time that she came with me. She would walk the course with me, inside the ropes, every tournament round I played, and the usual Wednesday pro-am . . . one time she got to meet Huey Lewis; she loved that . . . but Monday and Tuesday, when I was on the range or playing a practice round with some guy or other that I knew from the college circuit, Sandra would go sight-seeing in whatever city we were at. She'd be away all day, and when she came back there was always a sense of achievement about her. In fact there was one time, the last time in fact, when she came back from Philly, she had that glow about her. I remember I said to her, "Good day?" and she smiled, and nodded and said, "Yes indeed. That's another box ticked." I only smiled myself at the time, but now when I think back to what she said about researching in Europe, I'm wondering if she was doing the same thing then.'

Haddock nodded. 'Me too. I will get all this back to my people in Glasgow, and have them follow it up.' He rolled his driver, which he was still holding, in his right hand. 'Thanks for your help, Ryan. I'll keep you informed about the progress of our investigation.'

'I'd appreciate that,' Pilgrim said. He took a ball from the dwindling stack, and a tee, and handed it to the Scot. 'While I'm here,' he murmured, 'set up again for me. There's a very small change you could make to your takeaway that I reckon would get you those three shots back off your handicap.'

'Can you teach me to putt too?'

'Only God can do that,' the golfer replied, 'and even He might be a little shaky over a four footer down-hill with a left to right break, to win the Masters.'

Sixty

'Jackie,' Lottie Mann exclaimed. 'I don't know what to make of this, but I've just had a message from The Accidental Tourist.'

'Who?' Wright exclaimed.

'The boss; Sauce. It's what I'm calling him after his gesture in self-funding the Bahamas leg of our investigation. It was my mother's favourite book when I was growing up. She tried to get me to read it, but it wasn't quite my thing.'

'What was?'

'Terry Pratchett, believe it or not. Later on when I met my Dan, all scruffy as he used to be, I had a theory that the character Vines was based on him. Dan says that's rubbish: he was the model for Nobby Nobbs, he says. Anyway, the AT's forwarded a string of WhatsApps that he got from Sandra Bulloch's golfer boyfriend.'

Stirling overheard her. 'They were just good friends, according to Gordon,' he volunteered.

'Not according to her last message,' the DCI countered. 'I think absence might have made the fart go Honda as the old joke used to say. Anyway, these WhatsApps: I'll send them to you and John. Take a look at them, the pair of you and tell me what you think.'

She retreated to the privacy of her office where she forwarded the messages, then studied them herself, on-screen searching in vain for a common factor or any kind of link to the investigation. She had been studying them for five minutes when she was interrupted by a call, from within the police network.

'Lottie,' the caller began. 'It's Jenny Bramley here. There's been a development that might be significant . . . or then again might not. Do you remember the slip of paper thet was recovered from the pocket of the victim's jacket?'

'Yes,' Mann said. 'The piece that was useless because it had been made unreadable by bodily fluids.'

'Yes, and I doubted that it could be recovered. I was too pessimistic,' the scientist confessed. 'I could tell you that was because I didn't want to build up expectations, but the truth is, I underrated the skills of my people. They have managed to make it legible. I'm sending a scan to you.'

'Well done your team,' the DCI told her. 'Now, back to significance. What is it?'

'It's a ticket of sorts, a receipt for a deposit made in a self-storage facility in Alloa, Clackmannanshire. There's no number on it; just the address and a QR code, nothing to give a clue to the contents. Over to you, Lottie.'

'Just what I wanted,' she declared, 'a trip over that new bridge. I can't wait, it's like a lucky dip.'

Sixty-One

'You're chuffed with yourself, Dad,' Jazz Skinner observed. 'What have you done?'

'You know me too well,' his father replied. 'I had a very good result at work. I actually did, no to be honest, I directed, a very good piece of investigative journalism, that led to someone being arrested and got InterMedia a front page lead that's gone national and left our rivals spitting feathers. So yeah, I'm chuffed with myself. But,' he continued, 'that has nothing to do with the subject of this family conference. We've moved, you've started school. What are your initial impressions, you and your sister?'

'I love my school, Daddy,' Seonaid said. 'It's just great. Not that Gullane wasn't; I like the teachers and I miss my friends, but I've made three new ones here so far and my teacher's nice too.'

Bob turned to her brother. 'And you?'

'Same here,' Jazz declared. 'It's smaller than North Berwick, and the facilities are better. The subjects are a bit different too.'

'You realise you're a year behind the other kids? The new school's on an English A level stream, that starts at eleven not twelve.'

'Yes, but to be honest, I'm not struggling with anything. My science teachers at North Berwick knew that I was moving, so they ran through our first year stuff with me. The rest, English is English, I've been speaking Spanish here since I was old enough to play with other kids on the beach, and we're all beginners at Mandarin Chinese.'

'That's good to hear,' their mother said. 'Now, about where you're living. We're a very lucky family. We have the option of two homes in Spain. In Girona, we're closer to the schools, in . . .'

'We want to live in L'Escala,' Jazz declared cutting her off. 'Dad, I'm sorry. Seonaid and I have talked about this. I know you like this place, but it's a man cave. It's a big one, yes, but it's still a man cave. Seonaid needs a garden, Mum needs a pool, although she won't say so, and so will Dawn when she gets bigger. I like living near a beach; it's all I've ever known. Yes, we're lucky to have a choice, but that's ours.'

'You won't mind the commute?' Bob asked.

His son peered at him from beneath thick eyebrows. 'Dad,' he chuckled, 'have you ever been on the North Berwick school bus?'

He laughed. 'Okay,' he said, 'done deal. I'll still be here for much of the week, but your mum and I will handle the commute between us. All as from next Monday. Now, bugger off and do your homework.'

'Thanks,' Sarah whispered as they left. 'I didn't prime him to say that, honest, but Jazz is right. This is a man cave, of sorts. Just make sure it stays men only, when I'm not here.'

'Will it be all right for your schedule?'

'Sure. I'm a teacher in Barcelona, not a forensic pathologist. For the first time in most of my professional life I have regular hours.' She paused. 'Changing the subject, did you tell Raul Sanchez that you'd caught the Sister of the Trinity?'

'No, but Inge called me just after the story broke. He's away on business; we'll catch up when he gets back.'

'And meet them? Both of us and both of them?'

'Yes, we must. Let's go to Mad . . .' His ringtone drew a frown of annoyance, but it vanished when he saw that his oldest daughter was calling.

'Hi Pops?' Alexis Skinner exclaimed as he took her call. 'How's the big move gone? I'm calling from your house in Gullane. Dominic and I are here for a couple of days, to stop the place from feeling lonely. It turns out we needn't have worried. We're not alone. Ignacio and Pilar are here too, in the warren above the garages that you built for him.'

'What about his radio show?'

'His mum's doing it for a couple of days. There may have been a falling out, I'm not sure. I asked Nacho if everything was good, but he just grunted.'

'If he wants to talk to me,' Bob said, 'tell him I'm here for him. I know,' he conceded before she could make the point, 'we maybe need to bond better than we have, but he's still mostly his mother's son . . . and where Mia's involved,' he added, 'I find it best to keep my distance.'

'Wisely so,' Alex agreed. 'I could have told you that twenty plus years ago, when you brought her home, but let's not go back there. Instead, my first question, how is the big move?'

'The schools are great, the accommodation less so. Jazz has just told us it's a man cave and that he and Seonaid want to live in L'Escala and commute.'

He heard her gasp, then laugh. 'Pops, of course it's a fucking man cave. I've known that since you bought it, so has Dominic, and so . . . put me on speaker . . .' He obeyed. 'and so has Sarah, from the start. Jazz is the only one with the nuts to tell you.'

Until then Bob Skinner had never known a moment in his life when he had felt cornered; it was a strange and slightly unnerving experience. 'It was a good buy,' he protested. 'I had to do something with the bonus that the company insisted on paying me.'

'Insisted nothing,' she exclaimed. 'The company had an obligation: I told you that at the time. It was performance related, as set out in the contract that I looked through before you signed it. But there was nothing in it that said you had to buy a lavish crash-pad near the office.'

'There were tax reasons,' he argued, lamely.

'The way round that is to pay the fucking tax, Pops. Accountants never tell you that; they're too busy charging you fees for saving you approximately the same amount of money that they cost, then minimising their own tax hit through their own tax avoidance schemes. If they were all liquidated overnight, the world's developed economies would suddenly be five per cent richer.'

'That's pretty fucking profound, daughter,' Bob growled. 'What do you suggest I do with my strategic property investment?'

'Let it grow in value for a couple of years, sell it at a significant profit, and employ the same accountants to design you another perfectly legal tax avoidance scheme to minimise the capital gain, before they recycle your fee through their own perfectly legal . . . etc. Geddit?'

'Yes, I get it. Then where do I stay when I'm too late at the office to get back to L'Escala?'

'In the hotel you stayed in before you bought the cave. Actually, you'd be better to buy it; that would be the smart thing to do fiscally. But one thing you do not do. You do not fuck with the Spanish tax man; he's a killer and he loves feeding on ex-pats, as several footballers have discovered.'

'The company has me covered there,' he said, suddenly serious.

'Okay,' he chuckled, 'now you've put me through the wringer, is there anything else you want to ask me?'

'Yes, there is actually. It's the burning question in Scottish law enforcement circles. Who killed Detective Chief Inspector Sandra Bulloch?'

'You're asking me? I'm in Spain.'

'What difference does that make?' she countered, cheerfully.

'Let's just say I have my suspicions,' he replied.

'What are you doing about them?'

'I'm in Spain, love. What can I do?'

'I don't know, but I do know this. Sandra Bulloch was your former executive assistant and you liked her. There's no way you're just sitting on your hands.'

Sixty-Two

'The last hint of summer's gone,' Lottie Mann observed to Maya Smith as she stepped out of her car into the morning chill. 'Or maybe it's always like this in Alloa.'

'It's not,' the detective constable protested. 'My Uncle Bill lives here. He's always saying how nice the weather is in the summer.'

'What does he say about the winter?'

'Now that I think about it, very little.' She looked up at the sign on the building at which they had arrived. 'Paradigm Storage,' she read, stumbling over the first word. 'What does that even mean, ma'am?'

'It means "Try and pronounce this, folks." Beyond that I have no idea. Somebody probably saw it in a crossword and thought it looked nice. Let's go.' She led the way through the half-glazed entrance door into what was basically a huge metal hut.

Inside that hut was another, with a window and a fully glazed door; it was much smaller, standing within a tightly enclosed square area. Smith was claustrophobic, an issue that she had not disclosed when she was recruited; instantly she felt compressed.

'Ladeez,' a bearded man exclaimed, loudly, as he stepped out of the box. 'How can I help youse?'

'Police,' Mann said curtly, displaying her warrant card, thrusting it towards him, almost forcing him to read it.

'Sorry,' he murmured. 'How can I help youse, Officers?'

The DCI took a clear plastic envelope from her pocket. 'You can open the box this ticket refers to. That'll do nicely.' She knew that she was not at her most reasonable, but something about the guy grated on her. It took only a few more seconds for her to realise that he bore an unfortunate resemblance to her former father-in-law, the man who had tried to seize custody of her son. '*Not his fault,*' she thought, '*but still.*'

'Would youse have a warrant?' he asked.

The space seemed to become even smaller; Maya Smith neared panic point.

'We're investigating a homicide,' Mann growled. 'That ticket was found on the body of the deceased. We don't really need a warrant, but if you play silly buggers, I'll dig up the nearest Sheriff and get one that gives me the authority to open every box in this place. Do you know what's in every box, Mr . . .?'

'Mr Grater,' he said, with the fading confidence of a man who could see a light approaching fast from the end of a tunnel, too fast to be signalling any good news. He squared his shoulders. 'Always happy to help the police, ladeez,' he murmured. 'Can I have a look?'

Mann handed him the envelope.

Mr Grater peered at it. 'Ooh,' he murmured. 'That's a wee bit degraded.'

'If you'd been through what it's been through,' the DCI told him. 'So would you be.'

'Come into the office and I'll try the QR code reader,' he said. 'Just follow me.'

Mann did. Smith held back, crushed by the thought of three people in that tiny space. 'I'll stay here,' she called out.

'I'll have to take it out of the plastic,' Grater declared. 'Is that okay?'

'Do what you have to,' the senior detective replied. She watched as he slid the ticket and laid it on a table, then took out his phone.

'This'll generate a code,' he murmured as he focused on the tiny image, 'but only I can read it.' He hesitated steadying his hand. 'Success!' he exclaimed. 'There you are, unit four plus two. Contents deposited here on the tenth of March, not accessed since.'

'Unit four plus two. What does that mean?'

'It means follow me.' He squeezed past her and out of the tiny office, then led the detectives to and through another door, one that opened on to the main space within the great hut. Storage boxes were set out in long lines, somehow military in appearance. 'You can see they vary in size. You can store anything from a thimble to a motorbike in here. Units one to four are for wee things,' he paused. 'And this is unit four. Plus two's right there. The lower cabinet of the first pair.'

'How do you open it?' Smith asked.

Grater held up his phone. 'With this amazing device here my dear. I can program my bloody microwave wi' my phone.' He crouched beside the door, focused the camera on a small square window and pressed the side button. There was a click and the door opened; an inch, no more. The man stepped aside. 'Ah'll leave youse to it,' he said. 'We give our clients privacy when they fill and empty their boxes. For very good legal reasons,' he added.

'I'll bet,' Mann murmured as he stepped away. 'Maya,' she

murmured, 'come here. I need you to witness what I'm going to do now, for the very same legal reasons.'

The DC moved closer, until she could see the closed door of the unit, and watch as her boss swung it open. 'Jesus,' the DCI hissed as they saw what Sandra Bulloch had deposited. 'It's a phone. A mobile bloody phone. Why the hell would she leave that here?'

Sixty-Three

'How is this thing going, John?' Jackie Wright asked her colleague. 'What's your feeling for the investigation?'

Stirling twisted his body round in his chair, facing her as far as he could. 'Compared to what?' he asked. 'I'm a relative new boy at this level: serious crime when everything in my career's been petty until now.'

'How far do you think we've got?'

'Honestly? Not very. To be honest with you, we seem to be starting to repeat ourselves, and that can't be good. Faye Bulloch being the classic example. She was the first person of interest, then she wasn't. Then we took another look at her, now she's off the list again. Say something once, why say it again?' He sang the last few words, taking her by surprise.

'What?'

He smiled at her reaction. 'I'm a huge Talking Heads fan. Their song, "Psycho Killer"; I've always interpreted that as being about someone running around not really knowing what they're doing. I'm worried that's us.'

'Don't let the bosses hear you say that,' Wright warned.

'Don't worry, suicide is not in my forward career plan.'

'Neither is patience from the sound of things.' She paused. 'I never really knew him, but your predecessor, John Cotter, he had trouble settling in too. I don't think he and Lottie got on too well at first, but he persevered and eventually he cracked a case. It was more by luck than judgment, but he cracked it. He came up with a suspect that nobody would have guessed at in a hundred years and he got all the credit. Having done that he buggered off, back home to Tyneside.'

'And the DCI got me.'

'So don't let her down.'

'Hopefully not,' he said. 'She's just called, in fact. She and Maya are on their way back from Alloa with something she wants me to look at . . . with my special skills, she said. I didn't know I had any.' As he spoke, a phone rang, in Mann's private office. 'Better get that,' he muttered, springing from his chair. He strode the short distance and snatched the handset from its cradle.

'Lottie?' a voice exclaimed as he put it to his ear.

'No, DS Stirling. The DCI's out.'

'Ahh. Should have guessed when she didn't answer her mobile. Out of signal, I suspect. John, this is Superintendent Haddock. I'm just calling to give Ms Mann an update on what's happening out here. The main thing is that we've recovered Sandra Bulloch's computer from her house. Officers here are going to try to get into it. To help them do that, I need to have her fingerprints emailed, best quality, to an address that I'll text to your mobile. I've got your number. If they find anything relevant, I'll find a means of getting it to you.'

'Sir,' Stirling began, then thought better of it. 'No, nothing.'

'No, go on. The last thing any team needs is a member that's scared to say what's on his mind.'

'Well, okay? I was going to ask, sir, how you'll actually know what's relevant, given that things are moving forward here all the time?' '*Even if it's at a snail's pace,*' he thought.

Haddock's laugh came as a great relief to the DS. 'True, I can't know that. Everything that's on the machine will be sent to you. Right, the rest: I've done a quick two-person search of the Bulloch residence and found nothing apart from that iMac, but I'm going back in there this morning with more support to see if we overlooked anything. Beyond that . . . Sandra had a friend here, a golf pro. She followed him to a few events, and did some sight-seeing, like she did in Europe with Gordon Pollock. I'll send you the list of venue cities. You can add them to the places they saw.'

'Will do, sir.'

'John,' Haddock said. 'Go easy on the "sir". I'm not that fucking precious. Boss, gaffer, Sauce or just nothing at all. I know when you're talking to me, I don't need to be told. Okay?'

'Okay.'

'Good. Now one last thing. Was anything found in the motor home? Anything at all?'

'Only a ticket for a self-storage facility. That's where the boss is just now, seeing what's there. Apart from that nothing. Why?' He stopped himself from adding 'sir'.

'Ach, it's just something Ryan, the golfer told me. Apparently Sandra always wore Leo's Olympic silver medal. Maybe I'll find it in the house, or maybe Lottie will, in the storage. For now, you send those prints to the address I'll send you. I'll be in touch again when I have something new to tell you.'

Sixty-Four

'Sauce gets the Bahamas,' Jackie Wright observed as she stepped from her car. 'I get bloody Biggar.'

But it could have been worse, she conceded, as she looked around. In truth the small south Lanarkshire town was an attractive community, a mix of urban and rural with its own distinct character. She and Kate, her partner, had visited the place once, for an author event in its celebrated bookshop.

'Later Era Care Home,' she read on the sign beside the entrance to the building, which stood adjacent to the square that greeted those arriving from Edinburgh and bade farewell to those heading for the capital. She had checked it out before driving down from Glasgow, a relatively short journey, since most of it had been by motorway. It had appeared in its web material to be purpose built rather than an older building adapted, and her first sight confirmed that. The website had a professional look to it, rather than something thrown together amateurishly by the owners, as she had found frequently in the research that had led her to Later Era.

Its double doors had a keypad for regular visitors. Wright pressed the buzzer beside it and waited. A few seconds later there was a click and one swung open. She stepped into an enclosed space with two more doors. As she waited it made her think of an airlock. Finally the second doors opened, admitting her to a spacious reception area.

'DS Wright,' she said, announcing herself to a dark-skinned man behind a circular counter.

He frowned back at her. 'Yes?' he replied, cautiously. 'You're police?'

She nodded, displaying her credentials for inspection. 'I'm here to see Mrs Crawford, Sally Crawford. I did call to let you know I was coming.'

'Nobody made me aware of that.' His accent was thick. He was African; Nigerian, she guessed with little certainty. A badge on the chest of his blue uniform told her that his name was Efe.

'Not my problem, I'm afraid. Where can I find Mrs Crawford?'

'I will have to ask my manager,' Efe grunted. 'Can you sign in please?' He pointed to a visitors' book then walked away, leaving her with nothing to do but comply with his request.

She was adding her arrival time to her signature when another blue uniform appeared, worn by a man whose turban colour-matched it perfectly, and who sported a well-trimmed, grey-flecked beard. 'My name is Hardeep,' he announced. 'I am the assistant manager. Mrs Crawford is in room two thirty-nine,' he announced. 'I will take you there.'

'I'm sure I can find it,' Wright said.

'I will take you there,' he repeated.

Unbidden, the phrase, 'Look Jimmy, I'm the polis,' formed itself in her mind. It made her wonder whether she had been too long in Glasgow already, but she left it unsaid, instead following her escort towards a silver-doored lift. They rode silently to the second floor, where, emerging, she was led to the right and to the second door in a long corridor.

'Sally Crawford.' The resident's name was displayed on a plate beside the door, which was open. Within, a very old lady was seated, looking out of the window, with the remnants of a meal on a table beside her.

'Mrs Crawford,' the man called out, 'you have a visitor. A police person.'

She looked round, slowly, smiling. 'Have I, Hardeep?' she exclaimed. 'How nice.'

Having read Sandra Bulloch's detailed HR file, Wright knew that her father had died at the age of eighty, seven years earlier. She guessed that his sister might have been half a dozen years older than him. She turned to thank her escort, only to see that he had followed her into the room, and was closing the door behind him.

'You can leave,' she told him, firmly.

'It is my duty to stay with my patient,' he declared.

'Are you a nurse?' Wright asked.

'No,' Hardeep replied. 'As I told you I am the assistant manager of this residence.'

'Then she isn't your patient, as such,' she pointed out, 'she's your client. Do you hold a lasting power of attorney for the lady?' She sensed hesitation. 'One phone call to the Public Guardian's office, and I can find out, so tell me the truth.'

'No,' he admitted, '. . . but it is my duty to remain.'

Wright turned to the old lady. 'Mrs Crawford,' she began. 'I'm Detective Sergeant Jackie Wright, from Glasgow. I'm looking into the death of your niece Sandra, and I'd like to speak with you, in private. Do you understand what I'm saying to you?'

'Yes dear, of course I do,' she said, nodding. The peaceful smile was gone. 'Poor Sandra,' she sighed. 'When they told me she was dead I was hoping it wasn't true. She looked so well when she was here.'

Wright blinked at the remark. 'You're happy to speak with me in private?' she repeated.

'Yes dear, of course.'

'It is my duty . . .' Hardeep began but she cut him off.

'It'll be my duty to arrest you for obstruction if you don't leave the room, right now. And I'll be happy to do that, make no mistake.'

Sixty-Five

'Sir,' the Bahamian sergeant said, 'we've been ordered to assist you and we are privileged to do that, but the fact is, we work as a five-person team. We're well organised and very efficient. The addition of a sixth person would not improve us in any way; if anything it would hamper us, as I'd be looking over my shoulder all the time to see what you were up to.'

Haddock smiled. 'You're telling me, very politely, to stay out of the way.'

'No, sir, no,' the team leader insisted. 'It's not my place to tell you anything. But if I was goin' to make a suggestion, that would be it. It's a lovely morning, not too hot yet, so how about you sit in the garden and enjoy the ocean view? There's a yacht race going on out there and I bet you don't get to watch too many of them back in Scotland.'

'Not in this weather, no,' he agreed. 'I'll take your advice. Too many cooks and all that.'

'I'm sorry, sir?'

'No, I'm sorry. A stupid British saying, Sergeant.'

'Thank you sir,' she said. 'Is there anything in particular that you want us to look out for?'

'Everything. Okay, forget cleaning products and stuff like that;

forget clothing unless there's an item you think I should see. Otherwise, everything you find in there, I'd like to look it over. When Superintendent Dossor and I went over the place we saw very little. But we didn't have time to open every drawer or cupboard. That's why you're here. Look in the garage too, please. We didn't do in there at all. Oh yes,' he added, 'and one more thing. A medal, an Olympic silver medal. I'm pretty sure we'd have noticed it first time around, but just in case the owner left it in a drawer when she went away, look out for it, please.'

'Understood, sir. You take the weight off your feet and we'll get on with the job.'

Haddock took her at her word. He went into the garden and settled into a cushioned lounger beside the pool. There was only one other chair in sight, proof if any was needed of how much of a loner their late owner had been. He looked out to sea, counting a dozen yachts. They were all moving fast, in full sail. Impressive, he thought but as for the race, without any proper course markers, any one of them could have been in the lead. In truth, he didn't care. Samantha had been fractious through the night, and he had carried his share of the load. He reclined the chair, adjusted his Maui Jim sunglasses, fitted his earpods, found a Joe Pass album on Apple Music, put it on shuffle and let the moment absorb him.

Joe was playing 'Ode to Billy Joe' when he felt a hand on his shoulder, shaking him gently. 'Sir,' the sergeant said, waiting for Haddock to waken from his slumber and rise from the lounger. 'That's us done. There is no more to find. The lady seems to have kept very little domestic paperwork. We shook out all the books, but only a couple of markers fell out. The trophies and stuff in the hall: we found a catalogue, I checked it and everything's in its place, apart from the medal, although it is

281

listed. We didn't find it anywhere else. There's a Cadillac Lyriq, that's an American SUV, in the garage, a surfboard and golf clubs. Her bathroom checked out clean; we found over-the-counter drugs only, no recreational stuff. There was one ladies' personal item,' she added, discreetly, he thought, 'but that's nothin' unusual for us to find. Anything I thought might interest you,' she said, 'I left in the kitchen area. Let me show you where.'

She led the way into the house, and through the living area to the kitchen. On a work surface Haddock saw three items, side by side.

'We'll wait outside while you examine them,' the sergeant said.

'No,' he told her. 'We're good. You and the team can go. Thanks for your help. I'll make sure Superintendent Dossor knows how efficient you've been.'

As she left, he turned to the results of their work. The first was a pile of papers; on closer inspection turned out to be household bills, from energy suppliers and from the community's management company. There was nothing significant. The second was a photograph album. As he opened it the detective reflected on how times had changed. His own photographic collection was all digital, most of the images taken with a phone camera, with only a few scanned from prints. He made his way through Sandra Bulloch's book of memories. There were a few of previous generations, her parents, he assumed, and possibly grandparents. After those came two of Leo Speight, one of them taken in the ring after a fight, a second showing him in casual dress, against a rural background, and two of the boxer and Bulloch as a couple. They were prints from selfies; he recognised one as the wallpaper on the iMac. Finally there was a series of images of Leonard and Jolene Bulloch, her nephew and niece, at different ages and stages.

Nowhere in the collection, Haddock noticed, did her sister Faye appear. The hatred was mutual, evidently.

The third item was an envelope. On the outside she had scrawled a single word: Will. He tore it open and removed a single folded sheet of paper. 'Well, well, well,' he murmured as he read it. 'Are you all for a surprise.'

He scanned the document with his phone and emailed it to Stirling's address.

Sixty-Six

'The care home denied all knowledge of Sandra Bulloch,' Jackie Wright declared. 'They even showed me their sign-in book to prove it. But Mrs Crawford was adamant. She insisted that Sandra came to see her in March, stayed for a couple of hours then left, promising that she'd come back before she went back to the Bahamas.'

'How good is the old lady's memory?' Lottie Mann asked.

'It seemed pretty good to me. She knew all the staff by name, and,' she continued, 'her room overlooks the bowling green and she could tell me the names of a couple of the folk who were playing.'

'Could the visitor records have been tampered with?'

'It's a physical book, boss. Every visitor fills in their own details, with their time of arrival and departure. The only way you could tamper with it would be by ripping out a whole page, but there were no gaps. I checked every week, for the whole year, not just March.'

'Still Jackie,' the DCI persisted, 'Aunt Sally's ninety plus. Your time frame can get distorted when you're old. Wishes can become reality.'

The DS shook her head firmly. 'I've met the woman, Lottie,

you haven't. She's still quite mobile, with a three-wheeler walking aid. She goes out, to the bowling green or to a cafe across the road. She and Sandra went there, she told me. When I left, I checked the place out; I showed the owner a photo of Sandra. He remembered Mrs Crawford coming in with someone around that time, and he was fairly sure, couldn't be certain, but fairly sure it was her.'

Mann shrugged. 'She must have by-passed the sign-in, that's all there is to it.'

'And the sign-out?' the DS countered. 'Later Era's a closed institution; it's like a bloody jail, only without your stuff being scanned for weapons and drugs. If she'd been a regular visitor and had known the codes for the keypads . . . they have four, two on each door, one in, one out . . . yes she could just have walked in, otherwise she'd have been processed.' She sighed. 'There's something about the place, boss, something I just didn't like. When I showed the first guy my credentials, he decided I was above his pay grade and went for a manager. When he came he was worse; he tried to sit in on my visit. It was as if he was worried about what Mrs Crawford might say to me. I had to chuck him out. When I left, yet another manager appeared, a woman named Amina, to see me off the premises. All a bit weird and worth looking into.'

'Okay, it's a mystery, but not a priority. What did Mrs Crawford have to tell you? Did she say anything useful about Sandra?'

'She said she seemed very happy, very positive. She said that she talked about her niece and nephew . . . Mrs Crawford's great-niece and great-nephew, she was at pains to point out, although she told me she's never met them.'

'Faye doesn't visit her?'

'No, never, she said. I checked that with the staff too. Other than Sandra, her only visitor's her stepdaughter; Chris, she said her name is, her late husband's daughter from his previous marriage. She did refer to her as Sandra's cousin. "Sort of cousin," she said, actually, but she added that they did get on with each other. No, the last time she saw Faye, she told me, was at her brother's . . . Sandra and Faye's dad's . . . funeral, about twenty years ago. Sandra told her during her visit that Faye wouldn't let her see the kids, and she was sad about that, but otherwise she'd been very up all along. She told her she'd been looking at places in Europe with someone called Gordon. Mrs Crawford wasn't quite sure how he fitted in but she didn't think he was a boyfriend because she mentioned having one of those in the Bahamas. That last part confirms the WhatsApp Sauce sent us.'

'Yes it does,' Mann conceded. 'Jackie, see if you can contact this Chris Crawford. Maybe Sandra visited her.'

'I was planning to. I got her contact details from the home. That wasn't easy; I had to threaten the Amina woman with an obstruction charge as well. There was a big bloke lurking in the background too. I thought he might have been potential trouble, but he didn't get involved.'

'Did the old lady say anything else of interest?'

'Just one thing. She said that when she and Sandra left the tea room, Sandra had already signed out of the care home, so she didn't go back in. Instead she left, in her car.'

'Her car?' the DCI exclaimed. 'What bloody car?'

'Exactly.'

Sixty-Seven

'Well? Did the detailed search turn up anything unexpected?' Superintendent Dossor asked, as Haddock was shown into his office.

'Only one thing,' he replied. 'Sandra drew up a will, before she left. It was hand-written, signed and properly witnessed, by Jane Way, the community manager, and left in an envelope in one of the drawers we didn't look into, along with what household paperwork there was.'

'How did we miss it?'

'The drawer was concealed, in the computer table. It was easily done, so thanks to your team for finding it. How about the computer?' he asked.

'My people are still struggling to get into it,' Dossor admitted. 'I have one guy who is ace at these matters. Unfortunately he got himself married last week, and isn't expected back for another two. We may need to fly in a specialist.'

'Or take the mountain to Mohammad,' Haddock suggested.

'What do you mean?'

'I mean fly the fucker back to Glasgow. My outfit has all sorts on our crime campus, among them cybercrime specialists. The simplest solution might be to use an overnight air courier, or as close to overnight as we can find, and just send the computer to Scotland.' He nodded, making a decision. 'Yes, let's do that. Let me get on to my colleagues and tell them to make the arrangements.' He paused. 'No, I'll do it myself: save time. If you can have it securely packaged that would be great.'

'I can do that,' Dossor told him. 'Truth be told, I always prefer the easy option. How about the will?' he continued. 'Is that relevant to your investigation? Could she have written it because she felt under threat?'

'I don't know, can't know, for sure, but my inclination is no, to each of those questions. I think she wrote it because she'd reached a decision about her future, once she'd sorted out any issues she may have had.'

Sixty-Eight

'John, I'm sorry,' Lottie Mann declared. 'I've been remiss. Okay we're in exceptional circumstances but that's no excuse. You're still a relative newcomer to the team. I should have spent more time with you, making sure you're comfortable in your role, and that you're settling in. I made that mistake with John Cotter, my last DS, and now I'm in danger of repeating it with you.'

Stirling smiled and shook his head. 'No, boss, you're not. I'm comfortable in my role. I feel like a valued member of the team, and that I'm contributing to the investigation.'

'What do you feel your role is?' she asked. 'That might sound like a daft question coming from a team manager but I believe in letting people find their own strengths and play to them. If Pep Guardiola worked that way, Man City would be midtable at best. He sees things that nobody else does, he has a clear object-ive and every member of his team's placed where he's likely to be most effective. I'm no Pep.'

The DS laughed out loud. 'Gaffer, I'm a St Johnstone fan. You're speaking a language I don't understand. I'm quite happy with the way things work here, and I'm quite clear what my role is. You're a hands-on boss; if you want to stick with the football analogy, you're a player manager. Jackie's your deputy, your strike forward, someone you send out to probe weaknesses in the opposing line-up. Me? I'm your holding midfielder, your co-ordinator, the guy that all the information that the DCs gather is channelled through, and that the attacking prompts come from. I'm not going to score too many goals but I'll set plenty up for the rest of you. The fact is, I still play real football at a decent level, and that's what I'm good at, so I'm fine with the equivalent here. By the way, no offence to the present incumbent, but if the St Johnstone job fell vacant, I'd be happy if you got it.'

'Mmm,' Mann murmured. 'I'll tell my lads that, Dan and Jakey. They think I don't know the difference between a football and a suet dumpling. How about Sauce?' she asked. 'Where do you see him in this set-up?'

'Easy. He's the director of football; that's what he's doing right now. Off scouting in a different league, and feeding knowledge back to us. For example Sandra's WhatsApps to the guy Pilgrim; they were useful.'

'How? In what way?'

'They tell us that she was intending to go back home, to the Bahamas, and for a very good reason. The will that the director of football sent me: that backs it up.'

'True. Is it relevant otherwise?'

'I can't see how,' Stirling said. 'She wrote it herself, had it witnessed, and left it in a drawer, according to Superintendent Haddock's email. That means only two people knew about it, Sandra and the witness, whose job's only to verify the signature, not the contents.'

'Point taken, Midfielder. Now I've got another job for you. I'd like you to research the Later Era care home. Jackie says it felt a bit niffy. Let's see if we can find out where the smell's coming from.'

Sixty-Nine

Jenny Bramley liked Scotland, for several reasons. Having moved from the virtual horror show that London had become, her working environment had been transformed. As chief scientific officer of the Scottish national police service, she had reached the top of the ladder, one that it might have taken her another fifteen years to climb in the capital. In practice she was her own boss, providing specialist services to the police but not part of its command structure. In moving home from Muswell Hill to Glasgow, she and her husband had swapped their cramped and mortgaged terraced home for a wholly owned four bedroom villa in a cul-de-sac that was less than a mile from the motorway network, a short walk to a very good primary school for their seven year old daughter and a twenty-minute drive away from the crime campus where she was based. Alongside these plus points, she had discovered since her arrival that the fact that her mother had been born and spent the first two years of her life in Scotland made her eligible for a place in its Commonwealth Games rifle shooting team . . . if that gathering ever took place.

Her happiness was elevated by her excitement as she looked at her computer screen, and the tanned features of Charlotte Mann, one of her favourite colleagues.

'You look well chuffed, Jenny,' the DCI observed.

'Oh I am, Lottie, I am. Normally when I get to give you results it's all technical stuff, of which, let's be frank, you only understand the headlines and not the detail. This time, it's different. This time I am smiling in anticipation of your reaction to the bloody great monkey wrench that I'm about to throw into your investigation.'

When she put her mind to it, Mann's deadpan reactions had been compared favourably by colleagues with those of Chic Murray, the late great Scottish comedian. The fact that her right eyebrow rose only increased Bramley's pleasure.

'Do your worst,' she challenged. 'This is about the phone I dropped off with you, I'm guessing.'

'It is. First, the routine stuff. Fingerprints and DNA lifted from the device confirm that the only person to handle it, and therefore the person who deposited it with Paradigm Storage was the late Sandra Bulloch. That's the routine part, what we all expected. This isn't. My IT colleagues have been able to access the phone, using the facial recognition biometrics that were held on Bulloch's file. Given the time that's elapsed since she left the police service, I was doubtful they'd work, but they did; even more bonus points to my people. It was when we got in there that everything stood on its head. The profile of the user, it isn't Sandra Bulloch. It's someone called Alexandra Vernon, with a different date of birth, different registered email, different everything, other than Sandra Bulloch's face. There are photos in there too. It's for your people to go through them in detail, but mine took a look. One jumped out at them; an image of a driving licence, in the name of Alexandra Vernon, with her birth date and an address in Bath Street, Glasgow. We can't say for sure that it isn't a fake, but it looks genuine. As we speak, the device is on its way to your office, in the pocket of a cop on a motor cycle. It should be with you directly. Good luck with it Lottie, and thanks for making my day.'

Mann gazed back at her from the screen; deadpan. 'Thanks for making mine,' she countered. 'Until now, all traces of Bulloch vanished after she fuelled her vehicle at a filling station on the border. Now we know; she didn't disappear. She became some-one else. Thanks to you we should be able to trace what that person did. The question is, where the hell did she come from?'

Seventy

'I've booked it top priority overnight international,' Sauce Haddock said. 'For what it cost, it would have been a lot cheaper for us to bring it back as hold baggage and pay the excess charges. Although,' he added, 'there might not have been any. To use up our total allowance Cheeky and I would have needed to put lead weights in our suitcases.'

'When's it being picked up?' Stirling asked.

'Within the next half hour, the courier company promised. Guaranteed delivery to your office by nine tomorrow morning. I could have had it sent to Gartcosh, but Dr Bramley can send one of her specialists to you, to effect an entrance, so to speak.'

'What do you think we'll find on it?'

'I do not have a Scooby, John,' Haddock said. 'Maybe nothing, maybe everything. This investigation's been full of uncertainties from the off, a fistful of loose ends needing to be tied together. The latest being that list of cities that Ryan Pilgrim said Sandra visited. What we need you, or somebody, to do with that, is add it to the places she and Gordon Pollock visited on their Grand Tour, and see if you can find a linking factor, common ground in every one of them.'

'Maybe she just liked cities, boss.'

'Maybe she did,' he conceded.

'I'll do that,' Stirling continued, 'put the two lists together, but analysing them'll have to wait. I'm doing some other research for the DCI and that has priority. I could put a DC on the cities,' he suggested.

'You're there, I'm here. You make that decision. What's Lottie's priority job?' he asked.

'I'm looking into the ownership of a care home.'

'Care home?' the superintendent repeated. 'What the fuck are we doing looking into a care home?'

'Sandra Bulloch's aunt lives there. Jackie Wright went to talk to her and got bad vibes off the place.'

'Is it a new line of enquiry?'

'That could be, boss; but the truth is we've barely got a first one yet. A list of places, that's all. That, and Jackie Wright getting a dodgy smell off a residential home: neither's anywhere close to telling us who killed our victim. Or am I missing something?' he added.

'From the sound of that, you're not,' Haddock admitted. 'But don't go asking the question aloud if there are any journalists around. You don't want to be doing ten rounds with Lottie Mann. Where is she just now?' he asked.

'She's just finished a video call. I can see her from my desk. I don't know who was on the other end, but whoever it was, the DCI is not looking very excited.'

'There's a school of thought, John, that Lottie Mann would not look excited if she was on the Titanic and saw an iceberg approaching. Cheers.'

Seventy-One

'How's it going, Sir Robert?' Chief Constable Neil McIlhenney asked, smiling. 'You look pretty healthy, or do you have a filter on your camera?'

'Make-up,' Skinner shot back. 'InterMedia has TV stations, one of them in this building. All I have to do is make one call. You're looking a bit pale yourself, Neil.'

'That's what happens when you have a fucking desk job. You of all people should know that.'

'Why should I?' he countered. 'When I was a chief I delegated all the boring stuff to Brian Mackie, because he was better at it than me, and got out of the office, turning up at crime scenes and pissing you guys off. Brian's still there, you should use him more.'

Mario McGuire contradicted him. 'No he's not,' he said. 'Brian retired last week. He's gone to be head of security with an energy company in Australia. He's been replaced by Morven Guard; she was a chief super in Inverness.'

'Nobody told me that,' Skinner complained. 'I'd have chipped into his leaving present.'

'It all happened very quickly,' McIlhenney explained. 'The opportunity came up and he took it.'

'Head of security?' he laughed. 'Brian couldn't secure a freezer door. Administration was his strength. Unless he gets to patrol sites with a weapon,' he conceded. 'He was the best shot on the force.'

'We have a better one now. Jenny Bramley, she's international class. Unfortunately she's a scientist, not a cop. You got any openings?' he asked. 'Mario and I are always on the look-out for offers we couldn't refuse.'

'How's your Catalan?'

'Wanting, I'm afraid,' McGuire replied. 'My Italian's fluent, though, as you know. I speak it like a head waiter.'

'So what?' Skinner countered. 'I never met an Italian waiter who didn't speak English. Anyway, a call from the Glimmer Twins is always a hoot, but is there a reason for this one, beyond bullshit?'

'There is actually,' McIlhenney said. 'There's been an odd development in the Sandra Bulloch investigation. Since you were her direct boss for a while, we thought we'd pick your brains. I'm sorry,' he added, 'we should have made an appointment.'

'Fuck you. What's the development?'

'This,' McGuire exclaimed. 'The one lead we got from the crime scene led us to a self-storage facility in Alloa. There, Lottie found a phone that Sandra had deposited. When Bramley's people got into it, they discovered that she had a second identity. It was sophisticated; she had a driving licence in that name, even a National Insurance number. Why she used it we don't know, but she seems to have switched to it when she got back to Scotland after touring with the Pollock boy.'

'What did she call herself?'

On screen the two officers saw a light, a flash of expectation creep into Skinner's eyes. 'Alexandra Vernon,' McIlhenney said.

The light became a laugh. 'Ah Christ, I knew it was daft at the time.' He sighed. 'When I was appointed chief in the Strathclyde force, it was like becoming President, or Prime Minister. You'll know, Neil. You'll have had much the same. They give you the equivalent of the launch codes, secret files, stuff like that. One of the things they told me was that my late unlamented predecessor had the bright idea of designating two Special Branch officers, one male, one female, for undercover work, in certain situations. For this purpose, two false identities were created, although in fact they were never used. The ACC overseeing Special Branch at the time, Matt Allan, gave them names, and backed them up with apparently real but actually fake documentation: birth certificates, driving licences, national insurance numbers, the lot. I think he even fabricated degrees for them at a couple of universities, places with lots of students where two ghosts could be slipped on to the graduate roll without anyone noticing. The male entity was called Martin Littlewood, and the female was Alexandra Vernon. Get the picture?' he asked.

McIlhenney stared at him. McGuire shook his head.

'Of course Matt was taking the piss,' Skinner continued. 'You two seem to have forgotten, but Littlewoods and Vernons were the names of the two big football pools, the coupons that your fathers and their fathers probably filled in every week of their lives. I can't recall the name of the designated male officer, but the female was Sandra Bulloch, who was then a Special Branch sergeant. As soon as I heard about it, I told the head of SB to wrap up the silly project and burn the files. But he was a lazy bastard; a mate of old Jock Govan, the previous chief plus one, who'd been put there as a favour, or maybe just to keep him out of sight. My guess is, that bloke passed my order on to Sandra, and that for whatever reason, rainy day or whatever, she held on to her alter ego. If I were you guys, I'd be doing a check now to make sure that Michael Littlewood isn't running about somewhere, getting up to God knows what!' His laugh became a frown, as his phone's ringtone sounded. 'Got to go, guys,' he exclaimed. 'I have a call coming in, and I need to take it.'

His friends froze on screen then vanished as he picked up his mobile and clicked 'Accept'.

'Señor?' Jordi Poch exclaimed. 'You can speak?'

'Yes,' he confirmed. 'I'm good, go ahead.'

'The project you gave me. I have results, detailed results. I am still in Girona. Can I come to your office?'

'Do that,' Skinner said. 'As fast as you can.'

Seventy-Two

Wright would not have sworn to it in court, but she was certain that Hardeep's beard quivered when he looked up and saw who it was that he had buzzed into the building. 'Hello again,' she said, brandishing her warrant card. 'We have new information. I need to check your visitors' register for another name. Can I see it, please?' Without waiting for a reply she took the book from the counter.

'You cannot do that!' he protested.

'I can, and I will,' she replied, calmly.

'I will fetch Amina.'

'You can fetch the Highland Light Infantry, but it's not going to stop me looking through this book.' She took it to a table by the entrance door and began to go through the pages for the period when Sandra Bulloch was believed to have visited.

She had cleared two when a male voice, the accent broad Yorkshire, rang out behind her. 'Detective Sergeant, please stop that.'

She turned, to be confronted by a heavily built man wearing a tweed jacket and camel-coloured chinos and a trouser suit, similar to her own, with a head covering. 'Who would you be, sir?' she asked.

'My name's Gregor Rutherford. My wife and I own this place. All of that material, it's confidential. Data protection.'

Wright stared at him, then laughed. 'Are you kidding me?' she exclaimed. 'It's an open register, hand-written, plus, it's one that you're not obliged to keep at all.'

Rutherford tried another line of attack. 'Our residents have a right to privacy,' he said, his voice rising. 'Their friends and families have rights.'

Wright looked back at him. 'One of those family members had a right to life,' she murmured. 'Somebody took it away from her.'

'It wasn't taken away here.'

'We're not suggesting that it was, but we are trying to piece together her movements in the days before her murder. Please don't be obstructive, or this situation will escalate.' She held the man's gaze, until he turned and walked away.

The sergeant returned to her search. It was on the seventh page that she found Alexandra Vernon, the name printed in capitals, rather than in autograph style. 'March the first,' she murmured. Taking her mobile from her pocket she found the photo of the bogus but authentic driving licence in the name of Sandra Bulloch's alter ego. She took it back to the desk and showed it to Hardeep. 'This woman,' she said, 'is showing as signed in about six months ago, registered as visiting Mrs Crawford. Does she ring any bells now?'

He gazed at the image for several seconds. 'Maybe yes,' he conceded. 'But then again, maybe no. If she was signed in then she was here, was she not?'

Wright nodded. 'Yes, and from that I need to speak to anyone who interacted with her. I need to know everything she said; there's always a possibility that it might give us new information that might take our investigation forward.'

'She would not have spoken to anyone here,' Hardeep declared. 'It is not allowed.'

'Why not?'

'It is not allowed, that's all I can tell you. If you were not police I would not be talking to you.'

'Nonetheless, I would like to speak to other staff members.'

He shook his head; the turban stayed firmly in place. 'They cannot be made to speak to you, made by you, or by me, or by Amina. And they would not, because they all know it is not allowed.'

The DS knew that he was correct. When it came to staff interviews, she had no powers of compulsion. Threats of an obstruction charge only worked at a certain level, and they had to be real and enforceable. 'If you say so,' she said. 'But I will go up and see Mrs Crawford.'

'You cannot. Mrs Crawford, dear lady, is ill.'

Wright stared at him. 'When did this happen?'

'Last night.'

'That's too bad.' She was genuinely distressed; she had liked the old lady. 'Where is she?'

'She is at the hospital in the town. The doctor said she had to be taken there.'

'Has her stepdaughter been told?'

'That would be the business of the hospital. She is their patient.'

'F . . .' Wright bit her tongue, almost literally. 'Then I'll go there,' she snapped. She slammed the visitors' register on to the counter. The first of the two doors was swinging open even before she reached it; triggered by Hardeep in his haste to get her out of there she imagined. It was only when she was in the street outside that she realised that she had no idea where the hospital was.

Maps would have told her in a few seconds; instead she walked the few yards to the tea room that she had visited the day before. The owner, a portly middle-aged man, recognised her at once. She was going towards him, until her eye fell on another familiar face; Efe, the person who had admitted her, then bolted to summon help, at a table with another African, a woman, also in a Later Era uniform.

She stepped over and flashed her warrant card again. 'Remember me from yesterday?' she asked.

Efe nodded. His chair squeaked on the wooden floor as he moved in it.

'Can you tell me where the hospital is?'

'Sure, it's down that road over there,' he grunted, pointing towards a junction a short distance away. 'It's called Kello. You can't miss it.'

'Thanks. What happened with Mrs Crawford?' she asked. 'Do you know?'

'She just went ill, poor lady,' the woman said. Anne: her name badge identified her. 'It's a shame, she was fine when she had dinner with the rest, then less than an hour later, she was distressed. It's a shame,' she repeated. 'A lovely lady.'

'Does that sort of thing happen often?' Wright sighed. 'I suppose it must, given the age of the residents, and their general condition.'

'Not like that,' Anne told her. 'When an old person is ready to go, you can tell, at least I can. I can look at them and say, "This person will not be here in a week", and you will usually be right. But not Mrs Crawford. You will say she will live to be a hundred.'

'Honey,' Efe murmured. 'Shut up please.'

'Why should she?' the DS challenged.

'She's not allowed to talk to you,' he said.

'It's our contracts,' the woman explained. 'These contracts we all signed when we were brought here from Africa. They say stupid things, set down stupid rules and if we break them they . . .' She frowned. 'He's right, I should shut up. And I will.' Then she smiled. 'But only because it upsets him. He's a good guy really but he's chicken-shit scared of the people we work for.'

'Not all of them,' Efe protested. 'Hardeep is okay. But Amina . . . And Gregor, no you don't want to mess with them.'

'Who's Gregor?'

'Amina's husband,' he replied. 'You don't see him there much, only when there's trouble, like with Francis.'

Wright guessed that she had just met Gregor. 'And who's Francis?' she asked.

'Another of the workers, our friend. He's from Nigeria like me. He complained about . . .'

Anne laid a hand on his arm. 'Now it's you should shut up, Efe boy.'

He nodded. 'Yes, yes.'

The detective sergeant took a card from her pocket and placed it on their table. 'If you ever want to talk about it, I suggest that you show your contracts to Citizens Advice. If they say that legally you can, call me on that number.'

Anne nodded, picked up the card and pocketed it. 'Don't let no-one see that,' Wright heard Efe warn, as she walked away.

Kello Hospital was less than half a mile away, a grey two storey building with many windows that might have pre-dated the National Health Service by as many as twenty years. The building was dual purpose, part district hospital and part minor injuries unit. She followed a sign to the wards, feeling slightly lost until she encountered a nursing station where a woman was keying data into a computer.

'Excuse me,' the DS said, showing her credentials yet again. 'I'm looking for Mrs Sally Crawford, a resident of Later Era. I believe she was admitted last night.'

The nurse looked up. 'Yes. That's right. The GP sent her in after she had an incident. If you go to Ward Two and ask for Dr Wu, he'll update you. Along the corridor and you'll find it facing you.'

She followed the directions, towards an open double door. Wright's idea of a hospital ward was drawn from Edinburgh Royal Infirmary, a four bed unit that would normally be all female or all male. Ward Two in the Biggar hospital was old fashioned, open and mixed-gender with six beds on either side. Two were vacant and curtains were drawn around another three. At the far end she spotted a young Chinese man in blue scrubs with a stethoscope round his neck. *'Don't have to be a detective to work that one out,'* she thought, as she headed towards him.

'Can I help you? She was halfway there when a voice interrupted her. She turned to see another Chinese, also with a stethoscope, but older, taller and in green scrubs.

'Are you Dr Wu?' she asked, a Steely Dan refrain from one of her playlists running through her mind.

'That's me; I'm the medical registrar. You were heading for Dr Li, my junior colleague. And you are?'

'Detective Sergeant Jackie Wright, serious crimes, Glasgow. I believe that Mrs Sally Crawford's your patient.'

He nodded. 'She is. Can I ask, what's your interest in her?'

'We're investigating the murder of her niece. I spoke to her yesterday afternoon. I want to follow up that chat, ask her a couple of questions. Can I see her?'

'You can see her,' the physician replied, 'but you won't be asking her any questions. Mrs Crawford is asleep; she's on end of life care.'

'Eh?' Wright gasped. 'How come?'

'Because her time is almost over. She was admitted here last night at the request of Dr Rankin, a partner in the medical practice that serves the Later Era home. Dr Li handled her admission; I saw her for the first time when I came in this morning. You say you spoke to her yesterday afternoon. Was she responsive?'

'Responsive? She was watching a bowls match through her window and she'd just finished her lunch. I think she'd have taken me for a walk round Biggar town centre if I'd asked her. Now you tell me she's dying. I'm having trouble getting my head round that, I'm afraid.'

The doctor winced. 'Maybe she was having a good spell when you saw her. But deterioration can be very rapid in older people. Mrs Crawford is ninety-two. Were you aware of that?'

'I knew she was getting on,' the DS said. 'I didn't know she was that age, but it doesn't surprise me. Still . . . I hear what you're saying Doctor, but twenty-four hours ago she was full of life.'

'Come with me,' he murmured, then led her to one of the closed cubicles. They slipped between the curtains. 'There. See for yourself.'

Sally Crawford was indeed asleep, peacefully; her face was slightly flushed, but she was serene, her white hair spread on her pillow. Her bed was very slightly inclined, and its cot sides were raised, unnecessarily, Wright thought, for it was clear that she would not be going anywhere. 'Is she on medication?' she asked.

'Of course,' a third voice answered. The detective had been unaware that another person had joined them. 'I'm Dr Rankin,' she explained. 'I sent Mrs Crawford here last night, from Later Era. I just looked in to see how she was doing.'

'How do you expect her to do?' Wright asked.

'We expect her to die, Sergeant,' Dr Wu replied. 'Soon.'

'Medication,' she repeated. 'What's she on?'

'Morphine and midazolam. They're both standard at this stage. The first for pain control and the second to give the patient peace of mind.'

She turned to Rankin. 'When were you called in by the home?'

'It'd have been about seven thirty, I suppose. Yes, a wee bit before eight.'

'How was she when you arrived?'

'A little agitated, but much as you see her now, sleeping.'

'Did you medicate her then?'

'Of course; I gave her the drugs that Dr Wu described. Later Era don't have any staff qualified to give injections. They don't hold stocks of those drugs either: not allowed to.'

'Did anyone say anything about the onset of her distress?' Wright asked.

'When he called me, Hardeep, the assistant manager said that she'd had her evening meal, in the dining room as usual, and then gone back to her room. One of the carers found her there not long after, drowsy and unresponsive. I medicated her then agreed to send her here.'

'They asked you to?'

Rankin nodded. 'It's normal practice. Truth be told, Later Era don't like their residents dying on the premises. They think it disturbs the rest, so if someone is end of life like Mrs Crawford, they prefer it if they can send her here, for proper nursing care.'

'Hold on,' the DS protested. 'I lost someone in my family a couple of years back. She wanted to die at home and she did, with care from the district nurses. They could go into Later Era, surely.'

'They could, but the management discourage it. Look,' she declared, 'it's not my job to moralise. I treat the patients and that's it. The care in this hospital is excellent, so Later Era's approach might be the best option for the residents.'

'And might not, if they don't want it. Has Mrs Crawford's step-daughter been contacted? She's next of kin.'

'She has,' Dr Wu confirmed. 'I called her myself. She's very upset but unfortunately she's still recovering from a car accident and isn't mobile.'

'That is unfortunate,' Wright agreed. Her brow furrowed, as she assessed the situation for a minute or so. Finally she looked at the registrar. 'Did your colleague, Dr Li, do any blood work when she was admitted?'

He shook his head. 'No. Why would he? The situation was obvious.'

'To him, I don't doubt, but it's not clear to me. I'd like a full blood analysis done now.'

'That'll take days,' Rankin said. 'The lab goes at its own pace.'

'You'll send the samples to the police lab at Gartcosh. They'll be prioritised there. While we're waiting for them,' she added, 'I want you to do something for me that you might find difficult. The drugs you're giving Mrs Crawford are helping her to die. As a police officer, I remain to be convinced that she actually wants to.'

'I can't do that,' Dr Wu insisted. 'She's my patient, I have a duty to her.'

'So have I,' the DS countered. 'Based on the person I saw and spoke with yesterday and that I'm looking at now . . . let me put it this way. If Sally passed away now, I would be reporting it as a suspicious death. The fact that she's still alive doesn't remove those suspicions. Unless you see signs of physical pain, and I'm not just talking about bedsores, I'd like you to stop the morphine. Do that please, and let's see what happens.'

'That's cruel, Sergeant,' he protested.

'Doctor, I'm asking you, not telling you: I don't have the authority to do that. But I will be reporting the situation to my boss. Based on what I tell her she's likely to open a formal investigation into Mrs Crawford's situation. The old dear's had ninety-two years already, let's give her another day, and hopefully she may have a lot more.'

Seventy-Three

'He agreed?' Mann asked.

'Yes, he did,' Wright replied. 'He and Rankin did a bit of verbal pushing and shoving over whose patient she actually was, but when I suggested that if I placed her in protective custody that would make her mine . . . bullshit, boss, I know, but they're doctors not lawyers . . . common sense took over. Dr Wu's going to monitor her over the next twenty-four hours. No morphine, a wee bit of midazolam if it's needed to keep her settled but that's it. I'll look in on her tomorrow, after I've seen the step-daughter, Christine McGhee, Crawford as was. She's fifty-four,' she added. 'Divorced, music teacher in a school in Lanark, one son who's an RAF pilot, currently posted in Cyprus, she thinks; she's not sure.'

'Where does she live?'

'Dolphinton: that's just along the road, towards Edinburgh. My guess is that's why Sally chose Later Era, to be close to her.'

'She was in an accident, you said. What's up with her?'

'A broken leg; a neighbour's looking after her, she told me, until she's mobile again.'

'Did you ask her about Sandra?'

'I'll leave that until tomorrow,' the DS said. 'Hopefully we'll have had the result of the blood analysis by then. I took the sample straight to Gartcosh on my way back here.'

'What d'you think the analysis will find, Jackie?' Stirling asked.

'I know it'll find traces of morphine and midazolam. It's what else might be in there that interests me. I know who I met yesterday and age notwithstanding, she was a long way from the person I saw in that hospital today.'

Her colleague scratched his chin. 'If a punter walked into a police office and reported that a ninety-two-year-old relative in a care home had suffered an unexpected physical collapse and was pushing hard at death's door, how far up the priority scale do you reckon his complaint might be?'

'About halfway,' she conceded. 'On a slow day. But frankly, John, I don't give a fuck. Sally isn't a rellie and I know what I saw.'

'And I'm going to back you,' Mann promised. 'John, what have you found out online about Later Era?'

'It's incorporated,' he replied. 'Later Era Residential Limited's a company registered in Scotland. The accounts don't tell you a hell of a lot, only that it has chunky asset base, shareholders' assets just under four million quid. There are two directors, Gregor Rutherford and Amina Rutherford, ages forty and forty-two respectively. I found Facebook pages for three Later Era Homes, the Biggar one and others in Newmilns, East Ayrshire and Blackburn, West Lothian. Read them and you'd want to check in, regardless of age. There's a website as well. Here's what it says about Biggar.' He turned his monitor around on his desk, so that they could see it.

Wright leaned in studying it. 'I don't know where that garden is,' she murmured. 'The place is in the centre of the town. There's a patch of grass at the back, but that's all. And I'll tell you something else that's dodgy. The staff you see there, they're all white.

I didn't see a single white person there. Hardeep and Amina, they're probably both Indian, Efe and Anne, they're African. And they've got them on a pretty short leash.'

'You're right; Amina is Indian,' Stirling said. 'I found her on LinkedIn. And she is actually a doctor, according to her bio. But really she's a BUMS.'

'A what?' his colleagues exclaimed simultaneously.

'BUMS,' Stirling repeated. 'Bachelor of Unani Medicine and Surgery. That's her degree. Unani is traditional medicine, sort of homeopathic, you might say, with a bit of yoga included. Real doctors call Unani doctors quacks, but it's widely practised in India and Pakistan. Not by her, though, and not for long. She graduated aged twenty-three and came to Britain a year later to work in the care industry. That's the phrase she uses; care industry. She's a British national now, and has been for fifteen years.'

'How about Gregor?' Mann asked. 'Have you found anything about him?'

'He's on LinkedIn too. According to his biography, he's from Rotherham originally. He's an ACA, same as a chartered accountant but with less clout. Speaking of clout, I found a conviction for assault on his record, an incident involving a bus driver in Doncaster, when he was twenty-four. The vehicle was in a queue of traffic. Rutherford was in a hurry and asked the driver to open the door so he could get out. The driver refused, colourfully, according to Gregor's lawyer, and Gregor thumped him.'

'What did he get?'

'Community service, boss. The report I saw quotes the judge as saying the driver acted unreasonably.'

'What about his career since then?'

'LinkedIn says he worked for a small accountancy firm in Wetherby until he was twenty-eight, then moved to a similar job in Edinburgh. Four years after that he shows up as a director of Later Era, the same year as the company was registered.'

'Are the pair of them involved with other businesses?'

'None that I can find.'

'Keep looking.'

'Yes boss,' Stirling said.

'And John,' Wright added. 'When you have time, can you find someone at HMRC who can tell us a bit more about the Later Era employees? Let's see if we can find those shiny white faces on the website, because none of them were obvious to me.'

Seventy-Four

'We've found Alexandra Vernon.'

'What do you mean, you've found her?' Haddock exclaimed. 'Are you saying she's a real person, not the fake that the DCC said she was?'

'No, sorry, Sauce,' Mann said. 'The day's dragging on, I should have made myself clearer. Maya Smith, one of the DCs, found a trace of economic activity by the Vernon entity. We got information that when Sandra visited her aunt in the care home in Biggar, she was in a car, not the motor home. We assumed it was hired and Maya was tasked with finding it. With that as a starting point, it didn't take her long to find a Europcar place in Hamilton, South Lanarkshire. She checked both identities and found that on the twenty-ninth of February, Alexandra Vernon hired a Ford Fiesta. It was returned, by her, on the eleventh of March, having done three hundred and forty-seven miles. Now Maya's a smart girl. She didn't have to be told that the motor home had to be close to Hamilton, so she went looking for caravan sites. She found one at Strathclyde Country Park, between Hamilton and Motherwell. Its record showed that the thing was parked there from the twenty-eighth of Feb, until the thirteenth of March.'

'Do we know, did she live there or just park it?'

'No, it seems that she lived there. The manager remembered her, because he doesn't have many long term parkers at that time of year, usually just overnighters, and also because of the motor home itself. It was German registered, he told Maya, and he said he'd never seen one like it. It wasn't just parked there. It was lit most nights . . . the guy couldn't swear that it was every night, but most, he said. However there was one oddity: she booked and paid for three weeks in advance . . .'

'How?'

'By a debit card. We don't have the paperwork for that yet, but he's looking it out. Anyway,' she continued, 'the odd thing was that she'd booked until the twentieth of March, but she didn't stay until then. When the manager came into work on the fourteenth, it was gone, unplugged from the services and gone.'

'What's your thinking?' he asked.

'That she was probably killed there, moved somewhere else for the clean-up, then dumped in Irvine.'

'That fits. Any thoughts on where it might have been taken?'

'Somewhere quiet,' Mann replied. 'Most likely private land where everything incriminating could have been removed without anyone being aware.'

'That fits into our suspect profile too,' Haddock agreed.

'I'll bear it in mind,' she said, 'when we have one.'

Seventy-Five

As Christine McGhee opened the door of her bungalow, Jackie Wright was seized by a feeling of guilt. The woman's right leg was in a heavy cast and her weight was borne by an elbow crutch, with another one hanging over her left wrist as she gripped the door handle.

'DS Wright, Glasgow,' she said. 'Mrs McGhee, I'm so sorry to be inconveniencing you like this. I was told that a neighbour was looking after you.'

'She is,' the woman agreed, 'but she's out walking my dog. They come first, after all, need to get out to do their business.'

'That's what your back garden's for,' Wright, no animal lover, thought, although she replied, 'Of course. What happens to their humans is none of their concern. Let me help you.' She stepped into the house supporting her as she slipped her arm into the second crutch.

'Come this way,' Mrs McGhee said, as she regained her balance, swinging ahead of Wright with a degree of expertise, skirting a piano as she led them into a small sitting room, where she backed into an armchair and let herself settle, awkwardly.

'Can I get you anything?' the detective asked.

'A coffee would be nice,' Mrs McGhee admitted.

'Not a problem.'

'Thank you so much. The kitchen's through that door: you'll find everything you need through there. Milk, no sugar for me.'

The coffee was supermarket instant, but Wright gritted her teeth, took two mugs from a tree and completed her mission.

'Thank you,' the woman said again as she rejoined her, laying one of the mugs on a table beside her chair. 'Would you like a biscuit or anything?'

'No, I'm good thanks, Mrs McGhee.'

'Chris, please. Makes things more friendly.'

'It does. I'm Jackie.'

'Not Jacqueline?'

'No, definitely not, never have been.'

'Well Jackie, you're here to talk to me about my poor cousin, Sandra. Such a terrible shock . . . although it shouldn't have been. As soon as I was told, I just feel so, so . . . so bloody guilty.'

'About what, Chris?'

'About those people, in that bloody care home! What they were doing! I should have spoken out right away, more so when she didn't come back to me, but to be honest, I thought they must have done to her what they did to me. But no, it was worse. And now my stepmum . . . Och, it's . . .'

'Chris,' Wright said quietly. 'Drink some of your coffee, calm down and tell me what's happened.'

She nodded, did as she had been told, then stayed quiet for a few moments, until she drew a deep breath and said, 'I think they've killed her, Jackie. Those two in the care home. The Rutherfords.'

The DS remained impassive, as far as she could. 'Why would they do that?' she asked.

'Because of her investigation. And it's my fault, my damn fault, I started the whole thing off.'

'In what way?'

Chris pursed her lips. 'I told her I was concerned about the care home, the way it was being run. I'd been noticing for a while that there didn't seem to be a lot of staff on duty whenever I was there, and not just that, that some of them didn't appear to speak English well enough to understand what the residents were saying to them. Before you say anything, yes, there are people in there with dementia but most of them are like my stepmum, well switched on. Sandra and I, we speak, spoke occasionally on WhatsApp, and finally, oh, about a year ago . . . I could tell you the exact date from my chats . . . I opened up to her about it. She told me that she was planning to come back to Scotland for a visit, and that when she was there she'd look into it.'

'Did she give any specific reason for coming back?' the DS asked.

'Yes and no. She said she was in cop mode and needed to check a few things, but that was all.'

'No more than that?'

'No. She didn't mention anything specific when she came here either, other than to say, the first time she was here, that somebody was in for a nasty surprise.'

'Somebody? No gender? Not he, or she, or they?'

'No, just somebody. Anyway, on her first visit, it was the first Saturday in March, just after leap year day, we talked about my concerns. By that time I'd raised them with the owners, and been more or less brushed off. They said that their homes . . . they have more than one . . . had all been given excellent reports by the Care Protection Agency, and that if I wasn't happy I could take my stepmum home with me that very day. I told Sandra all this, and she said to leave it to her. She also said that the Care Agency's unreliable in cases like this, because they give advance warning of their inspections, letting the owners fill the place with agency temps if they're running short-staffed.'

'I didn't realise that,' Wright murmured. 'When did you see her next?'

'Two weeks later. She came back on a Sunday, and boy had she made progress. She told me that she had established, by talking to those staff members who would speak to her away from the premises, that the Rutherfords, in their three homes, employ a total of eighteen care assistants, about one third of the number they should have. There are also three assistant managers, Hardeep and two others, who are all related to Amina. They're on salary, but the care assistants, she told me they're all imported from Africa, on work visas obtained through the Home Office. And, all of them have got contracts that say they have to remain for five years, and that if they leave or even try to, they'll be taken to court. Sandra reckoned they were legally unenforceable, but the poor folk were just terrified. They sleep in dormitories and they're paid cash in hand . . . not much cash either. One of them though, a woman called Anne, she let slip about a guy in the Blackburn home who'd complained to Gregor. There had been a confrontation that had got physical, and, Sandra's informant said, the man had never been seen again.'

'Was his name Francis?'

Chris McGhee frowned. 'Yes, I believe it was. All this, Sandra told me, she could prove, and was going to. She was going to see them, she said, and if they didn't fall in line, then she knew a man, Bob Skinner she said his name was, that she could rely on to blow the whole thing open.'

'In which case she was silenced before she could do that,'

Wright observed. 'If she had done, it would have been blown wide open, trust me.'

'Maybe she did and this Bob Skinner killed her? Could he have been in on it?'

The DS laughed, quietly, grimly. 'No, if she had involved him, it would have been the Rutherfords that were in danger. Chris, we think that Sandra died a very few days after she saw you. Did she leave you a written record of her findings by any chance?'

'No. I'm afraid not, but I'm sure there was one, from something she said. Jackie, they killed her, I'm sure. She confronted them and they killed her.'

'That's an extreme conclusion, Chris,' Wright cautioned, although she doubted her own words as she spoke them.

'No, it's not,' she countered, 'because they tried to kill me.'

'What do you mean?' the DS gasped.

The woman tapped her cast. 'Jackie, this isn't new,' she said. 'This is me recovering. Toward the end of March, just before the Easter holiday, I was coming home from work when I was run off the road, near to Thankerton. It was nearly dark, and I don't remember much about it, but I'm sure that another car, a big car drove up alongside me and forced me off the road. After that I just remember tumbling down a hill side, there being a big bang, and then nothing. Next thing I knew I was being strapped to a stretcher, and screaming in agony. Someone must have given me a shot, for the next thing I remember is waking up in Wishaw General Hospital; a week later, I found out afterwards.'

'Did you report this to the police, when you were able?'

'Jackie, I was pretty much out of it for a fortnight after I woke up. They had me on such strong painkillers that I didn't know where I was. All I did know was that both my legs and my right arm were in plaster and I couldn't breathe very well because I had several broken ribs. The police never came to see me, but if they had what could I have told them? It was a big black car, that's all I could have said. Sometimes I think that I saw the driver and that it was Gregor Rutherford, but that could just be my mind showing me things I want to see,' she tapped the side of her head, 'in here. At least that's what I thought until Sandra got involved, and I heard she was dead.'

'Bloody hell,' Wright murmured. 'Look there must have been a police report of the accident, I promise. I'll call my boss right away, before I go to the hospital to see how Mrs Crawford is. She'll find it and if I know Lottie she'll go ballistic when she hears it was never followed up.'

'One of my nurses said, when I was a bit more compos, that when I was brought in one of the paramedics said the police had told them they thought I'd fallen asleep at the wheel,' McGhee said. 'They were right about that . . . but only after my car had turned over three or four times.'

'Chris, if Sandra hadn't turned up would you ever have done anything about this?'

'No, Jackie, I wouldn't. Maybe they weren't trying to kill me, just warn me off. If they did it worked. I've been scared shitless ever since, and I was until you walked through that door. Now, I want to nail them to the wall.'

Seventy-Six

'What's your problem, Mann?' Superintendent Steve Murphy barked. 'My station inspector in Lanark tells me you've been giving her grief about some six-month-old RTA. What's that got to do with CID, and why's a DCI involved? I've heard about you, by the way,' he added.

'I've heard about you too,' Lottie Mann thought but did not say. 'One of the last of the old Strathclyde time servers that should never have made it beyond sergeant but wound up running a division in Andy Martin's time.'

'A DCI's involved, sir,' she replied, slowly, for him to hear every word, 'because that six-month-old RTA's just become a potential attempted murder, linked to the very successful murder of one of our former colleagues, who might just still be alive if the officers under your command, the two that attended the scene, had done their jobs and followed up the incident as soon as the accident victim was fit for interview . . . even though that might have taken a month.' She paused. 'And now,' she continued, 'rank set to one side, I don't know what you've heard about me, but whatever it is you'd better fucking believe it and co-operate. Otherwise, the next voice you hear's likely to be that of DCC McGuire. While I might like to stick you in one of your

322

own patrol cars for the rest of your career, he's actually got the power to do it.'

'True enough,' Murphy sighed, wearily. 'You're everything I was told. You try and do my fucking job, DCI Mann, with the resources I've got.'

'At least I would try and fucking do it. Now, I want the names of those attending officers, within half an hour, and I want the pair of them in my office within an hour after that. They come to me, I don't go to them. Sir.'

As she slammed the phone back into its cradle, she was aware of John Stirling, standing in the doorway. 'I love the smell of napalm in the morning,' he murmured.

'You what?'

'A line from one of my favourite movies: *Apocalypse Now*. There's this mad air cavalry colonel, his helicopters wipe out a Viet Cong encampment and when they touch down that's what he says. Robert Duvall. When I heard you there, I thought of him right away. Whoever that was. I can smell his arse burning from here.'

'Robert Duvall,' Mann repeated. 'I remember him in a film called *A Shot at Glory*, when I was a teenager. He had probably the worst Scottish accent I've ever heard, but I still remember the movie. Ally McCoist was in it.'

Stirling's gaze was incredulous. 'He was? Acting?'

She nodded. 'Yes and no. Yes, he was the co-star alongside Robert Duvall, but no, he was just himself. Right John,' she exclaimed. 'Your audition's over and you've got the part. What do you want?'

'We've had a delivery, boss,' he replied. 'International, all the way from the Bahamas. It's a computer. I didn't have a chance to tell you it was coming. It's Sandra Bulloch's. Detective Superintendent

Haddock found it in her house, and decided it was best if he sent it here.'

'How kind of him,' Mann murmured. 'Okay John, get on to the cyber-nerds at Gartcosh and ask them to send a specialist here. Maybe they'll get more from it than they've managed to squeeze out of that mobile.'

Seventy-Seven

'*Biggar's quite nice,*' Jackie Wright thought as she parked outside Kello Hospital. '*I wouldn't mind living here.*'

She filed the idea for future consideration, and possibly discussion with her partner, and walked into the building. She was heading for Ward Two when Dr Wu stepped out of a side room.

'Detective Sergeant,' he called out. There was a look in his eye that she could not quite interpret, but it seemed portentous. 'Do you have the lab results yet?'

'I do,' she replied. 'They hit my email just as I left my last appointment, but I haven't looked at them. Here, you do it.' She took out her phone, opened the message and clicked on its attachment.

The registrar took the device and put on the spectacles that hung on a lanyard around his neck, along with his stethoscope. He peered at the screen, nodding and murmuring as he scrolled through the report. When he was finished, he whistled.

'Not a surprise,' he said as he returned the phone. 'It shows a significant level of morphine, far more than was necessary therapeutically, and far more than it should have been even allowing for the medication she was given here. Dr Rankin's blameless here,' he added. 'She was called in and saw what she was meant to see, a very old person who had suffered a perfectly natural collapse, someone who had simply reached the end of her days, like her late Majesty, for example, who simply died of old age.'

'We're clear about this, are we?' Wright asked. 'It's your opinion that Mrs Crawford was given an overdose of morphine? Yes?'

'Yes.'

'Could it have happened accidentally?'

Dr Wu shook his head. 'I can't imagine that circumstance. That was a good call you made yesterday, Sergeant, when you told us to stop the medication. If we hadn't she'd probably be dead by now.'

'Will she make it?'

'Come and see.' He turned on his heel and walked towards the ward, so quickly that Wright had to lengthen her stride to keep pace.

Sally Crawford's bed remained curtained off, but Dr Wu slipped into the space, with the detective close behind.

'Hello dear,' the old lady said. She was sitting up, against a stack of pillows; she looked fragile but she was wide awake. There was a tray in front of her, with an empty cup in its saucer and a KitKat wrapper on a plate beside it. 'What a surprise,' she exclaimed, with a gentle smile. 'How nice to see you again. I've had a nice rest, the doctor tells me. Have you come to take me back home?'

'Maybe in a day or so,' Wright told her, hoping that she was hiding her surprise. 'But first, there's something I need to ask you.'

'Tough old bird,' Dr Wu whispered in her ear. 'Do you need me any longer?'

'I do,' she murmured, 'very much, as a witness.' She turned back to the recovering patient. 'Mrs Crawford, can I ask you what happened after I visited you, two days ago. Do you remember that?'

'Yes, of course I do. You asked me about Sandra, poor thing. I'm not senile you know,' she scolded.

The DS laughed. 'You don't need to tell me that. But I meant what happened after I'd left. They told me you had your dinner in the residents' dining room, and then you went up to your room.'

'That's right,' she confirmed. 'I was there, watching the bowlers, and Amina came in. She said that the doctor, that nice Dr Rankin it would be, that she'd changed my medication, and she'd asked her, Amina that is, to give me a jag. I wasn't aware I was on medication, but the doctors know best.'

'Of course they do,' Wright agreed. 'Okay, that's all I wanted to ask. I'll need to go now, but a day or so and we'll get you out of here. Doctor Wu,' she said, 'can we draw the curtains back now, and let Sally meet the other patients?'

'Of course.' He pulled back the first screen; a nurse rushed across to complete the process, and he and the detective left the ward.

'You heard all that,' she said, in the corridor outside.

'I did,' he confirmed, 'and worry not, I will say so in court if I have to.'

'Good. Here's something else you'll probably be asked. Having seen the lab findings, do you believe that Amina Rutherford intended to end Mrs Crawford's life?'

'Let me put it this way, I believe that was the probable outcome of an injection of that size, and anyone with even rudimentary medical knowledge would have known that.'

'Thanks. Don't let anyone in to see her yet. Amina mustn't know she's recovered.' She took out her phone and called Lottie Mann's direct landline number. 'Boss,' she exclaimed.

To her surprise, John Stirling answered. 'Jackie, sorry, the boss is busy; she's put her calls on divert.'

'What's she doing?'

'Having an early lunch from the looks of it. Two patrol cops from South Lanarkshire that she ordered in to talk to her about a possible hit and run. I can see in her office; they're standing she's sitting, which does not look good for them.'

'I know what that's about,' she said, 'and I hope they enjoy every moment. Since she's busy this is down to you, John, and it takes priority over whatever else you're doing. I'm about to go to the Later Era care home to arrest one of the owners on suspicion of attempted murder. I need uniforms there, soonest, to take her into custody. Also, if he's there, I'm going to detain her husband, Gregor Rutherford, for questioning over the possible hit and run that Lottie's savaging those two cops about. And also because he's a cunt,' she added, gratuitously. 'We won't put that on a charge sheet, but I doubt that his wife ever acts alone. If he's not there I want him located . . . maybe at one of the other two homes. While that's happening I need an urgent warrant from any sheriff you can find, to let us search all three Later Era homes for illegally held drugs.'

'I'll do all that, Jackie,' he promised. 'At once. Now you do something for me.'

'Okay, if it doesn't take long.'

'It won't. I want you to take a deep breath, calm down and get a hold of yourself. I can hear the anger in your voice. When you arrest these people, you need to do it calmly. You say one word to them that could prejudice their trial . . .'

Even as he spoke, Wright felt the tension begin to ease out of her as she acknowledged the truth of his words. She realised, for the first time in their brief acquaintance, how much she liked John Stirling.

'Absolutely,' she sighed. 'You're right and I'm doing that right now. The arrests will be by the book. That doesn't mean that Gregor isn't a See You Next Tuesday, but I won't tell him, honest.'

'Good. Because while you've been working yourself into a lather, a specialist colleague and I have been looking at something that Sauce Haddock's had flown over to us from the Bahamas. It looks like a gold mine; it's Sandra's and all her stuff's accessible there. I've only just scratched the surface of what's in it, but already I've found something that you're going to love.'

Seventy-Eight

'Standing will be fine,' the detective chief superintendent said, from her chair, behind her desk, in the fish-tank office that was in full view of everyone in the busy CID squad room.

That was the moment at which Constable Drew Renwick, the senior of the two patrol officers, knew for certain that they had not been sent to Glasgow 'probably to pick up an urgent off-the-books parcel for the chief constable's wife,' as their station inspector, Grace Kelly, had suggested. His colleague, Constable Sanjeev Kohli, had not believed that for a second. He had read the current chief's biography on the police service website; that spoke for itself of his integrity. He glanced down at the triangular block on the desk. 'DCI Charlotte Mann.' *I think I've heard of her,* he thought, as he strove to keep his most innocent, wide-eyed expression on his face.

'Yes ma'am,' Renwick grunted. 'Would you like us to stand at attention?'

Her glare froze Kohli, even though it was focused on his colleague. 'No,' she growled. 'If you did that you'd probably strain muscles that you haven't used in years, and then go on the sick for a couple of weeks. What I want you to do is think back six months, to March and an RTA that you two attended on the road from Lanark to Biggar. A vehicle went off the road, a long straight road, and down a hillside. The only occupant was the driver, female, fifties; she was badly injured. Remember it, Constable Renwick?'

'Vaguely.'

The DCI leaned forward, with eyes so cold and a frown so deep that from Kohli's vantage point there could have been snow in its furrows. 'Vaguely?' she murmured. 'Vaguely?' The murmur became an incredulous bark. 'The woman went off the road, which had to be dry as it hadn't rained for a week before the incident with temperatures well above freezing, up a small grass bank, took out a three strand wire fence, and turned over several times before coming to rest in a small copse of trees. You know where I got that description?' she snapped. 'From the victim herself, and from a report by an insurance company assessor. Where I should have got it, Mr Renwick, is from your incident report. But I didn't, because that's a mere twelve words long. "Attended. No other vehicle or persons involved. Driver, female, removed to hospital." That's it.' The icy eyes fixed even more firmly on Renwick. 'Is your memory a bit less vague now?'

'Okay yes,' he conceded.

'Okay yes, what?'

'Okay yes, ma'am,' the constable muttered.

Just when Sanjeev Kohli thought it was safe to take a breath, her attention turned to him. 'And you, Constable? No, your cloak of invisibility isn't working. I can actually see you. What's your recollection of the incident?'

He gulped. 'The same as my colleague, ma'am.'

'How do you know that? He hasn't told me anything yet. What's your recollection?'

'Can I refer to my notebook, ma'am?'

The frown relaxed, became less deep. 'Does it go that far back?'

'The current one no, but I brought the one before as well . . . just in case, like.'

'Okay, dig it out and tell me what it says about the incident.'

Not daring even to glance at Renwick, whom he could sense was quivering with anger, Constable Kohli produced two notebooks from a pouch in his tunic, inspected them, held on to one and returned the other. 'Give me a minute, please, ma'am,' he murmured.

She nodded.

'Here it is,' Kohli said, then began to read. 'Called to a reported RTA at seventeen forty-two, A73. Informant was a householder whose dwelling overlooked the scene. No skid marks on road, but found a break in the fence. Vehicle at foot of a steep slope. Wedged between two trees by small river, with severe damage. CR . . . Constable Renwick, ma'am . . . ordered me to check. CR remained by police car. On inspection found female driver severely injured, apparently unconscious. Summoned ambulance and remained with driver until arrival, and as she was removed by paramedics. Driver recovered consciousness during removal. Immediately sedated by paramedic. Spoke with householder, Mr Gordon McLennan, male, elderly; home other side of wee river, near vehicle position. Advised he had seen vehicle rolling down hill, unable to render assistance because of age and river. Assisted with physical removal of victim on stretcher. Returned to LPS . . . Lanark Police Station, ma'am . . . CR submitted report. That's it ma'am.'

'Was it you who told the paramedics that the driver had fallen asleep at the wheel?' Mann asked.

Kohli shifted on his feet.

'No ma'am,' Renwick said. His posture had altered, from aggressive to submissive. 'That was me. I took a good look at the road while I was waiting for the ambulance. There was no sign of her trying to stop at all. If she had, the fence posts would likely have been strong enough to keep her from going through it.'

Mann's glare returned. 'That was the extent of your investigation, was it? You never considered any other possibilities before you made your twelve-word report?'

'Such as, ma'am?' the constable protested. 'There were no other possibilities.'

'Wrong, there was one: that she might have been forced off the road by another vehicle. Because,' Mann paused to let her words sink in, 'that's what the victim's saying now.'

'How were we . . ?'

'To know that,' she exclaimed, 'when she was sedated for weeks after the accident? Only one way, and that would be by interviewing her. But you never did. Nobody did. A potential attempted murder's gone un-investigated for six months because you submitted a report that was disgracefully inadequate, yet your senior officers didn't spot that and follow it up.'

'I submitted my report, ma'am, to my station inspector. Ask him why it was never followed up.'

'How would he have done that?' she barked, her fire refuelled. 'There was nothing in it. What was her name?'

'Pardon ma'am?'

'What was the driver's name? Your RTA report doesn't even include that. What was the vehicle registration number?' Her eyes latched on to Kohli. 'I bet you know, Constable.'

His gulp was both audible and visible. He reopened his notebook. 'The vehicle registration was Sierra Mike seven three Juliet Zulu Uniform, ma'am,' he read, with an apologetic glance to his left. 'Registered to a Christine McGhee. I did a DVLA check when I was waiting for the ambulance. But it's my fault,' he added. 'I didn't mention it to Drew, er, Constable Renwick.'

'You shouldn't have had to mention it,' she retorted. 'Renwick was the senior officer. Identifying vehicle and driver's a no-brainer; which begs the question, does he have . . .' Mann stopped in mid-sentence. 'Dismissed, both of you. Kohli, you take the vehicle you came in back to Lanark. Renwick, I'm opening a disciplinary into this. You stay here and report to the office directly below this one, where you'll be interviewed by officers from Professional Standards. They'll decide whether you should be suspended or not.' She looked at Kohli. 'You don't get a free pass on this,' she told him. 'As far as I can see you did most things right, but you'll still need to be interviewed. Not today, though; get on your way now. Renwick, wait in the outer office for a couple of minutes, to let him get clear. There should be no further contact between the two of you until this is sorted.'

Soon as Renwick had left the squad room, she stepped out of her office in search of fresher air. The window had been slightly open but three people in its confined space had been at least one too many. As she moved towards the refreshment table, coffee in mind, Stirling was ending a call. 'Thanks,' she heard him say. 'I'll have it picked up.'

'What?' she asked.

'A search warrant for the three Later Era care homes. We're looking for any drugs that shouldn't be there. Jackie's got grounds to arrest the Rutherford couple on suspicion of attempted murder, and she's doing that now. I've asked Maya, and two other DCs to get down there, search Biggar first, then do the other two.'

Mann nodded. 'Proper,' she murmured. 'And we can link them with Sandra Bulloch, yes?'

'Very much so, boss, given what we've found on her computer.'

'You got into it that fast?'

'The IT guys have an AI system that generates likely passwords,' he said, nodding to his specialist colleague, who was at a separate table leaning over the iMac. 'One of them worked. With that and the mould of her fingerprint that we had done, he cracked it. I'll . . .'

As he spoke the DCI's ringtone sounded. She checked the caller, raised a hand in apology to Stirling, and returned to her office. 'Sir,' she murmured as she closed the door behind her. 'I wasn't expecting . . .'

'I know,' Bob Skinner said. 'Is this a bad time?'

'Ten minutes ago it would have been,' she replied, 'but I'm clear now.'

'What were you up to?'

'I was reaming a couple of uniforms, one in particular, for something that might just have put us on Sandra Bulloch's trail six months ago, if it had been properly followed through.' She explained the circumstances of Chris McGhee's near fatal accident and the reason for the delay in their discovery.

'Not good,' he agreed. 'I could say that would never have happened in my day, but I'd be kidding both of us. Of course it did; you can't root out all the wormy apples. Who does this go back to? The station inspector, obviously.'

'Yes, and maybe her boss too, a superintendent called Murphy.'

'Ah,' Skinner exclaimed. 'I remember him from my Strathclyde time. He was on my hitlist but I wasn't there long enough. He'll likely wriggle out of the professional standards complaint, but if you give Mario McGuire all the details, he'll make sure that what's for him doesn't go past him.'

'I hope so,' Mann said. 'It's the second time we've encountered something like this on this investigation.'

'Then make sure Mario knows,' he repeated. 'Neil McIlhenney's facing manpower cuts. I know he's keen on using that to get rid of the dead wood, and hold on to the best people.' He laughed. 'Those two; the stuff they tell me, I'm sure they forget that I'm a working journalist these days.'

She smiled. 'Should I be talking to you?' she asked.

'No, you should be listening to me. Being a working journalist is actually a lot like being a detective. You investigate things and find answers maybe quicker than you would if you wore some of the handcuffs that cops have to.'

'You mean search warrants and the like? My DS Stirling's just had to pull one of those to look for evidence against a couple whose names came up in the Bulloch inquiry. We might have been able to exercise hot pursuit searches, but with defence counsel involved, and some of the judges we have these days, no way would I chance that. Still,' she added, 'you're talking to a seriously satisfied officer because once it is all done, and all the bits are fitted together, we may very well have found Sandra's killers. They're prime suspects at the very least.'

'Oh,' Skinner said, in a tone that curbed her enthusiasm, instantly. 'I hate to spoil your day, Lottie, and maybe I'm not going to, but, going back to my new role and the freedom of action it gives me, I've been using a resource of mine to chase, let's call it this story. On the basis of what he's told me, the people you're talking about aren't your only prime suspects. Let me fill you in on what my guy's discovered.'

Seventy-Nine

'Was all that necessary?' Gregor Rutherford demanded. 'Handcuffing us like common criminals and marching us out of our own properties, in front of our staff and our clients? And bringing us to Glasgow? What's that about?'

'Standard procedure,' Wright told him, calmly, 'in any homicide investigation.'

'Homicide?' he exclaimed. 'You're having a laugh.'

'We don't do stand-up here,' the DS said, 'as Ms DaCosta will confirm.'

Lottie Mann gazed at the live feed from the interview room as it played on her computer screen. John Stirling was beside her, seated on a chair in a space that was barely big enough to accommodate it. The images came from a camera set high on the wall behind a table at which sat five people. On one side, facing the lens, Gregor and Amina Rutherford, flanking their lawyer, Johanna DaCosta; on the other, Jackie Wright and Maya Smith.

'Who's the solicitor?' Stirling asked.

His boss corrected him. 'Solicitor Advocate. She's an associate of Alex Skinner KC, newly installed. She works out of Alex's office. Ms DaCosta might act as her junior in a really big criminal case, but mainly she operates independently.'

'Are you saying this isn't a big case?'

'No I'm not. It may very well become one, but Alex won't be involved in it.'

'Why not?'

'Too close to her dad.'

'She's . . .?'

'Yes, now shut up, listen and learn. You're here to learn, just like Maya is, in that room.'

As a whispered conversation between lawyer and clients ended, DaCosta looked across the table. 'Mr and Mrs Rutherford are confused about the reason for their arrest, DS Wright. Will you enlighten them? Also, what Mr Rutherford was trying to say was that it seemed to be precipitate. Can you explain that also?'

'Of course,' Wright assured her. 'I'll deal with the second question first. We moved to arrest Mrs Rutherford because we have evidence that two days ago, she attempted to murder one of the residents in the company's Later Era residential home in Biggar, Mrs Sally Crawford, aged ninety-two, by injecting her with morphine. As I'm sure you know, that's a controlled drug to be administered only on the instruction of a physician, and by a medical professional.'

'I'm a doctor!' Amina Rutherford protested. Nothing showed in DaCosta's eyes but she leaned to her left and whispered in her client's ear.

Mann could only imagine Wright's smile, but she knew it was there as she replied. 'Only in India, and even there your degree's only in alternative medicine. By the way, as I'm sure you've just been told, it's never a good idea to incriminate yourself this early in an examination. Are you saying that you injected her, because you're qualified to do so? If you are, that defence didn't do Dr Shipman too much good.'

'I am saying nothing.'

'I'm not asking you to, for now. I'll continue, will I? We believe, Ms DaCosta, that your client did this with a degree of urgency that was triggered by my visit to Mrs Crawford earlier that day. I went there to talk to her about her niece, Sandra Bulloch, and a visit she paid to her in early March. Staff at the home denied any knowledge of this, but it happened. This is proved by the home's visitor registration book, which we've seized as evidence.' She paused. 'That's charge one. The second relates to the illegal possession of morphine and midazolam, discovered in searches under warrant of the Rutherfords' three establishments. It's our intention to charge both of your clients with that. That's already been authorised by the fiscal, as has the attempted murder charge.'

DaCosta nodded. 'Charges to which they will respond in due course, but for now it'll be no comment.'

'Fair enough,' Wright agreed. 'But there's more: modern slavery, tax fraud, coercion. The Crown Office hasn't worked out all the charges yet, but trust me they will follow.'

'Noted,' the solicitor advocate said. 'Still, those charges don't explain Mr Rutherford's speedy arrest.'

'They don't. But I'll get there. What I propose to do now is to play a voice recording that's been recovered from Cloud storage on a computer owned by Sandra Bulloch, whose murder we are also investigating. When you've heard it, Mr and Mrs Rutherford, I'll let you have a private discussion with Ms DaCosta to consider your response. DC Smith, if you would . . .'

A laptop computer sat on the table. Maya Smith opened it, scrolled through its contents, clicked on a file and leaned back. Looking on remotely, Lottie Mann smiled. 'Listen to this, John,' she murmured. 'It'll be like throwing a hand grenade into a loch.'

'Mr and Mrs Rutherford.' Another voice was picked up by the

microphone in the interview room; mature, strong and confident. 'Thanks for meeting with me.'

'Fair enough,' Gregor Rutherford, disembodied, was heard to say. 'But we're short of time, so get on with it.'

'I will, but time won't be an issue. I'm your top priority. You know me as Alexandra Vernon, the name under which I visited Later Era Biggar. In fact my real name is Sandra Bulloch, I'm a former police officer, detective chief inspector, and I'm the niece of Mrs Sally Crawford, one of your oldest residents. I've lived in the Bahamas for the last five years, but I've been touring Europe on business for the last few months, with Scotland as my last stop. I'd been planning to visit Aunt Sally anyway, but then I had a message from my cousin Christine, her stepdaughter and her legal next of kin. What she told me made me change my plans. Instead, I became Alexandra Vernon, a name that I use for business purposes, and signed in as her when I visited. While I was there I kept my eyes open, I observed a few things and I asked a couple of questions of staff. They brushed me off; they all told me the same story, that they were not allowed to speak with family members or any other visitors. While I was asking those questions, I had one of Chris's observations in mind. Every person I spoke to was of African origin, apart from the assistant manager at Biggar, who was Indian. His name is Hardeep and I've discovered that he's your nephew, Mrs Rutherford. You have a big family; the assistant managers at your other two homes are his brother and sister. That one visit told me that Chris was right. Once a cop always a cop, and so I followed up on her concerns. I put each of your homes under observation, watching staff arrive and leave. I saw that apart from your family members, all of them were indeed African, and remarkably that they all lived in the same three places, each one a former council house with only basic modernisation. I was able to speak with a few of them. Three of them told me how things really are, about their contracts, the slave wages they're paid, the temps that are brought in when they get advance warning of visits by the Care Protection Agency. Those eighteen Africans and your family members are all you've got as full-time staff. Bottom line, every one of those elderly clients you have, each one paying you a minimum of five grand a month, are being defrauded.' As Sandra Bulloch told her story, anger was mounting in her voice. She paused. When she resumed she was as calm as she had been at the outset. 'In case you think I can't prove this,' she continued, 'I can. When I was in the police I had a spell in Special Branch. I still have a contact in the Home Office, who gave me details of every visa that's been issued under your sponsorship. I still have another in HMRC, who told me what you've been reporting as payments to your staff. Only you haven't been paying them anything like that. You've been putting them through the books on a minimum wage, but keeping half of their net earnings to cover accommodation. You disgust me, both of you. All of my instinct and all of the professionalism I have left makes me want to turn you in. But you know what? I don't intend to. If I did, and you were closed down, as you would be for sure, a hundred and fifty old people would be homeless. Those poor sods that you're exploiting with your bogus contracts and your threats would probably be deported. To avoid all that I've got another solution.'

She paused. There was silence, then a sound that could have been furniture, a chair, moving until Amina's voice was heard. 'No, Gregor no, sit down. You can't touch her. Someone will know she's here for sure. Let her continue.'

'Wise,' Sandra Bulloch said. 'You wouldn't like being tasered. Okay, this is it. You will sell your business, the company and the property it owns, to me. Effectively all that means is the bricks and mortar, because the business itself is so enmeshed in illegality that it's worth less than nothing. I know what you paid for the properties; that's on the Land Register. That's my offer; non-negotiable, take it or take it. When you're gone, I'll put managers in place to run the three homes properly. I'll continue the employment of the present staff, with proper pay and conditions, and hire as many additional workers as it takes to give the clients the service that they and their families are paying for. That's it. I'll instruct my lawyers, James Bonar and Marco Gialini, to complete the deal. One of them'll be in touch within a week. As of tomorrow, you will hire agency workers to bring the staffing levels immediately up to what they should always have been. Meeting over. I'll see myself out.'

The interview room fell silent. Mann in her office, grinned at her sergeant. 'Game and set,' she said, 'but there's a bit to go in the match.'

Wright's voice cut across her. 'That's it, Ms DaCosta, the foundation of our case against your clients. We've got no grounds to hold Mrs Rutherford's family members, or any evidence against them. However, by now they'll have been suspended by the managers that the Care Protection Agency has sent in to take over the running of the three places. That's an unusual thing for them to do, but this is an unprecedented situation. Do your clients have anything to say at this stage?'

'If they follow my advice, my advice would be not to comment, but . . .'

'Absolutely,' Gregor Rutherford exclaimed. 'We're saying nothing.'

His lawyer put a hand on his arm, but he shrugged it off, angrily.

'Behave yourself,' Wright warned, 'or you'll be back in handcuffs. What were you going to say, Ms DaCosta?'

'I was going to ask whether you have any actual evidence, other than that recording, which was I suspect made without my clients' knowledge.'

'Oh yes,' the DS said. 'DCI Bulloch was a good officer. All of that's documented on her computer, including the Home Office visa list. I should tell you also that as soon as the arrests were made our officers began to interview the staff. Once they were promised that they wouldn't be deported and that they'd stay in post with better wages and conditions, they started . . . what's the phrase? . . . singin' like linties. Good luck with the plea in mitigation, Johanna. Can I go on with my story now? Because we're not done, far from it.'

'Please do.' Mann, looking on, suspected that the solicitor advocate's interest was moving beyond professional.

'A few days after that recording was made . . . I'm taking that from the date of the upload to the computer . . . Sandra Bulloch was murdered. This was not discovered for six months, because her body was hidden in her motor home. Three months ago that was moved to a location in Ayrshire. It took that long for it to be opened. Two weeks after the recording, maybe ten days after Ms Bulloch's murder, her cousin, Christine McGhee, who blew the whistle on the residential home, and knew the broad outline of Sandra's findings, was driving on the A73 late one evening, when she went off the road, in good weather conditions and was severely injured. For reasons I can tell you are being investigated internally by our performance standards department she wasn't interviewed until a couple of days ago, by me. At that time she told me that she'd been run off the road by a large black vehicle. There was one witness to the incident, a householder a few hundred yards from the road, who called it in. He wasn't formally interviewed either, until this afternoon. This all happened six months ago, so his memory just can't be a hundred per cent but his recollection now is that there was another vehicle on the road when Mrs McGhee went off.'

'Not reliable though, as you say,' DaCosta observed.

'No,' Wright agreed, 'but: Mrs McGhee's car hasn't been pulped yet, because the insurance claim hasn't been settled. Insurers being insurers, Mrs McGhee's are doing their best to find her at fault. The vehicle's been recovered. It'll be taken to the police resource centre in North Lanarkshire, where our specialists are going to examine it for traces of paint from another vehicle. I believe that Mr Rutherford drives a black Range Rover. Tomorrow morning, again with a warrant from the sheriff, we're going to look at his bank statements and invoices to see whether he had any bodywork repairs done.'

The camera feed was high definition; viewing, Mann and Stirling saw the colour drain from Gregor Rutherford's face. As it did, his wife leaned forward glaring past their lawyer and at him.

'You idiot,' she wailed. 'You told me that we didn't need to worry any longer, but you didn't say that you'd done anything as reckless as that. Someone scraped you in Sainsbury's car park you said.' She looked across the table, towards the two detectives. 'Sergeant Wright,' she said, urgently. 'Yes, I injected that woman, but I did it because Gregor told me to. Old or not, he said, she was still a credible witness. I knew nothing about any road accident and I know nothing, I promise you about the death of the Bulloch person. But I cannot speak for Gregor, he is reckless and he is dangerous and he is capable of anything.'

'Mr Rutherford,' DaCosta exclaimed, as he moved towards his wife and before Wright could intervene, 'it's in your best interests that you do and say nothing at all.'

Eighty

'Was that a result or what, Sauce?' Mario McGuire exclaimed, looking at Haddock on screen, part of him trying to recall what the world had been like without Zoom and WhatsApp. 'Nailed to the fucking wall by Sandra Bulloch, God bless and keep her. Between us, she never pulled one like that when she was a serving cop.'

'Possibly because she never had the chance,' he replied. 'Does that mean you'll reimburse me for the cost of an intercontinental overnight air courier? Even Cheeky raised her eyebrows when I told her.'

'I think I can get the CFO to sign off on that one; after all, I am the deputy chief and she does report to me. You enjoy the rest of your holiday with Cheeky, and golfing with your new mate. All this stuff apart, you deserve it; you've been working like a dog for a while, without a break. And a word of advice: don't make any more calls to the office. This one's not done yet. Lottie and the team are doing a great job in Glasgow, and Tarvil Singh's looking after your patch in Edinburgh. Let them get on with it, without them feeling that you're looking over their shoulders.'

'Yeah fine,' Haddock agreed. 'Where do they go from here though? Will they ever prove that the Rutherford man killed Sandra to shut her up.'

'Dunno,' McGuire admitted. 'It all fits, the dates, the stuff on the computer, two attempted murders to cover up the way they were running their homes. They're in court tomorrow for the attempted murder of Sandra's Auntie Sally; he'll be remanded to prison for sure. She might get bail, as she's going to plead guilty and incriminate him. Gregor, not a chance. As well as the Christine McGhee charge, which still depends on Gartcosh finding paint traces on her car to corroborate what the wife said, plus the likely immigration and tax fraud charges, Lottie's looking into the disappearance of a Nigerian man, Francis Okolie. He had an argument with Gregor one day, and was never seen again. And yes, he is well in the frame for Sandra. He could have followed her to the motor home and killed her. Their home in Ayrshire has plenty of ground around it; Wright's suggesting that he could have stashed it there for a while.'

'On his own property?' Haddock asked, sceptically.

'I know,' the DCC admitted. 'He's not a deep thinker by all accounts, but yes, I hear what you're saying. There's also the consideration that if he did, then the mood Mrs Rutherford's in right now, she'd have shopped him in a heartbeat. One thing's for sure though. If he did follow Sandra from that confrontation, he didn't kill her that night. We know that because she returned her hire car in Hamilton the next day. If it was him, he used public transport to get back to Strathclyde Park, so that he could drive the motor home away.'

'Or he had an accomplice?'

'Not the wife, for certain.'

'How about the missing man, Francis?'

'Mmm. A line of enquiry that I will suggest tactfully to DCI Mann.'

'Without mentioning me, I hope.'

'Absolutely fucking not, Sauce, absolutely not. Any other bright ideas?'

'Just the one. Sandra was planning to go home when she died. How?'

'We may have covered that,' McGuire said. 'I'll enquire and if not, it'll be done, as my suggestion again.'

'Cheers,' Haddock chuckled. 'Good luck with nailing Rutherford to the wall.'

'Mmm. That's if it's him. Thing is, Sauce, there's more than one dog in the race.'

'What? How the hell did that come about?'

The DCC smiled, and shook his head. 'Inevitably,' he said, 'we have to thank Bob Skinner. Lottie asked me if I wanted to be involved when she interviews the other person of interest. This one's no reckless clown like Rutherford. This one's on a different level, altogether. But I told her no, she should deal with it, her and Jackie Wright. It's her show, all the way to the end.'

Eighty-One

DC Maya Smith was still tingling with excitement, in the aftermath of her initiation in the interview room during a serious crimes investigation. When she had been posted to the Glasgow office after a year as a local CID officer in Galashiels, she had been full of self-doubt.

She had heard of Detective Superintendent Haddock, and of DI Tarvil Singh, but only on the police grapevine, after the spectacular arrest of a suicide bomber that the pair had made together. The other members of the squad were unknown to her, but she assumed they would all be high flyers. One of the uniforms in her office, a veteran sergeant had warned her to look out for Lottie Mann. A formidable woman he had said, and still a legend for once attempting to chuck Bob Skinner out of a crime scene.

'I was bricking it,' Maya had told her mother, after the first day of her new job. 'But it was all right. Everybody was really friendly. DCI Mann was just back from Spain, not from holiday, from an assignment there that nobody either knew much about or was about to discuss with a newbie. And Sauce Haddock came through from Edinburgh.'

'Sauce?' her mum had exclaimed.

'That's what they call him, although I heard another DC call him Sherpa. He said it was because he's climbed the ladder so fast. He was there to catch up with DCI Mann, but he said hello to me too. He made me feel that he was there just to welcome me, although I know that he couldn't have been. There was another guy too, a DS called John Stirling. Well, nearly new, he started a week ago. Quite fanciable, actually, but I think I heard him mention a girlfriend.'

She was still uncertain of his status as she walked over to his desk, although they had moved on to a first-name basis. 'John,' she said. 'Do you know if the boss is in?'

'Not,' he replied. 'She and Jackie are on their way to Fife.'

'Fife? Why Fife?'

'To interview someone. That's all she said: she was unusually coy about it, and I know better than to press her. Why are you asking?'

'The job that she gave me last night. I've got a result. Sandra Bulloch had a flight booked back to the Bahamas, British Airways, business class, one way but flexible on March the sixteenth, via Heathrow.'

'As Sandra Bulloch, not Alexandra Vernon?'

'Bulloch.'

'Well done you,' the DS said, with a glance that made her feel good. 'That would fit with her promise to visit Gordon Pollock in London. March the sixteenth,' he repeated, 'two days after we think the motor home left the site at Strathclyde Park.'

'Should I ask BA to check whether . . .' she began in a flood of enthusiasm, before his smile made her stop short.

'Whether she caught the flight?' he suggested. 'That would have been difficult if she was dead, and by March the sixteenth she probably was.'

She felt the colour rush to her cheeks. 'Oh Christ,' she moaned. 'I'm so dumb.'

'No you're not,' Stirling assured her. 'Technically she could have taken her flight, then flown back a couple of days later to meet her . . .'

'Her death,' Smith said.

'I was going to say her appointment with fate, but I do have a tendency to over-dramatise. Look, Maya, cover yourself against a fussy fiscal by confirming that she never caught it, and after that . . .' He hesitated.

'What?' she asked.

'Do you fancy a bite of lunch?'

Eighty-Two

As he opened the heavy wooden door of his baronial home, Charles Baxter's expression was one of weary forbearance. 'Good day to you Chief Inspector Mann,' he said. 'I hope you had a pleasant journey.'

'We did,' she replied. 'The roads were relatively quiet.'

'I don't think I've met your colleague.'

'There's no reason why you should have. Detective Sergeant Jackie Wright.'

'Charmed,' Baxter murmured, extending his right hand in a way that made the detective unsure whether she was expected to shake it or kiss it.

'That said, your face is familiar,' he continued. 'Have we actually met? Is that possible?'

'A dinner,' she replied, 'a year ago, a professional awards bash, one of those dos where people say nice things about each other laced with acid, a few awards are handed out then everyone gets pissed.'

'I couldn't have put that better myself,' he conceded. 'What took you there? Was someone under investigation?'

'My partner took me,' Wright explained. 'Kate Gardner: she'd just become a partner in another practice: much smaller than yours, though.'

He frowned. 'Kate, Kate, Kate,' he muttered. 'Oh yes, I know who you mean. I remember seeing you two at that bash now. A few of the boys were quite surprised. A bit of a dish, your Kate.'

'A bit of a dish,' she repeated. 'Is that your way of saying it's a pity she's gay?'

'Absolutely not!' He laughed, but it was forced, making it clear that she had hit the mark.

'*Good for you, Jackie,*' Mann thought. '*Unsettle the smug, sexist bastard.*'

'Come on in,' Baxter said, moving on as quickly as he could and leading them into the house. 'Let's use the living room; my study would be a bit tight. Lydia's out, I'm afraid; our Josephine has a school hockey match. Her mum and her brother are great supporters. I'm trying to persuade her to follow me and play rugby, but no luck so far. I was a Scotland cap, you know.'

The DCI nodded. 'I did know that. Sir Robert Skinner told me he saw your entire international career, all twenty minutes of it.'

'*Twist the knife, Lottie,*' Wright thought.

'Yes, too bad that,' he sighed, glumly. 'I picked up a knee injury in that short period. I was never the same again. Otherwise,' he implied. 'All that's history, though,' he continued. 'What's this visit about?' The faux laugh again. 'Do I need a lawyer?'

'Not yet,' Mann replied, summoning her best deadpan, wiping the smile from his face. 'I'll stop the interview if we get to that stage.'

'Best get on with it then,' Baxter said sharply, as they sat. 'What's it about?'

'Sandra Bulloch.'

The mention of the name seemed to freeze him for a second. 'What about her?' he murmured, cautiously.

'We'd like to know what you spoke about when she visited you here on the tenth of March.'

'What makes you think she did that?'

Jackie Wright intervened. 'We don't think, Mr Baxter, we know that she did. You don't have the maker's name beside it, but your security camera is fairly obvious. It's monitored too, as all three of us know. With these systems the surveillance footage is always stored, not on site but remotely.' She pointed upwards. 'In the Cloud.'

'Confidentially, surely.'

'Sir,' the DS said. 'We're investigating a murder. In these circumstances we can look pretty much anywhere.'

'I can imagine, but why look here, why look at me and why look at my home.'

'Because,' Mann intervened, 'when you told me that you hadn't seen Ms Bulloch, I didn't quite believe you. Your office manager did run a check for me and assured me that she hadn't been there, but I didn't leave it at that. Your office has visible security, so I ran a check with the same supplier and found that you were a private client too, both here and at your fuck-pad in Glenfinlas Street.'

'Wait a . . .'

She cut off his protest. 'A one bedroom flat two minutes' walk from your office, registered to the firm. One minute from the Cambridge Bar . . . yes, that one, not the other . . . where my colleague Tarvil was told you are a regular, with a number of lady companions, none of them called Lydia. Do we have your full attention now?' He glared at her. 'Good. Under a warrant from the sheriff we checked the stored surveillance from last March, at both addresses, Edinburgh and here, and we found very clear footage of Sandra Bulloch, arriving here on the evening of March the tenth. You lied to me, Mr Baxter. It's so annoying when somebody does that. It wastes time, it costs manpower and money, and frankly it insults me that folk think I'm not going to find out anyway.'

'*Mea culpa*,' Baxter growled.

'Why did she visit you?'

He shook his head. 'This is where we're getting into lawyer territory.'

'No, we're not, because you haven't been cautioned or charged. You don't have a right to a solicitor, but you do have the right to refuse to answer my questions.'

'Which I will exercise.'

'Fair enough. I'd anticipated that you would, so I'll tell you what I know. Sandra was island-bound for well over three years, until she started to spread her wings. First it was the US, under the pretext of following a golf pro she knew. I say pretext because something linked every venue. Then, a year ago, she decided to come back to Europe, bought a motor home, and invited Gordon Pollock . . . Leo Speight's son, remember . . . to join her on a winter tour of Europe. They visited several cities, apparently at random but again with a link. In every one of them, Sandra owned property, office buildings that you manage for her. When the two of them, she and Gordon, were in Luxembourg, he heard her say something along the lines of, "I must ask him about that". She didn't say who "he" was but I think it's a racing certainty it was you. These property holdings were part of her inheritance; the most significant part as it happens, because they're well sheltered. The North American properties and the European ones are each owned by limited companies wholly owned in turn by

Sandra and registered in tax friendly environments. Each company is managed on her behalf by LJMcF. With that in mind, we can't know for sure why she visited you that night, but I doubt that she'd driven all that way just to look you up. She was a private person. She didn't do social calls. So?'

'So you're correct,' Baxter sighed. 'Well done, detectives. My client, Ms Bulloch, wanted a meeting. The tenth of March was a Sunday and she was tight for time on her trip, so I suggested that she come to the house rather than have me go all the way into Edinburgh.'

'What did you discuss?'

'She wanted a briefing on her portfolio, as simple as that. I gave her a rundown on rental income, property values in every location, and there are several. Leo invested the bulk of his career earnings in commercial property; what was shown in the will was only around twenty per cent of his real wealth. The will was legal though, everything that had to be declared was. Mrs Herbert, the Glasgow lawyer made damn sure of that.' He shifted in his chair, readying himself to stand. 'If that's it . . .'

'Not quite,' Mann said. 'I knew all that before we walked in here. We've been given access to research that someone else has done, on our behalf. He's actually looked inside those two entities, what are they called? Speight of Hand Inc and Speight of Hand SARL. He's come across several property disposals in the portfolio, each one of them in a location that Sandra visited in her travels. He's a clever guy so he went further. He established what properties were selling for per square metre in each place, at the time of each sale. Having done that it was clear to him that each of those office blocks was sold at well below market value. Not only that; further investigation showed that the buyers had one thing in common. Every single one of them is a client of

LJMcF. Sandra Bulloch was a resourceful woman, Mr Baxter; plus, as this investigation has shown us, she was a better cop than she was ever given credit for. With Special Branch experience during her career, she had skilled contacts all over the place. So?' she continued. 'Did she work your scam out for herself and confront you with it? Maybe yes, maybe not, but she did prepare and leave behind on her computer an agenda for her visit to you. It doesn't prove that she knew, but it does show that she wanted answers to every one of the awkward questions.' She stopped, for breath it seemed.

Wright filled the gap. 'It might also explain,' she said, 'why the video shows that Sandra was calm when she arrived, when she left her body language was completely different. She was angry, furious. She more or less ran to her car and drove away.'

'I told her nothing,' Baxter snapped. 'She didn't know who the buyers were but she'd guessed well enough. So what? It's history now.'

'I'm afraid it's not, sir.' Mann was suddenly formal. 'No accusation has been made against you personally, and even if it was, it's clear that no offences have been committed on our jurisdiction. But,' she added, 'my senior officers . . . I hate the word superior; it's rarely appropriate . . . they feel obliged to pass the material that we have on to their colleagues in Europol, and to the FBI. They're pretty much bound to talk to the head office of LJMcF. If anyone at that level was party to this, they'll have to answer for it, to Sandra's estate at the very least but probably to the court. If nobody was in the know, you're on your own, Mr Baxter. Now,' she exclaimed, 'we're at the point where you probably do need a lawyer. I suggest that you find a very good one.'

He had sunk back into his chair. 'You're enjoying this, aren't you?' he whispered.

The DCI shook her head. 'No, I'm not. Really I'm not, because I don't care about you. Not one tiny bit. People like you, you're the sort of pond life that'll probably survive the next mass extinction event. You and your company, you'll probably slither out of this. No, there's only one more thing that still does interest me. We're not going to discuss it here. When we do, you will have been cautioned and you will have a lawyer. But I'll tell you now, it's this.

'Why, after the video shows Sandra Bulloch driving off into the night, does it then show you tearing off after her, no more than a minute later like a bat out of hell? God,' Mann sighed, as she rose to her feet, 'I loved Meat Loaf.'

Eighty-Three

'He said he had a date in Edinburgh,' Mann told Mario McGuire. 'He said he was meeting one of his ladies in the Cambridge later on.'

'Do you believe him?' he asked.

'Dunno sir. I might have fed him the alibi with what I told him earlier. It could even be provable, if he had a booking, paid by card etc.'

'Maybe so, but even if he did, he might still have had time to follow Sandra back to the motor home, if that's where she went, and go back to take care of her later. Where it does muddy the water, the way the fiscal will see it, is by introducing our old friend Mr Reasonable Doubt. We now have two viable prime suspects, Gregor Rutherford and him. If we charge either one, his lawyer will be straight in there with a special defence of incrimination.'

'Yes, I know,' she agreed. 'Which of them would you bet on?'

'I can't answer that 'cause I haven't seen either of them. What do you think?'

'Honestly, sir,' she sighed, 'I don't know. It could be either. Gregor's a brute and Charles is a sociopath.'

'I'll tell you what,' the DCC said. 'Let's get a third opinion.'

'Sauce?'

'No, I've ordered him to take some proper leave. It'll be a video chat like everything seems to be these days . . . Lottie, this bloody job! I've got to get out more . . . but another perspective won't do any harm.'

'Ahh,' Mann exclaimed, with a rare grin. 'Him. I suppose he did help us, even though what his "researcher" did might have broken a few laws . . . all deniably of course. Maybe we do owe him some feedback. If he does have an opinion, there's no way we'd ever stop him throwing it into the mix.'

Eighty-Four

'Pasta's my secret vice,' Maya Smith confessed, as she looked around the busy restaurant, then down at her empty plate. 'I'd be embarrassed to show you my half of the kitchen cupboard. It's stacked with tins of Heinz Spaghetti Hoops, them and Heinz Ravioli.'

'Whose is the other half?' Stirling asked, as casually as he could.

'My flatmate. Janice.'

'Is she a cop too?'

'Hell no, she works for the council . . . sorry, the cooncil.'

'Are you and she . . .'

Her frown was puzzled. 'What do you mean?' As understanding dawned her eyes widened. 'Are you asking if we're a couple? Bloody hell, John, I know society's changing but it's still possible for two women to live together without being,' she paused, 'you know.'

'Sure it is, but as you say, these days. Jackie Wright's gay.'

'Is she?' Maya said. She looked down for a second or two. 'Would I have guessed that if you hadn't told me? Maybe I would, maybe not, but to be honest I doubt that I'd even have asked myself the question.' She looked him in the eye. 'Do you realise that in Woke culture you could be cancelled for asking me if I'm gay? People might say it displays your inherent homophobia.'

He grinned, and suddenly her day seemed a little brighter than it had before. 'Those who don't give a shit about such people,' he countered, 'and still have freedom of thought, would realise that it's just a means of clearing the ground. I chose the police as a career but I have a law degree; that question was gentle cross-examination.'

'If the charge is being a lesbian, I plead not guilty. If your next question was going to be, do I have a boyfriend? the answer is also no.' She leaned forward, elbows on the table. 'Now it's your turn in the witness box. What are you? Gay, straight or undecided? Sorry, questioning? That's what the Q stands for, isn't it?'

'No question: I'm straight.'

'Girlfriend?'

'If you'd asked me that a week ago I'd have said yes.'

'Aw,' she sighed. 'What happened?'

'Got dumped. She whisked me off to Millport for the night to tell me she was seeing someone else.'

'If a guy had taken me to Millport,' Maya observed, 'I'd have dumped him.'

'Hey,' he exclaimed, 'Millport's nice. It's not all cycling round the island. It's got the narrowest house in Scotland, and the smallest cathedral in the world, and,' he added, 'it's got the Crocodile Rock.'

She stared at him. 'Are you saying that Elton John wrote it there?'

'Naw, of course not. It's a rock painted to look like a crocodile.'

'Seriously?' she gasped. 'Then I rest my case. I'm really sorry about the break-up, though.'

'Don't be. The thing ran out of steam a while back; we'd become each other's handbags really. We both knew it; she said it first, that's all.'

'You're hurt.'

'I'm not.'

'You are.'

He broke off his study of a stain on the table cloth and looked her in the eye. 'An hour ago,' he murmured, 'maybe I was, just a wee bit. Now, I'm grateful to her.'

Maya felt her insides turn to jelly.

Eighty-Five

'Where are you, Bob?' McGuire asked. 'Is that the sea I can hear?'

'We're in L'Escala,' Skinner answered, 'and the doors are open, so yes, it is. What's up? Have you bearded Baxter yet?'

'Yes,' Mann confirmed. 'Jackie Wright and I cornered him in his lair in Fife and confronted him with all the stuff your man uncovered. Thanks to his lead our cyber-crime team's following the same trail, officially so to speak.'

'And Sandra?'

'We put our video evidence to him. He offered an alibi but even if it's genuine, it probably doesn't rule him out as a suspect.'

On screen, Skinner laughed, softly. 'That may be why he approached my daughter an hour ago, asking if she would represent him in, I quote, "certain as yet unspecified charges". She called me as soon as he had rung off.'

The DCC shifted in his chair, his heavy eyebrows coming together. 'What did she say? Has she taken him on?'

'She asked me if she should, and if I had any idea what the charges might be. It's the first time Alex has ever done that since she switched to criminal law. I told her that my perception is that any corporate fraud charges will be brought in other jurisdictions.

Baxter might have been panicking, but he's not dumb. He'll realise that too, so he must have been thinking about possible charges in relation to Sandra's murder. Is he in the frame? Really.'

Mann nodded. 'Oh yes, he is. We're looking at time frame. Even if he did have a date in Edinburgh, we're driving the route to determine whether he could have followed her to the caravan site and still made it back there. He's in our thoughts, most definitely.' She frowned. 'But he's not the only one. There's Rutherford, the care home owner.'

'Yes,' Skinner said. 'Alex told me that her associate Johanna's representing him. I warned her she shouldn't talk to me, or her, about it as I'm too close. For the same reason I advised her . . . I stopped telling her to do stuff when she was fifteen . . . that she should turn Baxter down. I can see your problem; two main suspects with no connection to each other. Which one do you make favourite?'

'What would you have done?' McGuire asked.

'I might have taken everything to the Crown Office, and let them make the decision.'

'And if they knocked it back?' Mann countered. 'My inclination is to focus on Rutherford. We've got him for running the lady off the road, and his wife's thrown him under the bus for drugging Sandra's aunt. Nothing doing on the missing man, Francis Okolie, though. The Home Office gave us his home details and police in Nigeria have established that he's home. Still, Gregor would be my choice. His motive for killing Sandra's probably stronger than Baxter's.'

'Plus Baxter's a pussy,' Skinner declared. 'I've met the man. You've met him Lottie. Is he capable of doing what was done to Sandra, then driving her vehicle back to his acreage in Fife, keeping it there for a few weeks, and then abandoning it, far away?'

'And cycling off into the dark after he's done it?' the DCI added.

'Yeah what about that too. No, Baxter's not the man, not for me. Rutherford yes, but . . .' he stopped.

'What, Bob?'

He sighed. 'Guys, you're so wrapped up in the chase that you're no longer focused on its origins. I wasn't at the crime scene but I've been at too many others. Every killing has its own characteristics. I look at this one and the first thing I see is rage, sheer uncontrollable rage, to do what was done to Sandra Bulloch, at the time of her death and afterwards. The blow to the head, the plastic bag to make sure she was dead, and afterwards, keeping her body as it rotted before leaving it to be found and hopefully, in the killer's mind, never to be identified. No way did Charlie Baxter do that. Rutherford? He'd kill her sure, to shut her up, but the rest of it? Really? No, he wouldn't have done it in anger, only because it was necessary.'

'Well?' McGuire challenged. 'Who?'

'I look at the cast list,' Skinner replied, 'and I can see only one person who fits my description. I keep coming back to her. Faye Bulloch. She's always been my prime suspect, folks.'

'You're right, Bob,' Lottie Mann declared. 'We've looked at her twice, but not closely enough. Bugger protocol, bugger corroboration. I'm going there right now, I'm going to face her down and I'm going to break her, once and for all. No smarmy wee lawyer holding her hand and telling her to keep her trap shut. Just her, just me.'

'Is that wise?' McGuire asked.

'Are you ordering me not to, sir?'

'No, I'm not.' He shook his head. 'You'd probably just ignore me anyway, just as I probably ignored Bob in the same circumstances. Go on, Lottie, end this thing.'

Eighty-Six

As Skinner headed for the door, heart set on a beer in his favourite beach-side bar . . . . if he and Sarah could find a table that was not occupied by people speaking bad Spanish or Catalan in even worse accents . . . he imagined the final confrontation between Lottie Mann and her adversary, the detective full of hell, Faye Bulloch full of bravado and probably smug, knowing that if the police had any evidence that she had killed her sister, as he was all but certain she had, she would have been arrested and charged already. It made him think of a movie from his childhood, *A Gunfight*, in which Johnny Cash had outdrawn Kirk Douglas . . . or had it been the other way round?

He was almost there when his phone sounded. He was about to reject the call, until he saw the ID onscreen.

'Raul,' he said. 'You're back?'

'Yes,' Sanchez said. 'And Inge has told me what happened. Remarkable, Bob, remarkable. We can't thank you enough for uncovering it all.'

'Not me alone,' he insisted. 'I had help; very good help.'

'Nevertheless, if you had not taken it on, the truth would never have been discovered.'

'It probably would, Raul. The outcome would have been different, that's all.'

'Fifteen years, Bob,' he exclaimed. 'Will Emil Blazquez really spend fifteen years in prison?'

'Nah,' Skinner chuckled, 'but he can think that for a while longer. The most he'll get will be about three, and that's really for giving terrorism a bad name. How does your wife feel about it?' he asked.

'She's happy that the threat is over. Her business has even won out of it. I told you they resigned the account after the second incident? Well they've got it back. Sancho Blazquez contacted Inge and Andrea, her partner. He began by apologising for his brother's misbehaviour. As you would expect the sale of the business collapsed as a result, so he has no choice but to carry on and rebuild its reputation. However he is an ambitious man, still. He doesn't want to carry on being a run of the mill maker of fizzy drinks; he wants to build his company into one of the biggest in Spain and beyond, across Europe. To do that, Sancho said, he needs their help. They agreed; a three-year contract with a performance bonus built in. Inge couldn't be more pleased, and it's down to you.'

'No,' he repeated, 'it's not. It's down to a couple of clever and unconventional young people. As I said, I was only the middle man.'

'Take the credit my friend, please. Inge wants to know: these young people would they be interested in a career in advertising?'

'One of them, certainly not. She's being promoted within my organisation. Where she'll go, I'm not quite sure yet, but we're keeping her. The other, he has special skills, and it may be that he'd be useful to Inge and Andrea, as a freelance researcher.'

'You can tell her about him, when we meet for dinner, which

we must do soon, the four of us. There is something else that we would like to discuss. This time, it does involve a family matter.'

'Oh,' Skinner murmured. 'That sounds ominous. What's my son been up to?'

'It's not your son,' Sanchez said, 'it's his mother.'

Eighty-Seven

In all the years that they had spent together, more of them as colleagues than as a couple, Dan Provan could not recall ever seeing Lottie so down and defeated, not even in the darkest days of her failed marriage to young Jakey's father. She was slumped in her chair, staring at nothing in particular; the drink in her hand was not her first of the evening.

'Let it go, love,' he said. 'Not even Muhammad Ali won them all.'

'No,' she whispered, 'but the ones where it really, really mattered, he did. And Leo, Leo Speight, he did win them all. Maybe if he hadn't, if he'd just been a run of the mill fighter who did okay, made a few quid and then retired, none of this stuff would have happened, and Sandra would still be alive. They might have got together, might not. Either way she'd be a chief super by now, running a division maybe, and he'd be . . . whatever he'd turned out to be. But that wasn't to be, she is dead and we still owe her.'

'We . . . you . . . the police . . . don't owe her any more than any other murder victim.'

''s not the argument,' she slurred. 'I was so sure. Skinner was so sure that it was her. And the fuckin' awful thing . . . she wished it had been. I put it to her; she hated her sister. Yes, she said. She

369

wanted her dead, I said. Yes, she said, so badly that it hurt. So badly that even when she was with a guy, and there's been a procession of them over the last five years, she would lie there on her back and think of ways of killing her, each one worse than the one before.'

'She must be a great shag,' Dan murmured.

'Shut up you,' she mumbled. 'I put it to her that when Sandra came back, when she turned up after all this time, she just couldn't contain herself. She went to her motor home, she hit her with an iron, she put a placky bag over her head, tied it and she watched her die. Then she moved the van somewhere and kept going back there like a ghoul, until she decided it was safe to let her be found. And you know what, Dan? Everything I put to her, every rock I put on her cairn she smiled, wider and wider, and nodded, harder and harder. And then she said, she said,

"Yes, I did all of that and a fucking lot more in my head, and how I wish I'd been able to do it for real. But,"

'Yes there was a fucking but,

"But I couldn't, not because I was afraid for myself, but for those two next door. If I had what would have happened to them. Gordon Pollock might have looked after them because he's their brother or his mousey wee mother might have, but most likely they'd have been the richest kids in the children's home. That's why I couldn't have done it."

'And you know what Dan?' Lottie said with tears in her eyes. 'I fucking believed her. I was wrong, Skinner was wrong. She didn't do it. We still owe Sandra; bottom line, she was one of us, and we've failed her.'

He shook his head. 'No, you haven't, lass. You still have two major suspects, Baxter and your man Rutherford . . . he sounds like a right psych to me.'

'He is, and we've got him on half a dozen charges, but we're nowhere near proving that he killed Sandra . . . even if it was him, which honestly, love, I doubt. As for Baxter, he's just a . . .' She shook her head and held out her glass. 'Give's a top-up. You never know, you might get lucky tonight.'

'What?' he chuckled, reaching for the almost empty bottle. 'While you lie on your back thinking of ways to fit up Faye Bulloch?' He refilled her glass, and picked up his own Peroni. 'It's done, love. Some we just don't win.' He paused, for more than a few seconds.

'You know,' he murmured, 'thinking about everything you've told me, there's one question that as far as I can see nobody's asked, far less answered. If Sandra was flying back to the Bahamas, via London, what the fuck was she going to do wi' that great big motor home?'

Eighty-Eight

John Stirling had never been one for self-analysis. He had been content for all the days that he could remember; he had never experienced unhappiness, other than when his Grandpa Maclean had died, and that had faded as he came to understand that it was part of the natural order of things that a person could expect to happen in the course of a lifetime. One day his parents would go too and while he had never anticipated that in his thoughts, he knew that he would cope.

But as he drove west, heading for the St Mirren stadium and the Buddies' clash with his own beloved Saints from Perth, he knew that there had been a sea-change in his existence. His perspective on life was altered, irrevocably; his mind was altered, even his physical being felt different. He had no need to search for the cause of this metamorphosis. He knew it and he rejoiced in it. Her name was Maya Smith, and she felt the same way. He had moved beyond contentment, beyond everyday happiness, a way beyond that state. He, Detective Sergeant John Stirling, LlB, was thoroughly, completely in love. Everything in his life was perfect. There was no way St Johnstone were going to lose that afternoon.

But first, there was the call he had to pay, before the match.

Leaving the motorway, he made two turns and reached his destination,

By most people's standards, Stirling thought as Maps told him he was there, Trudi Pollock's house was tiny, the smallest in the street. It sat at the end of a cul-de-sac on the outskirts of Paisley, a red sandstone bungalow with a very small front garden, blue pots on white gravel flanking the path to the front door. He remembered Gordon telling him that Leo Speight had bought it for his mother and him with his first meaningful ring earnings, after the hated Grandpa Pollock had gone to make closer acquaintance with the devil he had carried within him through life. 'She could move any time she liked, but she doesn't want to,' Gordon had said. 'The place ties her to my dad and him to her. Once, I suggested that she sell it; just the once, but never again. She's not very big, my mum, but by God she can be fierce.'

Stirling pressed the bell and waited, but not for long. Trudi opened the door within a minute, with a small gasp when she saw him on the step.

'Sergeant,' she exclaimed, smiling, 'I wasn't expecting . . .'

'I'm sorry to spring a surprise on you,' he said. 'I was hoping to catch Gordon. Something's come up in the investigation that I wanted to tell him about.'

'You've arrested somebody?' she asked. 'That man Baxter, that your colleague mentioned to Gordon?'

He shook his head. 'No, I'm afraid not. I can't discuss individuals, Trudi, as I'm sure you'll understand. That said, though, there are a couple of possibilities that are still very much open. But what I can tell you, as I was going to tell Gordon if he'd been here, is that Sandra's left a will. It was found in her house in the Bahamas. It's hand written, but it was witnessed by the estate manager, and the lawyers say it's absolutely legal.'

373

'My God,' Trudi gasped. 'Come on through. I'm in the middle of cooking.'

He followed her inside. She led them to the back of the house, and suddenly it was much bigger. It had been extended to the rear, to create a dining kitchen and living space that was bigger than the totality of the small rooms facing the street.

'The will,' she said, turning to face him. 'What's it got to do with me?' It occurred to him that it was the first time he had seen her without her florist's tunic. Yes, she wore an apron but it was tied round her waist, smeared with white flour and with the top of a large pair of kitchen scissors showing from a pocket in front.

'Technically it's got nothing to do with you, Trudi,' he said. 'It's Gordon. I shouldn't really be telling him this but he's going to find out quite soon anyway. He told me he was going back south, but since I was passing close by on the way to the football . . . Paisley Saints versus the Perth Saints, may my team win . . . I thought I'd call in and give him advance warning if he was still here.'

'Tchh,' she tutted, 'that's too damn bad. Gordon left an hour and a half ago. He'll be on the London plane by now. What does it say? The will?'

'Most of her estate goes to Leo's children,' Stirling replied, 'equally, in four parts. As Gordon's the only adult, he's named as trustee for the other three.'

'Bloody hell,' she exclaimed. 'Most of it, you said. What about the rest?'

'There's an individual bequest,' Stirling replied. 'Sandra had a man friend in the Bahamas, an American professional golfer. She's left him five million US dollars.'

Trudi Pollock seemed to stiffen. Her hand went to her throat and for an instant there shone in her eyes a flash of the purest rage, he thought, that he had ever seen. And then it was gone, so quickly that he thought he must have imagined it.

'I see,' she said, quietly. 'She's left five million of Leo's money to some guy, some stranger. And she thought she was doing me a favour when she said she was giving me her swanky German motor home, as if you need one of them in fucking Paisley. I think I'll need to process that, Sergeant.'

Stirling frowned. 'She was going to what?'

'I told you: give me her motor home. What a gracious lady Sandra was,' she murmured. 'Her fucking motor home, indeed! It came from my Leo, like everything else in her life. Her and her bloody sister came out the same pod right enough. Leeches, the pair of them.' She looked up at the detective. 'You know son, I think a medicinal glass of Sauvignon Blanc's called for. Would you like one?' she asked as she walked past him, towards a large fridge freezer.

'No, I'm good, thanks,' he murmured, inexplicably disturbed. 'Trudi,' he asked, 'when did she tell you that?' Stirling felt that he had stepped out of one world and into another, one where gentle bonhomie had been replaced by something dark and dangerous.

'The last time I saw her.'

'When was that?'

'Work it out.'

As her voice came from behind him Stirling replayed that moment earlier when her hand had gone to her throat, in a reflex gesture, feeling for something . . . something missing. Feeling for the silver chain, that she had worn in the shop, around her neck, half hidden by her tunic.

And there it was, on the work surface, before his eyes, with its adornment, a circle of shining silver. He picked it up and stared at it; the words 'Jeux d'Olympique' screaming at him.

He turned towards her. 'Trudi,' he murmured.

'Sorry, son,' she sighed. Left-handed, she threw the contents of a wine glass into his face. As he recoiled, instinctively, she plunged the kitchen scissors into his abdomen, and upwards, twisting them as hard as she could.

John Stirling's last breath left him in a great gasp. He stared at nothing, his blood spurting on to her white blouse as he brushed against her in his fall to the floor.

She stood over him, eyes narrow, lips clamped together, breathing hard. After a few moments, as the blood flow slowed, she gathered herself together. She took her phone from the back pocket of her jeans. Her fingers worked its screen, until she found and called a number.

'Gino,' she began, calmly, as she was connected. 'I'm going to need your help again; not your paddock this time, but it's messy, not like it was with her.' She grinned, icily, at his reply, at his fear. 'What makes you think you've got a choice?'